BLUE MOON

Also by James King

Fiction

Faking

Non-Fiction

Jack, A Life with Writers: The Story of Jack McClelland
The Life of Margaret Laurence
Telling Lives or Telling Lies?: Biography and Fiction
Virginia Woolf
William Blake: His Life
The Last Modern: A Life of Herbert Read
Interior Landscapes: A Life of Paul Nash
William Cowper: A Biography

Co-editor

The Letter and Prose Writing of William Cowper
William Cowper: Selected Letters

BLUE

James King

MOON

A NOVEL

SIMON & PIERRE
A MEMBER OF THE DUNDURN GROUP
TORONTO · OXFORD

Editor: Marc Côté
Proofreader: Julian Walker
Design: Jennifer Scott
Printer: Webcom

Canadian Cataloguing in Publication Data

King, James, 1942-
Blue Moon

ISBN 0-88924-293-3

1. Dick, Evelyn, 1920- — Fiction. 2. Murder — Ontario — Hamilton — Fiction.
3. Trials (Murder) — Ontario — Hamilton — Fiction. I. Title.

PS8571.I99.3I52837B58 2000 C813'.54 C00-931905-0 PR9199.3K44215B58 2000

THE CANADA COUNCIL FOR THE ARTS SINCE 1957 | LE CONSEIL DES ARTS DU CANADA DEPUIS 1957

Canada

ONTARIO ARTS COUNCIL
CONSEIL DES ARTS DE L'ONTARIO

We acknowledge the support of the **Canada Council for the Arts** and the **Ontario Arts Council** for our publishing program. We also acknowledge the financial support of the **Government of Canada** through the **Book Publishing Industry Development Program, The Association for the Export of Canadian Books**, and the **Government of Ontario** through the **Ontario Book Publishers Tax Credit** program.

Care has been taken to trace the ownership of copyright material used in this book. The author and the publisher welcome any information enabling them to rectify any references or credit in subsequent editions.

J. Kirk Howard, President

Printed and bound in Canada.
Printed on recycled paper.

www.dundurn.com

Dundurn Press
8 Market Street
Suite 200
Toronto, Ontario, Canada
M5E 1M6

Dundurn Press
73 Lime Walk
Headington, Oxford,
England
OX3 7AD

Dundurn Press
2250 Military Road
Tonawanda NY
U.S.A. 14150

For Wayne Allan and Sheila Russell

PART ONE

Ernst Newman

1

Some things, I notice, never change. The simple pearl necklace. No earrings. No makeup except for the shiny magenta creamily applied to her bow-shaped lips. But her colours are completely transformed. A silvery, sparkling blouse made of the finest *mousseline de soie*. The black skirt classically cut to end three inches below the knees. The burgundy shoes sedately burnished. The multi-coloured shawl draped over her shoulders bearing the signature of Paloma Picasso. One discordant note: the nails bitten to the quick, the cerise polish bestowed on them calling attention to their shabby state. A splendid composition, so different from the young woman who arrived on my doorstep thirty long years ago. That person was also clad in black, as if in mourning. Widow's weeds?, I had asked myself that first day. The button-through wool dress had a fitted bodice, a dolman top with a stand-up collar, and a flared skirt with panels of knife pleats. Expensive clothing, out-of-date by almost a decade. She had little money in those days.

Like Elizabeth, I came to British Columbia fairly late: 1958. German born, I was a thirty-seven-year-old psychoanalyst whose wife and son had been extinguished in the great maw of history.

Friends are always amazed at how much I observe — and remember — about the appearance of my patients; what Mrs. X wore the other day, the loud necktie impulsively acquired by mousy Mr. Z (is there a transformation in progress? — something I have not yet heard in what he has been telling me?). I simply shrug my shoulders and confess I sometimes have very little else to occupy my mind hour after sometimes dreary hour. "A by-product of my profession. A psychoanalyst has to occupy his mind somehow when he hears the same stories endlessly repeated, often with no significant variation. So I study the exteriors of my patients, especially their costumes. If I know how they prepare themselves to greet the world, I get to know them better." Then I shrug my shoulders and make a little joke: "What I don't know about the history of clothing in the past forty years is not worth knowing!"

Elizabeth has never been to any of my flats. For ten years I met with her four days a week at my office in the Medical-Dental Building on Georgia Street, crowned at the corners by the glorious art deco stone effigies of doctors and nurses. One of the first questions she ever asked me concerned them: "Are they guardian angels or malignant spirits?" I was unprepared for that: "If you thought they were evil, would you have entered the building to see me?" She never appreciated my answering a question with a question. Sadly, that building was torn down years ago.

We are in her suite at the Hotel Vancouver. She hands me a glass of whisky and then mixes her own drink. Elizabeth is not one for small talk, but she observes how much the city has changed. "I loved my flat in The Manhattan Apartments on Thurlow. A wonderful place, Italianate, salmon pink brick highlights. In those days, I was in the city but not *of* the city. When I walked through the courtyard in the evening, I knew I could relax. I'd imagine myself in Florence, about to encounter Robert Browning on the stair. Now my beloved old flat faces *two* Starbucks — and Virgin Records and Planet Hollywood are just down the street on Robson."

"The Manhattan has survived many attempts to tear it down."

"I'm not surprised. Does it really belong anymore? It was built in 1908. Even in the sixties, it looked out of place. Now it's completely incongruous. A dinosaur caged by columns of steel and plates of glass."

It is time to change the subject. "You have become quite celebrated," I point out once she has begun to sip her gin and tonic. I am nervous and have not made a good beginning. Although I talk with Elizabeth on the phone three or four times a year, I have not seen her since she left Vancouver for Toronto in 1981.

"Celebrated? Yes, Ernst. But have I been your 'best' patient?" She asks the question tenderly, but the underlying hurt is easy to see. Still so vulnerable.

"We are friends. By definition, equals. I am no longer your confessor, *liebchen*." That is absolutely the wrong word. I have very dear feelings for her, but she is not "my dear one." I avoid flirting with patients, but I can tell by the soft glow on her face that she has been touched.

Elizabeth has become very famous, one of the most venerated novelists of her generation. She has agreed to return to her old stomping grounds to promote the release of all her novels in a uniform edition. Fifteen volumes. A tremendous achievement, one that necessitates a coast-to-coast tour encompassing both the United States and Canada. Vancouver is the final stop on the last leg — the Western portion — of a three week tour that has taken her to Calgary, Dallas, San Francisco and Seattle. "I shall be very happy to be home at the end of the week. If I can only survive the next four days."

"I am sure you will be fine, Elizabeth."

"Yes, Ernst, I endure. But recently I have asked myself about the cost. My life appears to have reached a natural conclusion, yet I am in a terrible muddle."

"You felt lost many years ago — and then you found yourself."

"Was there a real change? Or did I merely refashion myself?"

"As an analyst, I cannot answer those questions. As a friend, I can assure you that there was genuine change."

"You are a man of supreme tact."

The time has come for her to reveal the purpose of our meeting. She has never requested a meeting in all these years, although I am aware she has been in Vancouver at least half a dozen times since she "retired" to Toronto. "I have a very special favour to ask. An enormous one. I wish you to be the guardian of my papers. All manuscripts of the novels are at the Fisher Book Room at the University of Toronto. Most of my correspondence — letters to other writers. Financial records. That sort of thing. Nothing has been given away that reveals my true identity."

"You wish me to help erase your childhood and young adulthood from the annals of biography?"

"No. That is exactly what I don't want you to do. I want the truth to be told, but I want it done correctly. I can trust you to do exactly that."

"As always, you have too high an opinion of me."

She ignores that observation. "I can no longer write fiction. My new novel has become autobiography. Obviously unpublishable during my lifetime. I can't even give that book its finishing touches. I try to work on it but all I'm left with are orts, scraps and fragments." She collects herself. "Would you be willing to oversee its publication? Make certain everything is handled — tastefully? That is all I ask."

"A psychiatrist who tells on his patients is a pariah; a psychiatrist who prepares a patient's autobiography for publication is merely a servant of history. Yes, I think I'm up to that. But you will survive me; that unhappy task will never fall on my shoulders."

"Ernst — you have no idea how much comfort you have given me."

2

A clean break. That was my rationale for choosing my new home. Like many of my patients, I wanted to escape from myself but — instead — decided to escape the place where I was living. I always warn my patients about such follies, but, like everyone else, I have my own blind spots, my own defence mechanisms — ways of lying to myself about myself.

After I lost my family, I went to England, where I trained as an analyst (I had qualified as a doctor in Germany). I did not wish to return to Germany, had come — in fact — to hate my native language, the same tongue as our oppressors. I found England increasingly cold and damp. Having no interest in any other part of

Europe and suspicious of the Antipodes, I decided to immigrate to Canada and settled in the West because of its remoteness, its distance from Europe. Vaguely, I knew of the mountains and of the Pacific Ocean bracketing Vancouver. I knew there was little — or no — snow. I admit I ignored the warnings about the omnipresent rain. I imagined my chosen environment as a garden state, verdant, plentiful in fruits, vegetables and flowers.

I was dimly aware that Vancouver was a city attempting to find a cultural identity and, to that purpose, it did not mind making use of myself and other refugees from Europe, survivors of the madness Hitler had unleashed. An honest exchange many of us felt: our sophistication in books and music in exchange for the refreshing innocence of a culturally nascent city. Something to be gained on both sides.

While I was living in London, I had heard of the pre-eminent Herr Doctor Otto Klemperer's unfortunate Canadian sojourn just after the war. He accepted the leadership of the Vancouver Symphony Orchestra. The famous conductor, renowned for his majestic interpretations of Beethoven, Brahms, and Bruckner — who had escaped from Germany to the United States — was at that time suspected to be suffering from a rare condition, Gershwin's brain tumour. The powerful-looking but inwardly sheepish maestro had convinced himself that a nurse in California — at a sanatorium in Santa Barbara, where he had been a patient six years earlier — had offered herself to him as an inducement to remain there.

Shortly after his arrival here, he knocked in the middle of the night on the hotel door of Regina Resnik, the young Austrian soprano he had engaged to sing arias by Mozart and Beethoven. He did not make any advances but kept her talking for two hours. A few days later, there was a reception in his honour at the home of Amy Buckerfield, the chairman of the orchestra board. Discreetly, he asked her daughter to accompany him into the gardens where, attempting to be Adam to her Eve, he clutched her in a vice-like grip. She escaped with her virtue intact.

The conductor was also preoccupied with Lotte, his twenty-three-year-old daughter, who accompanied him to Vancouver. She placed sleeping pills in her father's soup, but his bouts of mania were unabated. The poor daughter had to collude with the hotel staff to co-ordinate the comings and goings of the many "women of the night" her father made assignations with.

The members of Mrs. Buckerfield's committee were so frightened of him that they once hid under the stairs when he announced his intention of attending one of their meetings. Within a fortnight, things came to a head when the great man demanded a villa complete with swimming pool as part of his remuneration. Mrs. Buckerfield balked. She did not have sufficient funds to hire the Villa Russe, the former home of a Russian Grand Duke and Sergey Rachmaninov, on the Crescent in Shaughnessy. In desperation, Lotte negotiated the cancellation of the contract and flew back with her father to Los Angeles. The European — not the North Americans — had misbehaved. The story intrigued me (I had heard Klemperer conduct many times before the war, and the name of Vancouver must have stuck in my mind). Subconsciously, I must have taken in that the Canadian city was in the process of trying to develop itself, had cultural leanings.

Those ambitions had literally soared a decade before Klemperer's brief sojourn and hasty exit when that twenty-five-storey art-deco-fantasy-made-bricks-and-mortar, the Marine Building, opened its doors in October 1930. The huge lobby was a cavernous Mayan temple as spectacular as the Ball Court at Chichén Itzá. But the swirling crabs, turtles, carp, and sea horses that graced the walls and brass doors were meant to remind the spectator of the nearer presence of the Pacific. These creatures were accompanied by designs of trains, ships, airplanes and zeppelins. All twelve signs of the Zodiac were worked into the corkoid — "battleship linoleum" — on the floor. The stained glass over the entrance way paid tribute to Captain Vancouver and his ship, *Discovery*. Doormen in bright scarlet and black uniforms opened the massive brass doors and then sailor-suited young women escorted passengers in five high-speed elevators — seven hundred feet per minute — to the top. But the building was a financial flop — it had cost $2.3 million, $1.1 over budget. Only the first four floors rented and, in 1933, the building was sold to the Guinness family of Ireland. The new manager's wife hated the two-storey, three-level penthouse, and that couple soon escaped. (A subsequent tenant of those lavish quarters was an affluent widow who treated her grandchildren to rides on a Shetland pony that galloped around the balcony and had his living quarters there.)

In the middle of World War II, the painter Lawren Harris moved to Vancouver and purchased the large white clapboard mansion at

4760 Belmont Avenue. He remained an inhabitant of the city until his death in 1968. It was here that his large brilliantly coloured monumental abstracts — so different from his earlier landscapes — were made. A wealthy man, he established a salon where all the "advanced" painters, writers and musicians in the area could gather. He terminated the soirées abruptly, however, when one guest had the gall to break into the house and steal his gramophone. No longer would he cast his pearls before swine. As the new directions he was taking in his career were not appreciated by the locals, Harris spent a lot of time on the train back and forth to Toronto. Committed though he may have been to the beauty of his adopted city, he never saw it as culturally advanced.

After the war, Vancouver's civic pride fell mightily. Few trees had survived in the downtown. Both Georgia and Granville Streets were filled with car dealers advertising their wares with plastic pennants and glaring billboards. The streets were littered with candy wrappers and wads of chewed gum. At night, the canyons created by the large Edwardian buildings were deserted.

Yet, by the time I arrived in the city, the refugees from Europe had made their presence known. There was the Bonton on Granville, where one could buy exquisite properly prepared pastries — Napoleons, Three Sisters, Rum Truffles, Gateaux St. Honoré — especially beloved by the Austrians, Hungarians and Russians who resisted the more ordinary fare available at other bakeries and confectioners. The marzipan animals at the Bonton bore the most amazing colours, colours even nature was too frightened to bestow. Nearby, on Robson, there were the Mozart Tea Room and the Schnitzel House. One could have one's fortune read in tea leaves and by Tarot cards at a host of small restaurants and cafés. The city had a *slightly* decadent feel to it, very much like sedate, high bourgeois Vienna. The Canadian character, however, deeply frightened at the prospect of going too far in the pursuit of pleasure, firmly resisted the debauchery of pre-war Berlin.

In July, a month after I arrived in Vancouver, the city, poised for yet another run at becoming a place of cultural significance, held its first International Festival. Since Otto Klemperer had been a mistake a decade earlier, there were some doubting Thomases among the committee that had decided to take a chance on Joan Sutherland — later affectionately nicknamed La Stupenda — the Australian soprano.

Could she really become another Jenny Lind, as the impresario Nicholas Goldschmidt predicted? Suffering from recurring bouts of sinusitis, elephantine swelling in both legs, and abscesses in both ears, she made the long air trip from London to Vancouver to make her North American debut as Donna Anna in Mozart's *Don Giovanni*. Most residents of the city were more interested in the visit of one of the Royals — Princess Margaret dedicated the Okanagan Lake Bridge on July 19. I found the visit of a member of the English royal family of little interest. I must admit that I attended all six of the singer's performances; my diary has entries for 26, 29 and 31 July, 5, 7 and 9 August. Even by my fanatical standards as an opera buff, I acted gluttonously, determined to feed on the soprano's overwhelmingly huge voice and thrilling, ornate trills.

I was ravished by the voice. Elegantly costumed in deepest black, Sutherland fully enacted the plight of the wronged, love-tormented and vengeful widow. In my diary, I see it was on the 8th of August — the day before her final performance — that I encountered the soprano on the street. In her street clothes and without makeup, she was simply a big, gangly, kerchiefed woman with a huge, monstrous jaw. All the magic was gone. The following night, she made me believe in her all over again as the wronged woman transformed into monster. Never before had I witnessed such discordance between an artist's imaginary existence and her real life.

My encounter with both Joan Sutherlands — the soprano whose voice was the incarnation of all strong human emotions and the unduly ordinary woman — sums up much of my own experience of my adopted city. And, as I was about to discover, of Elizabeth Delamere.

3

I had been in practice on Georgia Street for four years when Elizabeth phoned me. The voice at the other end of the phone was nervous, suspicious and peremptory — emotions I am used to hearing when persons call to inquire about becoming patients.

"I wonder if you have time in which to see me?"

"You are thinking of becoming a patient?

"Exactly. Do you have any spaces?"

"That is a negotiable."

"Would you give me a straightforward answer?"

"So much depends on your expectations — and mine."

"Your expectations?"

"Whether I am able to be of any assistance to you."

"Yes. Right. I see your point."

"Would next Monday at three suit you?"

A small, blond and exceedingly pale woman of medium height, dressed in a black frock, presented herself at my doorstep at the appointed time. I indicated she should follow me into the consulting room but, instead, she strolled down the corridor examining the prints on the walls. She seemed offended by them. When — a few minutes later — she entered the room and seated herself in the chair opposite mine, her disdain did not abate. She sniffed as if detecting foul odours. Then she looked at the couch behind her.

"I suppose you use that for all your clients?"

"Some patients are threatened by it; they feel utterly defenceless reclining there. They are afraid a predator might attack them. Others crave that space. For them, it is a refuge, a place of respite."

"You don't force the issue?"

"Exactly." The adverb was a lie. I consider the use of the couch essential. If a patient sits across the way from me, the interaction is inter-personal. My face is scanned for responses to what is being confessed. If the patient cannot see me, the therapy becomes inter-psychic. The patient, listening to the disembodied voice of the analyst, tends to internalize the therapist, make him a part of herself.

She abruptly switched the subject. "I suppose you believe everything Freud preached?"

"A great man, but I would not call myself a slavish follower."

"You think for yourself?"

I refused to be drawn in and allowed her to ask a further number of questions before I intervened. Could she tell me her name?

The request startled her, as if the matter were none of my business. "I am Elizabeth Delamere. I work at Duthie's, the bookstore on Robson."

I nodded my acknowledgement. Before I could ask her any more questions — her date of birth, her place of birth, the names of her parents — she proceeded to tell me she was an adherent of Jung rather than Freud. "Does that bother you?" When I assured her it did not, she elaborated a comparison and contrast between the writings of the two doctors. This oral essay filled the remainder of the hour. It was concluded by my interruption when I informed her that our time had come to an end.

Startled, she asked, "When shall I see you again?" I suggested the following Monday at the same time. She nodded assent, quickly rose to her feet and proceeded down the corridor and out the door. At the end of that meeting, I had uncovered only her name.

4

Any expectations I had of discovering more about my mysterious visitor were dashed in the next five sessions. Each time she wore a different dress: a bright yellow, a drab olive green, a florescent green, a dismal brown, a jubilant pink. Her sombre mood was constant.

Briskly, she told me she had been born in the province of Ontario, had been a widow since 1946 — seventeen years before — and had given birth to three children. She was now on her own. Any attempt on my part to obtain further particulars was deftly foiled. She complained of horrible dreams and when I attempted to learn something of the contents of these nightmares, she would turn the subject away from herself. She would speak of the dream worlds of heroines from literature — Queen Dido, Clarissa Harlow, Jane Eyre. Or she would speculate on Ginger Rogers' dreams in the film version of Kurt Weill's musical about psychoanalysis, *Lady in the Dark.* More annoyingly, she would speculate on the theories of Freud and Jung. If I attempted to shift the subject back to her, she would ignore me. My belief was that she was waiting to become comfortable enough to reveal herself unabashedly.

Elizabeth was a challenging patient. As I was not sure she had any clear inkling of what she was doing, I decided to bide my time. I would wait to see what happened next. Six weeks went by. She came once a week; I became convinced nothing of benefit was transpiring.

On the Saturday following the sixth session, I was walking from the bottom of Robson Avenue towards Thurlow. All of a sudden I noticed a blond woman — her hair worn up in a chignon — on the other side of the street. Dressed in a simple but severely cut grey suit, she strolled purposefully along, pausing every so often to scour the contents of the clothing and shoe shops along the way. The woman reminded me of Kim Novak as Madeleine in Hitchcock's *Vertigo*, as if the woman I was observing had deliberately costumed herself as some sort of homage to that film, which had been released just five years earlier. Fascinated by this incarnation, I followed her along until she reached the corner of Robson and Thurlow, at which point she turned the corner.

I stood there, amazed by what I had witnessed. A minute later, my attention was attracted to a large window on the second floor directly opposite me. The woman I had been following came to the window, looked out and then sat down at a table. She stared straight ahead. Suddenly, tears gathered at her eyes. She brushed them away, but she could not control them. Finally, she placed her hands on her eyes. Her entire body began to shake as unhappy feelings gained full entry. The woman now looked more like Judy — Kim Novak's second incarnation in *Vertigo*. I had become Jimmy Stewart — the deluded but ultimately cruel and vindictive suitor — who pursues Kim Novak in the film. The woman I was watching was my difficult patient, Elizabeth Delamere. Despite the chignon and the grey suit, I should easily have identified her and desisted from any attempt to observe her life outside my consulting room. Her sadness was touching to the same degree her resistance to the therapy she had initiated was infuriating.

Her reticence stymied me, made me livid at myself for my inability to elicit the truth from her. My feelings of frustration had led me to follow her and to deceive myself that I was simply intrigued by a mysterious woman on the street. Rather than acting professionally, I had been play-acting a stupid role: the analyst as private eye, conducting myself as if I were some latter-day Humphrey Bogart on the trail of an elusive Mary Astor. My unconscious was out of control and had to be brought to heel. I decided to be much more direct with my patient at our next meeting.

When Elizabeth arrived for her appointment the following week, the session followed its usual course for forty minutes until I intervened.

"You have never asked me to give you a prognosis. Indeed, you have never asked me to make any assessment of our work here together."

"I assumed you would speak when you wished to do so."

"You have not given me many opportunities to do so. In fact, you have carefully avoided giving me any chance to obtain the details I require to form the basis for any kind of opinion."

"I have spoken at great length in our meetings. Not a second is wasted."

"The sessions are certainly filled with your observations, but you have evaded me at every turn, refusing to talk about yourself in any candid or intimate way."

"I do not agree."

"How do you see it?"

"You provide me with an opportunity to talk about matters that are important to me."

"You can talk about books and movies with other people. In my opinion, you are wasting the time we spend together. I am not sure I am being of any assistance whatsoever to you."

The patient's face turned bright red. "I have had curious thoughts about what I have been doing here. I want to come here; I desire to talk about the things that torment me, but I am desperately afraid that I shall commit an unpardonable sin." She took a deep breath. "I am afraid that I shall lie to you. I was an awful liar as a young woman. I cannot act that way ever again."

"So you have been waiting for the moment when you can put falsehoods away and reveal the truth?"

"Perhaps. But the moment for honesty has not yet arrived."

"You must decide if that moment is to be reached. Our session is over for this week."

Elizabeth, dressed in pale chiffon lemon, began our next session in an exceedingly curious way, "Do you know about Janet Smith?"

"Should I?"

"A Vancouver legend. Her story bears some resemblances to my own."

"Then I am most interested to learn about her."

Elizabeth related a gruesome account of one of the most celebrated crimes in Vancouver history. In the twenties, the death of Janet Smith, a Scottish nursemaid, had stunned the city.

On the twenty-six of July 1924, the police were summoned to 3851 Osler Avenue, Shaughnessey Heights, the magnificent home of F.L. Baker, an exporter of pharmaceutical drugs. Wong Foon Sing, the houseboy, took the detectives to the basement laundry where they came upon the corpse of the young woman, blood from her right eye having oozed all over the floor. A .45-calibre revolver was at her side. Sing explained that he had been peeling potatoes in the kitchen when he heard a loud noise — like a car backfiring — come from the basement. He investigated and called Mr. Baker, who rushed home before summoning the police.

The coroner discovered some irregularities. The bullet wound alone could not have caused the massive damage to the nursemaid's head, there were burn marks all over her torso, and there was a dark stain on the index finger of her left hand. But she was right-handed and would presumably have taken the gun in that hand had she indeed shot herself. Despite many clues that indicated a murder had taken place, the coroner ruled the death a suicide. Within a few days, an uprising by the underclass was in the making. Several other housemaids — friends of the deceased — came forward: their friend would never have killed herself. Someone must have killed her. Perhaps to keep her quiet. Then the rumours really began to swirl. One claimed that Smith had been raped by someone from Baker's social set and then killed when she threatened to expose the culprit. Further accounts suggested the police had been bribed to conceal the truth.

A subsequent coroner's jury ruled that Smith had been murdered by a person or persons unknown. Things simmered down. Then, on the evening of March 20, 1925, a group of Ku Klux Klan vigilantes kidnapped Sing from the front lawn of the Baker house. For six weeks, he was shackled to the floor of an attic room in Point Grey and subjected to beatings and death threats in order to force him to tell the true story of what had happened. On April Fools' Day, a delirious Sing was found by the police on a lonely stretch of Marine Drive. Immediately, they charged him with Smith's murder.

The following day, the attorney general of the province told a newspaper reporter that everyone in his office knew the houseboy was innocent. The Crown wanted, he asserted, Sing's case to come to trial so that the real murderer could be flushed out. This admission led the Grand Jury to dismiss the charges against Sing. The police chief of Point Grey, four of his constables and three private operatives were subsequently charged with the abduction of Sing. In turn, they accused the attorney general of having instigated the kidnapping. Then, quite suddenly, all charges were dropped.

For the next decade, stories about the real way Janet Smith had met her end were in circulation. The common currency had several versions and scenarios. She had been bashed to death by the jealous girlfriend of a wealthy playboy who had seduced her. She had slipped on the floor during an argument with a boyfriend and fractured her skull on a plumbing fixture.

The story with the greatest purchase on the public's imagination centred on F.L. Baker. Before he emigrated to Canada, Baker had run a drug smuggling ring in England. According to this variant, he covered up the circumstances of Smith's death because he did not wish too glaring a spotlight to be placed on himself. For him, an accident was much better than a homicide.

In January 1926 — eighteen months after Janet Smith met her end — Wong Foon Sing returned to China. No one ever discovered if Smith had killed herself or been murdered.

Elizabeth told this story in considerable detail. She took virtually all the session to do so. At the end of the hour, I was no more ahead than before in penetrating her mystery. When I told her we had run out of time, she told me that I could — if I was sufficiently discerning — see her own plight in this account. A challenge had been made. Could I rise to it?

As it turned out, I was not clever enough to unwind precisely the strands in the strange true-crime story Elizabeth had given me. Had she, a servant in someone's house, been treated violently? Had she, like the servant, been falsely accused of a crime? Had she perpetrated a violent crime against another woman? My curiosity was more than unusually aroused by the time we met the following week.

"You must admit that the short, sad life history of Janet Smith is mesmerizing."

Not wishing to lose track once again of my elusive patient, I told her the truth: "The story is of interest to me only if it sheds light on your life history. Otherwise, it is a distraction and of no account. I have a penchant for cat and mouse games in the films of Alfred Hitchcock but do not believe they will be of any use to us in our sessions."

"Is that because you are accustomed to the role of cat?"

"You are accusing me of wishing to be in control. If I am not in that position, I am dissatisfied?"

"Exactly."

"Well, there is some truth in what you claim. You are the patient; I am the therapist. I have to play my role properly."

"And have I not played mine?"

"No."

Elizabeth's face turned a bright red. She fingered her pearls, something she had not done before in my presence. When she spoke, the words rushed up, as if to escape: "Elizabeth Delamere is not my real name. I was born Evelyn MacLean in Beamsville, Ontario, moved to Hamilton as a child and married a man by the name of John Dick. I gave birth to three children: a girl who died at birth, a boy who died ten days after he was born, and a daughter, now grown. I was tried, convicted and then acquitted of the murder of my husband. I was found guilty of the death of the baby boy. Before coming to Vancouver, I spent twelve years in the Kingston Prison for Women." I tried to mask my astonishment at what had been revealed.

"Like poor Sing, I was accused of a crime I did not commit." As if a terrible burden had been partially lifted, she looked me full in the face: "I have come here to plead for your help." She was on the point of expressing how lonely, frightened and miserable she felt.

Then, abruptly, she collected herself and began speaking in what was becoming her customary detached manner, very much in the way of a schoolteacher instructing a slow pupil: "Had I not existed, someone would have had to create someone like me. I was a great distraction — a wicked woman who drew attention away from what was really happening in the city of Hamilton.

"In 1946, as soon as World War II had ended, the Hamilton labour unions — which in the interest of national defence had been largely silenced in making demands — propelled their members' economic interests to the fore. One of the steel giants — Dofasco — never became unionized because the company took on the guise of the benevolent grandfather showering employees with picnics, Christmas parties and gifts. When this ploy did not seem to work, they introduced profit-sharing.

"The workers at the other steel giant — Stelco — were unionized. Their leaders called the tactics of their employer fascist and Hitler-like. This set the scene for the company's establishment of 'Slag Mountain Lodge,' wherein two thousand men who spurned the strike call were sealed inside the plant gates by union pickets; a special company newspaper — the *Stelco Billet* — "Rolled At the Hamilton Works By and For The Loyal Order of Scabs" — carried anti-union and anti-strike news from Hamilton and across North America.

"Louis St. Laurent, the prime minister, defended the scabs. The strikers and the police were at each other's throats. The wrestlers Whipper Billy Watson and the Sharp Brothers performed at Scott Park Baseball stadium, all the proceeds going to the union. American folk singers Pete Seeger and Woodie Guthrie appeared on behalf of the displaced workers. During the summer of 1946, thousands gathered daily at Woodlands Park to hear news of the strike. The union flew a small rented plane over the Stelco compound; the company then hired a larger plane to engage in mock dog-fights.

"After a long, sultry summer which threatened all manner of menace and violence, the Stelco strike was settled in early October 1946. The strike against the Southam group — which owned the *Spectator*, the city's major newspaper — was carried over into 1947.

"John Dick was murdered in March 1946; my various trials for his murder — and that of the baby — were held throughout the remainder of 1946 and in early 1947. I became a necessary distraction to remove attention from the various swindles being perpetrated against the workers."

As a recent immigrant to Canada, I had no means of judging the accuracy of what Elizabeth was telling me. Of more concern to me that afternoon was the pedagogical direction in which — after making her confession — she had turned attention away from herself. She was — once again — evading my analytical net by objectifying her experience. "That is the only way she has of dealing with painful matters," I told myself. But my job was not to allow her off the hook. I might have a more pleasant relationship with the patient if I did not confront her, but I would be abrogating my responsibility to her.

"When you tell me these horrible things that have happened to you, it is perfectly alright for you to become emotional, show your real feelings."

"Yes, I know."

"You may *know,* but you don't allow yourself to *feel*. The horrors of the past torment you. You are at liberty to become upset when you come here. You can even lose control."

She glanced at me as if I were speaking complete gibberish. Then, her eyes scanned my face for half a minute or so. I don't know what she expected to find. Then the dam burst. Hot tears coursed down her face. She simply sat in the chair facing me, making no attempt to control the flow or to conceal her now badly distorted face. On that day, the real work of therapy began.

5

Rumours had abounded since 1997 that Elizabeth Delamere might find the approval of the Nobel Committee in Stockholm: she wrote about the rights of women, had begun her career at a relatively late stage in her life and was now somewhat elderly. On those three scores, the politics of prize-giving favoured her. I had questioned her about such a possibility when we met for drinks in her suite. She shrugged her shoulders, smiled and then simply said, "There are far worthier writers than me."

Two days before the Nobel Prize for Literature was to be bestowed in October 2000 — less than forty-eight hours after my meeting with her — the concierge at the Hotel Vancouver refused to put phone calls through to her suite; the management assumed that she wanted to be by herself and would surface in her own good time. The following morning, I was phoned by Dolly Smith, Delamere's publicist at Penguin in Toronto. She could not contain herself.

"Something awful's happened to Elizabeth! She's not answering her phone."

"She has probably left on holiday for a day or two."

"She wouldn't do that. I'm very close to her. She would've told me. I'm very worried now that you tell me she hasn't rung you. I'm quite close to Elizabeth. I know about her relationship to you."

A bit startled, I asked her what she thought might have happened.

"She's had an accident. For all I know, she could be dead!"

"You are sure something is amiss?"

"I know it. She would've phoned me. We're like mother and daughter. Why don't you phone the concierge and demand to be let into the flat?"

"I do not like intrusive people, nor am I intrusive. Elizabeth may simply wish to be alone." There was a silence that propelled me to respond: "I shall see what I can do."

Three hours later, accompanied by Mario the concierge, I entered the suite, which had, as I remember it, intensely bright images on pastel-coloured walls. Mario, nodding in the direction of the bedroom, indicated he would only follow where I led. So it was I who discovered Elizabeth's corpse. The double bed was placed at the side of the room's only window. Her body, cradled slightly to the side, was swathed by a single sheet. The face of the corpse had a benign aspect, a serenity I had hardly ever glimpsed in any of my many encounters with the living person. Death did not obscure her excellent bone structure — it enhanced that aspect of her appearance. In rest, her features hinted at the beauty age had just begun to rob from her. There was a small writing desk opposite the bed and on it I noticed a handwritten page, which I discreetly placed in the breast pocket of my suit.

I felt a comforting stillness in that room. Warm, golden sunshine penetrated the chamber of death, and the body of Elizabeth resembled that of a pre-Raphaelite beauty. A gentle peace had somehow settled itself. Mario, obviously a devout Catholic, crossed himself and began to weep quietly. I felt I had inadvertently taken part in some religious rite.

That evening, the news of Elizabeth's death filled the airwaves, various commentators offering eloquent assessments of her place in world literature. The local press was not quite so compassionately inclined. Elizabeth's mysterious passing from — it turned out — a heart attack in her sleep was ludicrously compared to the sudden death of Errol Flynn in Vancouver in October 1959. Accompanied here by Beverley Aadland, a seventeen-year-old starlet, the fifty-year-old matinee idol had been at a surgeon's flat to receive treatment for a slipped disk. He regaled those in attendance with anecdotes about W.C. Fields and John Barrymore and then retired to a bedroom to relax before the doctor went to work. A few minutes later, Miss Aadland stepped into that room and returned immediately screaming in horror: "Something is terribly wrong with Errol — he's turned black!" Although adrenaline was injected into his heart, the actor died a few minutes later. After the autopsy, the newspapers gleefully reported that Flynn had the body of a tired old man. *Sic transit gloria*. In their accounts of Elizabeth's death, the local papers suggested that only persons with secrets to hide lost their lives in hotel rooms.

6

Although in the main retired, I still see a few patients; I could not leave for Toronto at once. I booked my flight a month ahead, fairly confident that I had plenty of time to deal with Elizabeth's remains. I was wrong. Two weeks after her death, I received a phone call from Richard Johnston of the Thomas Fisher Rare Book Room at the University of Toronto's Robarts Library.

"I'd like you to take a look at the papers found in Elizabeth Delamere's flat. I gather you are her literary executor."

"Correct. I shall attend to everything in due course. I was going to get in touch with you next week. Can we wait until then?"

This was, however, a personage who was not about to be brushed off. "The documents point in a fantastical but inescapable direction."

"Such as?"

"Elizabeth Delamere was not the lady's real name."

"Go on."

"Elizabeth Delamere was Evelyn Dick, the Hamilton prostitute accused of killing her husband and convicted of murdering her own baby."

"I am aware of Elizabeth's past. I was her analyst."

"So you were in on the secret?"

"I wasn't *in* on any secret. I was aware of her past."

"You realize that the existence of the typescript of her autobiography puts me in a difficult position. I suppose you intend to embargo this portion of the archive? You can count on me to be discreet, although I imagine that much more attention will be paid to her now that she has died and given the number of awards and prizes she has won. It's a tricky situation."

"On the contrary, Elizabeth was well aware the truth would eventually be revealed. She did not wish her real identity to be known in her lifetime. I'm not sure she would have wanted her autobiography to be published so soon. But she certainly wanted it published. She left it to my discretion as to when and under what conditions it should be released."

"You might consider sooner rather than later."

"I dare say there is a great deal in what you say."

7

In the popular imagination, Karla Homolka has replaced Evelyn Dick as the best-known female murderer born in Canada. Homolka's husband, Paul Bernardo, had a copy of Brett Easton Ellis's *American Psycho* at his bedside — whereas a decade earlier, Jon George Rallo, the Hamilton city hall supervisor who in 1976 murdered his wife and children, had used *Torso*, the book about the Dick murders, as a how-to-do-it manual. The mutilated body of Sandra Rallo was found wrapped in garbage bags in the Welland Canal; her daughter, Stephanie, in Jordan Harbour. The body of Jason, 6, has never been discovered.

In the late 1940s, Evelyn Dick had been accused of murdering her husband by chopping off his head and all four limbs. (The victim's large penis was his only remaining appendage, leading to the refrain: *How Could You Mrs. Dick?* Local wags answered their own question: *Hard to do.*) She was found guilty of the ghastly crime, but the conviction was overturned on appeal. In the midst of their investigation of the "Torso" murder, the police came upon the perfectly preserved body of a healthy, newborn baby boy encased in cement in a suitcase in Evelyn's bedroom closet. He had been strangled. She was found guilty of that crime, sent to Kingston Prison for Women, released after twelve years and then vanished into thin air.

"It's all so improbable" was Richard Johnston's summary of the situation. How could Evelyn Dick have become Elizabeth Delamere? How could she have perpetrated such a masquerade? How could Evelyn Dick have had the intellectual capacity to become a famous writer?

I saw how unsettled he was, but my mind wandered back to the improbable accusation in a recent biography that Graham Greene had once murdered a woman, stuffed her body into a trunk and left the trunk at a railway station in London.

There is also the exceedingly curious case of Juliet Hulme, which was made into the film, *Heavenly Creatures*. At the age of 15, the frail, tubercular English-born Hulme was sent in 1954 to New Zealand by her parents; they hoped the climate in the Antipodes would improve her health. There, Hulme formed a close friendship with Pauline Parker, whose mother objected to the closeness that developed between the two girls. When the mother took steps to separate them, the two friends brutally murdered the older woman — they hacked her to death in a public park. Hulme, who claimed to be on medication that was mind-altering, was convicted of murder and sent to prison. After that, she disappeared from public view. When the film, based on a true story, appeared forty years later, it was a hit on the art-house circuit. Journalists proceeded to track down the real Hulme. She had become Anne Perry, the highly successful writer of Gothic mysteries, who lived in comparative isolation in the English countryside.

Hulme had transformed her life experience into fiction. Was it so strange that another supposed killer, Evelyn Dick, had done the same? Delamere wrote of wronged, often overly passive women who, after great struggles, took charge of their lives. All of the heroines in her early novels murder someone.

Had she been writing about herself? That was Richard's very justifiable question. What did those narratives reveal, he was asking, about the relationship between art and life? Could repulsive behaviour be the foundation of great writing? Is all art a grand fraud?

Evelyn Dick was renowned as a very evil woman; Elizabeth Delamere was a very famous writer. What are the connections between the two strands? Or are there any links at all? Perhaps Evelyn Dick was a very damaged but ordinary — not evil — person? Perhaps she became Elizabeth Delamere to compensate herself for the injustices she endured? Despite my close association with her, I am left with many unanswered questions when I think of the supposedly sullied goods that became, in the eyes of the world, golden.

As I envisioned it, my melancholy task was to sort through Elizabeth's fragments of autobiography, assemble them in the most appropriate order and then find the best way to make the entire narrative flow smoothly. I hope I have done my job satisfactorily, but it is the reader who must decide. The reader of these pages will have many more difficult issues to resolve.

How did such a seeming monster of cruelty and passivity as the young Evelyn Dick become Elizabeth Delamere? Or — you may wish to put the question in a different way — how did Evelyn Dick overcome the deprivations of childhood and young adulthood to become a great writer?

In any event, here is the last book written by Elizabeth Delamere. I leave it to you, the reader, to make your own adjustments — as I did many years before.

PART TWO

Evelyn Dick

8

Almost every night, I take that drive. I borrow the black Packard sedan, once my car, from Bill Landeg, the garage owner to whom I sold it two years before. It is a late winter afternoon, twilight quickly descending as I drive up John and Arkledun Streets and up the Mountain — really, more of a hill — where about a third of Hamilton's population lives. Quickly, the sky becomes enshrouded in a sullen blackness. Soon, I leave the city behind and reach open countryside. Only a few lights draw my attention as the car sways on its appointed path. All of a sudden, there are only the lights from the car itself, and I have to pay close attention to the twisting road. There are no stars, no helpful points of light to assure me I am not alone in the universe. Snow begins to fall.

A rabbit jumps across the road, dexterously avoiding the car. Enormous rocks — boulders really — guard the side. They are the only real signposts. I labour to pay attention. I want to be safe, but I know this is impossible.

Is this how I felt *that* night, on 6 March 1946? Or is it my dream state that makes me aware I am soon to be confronted with some form of the unending horror?

All of a sudden, there is the other car — an Oldsmobile — on the opposite side of the narrow road, its headlights beaming. This is the rendezvous point, the Incline. I slam on the brakes, put my cigarette out, look automatically for a split second at my lips in the rearview mirror. The lipstick seems faded, but my face is pure white, much whiter than I ever try to make it. I brace myself, open the door and start walking towards Mr. Romanelli. He walks at a fast clip in my direction, searching for something — the expression on my face. He wants to know how frightened I am. He takes out a lighter, flicks it in my direction and seems satisfied at what he beholds.

He has mean, darting eyes. He is medium in height but looks much shorter, his height diminished by his thick camel-hair coat and a thick waist. I catch a glimpse of a brown striped suit under the coat. He is what we used to call a *real Dago:* Huge nose, a sinister twist to his large mouth, a line of moustache that could have been painted on, and dark, little pig eyes. Having located what he had hoped to find, he does not hesitate. "We are short of fellows, tonight. Plans have changed." He motions me back to the Packard.

"How changed? What does it matter if some of your men are not here?"

Now, he laughs. Really, he snorts. "Evelyn, you and I are going to take a ride." This is said as a joke. Now, I am even more confused.

"I was told John would be safe if I came to pick him up."

"Oh, John is going with us."

For the first time, I feel a semblance of relief. Perhaps I do not have to worry quite so much. Perhaps this horrible misunderstanding will finally be over. "I'm glad he's safe. I was sure this mess could be sorted out."

This remark seems to astound my companion. He tells me to wait. He will fetch John. He walks back to his car and reaches into the back seat. Slowly, he pulls himself back to the road, a huge Santa Claus bag trailing behind him. He walks slowly back to me, accompanied by a man carrying a large parcel in front of him. I expect the man to be John, but he is someone I have never seen before. Mr. Romanelli opens the back door of the Packard and slowly wedges the bag into the back seat, most of which it fills. His associate wedges his parcel between the back seat and the floor and makes his way back to the other car. I silently witness this dumb-show, not understanding what is happening.

Mr. Romanelli grabs my shoulder and tells me we have to leave immediately. He has to be in Niagara Falls later that night. "Where's John?," I plead.

He tells me to get behind the wheel as he opens the passenger door and slips in. I do as he says, awaiting more information. Any semblance of comedy has been drained from his face. "For a smart dame, you really play it stupid. You know very well he's dead. His body is divided between that bag and the parcel."

I cannot make sense of what he is telling me. "I was told to fetch John, that I could take him home."

Now a smile crosses his face. "That's exactly so. You are picking up John and, if you wish, you can take him home — part of him anyway. He's safe now — from causing you and a whole lot of other people trouble. We've put him out of business."

My anxiety vanishes, replaced by total bafflement. "What do you mean *dead*? I was told everything had been settled. He promised not to talk."

Mr. Romanelli looks at me slightly aghast, as if dealing with a recalcitrant child. "Things are never quite that simple, Mrs. Dick. Your estranged husband would have talked sooner or later, and I was instructed to prevent that from ever happening. In fact, I have been ordered to keep you quiet, but I don't have to worry about disposing of you because you're going to help me dispose of the body. You are an accessory to murder."

I feel myself trying to cry. Sorrow and grief try to assert themselves, but in their place is only numbness. Perhaps it is the instinct to survive.

"What are we going to do?," I finally ask.

"I knew you were too smart to waste valuable time. We're going to dump the torso, and I'll leave the remaining parts of the cadaver to your devices. Perhaps you can burn them at your house on Carrick Street?" He then explains that the boys were short of space in their car, hacked the arms, legs and head off the body in order to transport the remains to the customary dumping ground at Fort Erie. But it turns out that all the fellows are desperately needed at once in Niagara Falls and won't be able to take even a short detour en route. Therefore, I have been summoned to assist Mr. Romanelli.

"In fact, Evelyn, there's a couple of hundred bucks in this for you if you do as you're told." He tells me to drive along the Mountain towards Albion Falls. Half a mile beyond the Silver Springs Riding School, he orders me to stop, gets out, places the bag on the ground, and then uses his glove-covered hands to shake the torso loose. He then pushes it down the ledge and gets back into the car. My stomach is wrenching, now completely out of control. He pays no heed to my distress. "The rest of the body is your problem, my dear," he informs me. I drive him into the city and drop him off at the Royal Connaught hotel on King Street, drive home, steer the huge Packard down the driveway, and start a fire to incinerate the parcel.

Suddenly, my mother hurls herself out of the house — it is now about eight or nine. "That car's too large for the driveway! Get it out of here!" She never seems to notice the putrid stench from the fire. She is frightened by the distinct possibility the car will become stuck in the narrow path between my house and my neighbour's. She was probably more angered by the fire and the resultant odour than by the presence of the car, but she concentrates on the car. Complaining about the smell might lead to embarrassing revelations.

After telling her to mind her own business — she is a guest at *my* home, I remind her — I back the Packard up, drive to the gas station and pen an apology to the car's owner: "My little girl, Heather, was in a bad accident last night, and I had to drive her to Emergency. I'm leaving five dollars to pay the cleaning bill for the damage to the upholstery. I'm very sorry about this."

That is the story of the infamous torso murder — as far as I had anything to do with it. Even back then, I could not remember in any coherent fashion what had occurred, the resulting muddle explains in small part the secret behind the conflicting stories I told the police — each variant containing a sliver of a "truth" I myself could never put into any coherent whole. Now, when I no longer have to be concerned about what happened, I relive the story every night.

Some nights, I arrive at the Incline and no car awaits me. I wonder if I have arrived too late and John has been killed because of my tardiness. I wait ten minutes or so, get out of the car, walk across the road and begin searching for John and Mr. Romanelli. Perhaps I have misunderstood what the Italian told me, have gotten muddled about the meeting time or meeting spot? I stray into the wood, a strange mixture of dry brown brush and vivid green leaves are highlighted against the darkness. Suddenly, I hear a whimpering sound at my feet, look down and see a headless torso contorting itself on the ground.

On other nights, my wanderings take me to a deserted house with a weak light emanating from within. I walk around the building, which contains no windows. Suddenly, I spy a beam of light coming from where two rafters do not quite meet. I look through the opening into a room in which the only furnishing is an altar on which a torso is placed — suddenly, blood erupts from it.

At other times, a door miraculously appears and I can enter the room easily. Soulfully, I approach the torso, kneel and begin some sort of prayer. Then I become aware of a hidden, dangerous force in the room. I want to escape, but the walls of the room have become seamless. There is no exit.

Once, just entering the forest, I stumble across two figures near the ground. As I approach, I see John's body outstretched on my mother's lap. My mother, swathed in blue, looks up at me. At first, she smiles hesitantly and then her face becomes malignant in its rage. Another time, I come across John and my father blocking my way. I am suffused with happiness, but my husband looks at me warily and walks away. My shrivelled little father's face glares at me angrily and screams: "Whore!"

In my dark wood, no companion ever emerges from the darkness to guide me.

9

10 July 1942. The baby — a girl — came slithering out. A very aquatic-looking creature encased in see-through plastic covering. Effortlessly. One big push and swoosh. She was there.

My mother grabbed her quickly, as if she were afraid I might assert some sort of proprietorial right. "A healthy baby," she informed me, her voice filled with an equal mixture of disappointment and despair.

"Let me see her," I moaned.

"Not yet, Evelyn. You must save your strength," my mother bossed me. The burr in her voice firmly enunciated.

20 June 1943. The next baby was blue, a deep grey blue. She hardly moved. Even when she came from me, she showed no effort. The nurse looked at her sadly. "Not still-born, dear, but she might as well be." She died four hours later.

5 September 1944. The last baby was filled with energy, a wonderful lobster red. Energy emanated from him. He gasped the air as if he owned it.

The proud father of these babies was Mr. White, Commander, Captain and, then, finally — near the end of the war, Admiral White. In those days, I was Mrs. White. Evelyn MacLean was my maiden name.

White is a difficult, perhaps impossible person to describe. When I met him, I was only 21, he almost 40. I had gone with my friend, Rosie, to the Tivoli on James Street. The film was a revival of *Sweethearts*, the first three-tone Technicolor picture and the first time the romance between Nelson Eddy and Jeanette MacDonald was given a contemporary setting. I remember seeing MacDonald's bright red hair and deep green eyes for the first time. The couturier, Adrian, dressed her in pale pink shades throughout, except when she is clad in a gold sequined gown when she sings the title song with Eddy.

After the movie, we were trying to decide what to do next. Did we know anyone who would buy us a drink at the bar across the street? Not likely. We did not want the night to end, so enthralled were we by the rhapsodic, happy-ever-after glow the film had given us. We could wander over to King Street, to see if anyone was hanging around the Capitol, the other large movie theatre. In the midst of our discussion about what we wanted to do, a middle-aged man interrupted us: "Do one of you young ladies have a light?" I handed him mine. He lit his cigarette and asked if we were from Hamilton. We both owned up to that, although I informed him that, unlike Rosie, I had not been born there.

Under the garish lights of the facade of the Tivoli, the stranger reminded me of Franchot Tone, then a great matinee idol. He had that actor's high forehead, the steely, intense eyes and refined good looks. He was definitely too old for me. I was more attracted to the glow emanating from Tyrone Power or Errol Flynn types. I never much cared for the mustachioed Don Ameche or the mature look of a

Charles Boyer. I was fascinated by romance, by the prospect of meeting a man who, after a whirlwind courtship, would whisk me away to a glamorous-sounding place.

I did not expect the stranger to have much interest in us, but he asked if we were free to have a drink with him, perhaps in the bar at the Royal Connaught, where he was staying during his leave. He then explained that he was in Hamilton on navy business — mumbled something about security arrangements at the harbour — and did not know anyone in the city. The words "navy" and "security" having caught our rapt attention, we readily agreed to go along with him.

Golden-haired Rosie was a big, bouncy girl, someone who laughed easily and raucously. She was not what anyone would call beautiful, and she lacked what I was supposed to possess in abundance — allure or sex appeal. In reality, I was more shy than Rosie, had never "done it," whereas my companion had years earlier eagerly investigated the bodies of several boys from Cathedral High when the two of us were at the Loretto Academy.

At the bar, our new companion identified himself to us as Norman White, born in Shaker Heights, a suburb of Cleveland, Ohio. He had been in the navy most of his adult life. After high school, he had attended the naval academy at Annapolis, graduated a midshipman, and in only seven years had risen to the rank of commander. He hinted — but did not directly tell us — he was involved in espionage, merely assuring us he was doing liaison work with the Canadian navy in order to safeguard one of Canada's crucial ports, the conduit of much-needed steel for the Allied cause.

Any young woman would have been impressed. My problem was that I careened, displaying how very much in his sway I found myself. Rosie and I only had one drink and then told the Commander we would have to be on our way. He offered us a lift, but, fearing the parental disapproval that would have been showered down upon us, we told him we would make our way home by the streetcar which conveniently stopped in front of the hotel. He walked us out, waved us a gallant good-bye, walked back to the entrance and then turned around again just as our car pulled out.

Romantic allure. That's what I think Norman White exerted over me. The next day I could not keep my mind on my studies. After work finished that day, I told Rosie I was going to walk over to Eaton's to shop; my mother needed some wool and various other odds-and-ends. Not terribly excited by my mission, Rosie did not offer to join me. Instead of heading for the department store, I walked two more blocks beyond it until I reached the hotel. I had no other plans. I did not have the nerve to phone Norman's room. I guess I must have been hoping to run into him. And, of course, that's exactly what happened.

He emerged from the front of Connaught just as I reached it. "Evelyn, how heavenly to see you again!"

My face blanched, so startled was I to see him and by his welcome. Not knowing exactly what to say, I hesitated. But I need not have worried. He asked if I was free. "You must be out shopping. Are you finished?" In retrospect, this was a foolish question since I was not carrying a shopping bag. I agreed with him that I was indeed free, and we wandered to a tea room a block away.

As soon as we had ordered, he observed how much like Hedy Lamarr I looked. The resemblance had not gone unnoticed by me: I was an avid reader of *Photoplay* and had seen all of the Austrian-born star's films. The navy was not really a subject of conversation that day, although Norman mentioned he would be in Hamilton only for two more *nights*. He asked if I had a sweetheart or a "boy chum" I was close to. I assured him that was not the case. "Have you ever had a boyfriend?" He seemed upset when I told him no. Finally, he asked: "You've never had a physical relationship with a man?" I blushed, admitting that was the truth of the situation. After a brief pause, he whispered, "Would you like to? With me?"

To be honest, I wasn't interested in such things. I was enthralled by romantic love, but I had never been inclined to perform the kind of acts of which Rosie had spoken with unconcealed relish. For me, Hollywood and all its attendant culture about the glamorous lives of the stars was enough sex for me. Mr. White put me on the spot. If I said no, I would be closing myself off from a potentially interesting arena of human activity; if I said yes, I might be able to learn about such things from a real gentleman. So I said yes.

After he snuck me into his room that afternoon, things went very slowly at first. From Rosie, I had heard such expressions as "petting," "climax," and even "orgasm." In cruder moments, she had described "hand jobs" and "blow jobs." Mr. White was clinical in an extremely professorial way once we were seated on the sofa in his room. His penis was uncircumcised, he informed me, was medium size in length (seven inches) but extremely thick (such width being a special source of pleasure for his various partners). We kissed a bit and then Mr. White undid his belt, unzipped his fly, and proceeded to show me his "member" (another word he used frequently to describe his penis). He then asked me to take it in my mouth. I remembered Rosie had told me that boys with "big dicks" always cautioned her to be careful she did not allow her teeth to graze their instruments. When I confessed this knowledge to Mr. White, he nodded sagely in agreement. In addition, he instructed me to place the tip of my tongue under the cap of his penis — this would give him additional pleasure. I proceeded to "eat" (Rosie's word) my partner, but I was not prepared for the sour, salt-tasting phlegm which eventually filled my mouth.

Only after that dire event did we remove our clothes, move to the bed, remove the bed covers and slip under the sheets. Mr. White explored my vagina with considerable detail, poking his fingers into it assiduously. Very disappointed that I did not become wet, he asked me if I would play with his penis with my hands. I did this and he soon came to another climax. I was happy the white liquid was not deposited in my mouth this time. After about two hours, I told Mr. White I had to get home and would take the streetcar. He assented but made me promise to meet him the next day at the same time. I muttered something about not being sure I was what Mr. White wanted, but he assured me I was his darling girl and very much wanted to see me again.

The next day when I once again did not become wet when his hands caressed me, he said that maybe I was afraid of sex, afraid of having a man in my vagina. Perhaps he could use my "back door," even though some women found that painful. He would place Vaseline on his penis and an equal amount in my anus. I agreed to this and was soundly buggered that afternoon, even though I am sure the courtly Mr. White did his best not to hurt me. Later that afternoon, I endured vaginal intercourse for the first time. Although I did not become wet, Mr. White assured me I was so tight I had given him the greatest pleasure he had ever experienced in bed. During my last afternoon with Mr. White, we were very much like an old married couple. He placed his organ in my mouth, I sucked it, he then placed a rubber on his erection and then mounted me missionary-style on his way to orgasm.

Mr. White would be back in Hamilton in a month's time. We met in this way over and over again, his career in the navy leaping ahead by leaps and bounds until, just before V-J Day, he reached the rank of Admiral. Unfortunately, he was one of the last major casualties of the war in the Pacific. He never saw his daughter, Heather White, his later nameless still-born daughter nor his son, Peter David White.

There was never a real Mr. White. He is my first fictional creation. He was the person I invented in order to explain the existence of Heather, my first child. Of course, I told the medical and nursing staff at the Hamilton Mountain hospital of my wonderful husband (I doubt they were gullible enough to believe me) and, on the two subsequent occasions when I gave birth there, my husband in the interim had — I proclaimed — earned much-deserved promotions.

The existence of the man who never was went unchallenged by my few friends from Loretto Academy, and most merchants in the city were sympathetic to the plight of the wife of a naval officer, especially one stranded with a young child while her husband was fighting the Japanese in the Coral Sea. Even my account of the wedding in Cleveland, the Tommy Dorsey orchestra in special attendance at the behest of my wealthy in-laws, passed muster.

Of course my stories were preposterous. I cannot believe I could ever have been stupid enough to mouth such monumental untruths. Yet, the story has its own ring of authenticity, provided it is read allegorically. From the age of 21, I held a very special position in the city of Hamilton. I was a courtesan, specially trained by my mother to provide services to the upper-crust gentlemen of the city.

10

Habitually clad in a tweed skirt and a plain jumper, her crisply short mouse-brown hair flecked with white, a pince-nez attached to her nose, my mother was a formidable presence. She was also a consummate snob. Outwardly, she looked and conducted herself very much like Ethel Barrymore. She was large and officious and brooked no nonsense. Like the great American actress, she gave the impression that a heart of gold resided underneath a tough exterior. That was the most masterful of her many duplicities.

By any standard, Mother was a grand character. Even the way she pronounced her name, Alexandra (a name used by the Royals, she frequently pointed out), was theatrical: Al-ex-aaan-draaah. She would enunciate her given name slowly — at least five seconds — and then add MacLean quickly (one second). She was what is sometimes called a handsome woman. This is a difficult expression to define, but it usually refers to a woman whose sense of power is so immense that she can summon up a great deal of respect and admiration from others even though her appearance has a slight masculine edge to it.

My father was fifth business. He looked and acted like a man of absolutely no importance. Small, squat and rodent-like, he did not have a single good facial feature. His look was furtive, always studying situations carefully and guardedly. Usually draped in massively overlarge trench coats, he looked like one of those seedy, sweaty dirty men who populate Graham Greene novels. There were only two extraordinary things about him. He had a sudden, quick and violent temper, and he was an extremely possessive person. If he owned something, no one could remove it from him.

Father, who looked to passers-by on the street a small, inconsequential creature, had a fierce leonine strength which belied his size. He also had a magnificent tenor voice which he displayed at Christ Church Cathedral on Sundays; every other day of the week, the din of his puny, snarling speaking voice was heard at the seedy Balmoral Tavern, near the Hamilton Street Railway headquarters where he worked. When drunk, I later heard, Father would, when teased about his height, invite his tormentor to retire to the washroom where he could view his equipment, the proportions of which were suitable for a titan.

I was born in Beamsville on the Niagara Peninsula on 13 October 1920. My parents moved less than a year later to a modest two-bedroom house, which they had constructed, at 214 Rosslyn Avenue South in Hamilton. The house looked like a bungalow, but it had a large bedroom occupying the front of the house's modest second storey. Our end of the street faced into the side of the escarpment; if we looked up we could see one of the roads carrying cars up the side of the Mountain where many residents of the city lived. The property values on our street were low because three doors away from us — on Lawrence Avenue — was a brick factory and a railway line. The side of the Mountain had been savagely ripped away to make room for them. Four huge kilns belched smoke into the air night and day; the fog horn sounds of the trains blared mainly in the middle of the night.

My parents, in an attempt to pretend that they did not live in Canada, filled their new home with things from the old country. "Bonnie Scotland" would have been a good name for the house, every room of which contained splendid views of lochs, highland mountains, and men in kilts.

Hamilton was Canada's Steel City, very much in the mould of Pittsburgh in the States or Leeds in England. Although graced with an enchantingly beautiful harbour on Lake Ontario, columns of black smoke poured regularly out of a vast multitude of smoke stacks. The stink that often penetrated the air reminded Mother of the foul odours that had filled her nostrils when she had visited Leeds.

Like many other middle-sized cities in North America, Hamilton was largely blue-collar. The only difference between it and nearby Buffalo was the obvious English influence: the flags, the companies whose names ended in Limited and the fact that a significant portion of the adult population revealed British accents or Scottish burrs when they spoke. That group — placed in an uneasy middle between the rich and the poor — were the middle-management types: the foremen and the bank managers.

Never able to compete culturally with Toronto, nearly sixty miles away, Hamilton had in fact been sucked dry by the presence of the Metropolis at its doorstep. So it developed its own society based on a rigid segregation between rich and poor. The rich were the captains of industry and their attendant vassals; then there were the proles — Italian and Polish immigrants — who came to tend the smelters.

Toronto was considered to be a very fast place and so things were appropriately slowed down in Hamilton. In reality, this meant that Hamilton was even more strait-laced than puritanical Toronto, still unaffectionately called Hog Town in the twenties and thirties. The jealousy that Hamilton felt for Toronto surfaced early, in 1847, when *The Globe* dubbed Hamilton the "ambitious" city; the *Hamilton Spectator* promptly castigated Toronto as ostentatiously vulgar: "we cannot display here the paraphernalia of red coats and dashing equipages, but in all that betokens enterprise, public spirit, and future greatness, Hamilton will hold its own ... let us hope that as we walk ahead of our rivals, we shall not imitate their example, and look down with contempt on all who have the misfortune to exist beyond the prescribed limits of Canadian cockney gentility!"

Incessantly, Mother complained that she had moved to a country where pharmacies had replaced chemists, airy pubs had given way to dark bars. "A country of smoke shops is what the Dominion of Canada has become. Not really a country at all. Just a big, hulking colony." She did approve of Mackenzie King, however. But not because the prime minister fostered independence from Britain. Superstition ridden, he believed in the spirit world, often consulting his dead mother on crucial matters of state. "A dutiful son, he is, to his departed Mama."

My earliest memories go back to about 1925, when I was five years old. I remember playing on the lawn in front of our house. I cradle a small doll, who is being a bit fretful. I am trying to comfort her, but I am fighting a losing battle because my mother and father inside the house are screaming at each other. I assure "Nell" that everything will soon settle down. I say this without any assurance I am speaking the truth, for I know that the battles between my parents can go on for hours at a time. Eventually, Nell and I fall asleep by the door. Next, my mother shakes me awake. "You horrible little girl," she shrieks. "I thought you were in your room. I had the fright of my life when you weren't there." I mumbled an apology.

I remember riding up and down the James Street Incline Railway, a seventy-two second ride up or down the face of the escarpment. Sometimes, my mother and I would take the train at the Mountain View Hotel and then descend to the middle of the city. I was puzzled that a city could have a mountain where people lived. My mother scoffed: "They call it a mountain, darling, but it's really more of a hill plopped down in the middle of the city."

Then there was the elaborate, ornate, magnificent fountain in the middle of Gore Park a short walk away from Eaton's. Once — I must have been 6 — when my mother was less vigilant than usual, I escaped from her and managed to slip through the iron railing on the periphery of the fountain. Of course I returned soaked to the bone and received a severe dressing-down.

I have a vague recollection of being taken to the Sunken Gardens in front of McMaster University on Main Street. Fascinated by the huge lily pads floating in the long concrete reflecting pool, I considered the possibility of wading in to pluck one of the huge pink flowers but, weighing the consequences carefully, decided not to. I remember being dragged along in August 1930 to the British Empire Games (the first ever) at the Civic Stadium; there, in the pouring rain, I had to sit through a dozen or so foot races. Despite the awful weather, my mother purred delight: "This city is linked as never before with the Imperial family — the best family in the world."

Then there was the Farmer's Market where I can still see a pyramid of gleaming russet apples, a small hill of bright orange pumpkins, and hundreds of purple-flowering autumn cabbages. My mother was shocked when she took me to see the new Rock Garden made from what had once been a gravel pit. On the day we visited only a small sprinkling of tiny Alpines had established themselves. "In the United Kingdom, we have real gardens with real flowers, Evelyn. Never has the term 'Rock Garden' been more appropriately used to describe a rubbish pile." Almost out of control, she whispered loudly: "For the life of me I don't understand how your father sweet-talked me into this." That lament — repeated on a regular basis — would be accompanied by a majestic sweep of her right hand. Everything within her line of vision was an eyesore.

My recollections of childhood are fragmentary at best. I did not know precisely why until I read Virginia Woolf's *Moments of Being* where she provides an account of how her teenage half-brother placed his hands into her private parts: "I can remember the feel of his hand going under my clothes; going firmly and steadily lower and lower. I remember how I hoped he would stop." Those words haunted me as I read them, as did Sylvia Fraser's *My Father's House*, her account of growing up in Hamilton fifteen years later than myself.

At first, my father did not force himself on me. No, he was a subtle thief. He would fondle me, usually in the presence of my mother; when her back was turned — even for a moment — he would place a finger into my vagina. Or, he would take my hand and place it on his erection, a blissful smug expression crossing his face — as if he were a lover made happy because he was soon to arrive at the moment of orgasm inside his beloved.

A bit later — I would have been 9 or 10 — he attempted to penetrate me. He summoned me to the large bedroom at the front of the house shared by him and my mother. Summarily, he informed me it was a hot day. When I agreed with this observation, he suggested we remove our clothes and lie down on the bed. I knew this was an improper thing to do and when I voiced my reluctance to do so, he informed me I was like my mother: unforgiving and cruel. He had simply wanted to show some affection towards me, and I — like "the other female occupant of the premises" — was a cold little bitch.

As he said these things, he removed his clothes, revealing in the process his erect penis. He began to manipulate his member, pushing his foreskin up and down as if he were peeling and then re-peeling a very large banana. Then, he ordered me to remove my clothes. Frightened and confused, I began to cry. He walked over to me and began to pull my clothes away. I became hysterical and began to scream. He pushed me on to the bed. Just as he was about to have his way with me, the door opened and there was Mother. A migraine having descended upon her, she had begged off work two hours before her shift finished.

Swiftly and decisively, she commanded my father to leave the room. He was never allowed to sleep there again. The full force of Mother's temper was directed against me, however. "A fine little vixen you have become. A regular little temptress." She slapped me hard on the face and informed me that I would henceforth cohabit with her "in order to protect you from your father's filthy lust." She then sat on the bed for a few minutes and, in the process of adjusting herself and retrieving my torn clothing from the floor, commanded me to make her a pot of tea. "Strong, the way you know I like it." She dismissed me from the room. The incident was never discussed again.

My mother and father did not argue about sex. They had many other causes for complaint. Both of them had left Scotland — where they met and married — with the intention of "making a go of it" (one of my mother's favourite expressions) in the New World. In a good mood, she would become philosophical. She and Donald did not believe the streets in Canada would be paved with gold, but they had expected that Canada, in the wake of the promise of renewal engendered by the end of the Great War, would allow them to become prosperous, moderately well-off. Then the mood swing would come full circle, her face turning bright red: they had been mightily disappointed. Thus, the ensuing bickering about money. My mother would complain about my father's excessive drinking and my father would lament my mother's pretensions. He especially did not like her invention of the mysterious Lady MacLean, his aunt, who had married a peer of the realm. Since my mother did not have a fantasy world into which she could tap when inebriated, she imagined herself as having married into a family that had risen in the world. Many were the stories I was told as a child about my great aunt. At various times, her long dead husband was an inventor, a physician rewarded with a baronetage because of his exemplary service to the Royals when they were in residence at Balmoral.

Our neighbours in Hamilton — working-class Poles, Italians, and Irish — understood instinctively that my mother was mendacious, knowing full well that her anecdotes were a way of establishing some sort of dominion over them. As a result, my mother became an object of curiosity and of loathing. In effect, she segregated herself from everyone around her. In the process, she made me an outsider as well.

In my mother's view of the world, those born in any part of the United Kingdom and into any station of life there were inherently superior to those born in Canada. Soon after moving to Hamilton, she found her world-view in open conflict with the "natives." She joined a circle of women who purchased Limoges blanks from France and then decorated and fired the various vases and plates in their own kilns. Those women, she soon discovered, were uppity. She dropped out of the group. Then Mother attempted to infiltrate The Wynn Rutty Radio Writers who wrote and performed plays on CHML. Quite soon — when her ideas about scripts were not readily received — she denounced Mrs. Rutty, Mrs. Pettit and Mrs. Fuller as prissy village tyrants, colonials unappreciative of the finer points of theatricals.

Later, my mother would maintain I was queer, shunned by other children. But she was the cranky person who made me such. In fact, my mother had her own special way of reserving me exclusively for herself. If I became friendly, as I did, with Anita, three doors down, who was of German ancestry, my mother immediately became fixated on her racial origins. Like all Krauts and Huns, my friend was overly aggressive and warlike. Helen, a year younger than I, was a Kike, who came from a race famous for money-lending and various kinds of opportunistic cheating. Little, adorable, red-haired Bernadette, whose family had emigrated from the Emerald Isle, came from a group of rabid opportunists who had invaded England and Scotland, bred like rabbits, believed in witchcraft and made the United Kingdom uninhabitable for respectable Scots. The worse offenders — probably because they were more numerous — were the "EYE-tal-ians," slummy dark-featured people whose men were only interested in sex, whose women — after marriage — dressed in black for the simple purpose of annoying her.

Together, my mother and father — themselves usually clad in blacks and greys — resembled those tiresome comedians, Laurel and Hardy. Like Oliver Hardy, my mother looked overstuffed, her natural expression was a smirk, and her good-humour could quickly convert itself into what it did a bad job concealing: the rage that consumed every fibre of her being. My short, delicate-looking father was the perfect foil to her, a full partner in the *folie à deux* that was their marriage. In a manner similar to Stan Laurel when he provoked his partner, my father was an expert in passive-aggressive behaviour: he would play dumb at the very moment he said or did something he knew would incite my mother's anger. This would cause her to strike him, making her the perpetrator of spousal abuse.

So imbued was my mother with the silver screen that she even once (my father had corrected her pronunciation of an obscure word) re-enacted the celebrated breakfast table sequence wherein James Cagney pressed a grapefruit into the face of his moll. In his turn, my father seemed to receive a strange pleasure from inciting my mother to violence. As if he were proving something about her to himself. His face would become suffused by a sickly sweet smirk. My mother suffered no fool gladly, and she was especially prone to being goaded by my father playing that role. In essence, that was their relationship: she was testy, and he took a malicious pleasure in making her more so.

My parents were extremely indirect with each other. Mother knew full well that my father's pay from the bus company was far more than it should have been — she both ordered and controlled the activity. He knew — in his capacity as janitor and security guard —

the combination to the safe, and would, from time to time, remove huge amounts of tickets, and then sell them on his own improvised black market. The proceeds from these sales would then be deposited — usually in small change — at his two banks — a branch of the Bank of Toronto, the other a branch of the Canadian Bank of Commerce — which flanked the HSR offices at the corner of Wentworth and King Streets. Yet, this activity was merely hinted at in exchanges between my parents in front of me.

"Donald, we are very short this week."

"Yes, my love. I shall work on it."

"Don't work on it — do it!"

"Let me think about it."

"I've told you a hundred times not to think. Just do what you are told."

If my father kept quiet at this point, the matter would die a natural death. But sometimes he needled my mother.

"How do you propose I solve the problem, dearest? Our savings are very limited. I can only make so many withdrawals and our piggy bank will be empty." This would be said in a loud swaggering voice, a glint of mischief entering his eye. He would wink at me, making me a co-conspirator.

More and more, my mother's anger was vented on my father. In the process, I became an uneasy bystander, a pawn in their bitter war. To be fair, Mother hardly had an easy time of it. Her domestic chores were vast and complicated. She hand-washed all the laundry before laboriously placing it on the clothesline to dry. She also maintained a vegetable garden, chicken coops and rabbit hutches in the back yard. When the laundry was thoroughly dry, she ironed it all — even the sheets.

Briefly, she took a job at the Membery Mattress Company but quit when her legs could no longer bear the constant pumping on the foot pedal that powered her sewing machine (electrical power would have made the expenses of the company too heavy and thus uncompetitive). Before that, the sweat that poured down her face made it impossible for her to see, so blinded was she by the salt water that invaded her eyes. So, she had a towel draped over her shoulder, which she made constant use of.

At the time she came across my father and myself *in flagrante*, Mother worked as a "tinflipper" at the Stelco steel works, one of the few well-paid jobs for females in the steel industry because women, unlike men, did not become bored inspecting both sides of a tin plate. The supposition of the captains of industry was that women, after centuries devoted to knitting and sewing, had quick eyes and patient hands. This stereotyping obviously did not lead to any other kind of preferment in the factory.

My father had refused to walk through what he called the "gates of hell" at Dofasco and Stelco, the two big steel works, each giant accounting for thousands of immigrant jobs. These places — in his words — were "bloody, dangerous infernos." He was especially frightened by what he had heard of what could happen during a "bottom pour," when overhead cranes delivered the enormous ladles of burning, bubbling steel from the furnaces to the men who waited to guide the pour into huge moulds. The twenty dollars a week the men were paid for such work hardly kept them and their families above the poverty line, but my father settled for the lowly job at the street railway company which supposedly gave him only seven dollars a week (the steel companies paid twenty-five cents an hour: ten dollars for a forty-hour week). Before that, father had worked for a month or so at the huge Tuckett Tobacco factory on Queen Street, but he quit when he could no longer remove the accumulation of the thick juice of the demon weed from his hands.

According to my mother, father was a coward, who refused to do a real man's work. He forced his wife to work in factories because he was not man enough to do so himself. What kind of a husband did this to his wife? She, therefore, felt completely justified in demanding he earn "extra wages" (another euphemism devised for my benefit) by volunteering for overtime. So, both the battleground and the battle lines were firmly established. The fighting was constant, my mother taking on the role of the aggressor. My father obviously felt his manhood had been ripped from him, and my mother was certain, as she told me, that she did not have a proper husband even though her spouse had an "instrument of unnatural size not intended for normal sexual activity." She also reminded me frequently that I was not really a natural daughter. In more ways than one I was an orphan from an early age.

What was it like to live in that small house? The wallpaper had begun to disintegrate, falling in little strips to the floor; the glossy paint on the doors had chipped badly. I can still smell the cooking odours, the gas leaking from the oven. I do not remember much daylight ever penetrating those rooms. In my mind's eye, I am a large Alice — no magic potion at hand — trapped in a small, narrow room in which she cannot move.

My mother's domain was the bedroom; my father's, the makeshift space he cobbled together in the basement. Rightly suspicious of my father's easily assembled charm, I avoided him. I had only my sour mother for any kind of solace.

11

Roswitha (Rosie), the girl of my own age who lived across the street, escaped my mother's scorn because her parents were even more preoccupied with status than was she. Mr. and Mrs. Bauer were also fierce anti-Semites. So, Rosie's German ancestry was both tolerated and forgiven. Although she would not have wanted to admit it, my mother was entranced with the little bairn's snow-white hair and refined features. One day, in a moment of tenderness not usual to the way she normally conducted herself, my mother informed me that she liked seeing Rosie and myself playing together. "Like having two wee Scotch terriers, one white, one black." Such were the compliments that came my way.

Since Rosie was the only one of my acquaintances who was welcome in our home, she, not surprisingly, became my best friend. We played with dolls, but we were encouraged by Rosie's father to devote ourselves to more academic pursuits, such as stamp collecting. At school, we were diligent, willing pupils, although neither of us did particularly well. Discouraged by his daughter's poor results, Mr. Bauer decided to enroll her at Loretto Academy. Upset at the prospect of losing Rosie, I confided in my mother my distress. To my great surprise, she told me she was perfectly well aware of this turn of events. The Bauers had informed her of their decision.

"Evelyn, sit down, dear." I was surprised by the gushy, confidential, almost affectionate tone in her voice. "I have given the matter some thought, and I have decided that you shall accompany Rosie to her new school." I must have looked very startled because my mother stopped speaking and looked carefully into my face, as if trying to discover the full state of my feelings. "In fact, I visited two of the dear nuns at Loretto Academy yesterday afternoon. The Mother Superior and the principal. As you know, they do not like to take non-Catholics into their midst. The Bauers were born Catholic, although they do not practice that creed, as they have become Lutherans. Any kind of Catholic is acceptable to the nuns. No self-respecting Scotswoman is a Catholic, and I could not pretend your father or I were born into that faith. No, I had to take quite a different approach. When I mentioned that your aunt, dear Lady MacLean, would, if they accepted you, be paying your fees, their interest quickened. Seldom do they have the opportunity to be associated with members of the English peerage. I'd notice in the paper how that posh finishing school — Strathallan — has Lady Bessborough as its Patron. I offered the nuns their own Lady! That did the trick. You have been given a place for this fall."

I was vaguely aware that Loretto Academy was a society school. There were several other perfectly good private schools for girls in Hamilton. I also had some knowledge even at the age of 11 that the fees at my new school were outrageously high. I felt a bit guilty, as if I were putting my parents to an unnecessary expense. Not sure of what to say, I hesitated and then simply observed that Loretto was costly.

"Of course, it is my dear. Lady MacLean will help us out." I was already perfectly aware that there was no such person. In fact, I knew it was a code word between my parents, referring to the money my father routinely pilfered — at my mother's instigation — from the Hamilton Street Railway Company. Any reference to financial assistance by dear, sweet Lady MacLean was a reference to the resulting cache of money hidden away in my mother's bedroom closet.

So, with the assistance of my Scots relative, about whom I was questioned incessantly by the nuns, I attended Loretto Academy, the educational benefits of which were in my mother's eyes secondary to the useful contacts I might make there. I would meet girls from the right families, one of whose sons might eventually make a suitable match for me. Despite my mother's hatred of Popish ways, she had an even greater contempt for the solid core of wealthy, stodgy Presbyterians — the Hendrys, the Faircloughs, the Buchanans, the Burkholders — who controlled Hamilton, then a city of one hundred and fifty thousand inhabitants. Catholics were very much a minority and, in such circumstances, she hoped, a certain fluidity in outlook might prevail. A penniless young Protestant girl with good connections back in the old country might stand a chance of marrying a good Catholic boy.

"You are not to be at all concerned about the money, Evelyn. You must simply strive to do your best at your studies." Then, she changed her tone considerably and quickly: "So buck up, my girl! The nuns will assist me in keeping your wanton ways in check. I hope you will use your time at the school profitably. Perhaps you will attract the attention of a young man of your own age from Cathedral Boys' School." The issuing of marching orders always signalled the end of any conversation with Mother.

Lady MacLean's money covered the tuition at the square, squat building that was Loretto Academy, but it did not extend to an appropriate wardrobe. Visually, Rosie and I were very much out of place in the company of the wealthy Catholic girls. We were shunned and, later, ostracized. The nuns, who came from wealthy families, were also snobbish, but, at least, they were moderately civil to the two foreigners in their midst.

Although my mother had no deep sympathy for the Romans, she shared with the nuns a rigidity of outlook that made them, despite their differences, sisters. Since I had never been exposed to religious belief before, I was startled by the representations of Jesus. The

Sacred Heart was the most fascinating case in point. How could he have a heart exterior to his body? I wondered. Did he have two hearts: one inner, one outer? The denial of basic biology offended me.

Even more worrying were the crucifixes that adorned every single classroom. I was perturbed that Christ was almost naked, his private parts covered with a loin cloth. In some of these representations, the pain that filled his face seemed to be touched with a glimmer of pleasure. I sensed that those small sculptures mixed death, pain and sex perfectly: in some cases, a powerfully built Jesus had an athlete's body and the hint of a penis could be seen in the folds of the covering around his middle.

I must confess that the frequent references to Christ as the bridegroom of the nuns were extremely confusing. As we were walking home from school one day, Rosie said to me: "I don't know how he can be their bridegroom."

"What do you mean? They say they're married to him, spiritually."

"Yes. But the bridegroom does 'it' with the bride."

I pretended ignorance. "I don't know what you mean."

"Yes, you do. The groom gets his 'thing' big and then puts it into the bride."

"No, they don't mean it in that way. It's not about sex for them."

"It is so! They ask him to fill them."

"With grace."

"Yes, that's what they say. Really, they want his 'thing' in them, pushing in and out."

I told Rosie to hush, not to be stupid. She was, as usual, playing the clown to my Miss Priss. But, in her own way, she was, of course, quite correct.

With one exception, the nuns were ghastly teachers, much more interested in imparting their religious beliefs than instructing us in mathematics or history. The references to chastity and purity were constant. Sometimes the emphasis was on the opposite sex. Boys were ferocious beasts who preyed on innocent young girls. They could not help themselves. It was their nature to be out of control; it was the girl's responsibility to keep them under control. Sometimes, the talk was at this very elemental, psychological level. At other times, the euphemisms were slightly less pronounced. Boys were more outer than girls, who were inner.

Our biology teacher, however, refused to teach the chapter on the sexual reproduction of tapeworms. She told us the material was disgusting and would not, therefore, discuss it. But, since it might appear on the provincially regulated examinations, we should study it by ourselves. Once, when I asked my mother about such matters, she took it as an offence that such an enquiry would be made.

"Well, my dear, men always want to plant their seeds in women. It's their nature."

Surprised by her botanical turn of phrase, I asked her how the man planted his seeds. At the time, I did not remember that my father had been attempting to sow his seed in me.

"Eve-e-lyn, you are becoming too inquisitive and literal-minded. It's simply a fact of life, one of the chief facts of life. You are too young to think about such things. Do the nuns talk about such things? Why have you become interested in such matters all of a sudden?" She looked at me very suspiciously, obviously wondering if I was referring to my father's behaviour.

No, I assured her, the nuns did not talk of such matters. I could hardly tell her — I suppose I did not realize it at the time — that my new school was a hotbed of ripe sexuality. In a very strange way, it was a breeding ground for the vices the nuns ostensibly wanted to stomp on. My classmates — even those who did spectacularly well in catechism class — often spoke of what it would be like to be "eaten" by their boyfriends, many of whom seemed to be exceptionally well experienced in the pleasures of "finger fucking." Such was the contrast between the language of the nuns and the words of even their most devoted pupils.

Many of the nuns were mustachioed and a corresponding male brutality invaded their behaviour. If you forgot how to conjugate an irregular French verb or did not know the proper plural of goose, your outstretched hands could be subjected to brutal lashes from a thick ruler or strap. If you were unable to remember something assigned for homework, you were automatically assumed to be guilty of slovenliness and had to be punished accordingly.

Mother Patricia Francis was the epitome of the brides of Christ. Every morning, she lurched herself into the classroom like some huntsman certain that his prey was on the point of evading him. A member of a family whose considerable fortune was derived from Hamilton's steel works, this nun had absolutely no interest in us as young women. She would have preferred teaching at Cathedral Boys'. Her limited imagination, fixated on football players, was excited by the idea of manliness, qualities which her students were forever excluded from possessing and thus pleasing her. And, paradoxically, she seemed genuinely hurt and angry that we did not display such attributes. At the time, I had no comprehension of how her strange notions — especially for a girls' school — had come into being. Now, I am certain that she was sexually repressed and envied those of us who might, in time, receive the manly caresses from which her vow of chastity permanently disenfranchised her. As a child, she made me feel there was something inherently wrong with me because I was born female.

I was fortunate enough to have one excellent teacher during my eight years at Loretto. Mother St. John was small, thin, and pale. Her complexion was splotchy, her nose overly pointed, and she suffered so dreadfully from eczema that she always wore thin white gloves. That there was something exceptional about this awkward young woman could be first glimpsed in the majestic way she carried herself.

"Why do we read?" That was the first question she posed to the assemblage of sixteen-year-olds gathered before her. Without waiting for anyone to venture a response, she proceeded to answer her own query. Enjoyment was the first item on her list, although she passed over it quickly. Moral and spiritual enlightenment were mentioned but not dwelt upon. "To see into the creative spirit, the heart of the imagination?" she suggested. The tone in her voice revealed that, as far as she was concerned, this was the only real answer.

When she taught us, Mother stood still, at the dead centre of the front of the room. She spoke quietly but with great authority. If she were to offer a particularly new or startling insight, she would move to her far right and position herself by the window. "Emily Dickinson lived what from the outside seemed a humdrum existence. She was isolated in that large house in Amherst, Massachusetts. She knew first-hand the dreariness of so much of daily life, its essential emptiness. And yet she wrote her strange, contorted fragments of poems as protests against dreariness. They were tiny, isolated little screams, celebrating the radiance one can find in the everyday. Those lyrics were wrenched from her solitary heart." When delivering herself of such observations, Mother's voice became quieter than ever. With every fibre of my being, I longed to hear more, to find some entry into the mysteries of my own humdrum existence.

In those days, that irrepressible wild girl Emily Brontë was my ideal rather than her more careful elder sister, Charlotte. I knew that Emily's excess of life led to her early demise, but I could not help but be overcome with Catherine's devotion to Heathcliff, the way in which the lovers mirrored each other. At some level of my being, I understood the cruel sadism of Heathcliff, the many ways in which he is an outcast and a reprobate. In contrast, the gothic romance of Jane and Rochester seemed tame, too irrevocably adult. The explosive language of Emily spoke to my heart, already one filled with bitterness.

Later, it would be maintained by various investigators of my early life that I was little better than an idiot. Proof of this could be found, it was hinted, in my academic record at Loretto. This is not true. To be sure, my performance there was mediocre. There were extenuating circumstances, the indifferent teaching and snobbery of the nuns being the chief claim I can make to excuse myself. Yet, there was the afternoon Mother St. John called me aside.

This was the only time I ever saw her hands, beautifully shaped but marred by a myriad of tiny bright pink eruptions that had permanently invaded them. She was exchanging one pair of gloves — covered with chalk dust — for the much cleaner pair she kept in reserve. She was seated at her desk and motioned for me to sit down at the student desk closest to hers. For once, she seemed lost for words.

Hesitantly, she began. "Your academic work is not very good, Evelyn. Do you study at home? I know you do the work assigned, but do you actually study?" I assured her I did my best to comply with everything I was asked to do.

"Yes, yes. I thought that was the case. You are one of the strangest girls I have ever taught. You write like an angel, and in your essays you show considerable understanding of what you read." She stopped a bit abruptly, looking into my face to see if she could discover its secrets. "And yet, your exams display none of that talent. Do you have any idea why this is so?"

I, too, was puzzled by the discrepancy. Quite often, I was simply bored when I did my assigned tasks. At other times, they seemed futile pursuits, as if I were trying to catch trains that always pulled out of stations just as I arrived to board them. If I wrote an essay, I could bring my entire consciousness to bear, actually get lost in the enterprise. If I had to memorize something, I became easily and often permanently distracted. It was not simply, I increasingly realized, that I could not do the work: I did not wish to do the work. I shrugged my shoulders, unable to muster a suitable response to the kindly concern bestowed upon me.

The nun did not seem offended by my perfunctory response. In fact, a small, bright smile crossed her face. "Never mind, my dear, you possess some wonderful gifts. Eventually, they will see you through."

My mother and the Mothers. At times, this seemed the sum total of my teenage world. How could I be any kind of success when I frustrated all their expectations? None of the few Catholic boys I encountered had the slightest interest in me. I obviously was not a worthy niece of the great Lady MacLean, who must have been both baffled and aggrieved, the nuns imagined, when she read my school reports.

12

Towards the end of my time at Loretto, my mother became increasingly worried that I had not met a good Catholic boy whom I could marry. One day, she summarily informed me: "You're a very attractive young woman, Evelyn. I have no idea why you do not have streams of boyfriends in attendance."

My large, dark doe eyes gave me the look, Mother told me, of a young Bette Davis. This may have been so, but Rosie and I were segregated from the other students at Loretto — and from the young men who courted them. There was an invisible line that placed the two of us into a limbo of unacceptableness. We looked and acted like our peers, but there was something different. We did not take riding lessons, we could not afford to go to Europe during the summer. Our clothing was not from the finest shops in Toronto. Moreover, we were Protestants, the sworn enemies of Papists. Rosie, anxious to please, finally found a male friend. I did not.

Not someone to say no to adversity, my mother tried to find a way around a difficult situation. I was not invited to any events at the Catholic homes in Hamilton, and we certainly could not invite my schoolmates to our drab little house with its drab furnishings. The drapes and carpet were in shades of olive green, and the guts of the dark brown chesterfield were spilling to the floor. So Mother decided to hold a cotillion in Toronto. Such events had become a part of the social scene there. Large, first-floor rooms were rented out by various hotels for such events, which were often elegantly catered; small orchestras would play — melodies by Rogers and Hart and Cole Porter. In arranging such an event, my mother was placing herself in the forefront of modernity. The costs were high but, once again, Lady MacLean was summoned to the rescue. Only the best would do. In this case, the monumental chateau-like façade of the Royal York prompted Mother's choice: "Real class that is."

The small orchestra, the precision-cut sandwiches, the prim waiters, the austere gothic beauty of the hotel. They were perfect, but no one except Rosie, her boyfriend Stephen and her parents showed up at the appointed time. My mother, surveying the enormous room she had rented, gulped in astonishment but said little. She spoke in flat, unenunciated tones to Rosie's parents. My father helped himself to copious amounts of liquor. Rosie and Stephen took a few turns on the floor while the remainder of the small assembly watched. At Rosie's prodding, Stephen asked me to dance. After about an hour, the seven of us left.

The Bauers were quietly pleased by Rosie's acquisition of the Catholic boyfriend she had met at a Loretto dance. Stephen's parents were among the city's wealthy; their huge mock-Tudor home on Bay Street was an appropriate monument to their grand status. Unbeknownst to them, Stephen, who looked a very ordinary boy next door (mouse-brown hair, average height, unexceptional build) had the reputation among his peers of being an extremely successful sex fiend. His mild, unassuming exterior concealed a warped heart. On their first date, Stephen had been, according to

Rosie, a model gentleman. On the second, he stuck his tongue down her throat as soon as they began kissing. On the third, he ordered her to give him a hand job. On the fourth, he told her he would only see her again if she agreed to allow him to have anal intercourse with her: he wanted to take no chances of her becoming pregnant. So, this was the substance of their relationship, a meagre bowl of porridge.

I was not interested in having a similar relationship with a boy. Rosie thought this unwise and unnatural of me, but, if I am honest about it, her descriptions of sex frightened rather than intrigued me. Even the tender glow of love — so-called natural desire — offered me nothing. I thought I was cold, "queer" (to use Mother's word), to have absolutely no wish to investigate this realm of experience, which Rosie held dear despite the humiliation it brought with it.

Later, classmates at Loretto — when grilled by reporters from the *Hamilton Spectator* or interviewers from radio station CKOC — would recall how strange I was. "She was very beautiful," one said, "in an exaggerated way, almost like a film star. But she was not popular. Quite the contrary, no one liked her. Mind you, what makes this strange, is that no one envied her good looks. She was shy to the point of rudeness. She never had anything to say and when she did speak, she never talked the way we did. She never fitted in." Another, in breathless tones, confided: "Evelyn was not Catholic. This made everything difficult, certainly at first. But she never showed any willingness to become a member of the Loretto family."

As a teenager, I had nowhere to turn. On the surface, Rosie and I remained close friends, but I had started to study her as some sort of object lesson in wrong turns. I was fascinated by what she told me of her strange relationship with Stephen — I even quizzed her on all the intricacies of her sex life. I became the voyeur to whom Rosie happily confessed her intimacies. In the process, I was doing absolutely nothing to mollify my impatient mother. If I could not marry a wealthy man, exactly what did I propose to do, she asked me, with my sorry existence?

In the countless interviews with my former schoolmates, the reporters uncovered another thread. "Evelyn was always giving presents to the most popular girls, especially those a grade or two ahead of her. She was obviously trying to buy protection, perhaps affection. It was awfully pathetic. Sad, really." Another old chum offered this opinion: "The gifts were really expensive. She once gave me a set of pearl beads. I still have them. Not cultivated pearls — real ones. Worth a fortune now. She must have shoplifted them."

According to this wag, my criminal career began in earnest at an exceedingly early age. I was not that precocious. The gifts were purchased from Lady MacLean's fund by my mother at Birk's, Hamilton's most resplendent jeweller. Mother, after quizzing me on the power strata among the girls, determined the lucky recipients of this largesse (one receipt was for $2,761, a very hefty sum in those days). My parent, obviously a person whose conscience was easily bought off, did not realize that teenage girls might be of more independent frames of mind. What is of more interest is the intriguing question: what about the young girl whose only protector is her greatest enemy?

13

Even from the relatively safe vantage point of the past, I remain obsessed with my mother. She has been dead over forty years, and I loathe her. As a youngster, I did not have the luxury of hindsight. Precarious though it was, she was the only lifeline I had.

Since about the age of 8, I shared her bed, my father having been banished to the basement years before. Despite the frequent lashings-out of bad temper, Mother's was the only constant presence I knew. I could, God help me, always count on her to be her bad-natured self.

I was a deprived child who came to depend upon my depriver. Then, it did not seem so simple. I am not sure, on the other hand, that it was all that complicated. A child has to count on her mother for something. My mother may not have wanted to harm me, but in her increasingly twisted way she could not help doing so.

I had to make something of myself. She continually informed me. "You have to become someone important." Today, she might sound like some sort of proto-feminist. In reality, I had to become significant because she had never achieved prominence. I was her daughter, destined to achieve that of which she had been incapable.

Yet, there was no way for me to obtain the status she hankered for. We were poor. I had not done particularly well at school. My mother wanted to re-make me, to create a daughter she could admire and whom the world admired. As far as she was concerned, few options presented themselves. She did not have the resources of a wealthy bachelor like Henry Higgins.

There were moments of tenderness, especially when she joined me in bed, the sheets of which were of the finest Egyptian cotton. A huge, silk cream-coloured puff rested on top, as if creating an island of serenity in a turbulent world. "If you can't be comfortable in bed, you'll never be comfortable anywhere else" was one of her many truisms. In such moments, my mother would actually relax, sometimes allowing a wan smile to cross her face.

"Pet," she would plead, "you're such a good reader. Read a story to me. A nice one."

"Nice stories" were not usually of the passionate variety. They had to have quick, sudden turns to them as in O. Henry's "The Gift of the Magi" or they had to have an air of menace and comedy fused together as in the little Saki mysteries she adored. Since her attention span was limited and would not allow a narrative to be carried over from one day to the next, I was happy to chance upon the *Arabian Nights' Entertainments*. I read these to her over the course of many years because it took months to get through the whole lot, at which point Mother would have forgotten everything that came before.

In many ways, I became the perfect *lectrice*. As I came to know these stories intimately, I allowed myself to enter the world of the secret underground caves, hot desert sands, and forbidden harems. The voice of the resourceful Scheherezade became mine. Like her, I was trying to save myself from a depraved tyrant.

"You are so clever, darling," Mother would sometimes proclaim. "You read with such feeling, as if you had written those stories yourself.

You put so much of yourself into them." I nodded appreciation in the direction of my despot.

In addition to the *Arabian Nights*, my loving tyrant was most addicted to fairy tales. First, we read Hans Christian Andersen, then the Brothers Grimm. Perhaps I could not help seeing my own plight reflected in the fate of Hansel and Gretel, outcasts of their family home in the wake of their mother's death and consigned to wander the forest in the wake of their father's weakness and their stepmother's cruelty. I rejoiced when they outsmarted the witch who contrived the enticing gingerbread house in order to destroy them. Perhaps, like them, I hoped one day to get the best of my oppressors. I certainly saw my own plight reflected in the torments to which those two exceedingly resourceful children were subjected. Music is said to soothe the savage beast but, at an early age, I learned the power of the written word to accomplish this task.

14

I may not have looked like an Ugly Duckling, but I was made to feel like one. In every conceivable way, I was a disappointment to my mother. Since the prospect of alliance with an offspring of a wealthy Catholic family had come to nothing, I had to find some sort of employment. Hamilton was not fertile ground if one did not wish to work in a factory. I was constitutionally lazy. Or, to put it more accurately, since there were no interesting prospects, I became indifferent to my future.

I worked for just over three weeks at Westinghouse, winding coils for refrigerator motors. Two hundred and twenty women there had to deal with over thirty-two million feet of wire for transformer distributions. Unfortunately, I was not the wizard at winding demanded by the company; my fingers were much too slow.

My life seemed even more humdrum after I became a telephone operator — a much lower paying job. I was one of sixty women lined up in a row connecting callers with each other. Often I would hear frustration in a voice that was having trouble reaching its destination and thus pleading for my assistance; elation sometimes followed when I provided the correct information. At times, the voices were filled with terror, loathing, fear, apprehension, even disgust. Since I was party only to the request, I had no idea of the subsequent conversations. I heard many emotions, made the connections and then vanished from the ensuing scene.

Most days, I would meet Rosie at her place of work, the Hemming Brothers Travel Office in the Sun Building on James Street South. She always sat glumly at her desk, her long-handled telephone and typewriter her only accessories; glamorous photographs of ocean liners filled all the available wall space behind her. How often we fantasized about taking one of those huge ships to France or even sultry Morocco. Rosie never sold a single ticket that would carry someone aboard those streamlined, miniature cities. Her lot, she informed me, was to sell train tickets to Buffalo.

One Saturday she and I took turns riding in one of the small twin-engines at East Hamilton Airport. I remember screaming in delight and horror as the flirtatious pilot dive-bombed the city he was supposedly giving me a sedate aerial view of. He chortled when one particularly malicious swooping curve turned my face green. Rosie and I became well known at all the hot spots: the White Towers Snack Bar on Burlington Beach, at the Wonder Grove, the outdoor dance floor and bandstand in the east end, and at the Alexandra Ballroom and Roller Rink on James Street South.

There were some red-letter days. I remember seeing King George VI and Queen Elizabeth at City Hall on June 7, 1939. The King stuttered badly when he spoke; the Queen had a gentle, reflective smile. She waved directly at me when leaving the platform, our eyes locking together for a second or two. I attended the Victory Bond Rally in October 1944 — I even overcame my customary shyness by selling bonds door-to-door. I was one of the sweating, screaming thousands who gathered together at Gore Park to celebrate V-E Day.

These events were momentary distractions. My life centred on the films at the Tivoli and the real life adventures of the stars. My eyes feasted on the black and white and Technicolor images that flickered on the screen. I greedily devoured each issue of *Photoplay*, seeking excitement in the glamorous existences off-screen of my various heroines, such as Rita Hayworth, whom my mother contemptuously referred to as "that red-haired tramp" because of her quick real-life turnover in lovers and husbands. I was intrigued by how Rita, who began life as Margarita Carmen Cansino, a cousin of Ginger Rogers and the leading player in a series of frightful B-pictures, transformed herself into a siren. Not able to decipher fantasy from reality, I believed in the world Rita inhabited. I did not wish to be bothered with a succession of lovers, but I was bewitched by the jewellery, the furs, the clothing, and the fairyland California haciendas.

After the excitement of seeing the latest film at the Tivoli, everything around me seemed extraordinarily lacklustre, streets of broken dreams. Rosie, my companion on such outings, and I felt banished from the real world of Hollywood. We would wander down to Gore Park or, if we were in a particularly desperate mood, we would stroll into a pub, where we had to give the barman precise instructions — gleaned from *Vogue* — on how to construct a martini; and we had to always insure our drinks were served in the proper glasses. Our adulation of screen heroines also took us in the direction of imitating their clothing. Since we could not afford anything expensive, our best efforts consisted of realtering — and sometimes ruining — the dresses, skirts and blouses we purchased at Eaton's or Robinson's, the city's two main department stores.

Rosie continued her recitation of her various sexual adventures with Stephen, whose reading, confined to the Marquis de Sade, was assiduously put into practice. Despite Rosie's pleasure in any kind of sexual experience with him, he made any kind of orgasm forbidden to her. If, on the few occasions he penetrated her vagina, she gave any sign of experiencing pleasure, he would quickly withdraw. Stephen's cruelty provided her with a frisson all its own.

I have always been an overly tactful person, but I once or twice offered Rosie my opinion on Stephen.

She was defensive. "You simply don't understand. He's such a thrilling person. Always something new."

"But he's always hurting you."

"No, no. You misunderstand. He's wonderful to be around. I never feel bored. I can't live my life like yours — at a distance." She paused. "You are very beautiful. Yet you've never had a boyfriend. Stephen thinks you're a lesbo."

"He can think what he likes." I was not going to provide Rosie — and thus Stephen — with any information about myself, "Better a fantasy life than the reality to which you're addicted." Rosie would pout for a half hour or so after such an exchange. Then, we would gossip and speculate about the amours of the screen stars we adored.

Mother considered the girl talk between myself and Rosie a complete waste of time. "There is no sense in living in a dream world. Harsh, cold reality. That's what you need a touch of, Evelyn." Mother mouthed those words at the very same time she assiduously followed — and aped — the dress fashions in Hamilton. This was a strange undertaking.

As Mother discovered, staying abreast of the latest trends in the Steel City was a difficult task. First of all, most of the women of wealth bought their clothes in Toronto, which was always two or three seasons behind New York and Hollywood. So Hamilton had no genuine trend-setters. Eaton's department store in Hamilton was always a year behind Eaton's Toronto because the dresses not sold in the larger metropolis were simply sent sixty miles down the road to be offered a year later.

Much less sophisticated than Toronto, the smaller stores in Hamilton — realizing that their clients had less disposable incomes — would tend to imitate fashions a year or two out of date by rendering them in cheap materials. For instance, poor quality muslin would be turned into outfits meant to be made of raw silk. The refined angles of high heels intended for genuine Italian leather were manufactured of rough-looking, heavy rawhide.

Mother may have been a consummate snob, but she was herself victimized by her betters. On the streets of Hamilton, the women of the upper classes discreetly looked at each other's clothing, scanning for the quality of the wares on each other's backs. They knew good cloth when they beheld it, were aware of the imitations readily available. Mother often claimed she saw a snicker or a malicious smile made in her direction when she went shopping.

I never liked going to films with Mother, mainly because she was so completely unable to distinguish between the fictions on the screen and the fictions of everyday life. "That Ava Gardner is such a tawdry human being. Sleeps with anyone who comes along. A real vixen." Or, "Katharine Hepburn. She's never married. Something wrong there." Innuendo may have been my mother's strong suit, but she overdid it when she was unable to distinguish between a screen performance and the gossip surrounding a star. In fact, she blended the two worlds together uneasily, so that a crisp, sedate piece of acting by Gardner was mistakenly and immediately seen as an exercise in real-life vampery. Mother was a poor reader and an even more miserable critic.

My sedate life was transformed when we saw Bette Davis and Paul Henreid in *Now, Voyager*, one of the strangest films ever released by Warner Brothers. Bette Davis plays Charlotte, a repressed, mother-dominated young woman, who, with the help of an understanding and sympathetic psychiatrist, makes herself over into a stylish, confident and outgoing person. During a South American cruise, she meets and falls in love with a married man, whose love she renounces. Upon her return home to Boston, she becomes engaged to another man but, realizing the true direction of her heart, she breaks the engagement. Her domineering mother, aghast and enraged, suffers a fatal heart attack in the midst of an argument with her daughter. A despondent Charlotte returns to the sanatorium where she was helped, encounters a young girl very much like herself, aids in her transformation, and takes her into her own home. The girl, it turns out, is the married man's daughter. He renews his declaration and offers to leave his difficult, hypochondriac wife. True to herself, Charlotte renounces him yet again.

The film is faithful to the convoluted turns in the bestselling novel by the underrated Olive Higgins Prouty. I found the film deeply moving. So did my mother. As was her wont, she beheld only what she wanted to see.

"That Charlotte Vale was such a frump. Bette Davis must have had catfits when she was made to look so ugly."

"She probably didn't mind. She knew what was going to happen."

"Nonsense. No actress likes to look such a fright. Women like that are so careful about their appearance. Must have upset her to look like such a bedraggled Cinderella."

"I guess so."

"*Guess* so? I know so." She looked at me askance, as if the village idiot had dared to make yet another stupid utterance. "You know, dearest, you look a lot like Miss Davis, but you never really prepare yourself correctly. You always manage to look shabby."

"I do my best. I read all the fashion magazines."

"You read them — you don't *look* at them." Another significant pause as she halted, turning to face me. "You have great potential, but you never use it." Then she drew herself in, stared at me intently. "Those eyes of yours, those wonderful eyes. I wonder." We resumed walking, but, some flight of fancy having overcome my mother, she remained strangely silent on our bus ride home.

A few days later, my mother persuaded Mrs. Bauer to drive her to Toronto, from whence she arrived back with a large number of parcels, all from a small European couturier on Queen Street. My curiosity aroused, I asked her what she had purchased. "All in good time, my girl," she responded. The next day, she told me that her shopping expedition had been devoted to me and my best interests. She then revealed that she had spent a great deal of money at the cosmetics counter, where she had received excellent instruction on how the film stars in California did themselves up.

"You know, Evelyn, it's a closely guarded secret, but an actress like Bette Davis is made up one way for the cameras, and another for the still photographers. And someone like that has even more tricks for improving her appearance in public."

I nodded my head, indicating I understood what she was saying. Smiling, she continued: "Someone like you. You have all the raw materials for looking like a great actress, but you have to work at it."

My face must have betrayed my confusion, since I had no idea why this pursuit intrigued my mother. As was her wont, my mother would tell me no more, except to instruct me to wash my hair thoroughly in preparation for a treatment. Knowing it was useless to argue with her, I retired to our bedroom, slipped into a dressing gown and then cleaned and shampooed myself in the bathroom.

When I returned to the bedroom, I could see that Mother had removed the contents of several of the boxes. She had also placed the dressing table mirror on the floor so that I could not see — and thus object — to what she was doing. After combing my hair, she proceeded to put a number of noxious smelling chemicals into it. I was ordered to shampoo my hair again and return directly. The next stage was the curling of my hair with a sinister-looking electrical device. After that, my mother cleaned my face with another foul-smelling concoction, applied two or three different powders, and then affixed further markings by way of lipstick, eye shadow and a beauty mark on the right side of my face.

Then further parcels were opened to reveal dresses, hats and shoes, all elaborate concoctions. My mother chose a tiny white hat that she perched near my forehead, black patent leather heels, and a red but demure day frock. "That woman at Simpson's was right. 'Use simple colours and classical cuts. That combination will never go wrong.'"

"We're almost there," she exclaimed. "But I can tell practice is going to make perfect." Bending down, she retrieved the mirror and placed it back in its usual place. I did not recognize the person staring back at me. It was as if I were looking at a still of the rejuvenated Charlotte Vale from *Now, Voyager*. "You're a whole new person, my dear," Mother pronounced.

15

"Poppet, have you ever come across the word 'miss-u-a-gee' in your reading?"

"You mean *mizuage?*"

"The very word."

"In the geisha world, it is the first time a woman's vagina is explored by a man's penis. A high price is usually exacted for this privilege by the geisha's pimp."

"By her mistress in the geisha house," my mother primly remonstrated.

I was startled. "Why do you ask?"

My mother was not usually coy, but on this day a rather hesitant smile crossed her face. She drew her breath in slightly. "Well, Evelyn dearest, you are not making much at the telephone company. What if you were to offer your services here in Hamilton as a sort of geisha?"

"They're whores."

"That's a rather harsh word, dear. They are companions to men of wealth. Intercourse is rarely part of the exchange."

This conversation took place early in September 1941, a few months before Pearl Harbor, but there was already a great deal of anti-Japanese sentiment in the press. "Mother, this is not the time to be imitating the Japanese."

"You are such a literalist, dearest. I'm simply making a suggestion. We could make a simple adaptation of an old custom."

"What are we reduced to when you try to turn me into a prostitute?"

"A woman of pleasure, my dear. The bare truth is that we are in exceedingly difficult circumstances. Funds from dear Lady MacLean are in short supply. Your father has quarrelled with her. If you and I are to survive, we have to be inventive."

"What you are suggesting is immoral and disgusting."

Usually Mother would become blindly angry in response to such sauciness. Realizing she had overstepped the boundary, she backed down. "Just think about it, dear. It's not such a bad idea."

A few days later, my mother resumed her discussion. "Dear one, I did pay a lot for those cosmetics and a whole new wardrobe. Shame to let them go to waste."

"I had no idea why you bought all those things."

"An investment in *our* future."

"I am not a sexual being. The whole idea of sex with anyone is repulsive."

"Exactly. That is why you might be excellent at such a profession. You would have the necessary detachment. Besides, the men who visited with you would be more interested in intelligent conversation than sexual congress."

"Maybe. But I would still have to do 'it.'"

"Occasionally. Every little once in a while, sweet bairn."

A few days later, she returned to the subject. "We could rent a splendid flat, perhaps on James Street. You would have the most wonderful clothing. You would meet the best people. This would be the entry into society you always dreamed of."

"*That you always dreamed of.* More a hostile invasion than an entry."

"Still, you would have the company of some extremely intelligent men. Learn about the world."

Mother was skilled in Chinese water torture and slowly but surely my stone-like reserve gave way. I still do not completely understand why I went along with the whole preposterous scheme. I was bored. I was lazy. Still, most women suffering from those conditions do not become *belles de jour*. I suspect I was looking for excitement, some way of rebelling, although, God knows, the best form of rebellion might have been to say no to my mother. Nevertheless, I became her accomplice. When I agreed to the whole undertaking in a muted way, she nodded her head in sage agreement. "I'll take care of everything, sweet one."

Why did I really go along with Mother? Even today I ask myself that question. In those days I was an uneasy witness to my own life, very much like the movie-goer who stares uneasily at a grim happening on the screen but is utterly powerless to do anything, for instance, to prevent the nasty man from killing the heroine's fiancé.

A prostitute who hates sex? Some days I still make that apparently paradoxical query of myself. And yet who makes a better lady of the night than the woman who is detached from the acts she is performing? Perhaps she couldn't do them otherwise? Such a person is in a position to make herself into a good businesswoman. If an antique merchant loves his treasures too much, he will not be able to sell them readily. If, on the other hand, he cares little for the items eagerly collected by others, he has a good chance of making huge profits selling them.

I did not value myself; I could easily sell myself. That is the great sorrow of my early existence, of the silly, sad, vain woman I was. Some days, I loathe that empty-headed young creature. Other days, I pity her, even catch myself shedding tears for her.

In the first four years of my new life, the Royal Connaught in Hamilton and the Royal York in Toronto were my meeting places. A client would rent a room, telephone Mother with the number, and I would meet him there. My first client, Mr. Sinclair, Q.C., was a distinguished Hamilton attorney, specializing in corporate litigation. The agreed time was eight o'clock on a cold February night. He answered the door at once and ushered me into a large suite, two or three rooms. Exceedingly thin, he carried himself as if a huge burden sat uneasily upon his back. He was bald, although some specks of white hair clung to the crown of his head. His tiny, inset eyes betrayed a deep weariness.

"Good evening, Miss MacLean. It's very cold outside, is it not?" He helped me remove my coat.

I nodded agreement to his question. I was uncertain of what to say next.

"Well, we might as well get down to business. Let's go into the bedroom." He pointed at the room and followed me into it. "You can place your clothes there," he said, indicating a chair on the left of the double bed. He proceeded to remove all his clothing, observing me as I did the same. So there we were, both stark naked, standing in front of the bed. He indicated I should approach him. When I did so, he pushed me down gently on my shoulders, indicating that I was to perform fellatio. At the time, I had no idea what he wanted me to do.

"You've never done this before? You're more a novice than I realized. Lie down on the bed on your back."

I followed his instructions as he opened the drawer in the night stand, out of which he took a tube of ointment and a condom. He threw the tube at me. "Rub some of this down below. That way it won't hurt so much." As I followed his instructions, he fondled his penis until it was bright red and fully erect and then rolled the condom on to it. Without more ado, he walked over to the bed, mounted me, and entered me, slowly but vigorously. The pain was extreme, but he cautioned me to be quiet. He then moved his penis back and forth as if it were a metronome — two seconds in, two seconds out. This must have lasted ten minutes, at which point perspiration dotted his face, which turned a violent purple. Silent heretofore, he now spoke. "You little bitch. Daddy's filling your goddamn crack." Then, he began to moan, somewhat in the manner of a wolf bawling at the moon. Then, he stopped moving, at the moment he reached orgasm. A few seconds later, he removed himself from me and asked if I wished to bathe. I assented to this proposition.

When I returned from the bathroom, the bedroom was deserted. Hearing me, Mr. Sinclair summoned me to the sitting room, where he, clad in a smoking jacket, was having a drink. "Would you take a glass of sherry with me, Miss MacLean?"

Rather numbly, I assented. I silently took a sip or two. Looking intently at me, his eyebrows assuming a curious stance, he asked: "What do you like to read? Your mother informs me you are an avid consumer of all manner of literature."

Surprised by this twist in the conversation, I mentioned O. Henry, Saki, and Dickens.

"Excellent choices. Have you ever heard of D.H. Lawrence's *Lady Chatterley's Lover* or Thomas Hardy's *Tess of the D'Urbervilles?*"

I indicated the names of the authors were known to me, although I had never read anything by them. "You should seek out those two titles, particularly in your line of work. Essential, I would have thought." He then proceeded to tell me about the struggles that beset both writers in their attempts to write accurately and honestly about the entire life of any man or woman, of how the authorities had attempted to silence them. He proceeded to speak at length about both men, indicating, I now realize, a very sensitive aptitude for literary criticism. We chatted for about an hour, at which time he indicated he had used up my time, and I might leave.

From this encounter — and those that ensued in the following month — I learned a vital truth. Most of my clients wanted to have the act of sexual intercourse completed quickly in order to experience a chaste social intercourse. In such agendas, sex was an impediment to the real purpose of the encounter.

I also discovered several things about myself. Sex was merely a necessary inconvenience in being a prostitute. When I sucked or manipulated a penis — or had one inserted into me — I simply imagined myself somewhere else. My body was performing sexual acts, but my mind was always otherwise occupied. I also realized that my skills as a reader could help fill in the time in all these encounters. I began to ask clients if could tell them a story — or read to them. During a first encounter, most clients looked surprised but hardly ever demurred. So my specialty was soon established. I was never famous for sex. Among my clients, I became a renowned spinner of tales.

My retinue was wide and varied. For Mr. Justice Smith, who presided over countless probate cases, the subtle sado-masochistic manipulation of the patient Griselda by the Marquis Walter was perfect ware. A sort of busman's holiday. Sometimes, I dipped into the boring autobiography of Casanova in order to entertain those clients who thrilled to exploits they would never venture to undertake. On occasion, beautifully simple tales, such as "The Little Mermaid," calmed the anxiety ridden, reassuring them about themselves.

A good narrative requires a strong plot line, but so much more resides in the way the teller breathes life into it. Although I did not yet have my own stories to tell, I learned how to frame one, to select the right narrative to match the needs of my client. I was the voice who brought dead authors back to life.

16

My new profession exacted more time than even I expected. Whenever I left home, I had to be scrupulously groomed. Mother insisted that I always look my part. Sometimes, she would help me with makeup, but I soon learned to deal with this aspect of my toiletry. Endless shopping for clothes, especially undergarments, took up more hours than applying makeup and dressing.

Later, sales clerks — when interviewed — would recall the expensive blouses, slips and skirts I purchased. Maureen, a tiny loquacious sprite from Ireland who sold the expensive frocks (originals) at Eaton's, told *Newsweek*: "She adored black. Very classical. Almost severe taste. Always bought the best." She added: "*Looked* like a film star. Austere, full of herself. But that impression vanished as soon as she spoke. Very chummy. Always asked after my children. Remembered me at Christmas."

My role gave me a great deal of satisfaction. On a full moonlit night, costumed in black with a tiny pillar-box hat and veil, wandering down James Street to meet a client, I became Barbara Stanwyck setting off for an assignation with Fred MacMurray, whom she would inveigle — by means of wily female charms — into becoming a conspirator with her in an insurance scam. Or, on dark rain-splattered Main Street, I was Garbo setting off to rescue her lover from the clutches of the Gestapo.

Self-imposed illusions can provide wide ranges of comforts. Yet, as I wandered into Robinson's to look at skirts or walked over to the main post office nearby to buy stamps, I knew I had segregated myself even further from the common herd. I had become a woman of pleasure. I asked myself: surely my new occupation proclaims itself in the way I carry myself, in the look in my eyes? Always painfully self-conscious, I now interrogated every aspect of my existence. And yet, I seemed to Rosie — initially scandalized by what I was doing and then intrigued — much more self-confident, a woman of the world. Inside, I saw only the famished little girl.

In the world of the high-end prostitute, fantasy is the key element. I never took money from clients. When I arrived at a customer's hotel room, it was as if I were paying a friendly social call, which just happened to involve sex within the first few minutes. Mother handled the bookings; Mother received the money. In order to make our product known to those members of the public likely to purchase it, I frequented the city's two racetracks, the stadiums that were home to two football teams, the Tigers and the Wildcats, and would be seen in the afternoon and early evenings in the cocktail lounges at the Connaught in Hamilton and the Brant Inn in nearby Burlington. At those places I sometimes saw — but never spoke to — other women who practised my profession. Like myself, they were there to be seen, to be admired, and, at the appropriate time, to be purchased.

In later years, my attendance at such places would be turned decisively against me. According to the Powers, my neighbours on

Rosslyn Street, they once encountered me at a thoroughbred meet at Fort Erie. Mrs. Powers, a tiny, perpetually harried creature bedecked in a grey Persian lamb coat, lamented the lack of hotel rooms in that small city. She and her exhausted husband feared they would be forced to drive back that evening to Hamilton. "Here," I said, taking a key from my purse, "use mine." That much is true. I added: "I have to get back tonight." According to Mrs. Powers, I said: "I won't be needing the room. I'm sleeping with a jockey." No act of kindness ever goes unpunished.

The stuff of legends goes in even more ludicrous directions when it claims I offered my services to two entire forward lines and a couple of sets of defencemen from a local hockey team. Such gossip reeks of misogyny. There is also a neo-Freudian spin on my early existence. When my father first worked for the HSR, he drove a bus. This turn of events supposedly led me as a teenager to bed a number of HSR drivers. The nub of this thesis: Evelyn MacLean was desperately searching for a father-figure.

My mother had strict rules regarding my services. A new phone line and accompanying telephone was installed in the house in the name of Evelyn White, but only my mother was permitted to make or receive calls on it. A customer had to indicate his pedigree: who he was and how he had learned of my availability. Many called but relatively few were chosen. Mother preferred Gentile customers of Anglo-Saxon heritage, but she made exceptions if a Jewish or Italian client was sufficiently powerful or dangerous. She warned me about becoming involved with clients: I was not to write letters, and she intercepted the few that arrived at Rosslyn Avenue. Professional deportment, professional detachment: those were her standards. I was to warn her about any client who acted in a markedly strange manner. "You cannot be too careful, dear. These are well-placed men, but even such persons can get strange ideas. Fixations."

Once again, she was correct, particularly in the instance of tiny little Mr. Beasley, a well-heeled realtor from Oakville. Not more than five feet tall and inordinately thin, he looked the model of prissiness. On the three occasions I saw him, he was courtly when I arrived at his room. "Let's get down to business," he would then rather abruptly command me. This was a signal for me to remove my clothes, lie down on the bed, and touch myself in my private parts. Staring abruptly at me through his tortoiseshell-framed glasses, he would remove his clothing and begin to fondle his member, which, considering his height, looked worthy of a giant.

"You want me to put this in you, don't you?"

From the first, I guessed the script. Demurely, I responded, "Please. I'd really like that."

"You women are all alike. All you want is a big dick."

I nodded assent to this apparent truism.

"My wife says I'm too big for her. Hurts too much. Would a whore think it hurt too much?"

"It would hurt, but I'd enjoy it," I lied.

"Well, you can't have it." Mr. Beasley would then proceed to masturbate. When he was close to orgasm, he would wander over to the bed and then deposit his sperm on my vagina. All of this activity was accompanied by violent language. After he reached orgasm, he commanded the "dirty little bitch" to clean herself, to remove all the "spunk."

Many of my clients had unusual ways of experiencing sexual release. Mr. Beasley's particular predilection was not unknown to me — or frightening. His stories were disturbing. Rather than listening to anything I might say, he would tell me anecdotes about famous prostitutes from the past. One of the two most terrifying was about "Dusky Sally," the paramour of Thomas Jefferson; according to his version of history, the "black cunt" robbed a great man of political vigour, and, in the process, made him a willing dupe of the "niggers." The last time I saw him he related the sad life history of Helen Jewett, who lived in Manhattan in the 1830s and was known for her interest in serious literature. A coquette as well as a prostitute, she led some of her clients on, giving them the impression she entertained sentiments of love for them. Her big mistake was to make such a suggestion to a young clerk, who savagely murdered her with an axe while she was sleeping next to him. Having related that narrative, the realtor then paused, licked his chops and described in gruesome detail the autopsy performed on the still warm corpse, emphasizing in the process the removal of her "female innards."

When I mentioned this episode to Mother, she informed me Beasley was a "real nutter." After that, I was always booked or ill when he phoned. Although I never visited him again, I am relatively certain

I saw him following me one evening when, after returning from the Connaught, I alighted from the bus near Rosslyn Avenue.

If I took a day or evening off, or if I had my period, I would go to the pictures with Rosie. Occasionally, Stephen would take us driving. Westdale — the suburb near the university — was daintily pretty but dry. If we wanted to drink, we had to venture into the two adjacent small towns, Dundas or Ancaster. I could never be seen to be alone with a man, my mother had warned me. My clients liked to imagine they were the only ones who had access to me, and it was important to maintain this illusion. The presence of a boyfriend or suitor could destroy my public image and thus ruin my career.

Without doubt, I became a consummate story-teller, a consort worthy of King Shahriyar. Instead of using such skills to ward off death, I was deploying them to fill in the necessary time and thus distract my clients. Many of my elder clients became only interested with hearing my confabulations. Younger and middle-aged men were different. These were rapacious persons, filling their entire sessions in various forms of foreplay and vaginal and anal penetration. There were those who simply wished their manhood to be admired by way of sucking. And then there were those who wished to be beaten. Such clients provided their own instruments of torture. Mother made it clear to them that I was unwilling to be subjected to such humiliation.

My new profession was lucrative, but it came at two heavy prices. My father — ashamed that the legacy of Lady MacLean had virtually come to an end because of increased vigilance on the part of the bookkeepers at the Hamilton Street Railway — became deeply resentful of the entrepreneurial skills of his wife and daughter.

"You've made Evelyn into a common whore," he told Mother one day.

"Evelyn is well paid for acting as a companion to wealthy gentlemen," she briskly retorted.

"She has sex with men. Lets them put their things into her."

"Donald, you've always had a coarse way with you."

"I'm coarse? You've become a madam that sells her own daughter. In the old country, we called such people panderers."

Mother's temper, badly masked at the best of times, asserted itself.

"You're the first man who tried to put his privates into her! For all I know you did! You're the person who *spoiled* Evelyn, not me. You're the real whoremonger!"

She struck him and, like a character in a pantomime, he fell abruptly to the floor. Suspecting that there was not much wrong with Punch, Judy began to chortle, until she noticed the blood at the side of his head. A bit guiltily, she reached down to assist him, whereupon he pulled her down upon himself, scratched her in the face, and proceeded to mount her, as if to fulfill his conjugal duties.

"Help me, Evie!" my mother yelled in her most theatrical way. She was not so much injured as surprised.

"Daddy, let go of her!" was the best I could do as I reached down and pulled her up by both arms. Getting up quickly, he raised his arm at me and then thought better of it. His inset eyes, like fiery dark pieces of coal, fastened themselves on me. When he saw that I had noticed his erection, he quickly retreated to the basement.

Despite the rubbers that Mother insisted be worn by all those clients who performed vaginal intercourse, I was soon faced with pregnancy — the most feared and common side-effect of my calling.

Abortion was an especially dangerous option in the forties. No hospital would perform such a procedure on a young healthy woman such as myself, and Rosie had told me of the deaths and mutilations endured at the hands of some of the local practitioners of the dark art of ridding unwanted babies from unwilling mothers-to-be.

I wish I could claim to have been a good, even an adequate mother, to Heather, who was born in July 1942. From the start, she was really my mother's child, almost as if I were the father who went out to work to support his wife and child. I never gained much weight during any of my pregnancies, especially so in this instance. I saw clients until the end of May and then took a relatively brief holiday until after Labour Day that year. My clients were told by Mother that I was pregnant and that no special risks during carnal exchanges would be tolerated. Miss MacLean became Mrs. White, in large part to evade the scrutiny of the ever-vigilant Children's Aid Society.

Much has been made in the succeeding years about Heather's appearance. Some said she had a definite Oriental cast to her eyes, implying that I had slept with a Chinese or Japanese gentleman. This is untrue — there were no such men in Hamilton in those days. The claim may have been an overly subtle way of suggesting Heather was a Mongol. Also a falsehood. From the time she was a toddler, Heather was a very average child, not especially gifted or deprived intellectually. What is patently true is that my mother took Heather over, never allowing her to speak on her own.

This interference on my mother's part obviously made it difficult for my daughter to establish her own voice. I suspect that turn of events is the fount from which the various stories about the supposed slowness of my only surviving child springs. Less than a year later, another accidental child came into being, but that frail creature mercifully lasted only a few hours. I resumed my profession in October.

I was an overly dutiful but frightened daughter, a neglectful mother and a wayward woman. Less than a year later, the gossamer web carefully spun by Mother with my assistance began to disintegrate.

17

I fell in love. An unusual turn in a courtesan's life. Earth-shattering, as in *La Dame aux camélias* by Dumas *fils* or Verdi's version of it in *La Traviata*. In those long-ago days, that sad, poignant story was known to me only in its Hollywood version, Greta Garbo and Robert Taylor in George Cukor's *Camille*. Woman of pleasure finally meets the man of her dreams; his father is furious at his son's pursuit of an immoral woman; even the heart of the angry patriarch is melted by the beauty and integrity of Camille, who is dying of tuberculosis. A melodramatic, quasi-sentimental story perhaps, the classical rendition of the story of the prostitute with a heart of gold. Yet, in my experience, real life has a way of imitating even the most outrageous clichés.

My Robert Taylor was a man with the preposterous name of Bill Bohozuk. A year older than me, he lived with his sister on shabby Picton Street East where the houses were crushed together. He worked the open hearth at one of the steel mills, the Dominion Foundries, and rowed with the Leander Boat Club. Seems a rather nondescript existence. Yet, Bill was a celebrity eagerly received at the best homes in Hamilton. Achievement in sports cuts across all social lines, and Bill was a magnificent rower. In the past, his group had won Pan-Am, Olympic and World Championship medals; he was expected to lead his club to even greater glories. Physically, he was a splendid specimen. Huskily built, he had close-cropped dark brown wavy hair and straight eyebrows above small, narrow eyes. A strange choice to play Lancelot to my Guenevere, but that is exactly what happened.

Bill was obviously not a client. He was not the kind of man who needed to pay women to sleep with him. I first encountered him at Smithy's, the pleasantly seedy, always-crowded bar across the street from the Tivoli. Rosie and I had gone there after our weekly visit to the pictures. We had a booth to ourselves and were eagerly immersed in discussing Lana Turner's love life, as revealed in the pages of *Photoplay*.

As we were chatting, my eyes wandered to the back of a man seated at the bar opposite me. Maybe, it was his shoulders. Perhaps his hair. I became intrigued and waited impatiently for him to turn around. When he did so, it was to greet a woman who entered the room, advanced towards him and nodded, whereupon he stood up, took her by the arm, and left the bar with her.

The next time I saw this fellow was about six weeks later at Smithy's, when he walked by our booth on his way to the washroom. Rosie, noticing my interest in the stranger, asked me: "Bill Bohozuk isn't one of your clients, is he?"

"Of course not, I've never met him. How do you know him?"

"Local hero. Star of the Leander Boat Club. You must have seen his photo in the paper."

"I never read the sports pages."

"You shouldn't need to. He's often in the social pages. A real man-about-town. He's the sports star factory worker who dines with millionaires. He's competed all over the world." When Bohozuk walked past us again on his way back from the washroom, I must have seen him in a slightly different light, as a god in the Hamilton firmament.

I met Bill a month later at another watering hole, Haley's Hotel in Dundas, where I was waiting for Rosie to meet me. He asked if I had a match. I handed him my lighter, whereupon he exclaimed upon its beauty: a sterling silver Ronson. I thanked him for the compliment and off he went. I next encountered him at the cocktail lounge at the Connaught, one of my usual haunts. This time, he came right up to me.

"How are you today, Miss MacLean. Or should I say Mrs. White?"

"You know both my names. I didn't think you knew who I was."

"Everyone knows who you are. May I call you Evelyn?"

"If you prefer."

"Evelyn it shall be."

"Fine. What can I do for you, Mr. Bohozuk?"

"You know who I am?"

"Turn-about is fair play. A friend told me."

"I guess that's natural. A friend tells a friend. We're both celebrities."

"I don't follow you. No one knows who I am."

"Everyone knows Hamilton's most celebrated courtesan."

"I think you're being incredibly rude." Summoning up the little bit of dignity left to me, I walked out of the room.

My next encounter with Bohozuk was at the races, just as I was collecting my winnings at one of the pari-mutuel windows. Doffing his hat in a courtly manner, he bid me good day.

"You're looking especially lovely today, Evelyn. Really beautiful."

I thanked him, but, since I was with a regular client, I could only acknowledge his compliment and make my way back to my seat.

We continued to take sightings of each other at the movies, bars and other spots frequented by the demi-monde of Hamilton. On one of the rare evenings I went to the Tivoli by myself (Rosie had to accompany Stephen to a dance in Toronto), I encountered Bill as I was heading up James to catch my bus at Gore Park.

"Beautiful evening, Evelyn."

"Hello, Bill. Were you at the Tivoli?"

"No. I just caught you out of the corner of my eye as I was leaving Smithy's."

His breath smelled of whisky, and he was obviously not in the same jaunty mood he had been at the Connaught two months before. There seemed a bit of desperation in his voice — and in his eyes. "You really like the pictures?"

"It helps to pass the time."

He nodded in agreement. Then, he struggled with what to say next. He hemmed and hawed a bit and then asked, "Is there anywhere we could meet, have a real talk. Could I come to your house?"

"That would be dangerous."

"Dangerous?"

"A courtesan — to use your word — cannot be seen in public with handsome young men. It would put clients off."

"I understand. At least I think I understand. Perhaps we could have a drink at Smithy's? Sit in one of the booths out of the way?"

I agreed and suggested a day and time. He nodded and disappeared back down James Street.

At our next meeting a few nights later, on 10 February 1944, the so-called suave man-of-the-world Bill was much in evidence. If I had caught even the slightest hint of vulnerability in our last encounter, that side was absent.

"Well, Evelyn, how's tricks?"

I felt I might pass out. Seeing I was upset, he decided to change his approach. "How've you been?"

I nodded, as if to suggest I was well.

"Sometimes, I really play the fool. You have to forgive me."

I nodded again, not sure where the conversation was leading.

"Evelyn....?"

"Yes."

"Evelyn, love me a little." He added: "Please."

18

My friendship with Bill might possibly have transformed itself into an affair, except I discovered a few days after his declaration that I was pregnant for a third time. Here is an even stranger revelation: Bill was the only man to whom I was ever remotely sexually attracted, but I only slept with him once, and that was much later. Love rather than lust. A stunning claim to emanate from a prostitute. In retrospect, Bill is a difficult person to write about, perhaps because he seemed so perfect. Tall, magnificently built, and deeply handsome. Those qualities were obvious to anyone, but, beyond that, he seemed a remarkably generous and kind person.

Straddling the aristocracy and the working class, he was at ease in both environments. As I learned during one of our first encounters, Bill could be teasingly and mockingly cruel, but those sides of him vanished when we became friends, and when I confided to him I was with child and that my parents were furious with me. I do not mean to imply that Bill played the role of St. Joseph to my Mary Magdalene. No, he was, I am sure, far from chaste during the time we began to see each other.

Once or twice, we met at the White Towers snack bar at Burlington Beach, a spot that could be seen for miles away because of the huge rectangular Orange Crush sign that crowned it. Usually, we were more discreet. Every two weeks or so, Bill would take me for a drive in his powder blue Oldsmobile, usually to the outskirts of the nearby town of Ancaster where the chances of our being recognized were severely reduced. During our talks in the wood, I told him of my childhood and of my profession. He complained of his reputation as a local Renaissance man, of how everyone — his sister, his parents, his friends — expected him to be perfect. He had a semi-secret life as a ladies' man, but, since he protected the names and the reputations of all the women in his life, he was accused by some of his loutish friends of being priggish. In a way, his local greatness was a burden to him, a weight he did not like shouldering.

At first, we shared with each other our desire to abandon Hamilton. Later, we began to form a pact to leave the city together, to start our lives anew, perhaps in the south-west of the United States — Arizona or New Mexico. These vague plans became more concrete as my confinement approached. As soon as the baby was born, the three of us would escape.

I had already determined to leave Heather with my mother. My daughter represented a past I was then stupidly determined to destroy. This resolve was heightened by Mother's fiery anger at my carelessness in becoming impregnated yet again. A girl on the town must take steps to evade such an eventuality: Mrs. White, in a delicate condition for a third time, had gone beyond the accepted bounds of her profession. No matter what I said about broken rubbers, my mother assured me I was responsible. It was my responsibility to fit the condom on the client, to be certain he was wearing his envelope properly so that no nasty jism escaped.

At first, my father comforted his "wee lass"; he did so in part because it provided him with yet another opportunity to annoy his wife. As time went on — and the Lady MacLean funds were in short supply — he too became resentful of the income that would be lost. Although I was never large for dates, I did gain more weight during this pregnancy; I also became tired more easily. By May 1944, I could no longer work. Mother had to begin removing money from one of the three bank accounts that held what was left of my earnings, and she was loath to make any of the withdrawals accessible to my father.

By the summer of 1944, life at the cramped bungalow on Rosslyn Avenue became unbearable. There was the constant skirmishes between my parents. Things heated up when Bill came to pick me up. He simply parked at the front of the house and waited for me. At first, I did not mention him by name, but I didn't have to: my mother and father knew who Bill was.

In a wonderful ironical twist, Father condemned Bill, the man he claimed had impregnated his daughter. I explained he was neither client nor boyfriend, but my father refused to believe me. In his eyes, Bill was the culprit because he was young and attractive and patently not one of the elderly or middle-aged men father reckoned my clients to be. Bill was a genuine sexual threat, something my generous clients had never been. Not to be outdone, my mother accused me of being no better than a common whore, presumably because such women easily allowed themselves to become pregnant. She also resolved to protect Heather from the corrupting influence of her prostitute-mother.

I had to believe Bill was perfect — or nearly so. Except Rosie, I had no one in whom I could confide, let alone speak with. Politely but firmly, my mother refused all my old clients. "I regret to have to tell you that Evelyn has not been at all well." Although I am certain most of my patrons were well aware I was in the family way (I had informed many myself), Mother considered it a serious breach of protocol to make such a revelation. Very "ultra dig," she informed me.

During the pregnancy, I began to imagine the baby I was carrying had been fathered by Bill. My mind turned in that direction because I was in love with him and wanted him to be the father of the baby. He had also offered to become the baby's parent and, moreover, to assert that he was the natural father. I clung to this lifeline in the face of the constant disputes with my parents. In my father's view, I had betrayed him because I had fallen in love with another man; in my mother's view, I was a traitor because I had destroyed her careful plan to establish me as Hamilton's Madame de Staël. Financially, they were both bereft since my father's income provided an existence below the poverty line, and security at the HSR had been stepped up. We were three cornered rats clinging precariously to the same sinking craft.

The birth of the new baby would be a liberation, I assured myself. Although I had saved many pieces of Heather's infant clothing, I was convinced the baby I was carrying was a boy. I bought a few odds and ends at Eaton's, but I spent the last three months of my pregnancy knitting a huge assortment of sleepers and cardigans, mainly blue and white. My mother, herself an accomplished knitter, did not assist me.

I prepared for my final stay at Hamilton Mountain hospital as the anxious wife of Mr. White, who was still away at war. If they believed in the existence of Mr. White, the nurses must have thought it strange that he was in Hamilton to impregnate me but always away when it came time for birthing.

Steeling myself for a new series of lies, I entered the hospital just after Labour Day. Peter David was born on the fifth of September. A beautiful, strong baby, he weighed nine pounds, two ounces. As one of the nurses later recalled, I had no visitors but used the phone extensively in my private room and had a good supply of funds. That woman recalled I happily bottle fed the baby: she "seemed quite happy and did not seem to be suffering from the loss of her husband." My mother did not visit, I explained, because she had to look after my small daughter. The day before we left hospital, Peter was circumcised.

Bill, who was at work, was not able to pick me up at the hospital and so I took a Yellow Cab home. Although I had been on the phone with Bill a great deal (I had forbidden him to visit me because he would be recognized and then accused of being the father), I had spoken on the phone to my mother once; and to my father, not at all. When the taxi pulled up to Rosslyn Avenue, I was certain my new life was about to begin.

19

I had known the great cruelty of which my parents were capable, and their scorn for the baby was evident as soon as I opened the door to the bungalow. Only little Heather showed the slightest interest in her new brother, asking to hold him before I even had a chance to sit down. Mother avoided making eye contact with me, and father, in his habitual way, retreated to the basement. That night, I slept in Heather's room, Peter David's crib next to the bed; Heather, who had been sleeping with Mother since my confinement, was quite happy to continue usurping my place. The baby nursed his bottle vigorously and slept soundly.

I had arranged with Bill the day before to take a short drive with him in the afternoon the next day, provided the baby was settled. Bill arrived promptly at two, at which time the baby was soundly asleep. I informed Mother I would be gone for only an hour and asked her to warm a bottle for the baby should he awake. She sullenly nodded her head in agreement. My last memory is of the sleeping baby on his stomach, his parchment-thin perfect little hands moving rhythmically back and forth in reverie.

When I arrived home an hour later, the undercurrent of tension which had previously enveloped the house had vanished. Heather was sobbing inconsolably; my very distracted mother was trying to keep her quiet; my father was nowhere to be seen. Uncertain of what kind of domestic maelstrom I had entered, I looked at my mother.

"The baby's dead."

"Dead! How can he be dead?"

"Just after you left, he had some sort of convulsion, a seizure. His face became bright red, and he was screaming in a demonic way, like some sort of mad creature. I picked him up, trying to comfort him, but that did no good. I put him down on his back, he rolled over, tried to lift himself and then became very quiet. He must have died then." I rushed to Heather's room, where the corpse of the baby was on its side. I noticed the tiny red necklace-like marking around the neck, but I must not have wanted to deal then with this very obvious clue as to how the baby had really met his end.

I returned to the bedroom I had shared with my mother, threw myself on to the bed, and began to weep inconsolably. Quite soon, my tears dried up; my screaming stopped. Part of me did not wish to frighten my daughter. Another part knew I would receive absolutely no sympathy from my parents. The only real audience for my strong feelings was myself — that had always been the case throughout my entire life. That afternoon, I was rendered mute as if I were a silent witness to my own destruction. I would have to find a way of coping, of making my vulnerabilities invisible.

Only Heather offered me any comfort. I must have remained there for three or four hours, at which time I returned to my daughter's bedroom. The baby's corpse had vanished. When I asked my mother where Peter David was, she told me that my father had taken him to the undertaker, to be, as she put it, "disposed of." I was too numb to register a protest.

Bill tried to comfort me, but I could detect relief in his voice on the phone that he need not worry about another man's baby. The depression which now clothed me was a heavy one. I even found it difficult to move, as if I were walking through a thick fog that pressed against me, preventing me from moving forward. My screams may have been silent, but I uttered them to myself every day. I still do.

Three days after the death of my son, I met Rosie downtown at the restaurant in Robinson's, the department store. Her blond face was eerily white that day as I recounted the story of the baby's death. She grasped my hand, tears filling her eyes. I told her I had resolved to move on with my life, to turn over, as it were, a whole new leaf. For the first time, I confided to her the new plans Bill and I had made. We were going to escape Hamilton with Heather, marry and set out for Arizona or New Mexico.

Obviously worried about what I was telling her, she waited a bit and then blurted out, "Bill can't marry you. He has a wife."

"He told me he had a serious relationship, which he ended."

"What I know is that his wife, called Helen, abandoned him a few months ago because of his philandering ways. She now lives in the States."

"That can't be right. He would have told me if he was married."

"He lied to you." She paused: " You better think this matter through. He's a very attractive man with a wandering eye. With him, you might be going from frying pan to fire."

Upon my return home in the afternoon, I phoned Bill and arranged to meet him that night at Smithy's. I was waiting for him at our usual booth when he arrived. I had not seen him since the baby's death, although I had spoken to him on the phone numerous times. He took my hands in his huge paws and proceeded to kiss them. Without any preface, I confronted him with what Rosie had told me.

"Is it true?"

"Yes. Sort of."

"How can it be 'sort of'?"

"I am legally married to Helen, but our marriage is over."

"You never breathed a word of her existence. Why?"

"I thought it would complicate things. I don't know where she's living. I can't ask her for a divorce."

"So we can't get married. You knew that all along, unless you meant to become a bigamist."

"I was going to tell you. Before we left. I was waiting for the baby to be born."

"You're a gold-plated liar who's been stringing me along."

"No. Honestly. I've been waiting for the right moment."

"Well, you waited too long. We're over." With those haughty words, I got to my feet and headed out of the bar. If I had been in a better frame of mind, I might have listened to Bill, been willing to receive his assurances about his true intentions. In September 1944, I simply could not do that.

A few days after my break with Bohozuk, I informed my mother that I was going to change the course of my profession. I was no longer going to visit hotel rooms; from the 1st of October, I was going to rent one of Samuel Henson's apartments in a nineteenth-century converted mansion on James Street South, in the heart of Hamilton's most prestigious neighbourhood. I would continue to live with her and father, but I would transact my business from the new location, where a phone would be installed. I would handle all my own bookings henceforward.

My clients appreciated the convenience of being able to visit me in a location near their own homes. The stained glass and the mahogany pillars in the entrance way on the ground floor of the building reminded me of the chapel at Loretto. One of my Catholic clients told me he shuddered every time he walked through those portals: "It's gloomy, just like the vestibule in Christ the King Cathedral." For some of my clients, it was entirely appropriate that they were reminded of sacred things. They had, after all, replaced conventional religion with that of the body.

This new arrangement lasted nine months, until my father assaulted my mother on the seventh of June 1945. On that occasion, he almost murdered her. Faced with this horrendous possibility, Mother, Heather and I moved into the apartment. Mother and Heather would have to leave the apartment in the afternoons and evenings when I worked. In the afternoons, Mother would take Heather for strolls; in the evenings, the two would taxi to and from

Rosslyn Avenue. Old Mr. Henson later recalled: "I saw Mrs. MacLean more frequently than Evelyn White because the child, Heather, used to be taken out for exercise. I do not recall seeing Mrs. White with her as much as the grandmother." An innocent, kindly man, he concluded: "We considered them excellent tenants."

Our frail, festered lives continued on their precarious, uneven keel until I announced to my mother in late September that I was to marry John Dick, a streetcar conductor, on October 4, 1945.

20

Almost five months to the day of our marriage, John Dick was murdered. In all accounts of his existence, he is depicted as a frightened, bewildered, nondescript man waiting to be deprived of his life. He came by that reputation honestly.

Why would Hamilton's most celebrated woman of pleasure marry a mere bus conductor? If there is an answer to that question, it is at the heart of the Evelyn Dick mystery.

The common assumption is that I met John, who drove the Number 20 Belt Line, at the office of the HSR, where Heather and I had gone to meet my father. That is correct. That autumn, my mother and father were planning — at long last — to divorce; since violence was an integral part of their exchanges, I occasionally, in the role of go-between, visited with Father at the HSR.

Although descriptions of John emphasize his lack of distinguishing characteristics and the fifteen-year discrepancy in our ages (I was 24, he 39), he was a well-built blond, similar in physique to Bohozuk. He spoke in an awkward way because of his Silesian accent — he had immigrated to Canada when he was 17. Unlike most of my clients and Bill, John had a hesitant, almost self-effacing manner. I didn't think much of him or the encounter until I came across him three afternoons later as I was leaving a matinee at the Tivoli. He doffed his hat, asked about Heather and myself and suggested we have a cup of coffee at the nearby Liggett's Drug Store.

During our talk, I was impressed by his modesty, his seemingly chaste existence and — if I own up to the entire truth — his naivety. He indicated he was the heir to a small caning factory in Beamsville, where I had been born. He was only putting in time at the HSR before he came into his inheritance. He was so different from my clients, who often boasted about their remarkable successes as captains of industry, judges, lawyers, and professors. Unlike Bill, he was not a local hero, lionized by an appreciative audience. At this point, I was still determined to leave Hamilton, even if it only meant getting swallowed up in Toronto.

John's work experience was eminently transportable; he showed a great deal of interest in four-year-old Heather; he seemed to be a man who would make few demands upon me. Financially, his future seemed bright. Escape. The word filled my consciousness. I needed to show Bill I could make my way in the world without his assistance. I had no wish to see my father or mother again.

That afternoon, I courted John. My openness took him by surprise, as did my willingness, on the briefest of acquaintances, to confess I had fallen in love with him at first sight. He had an annoying nervous habit of pushing his thinning hair back, and that day he did it more than usual. Without any serious thought of the consequences, I used low cunning to entrap him. Over the years, manipulated by mother, I had become an expert in that art. I deliberately led John Dick on, giving him the distinct impression I was taken with him. I wanted to get married again, I assured him. It was tough for a widow to bring up a child alone, no matter how supportive her parents were. I needed a man because

Heather and I were essentially on our own. I appealed to his sense of duty and responsibility, realizing full well he was entertaining the fantasy of having an instant family. His heart melted; he asked me to marry him.

Rather than exacting revenge on those who deserved it (my parents and Bohozuk), I entrapped a seeming innocent. Unconsciously, I was preying on someone I thought was vulnerable, like myself.

From the earliest days of childhood I had been superstitious, convinced that the souls of the dead could provide guidance to the living as they tried to sort out the muddles of daily life. In this instance: like mother, like daughter. One of my mother's favourite activities as we snuggled up to each other in bed was to seek guidance from the ouija board. Since those spirits simply issued directives that underscored advice or orders already given by Mother, I soon realized that the various messages from beyond were really from her.

Nevertheless, I remained fascinated by the spirit world. Old Mr. Washington, a garrulous black man who was a conductor at the HSR, told fortunes using Tarot cards. He was a descendant of slaves who had escaped from the southern United States by means of the Underground Railway and had a considerable local reputation as a communicator with the world beyond.

Once a month I visited him and his family on Cannon Street. Since he liked me and refused to take any money for his services, I would descend upon the family with flowers and candies. The "readings," held in a narrow parlour at the back of the house lighted by a single candle, were usually inconsequential. Assurances of financial stability, vague promises of a better future. Yet I could always glimpse a deep sadness in Mr. Washington's eyes when he looked into mine. "He's worried about me," I would tell myself.

Mr. Washington and I had one common client — an accountant. One day, this man confided to me that the fortune teller had referred to me — with great sorrow in his voice — as "that poor woman." Washington's wife — overhearing this snippet — immediately leaped in: "Poor woman! She drives a new Packard every year, wears the finest clothes. What are you talking about?" Mr. Washington refrained from saying anything more, sagely nodded his head and walked Mr. Cunningham to the door.

The next time I visited Cannon Street, I had decided to marry John Dick. On that occasion, there was no jollity or banter as the cards were turned over by Mr. Washington. The whites surrounding his large brown pupils became immense and, for once, he was at a loss for words. "Cut the cards again, Evelyn." I did so. He turned three or four over. "Let's try again." I did as instructed. This time he uncovered only two. "Evelyn, I keep seeing the Hanged Man over and over again. He won't leave us alone. I've never seen such a bad fortune." Then he tried to make a joke of it. "Sometimes a really mean-minded spirit gets into this room and makes havoc of everything I'm doing. He's here today. No sense trying to make sense of the cards when he's around. Come back in a week or two." Two weeks was too long. I never had the opportunity to visit the Cannon Street house again.

My mother was flummoxed when I told her what I was about to do. We didn't need a cover or beard — we still had Norman White. That might be so, I assured her, but a recent widow was more vulnerable than a married woman. "But he's a lowly bus conductor, dear! Someone of no consequence!"

I assured her that made him all the more valuable in my profession. He was someone who posed no threat. I could not help but add that my father was an employee of the HSR. That observation really rubbed salt into the wound I was inflicting. Without wanting me to know she had taken this taunt in, she responded: "Your father hates foreigners. He'll kill him!" At that point, I suggested we keep the marriage a secret from him. When she saw my mind was made up — that I was beginning to conduct myself as her daughter — she ceased trying to dissuade me.

Even a diligent biographer like Jack Batten, who wrote the life of one of my lawyers, can get things wrong. After mentioning that the marriage took place on October 4, 1945, in the Church of the Ascension on James Street South, he continues: "The only two witnesses to the event were present by happenstance. A few days earlier, a nodding acquaintance of Dick's named Dominic Pollice had climbed aboard his streetcar where, to Pollice's surprise, Dick pressed him to attend the wedding. Pollice showed up with his fiancée, and afterwards the two couples went to a hotel room for a few celebratory drinks. During the subdued festivities Pollice leaned over to give Evelyn, who was sitting on a bed, a kiss of good wishes. Evelyn reached up her arms and locked Pollice in an embrace that lasted far beyond the respectable time for congratulations. Perhaps it was at this awkward moment, as Dick watched in confusion and jealousy, that he began to realize he'd stepped in over his head with a woman like Evelyn."

Having made his editorial interjection, Batten continues: "As for the bride, her enthusiasm for the venture into matrimony cooled that very evening. She and Dick ate dinner alone in a downtown restaurant and spent most of the meal bickering. Evelyn expected Dick to set up the new family — husband, wife and Heather — in a house, but Dick talked of a flat on Barton Street in the north end. 'With all those dagos,' Evelyn said. The north end wasn't her style, and before midnight she left both the restaurant and Dick and returned to Henson Park, where, since the apartment had only a single bedroom, she spent her wedding night in the same place she'd been sleeping for the previous four months — in bed beside her mother."

Most of the information Batten supplies is correct, but cause and effect become completely muddled in the description of the kiss I gave Pollice. I met the man and his girlfriend, Dorothy Jackson, on the day of my marriage. I did proffer him a sedate kiss, at which point he turned to John and whispered: "Have you squared this with Anna Wolski? She'll kill you."

After Pollice and his woman left, I asked John who Anna was and was told she was a girlfriend with whom he had recently finished. Shades of Bill Bohozuk arose before me, although I attempted to remain calm in the face of another betrayal. At our wedding supper, I told John about my wish to rent or purchase a home where our little family could be safely ensconced. He suggested shabby Barton Street; at that point, I might have made the racist remark attributed to me (I was such an ignorant hard-hearted young woman).

As the conversation continued, it became apparent my new husband was penniless: I would have to supply all the funds for our matrimonial home. At that point, I informed him there was no room for him on James Street; he would have to return to his boarding house at the corner of Emerald and Cannon. When I had first contemplated marriage to John, I had not dwelt on the prospect of conjugal sex. That night, the information he had just provided me with allowed me to banish that subject completely from the horizon.

Thus began what was essentially a non-marriage. Three days after the ceremony, Bill phoned me, imploring me to see him. I agreed to meet him at the Tivoli after the movie the following evening. We nodded to each other as we left the cinema; he waited a minute or so to accompany me on the walk up James Street back to the Henson Apartments. Suspecting I had married Dick in order to get at him, he offered an olive branch. We were now both guilty of the identical crime of linking up with unsuitable partners. Couldn't we resume our relationship and couldn't we both rid ourselves of undesirable pasts?

As we reached the Apartments, I continued to listen in grim silence to his protestations and was about to turn him down when suddenly John Dick leapt out of the thick bushes that fronted the property. He accused Bill of being a home wrecker, an unmanly propositioner of a recent bride. Speech deserted Bill, but I told John to leave immediately or I would summon the police. Stammering obscenities, he wandered down Herkimer, the street that intersected James.

My anger at John fuelled my lust: Bohozuk retrieved his nearby car, and we drove to his home in the north end, where, careful not to make any noise that would wake his sister, we had sex for the first and last time. In the morning on our drive back to my apartment, I told Bill I had no wish to see him again.

My first and only act of genuine sexual passion was generated by rage. As a young woman, I had been taught by Mother to suppress my emotions — especially anger; I was the perfect prostitute because I experienced no sexual feelings. All of a sudden anger and the pleasures of the body were uncomfortably fused for me. I chose not to believe that either of these basic instincts was part of me — I was obviously afraid of veering out of control. I also wanted to revenge myself on Bill, to make him think I had forgiven him. In one fell swoop, I got even with him and made the pesky John furious.

In quick order, John proved to be a dreadful nuisance on another score — money, once going so far as to ask my mother to loan him some. A few days after the Bohozuk incident, he showed up at my flat asking for me. Mother explained I had gone out with a friend.

"I thought she was ill in bed."

Such was the not the case, Mother ventured. Then she added: "How do you expect Evelyn to keep up with her social contacts if she doesn't go out, and doesn't have a nice apartment to entertain her friends in?"

At that point, the penny finally seems to have dropped for John. "Do you mean she earns money as a prostitute?"

Attempting to put the best face on the situation, Mother, as was her wont, gilded the lily: "I wouldn't say that exactly, but she has rich friends and she has to have a nice place to receive them."

A very distraught — apparently shocked — John Dick then took his leave. To his cousin, Alexander Kammerer and his wife, Anna, he told how he had been taken in by a whore posing as a helpless widow. He characterized himself as a victim of a manipulative woman and, to a large extent and to be fair to him, that claim was accurate.

Unfortunately, John Dick began to broadcast his discoveries beyond his own family circle. He also continued to hide in the thick bushes surrounding the flat; he noticed when Mother and Heather left the flat and a gentleman caller would arrive five or ten minutes later. Some of these men he recognized from their photos in the *Spectator*. As he began to voice his litany of complaints and to mention the names of the men he saw, he also learned from fellow HSR drivers that many of them suspected my father — in collusion with one or two executives — was robbing the company blind. He began repeating that gossip.

In an attempt to check any damage my new husband could unleash, I decided to buy a house where my mother, Heather and I could live away from James Street. My hope was that I could settle John there and then decide my next step. Under those circumstances, I purchased 32 Carrick Street, a modest three-storey red-brick house with a white veranda, a small garden, and a garage opening into a narrow alley in the east end of the city but nearer to the centre than Rosslyn Avenue. When the three of us arrived there on the morning of the thirty-first of October, John was sitting on the steps to greet us. Later, he would untruthfully claim I swindled him out of $1,300 as part payment on the house.

His paranoid turn of mind took further flights of fancy when he told Anna Kammerer, as she later recalled, of his domestic arrangements: "He said he was never allowed to have any private talk with his wife without the mother interfering. As soon as they would enter into conversation she would call Evelyn on some pretext or other. Evelyn and her mother also spent hours together whispering in a low voice so he wouldn't hear what was being said. He also remarked he was never allowed the freedom of the house, as one of them always made some excuse to accompany him wherever he went. He said there was a locked trunk and suitcase in the attic and when he asked to see the contents Evelyn always said, 'You wouldn't be interested. They are only my school things.'"

Just because one is paranoid does not mean one is not being looked at — or noticing the truth. John had given himself plenty of good reasons to be watching his back. My mother and I remained agitated about my father's wrath if he discovered what John was openly declaiming. We were also worried about my patrons and the obvious consequence of any gossip about them being spread about. Containment: this was the task to which I now had to turn my attention. I was not assisted by two mysterious visitors.

The first was a Ukrainian woman, who supposedly came in response to a classified advertisement in the *Spectator*.

"You have an apartment to rent it says in tonight's paper."

I assured her this was not true and retrieved that day's newspaper. In fact, I pointed out, there was no flat advertised anywhere on Carrick.

"Well," she remarked in broken English, "I think I make a mistake." She retreated quickly but Anna Wolski accosted John the next day on the streetcar: "I found your wife at home. You really are married."

The next visitor was even more sinister: a stout, dark Italian, elegantly dressed in a dark overcoat, a bright tie, and a large diamond ring in a claw setting. When I invited him in, he bowed, removed his gloves, and held his bowler hat in his hand. According to him, John was breaking his home up. If he did not desist from visiting his wife, he would fix him. I asked him what he meant. He opened his mouth wide, revealing glistening pearl teeth with gold fillings, smiled and then fixed me with his dark eyes: "You know what we mean by 'fix him.' We fix him all right, one way or the other. Get him sooner than later." With that, he bowed again, placed his hat on his head, turned slowly and let himself out of the house.

At close range, I now learned — as I should have known — that appearances can be extremely deceiving. My own skills in reading John had been minimal. He was a philanderer who kept a number of women on a string; he had lied about his financial prospects; he now showed little interest in Heather. He wanted me to *keep* him: he thought he had found a virtuous woman who would mother him, save him from himself and, at the same time, provide a ready source of cash.

When he discovered the nature of my profession, he acted the role of the generous, disappointed, betrayed lover whose expectations had been dashed. When that ploy did not work, he accused me of withholding from him what I gave to others. "I'm supposed to pay you? Just like the others? Otherwise, nothing?" Then he threatened Mother: "If my wife is a whore, I'll be the pimp. Where will that leave you?" When she tearfully informed me she did not like the tone in my husband's voice, I could appreciate both the irony and the comedy of the situation. John's self-effacing mannerisms — an elaborate charade — had totally vanished. Mother had met a man after her own heart.

I was badly frightened, realizing that I had created a situation that was quickly veering out of control. My fantasy was that I would rest easier if I did not have to see my spouse on a daily basis.

I told John he could stay at Carrick Street — sleeping by himself on the living room sofa — until after the Christmas holidays. After that, he was to find his own place. Our brief marriage, I instructed him, was over. Early in January 1946, he fled to the Kammerers, claiming he had heard gossip that both my father and Bohozuk were out to get him. On 28 February, he attended the funeral of his grandmother in Beamsville. On that occasion, he made — in his babyish yet pompous manner — a solemn declaration to his widowed mother: "If something does happen that I am missing, go after Mr. and Mrs. MacLean and my wife and you will get a lot more. But start there." Tears filling his eyes, he added: "Mother, I believe in prayer to the Almighty God, and He might get me out somehow from that bunch, but if something does happen, go after those three people." Ten days later, all that remained of John Dick was a headless, armless and legless cadaver.

21

"Any discussion of your guilt or innocence is a waste of precious time. You are patently innocent, my girl."

I felt very reassured by Mr. Sullivan, although he issued his declaration in an almost casual way. My lawyer loomed over me as I sat with him in the cubbyhole assigned to us. Refusing to sit down, the big, bluff Irishman, with the furriest, most outlandishly out-of-control eyelashes I had ever beheld, paced furiously.

"The physical evidence won't allow any jury to convict you. But the prosecution already knows that. In fact, they probably know the identity of the real culprits who hired Mr. Romanelli. That's irrelevant to them. They need a conviction and, by their lights, you must suffer because you began the whole godforsaken mess. You are a fallen woman and, in a twisted sort of logic, you must — as far as they are concerned — be punished. Now that the war is over, the newspapers are desperate for copy. A murder involving a call girl is perfect for them."

He handed me a copy of the report by the coroner: "Hair, eyes, ears, teeth and features were missing. The severing of arms, neck, and legs and a transverse cut 12-inches across — which penetrated the belly wall and caused three perforations of the bowel — had the appearance of having been made with a saw rather than with a keen cutting instrument. The right arm had been severed by a slightly diagonal cut and the upper arm bone partially splintered, as if the bone had been almost sawed through, then bent, splintering the remaining bone."

Perhaps against his better judgement, he next showed me the photographs. "It is obvious that a woman of your height and build could not have done this." In one picture — taken at the crime scene — the torso, surrounded by leaves, lies flat on its stomach, giving the impression of a doll that, having displeased its owner, had its extremities removed. On closer inspection, the area around the neck is blood-stained, the lower portion of the neck is visible, and the mangled remains of the right arm forlornly rests on the ground. In the morgue photo, the side of the body is shown — the pearly white skin of the upper torso contrasts sharply with the red meat-like look where the head, arms and legs were ripped off; the stomach area looks like a piece of liver one buys at a butcher; in his photos, the coroner has been careful to exclude the penis from view. He obviously did not wish to be accused of venturing into pornography.

My lawyer continued to whirl around the room, his felt hat in hand, his undone overcoat revealing beneath it a completely crumpled suit, a shirt with a week's worth of sweat on it, and a necktie that looked like a hangman's noose. I wondered if I so upset his Catholic-family-man approach to women that he could not bear to discuss the murder with me. Yet, as he declaimed, I realized that even more important to him was the desire to best the prosecution, to find a way to render them powerless.

"Evelyn, I have an idea. Your mother will have to help us, if she is willing."

"I imagine she'll do everything in her power to assist me."

He shot me a funny look, obviously not at all taken in by this vague assurance. "The way to win this case is to make you look like an innocent victim who has been manipulated to appear a guilty woman. Most of the jurors will know you worked as a call girl, a fact that will heavily prejudice them against you. I have to encourage them to overlook your profession."

Once again he paused, looking me over as one might a piece of cattle. Then, he smiled. "There's a lot of movie pictures in which a fallen woman is unjustly accused of a crime, often murder. Force of circumstances is always against such ladies, but they triumph over adversity when it becomes obvious that reputation and guilt are not one and the same. Do you follow me? A criminal lawyer can learn a lot at the Tivoli."

I smiled in agreement. "I understand what you're saying, but I'm not sure what this has to do with me."

"Everything. You look a bit like Bette Davis, one of the great wronged women in the pictures. She looks like a hard dame, but in the end she is shown to have a heart of gold. Wouldn't hurt a fly."

"I'm still confused."

"Every day of the trial you are going to be carefully dressed. Expensive, conservative clothes. Dark colours. Only your hat is going to be stylish. Some will have veils, some not. You will always wear white kid gloves. Your hair is to be marcelled every day after court has finished. You must be careful not to sleep on your perm, never allow it to be mussed."

"I still don't understand."

Without paying any attention to me, he continued: "You are never to look at the jury, even if you give testimony. You are never to appear even the slightest bit upset, no matter what any witness says. You are to have a slight — very slight — smile on your face, as if you are above everything that is happening around you. You speak only to me — and only when I signal you to do so."

"Sounds like a role in a melodrama."

"More of a movie. Think of it like that. You must do exactly as I instruct you."

"Do you think we can influence the jury?"

"Of course we can. If you sit there looking like a wronged Barbara Stanwyck, they will become convinced you're being framed. Which is exactly what is happening to you."

"Yes. I guess so. It seems overly contrived."

"Take it from me. All the best criminal lawyers do what I'm doing. Baiting the trap, it's called. We just have to be sure the trap doesn't get sprung on us."

So Mr. Sullivan prevailed upon Mother to be my wardrobe mistress and makeup artist; he paid one of my fellow inmates to do my hair. My costumes were chosen well in advance — usually three or four days — and I was given careful instruction on my posture and other aspects of my physical presence. My lipsticks were to be dark but never lurid: very deep reds, never scarlet. In place of the image of the fallen woman was substituted the picture of the wronged ingenue. On the eighth of November 1946, the columnist for the *Spectator*, a man with an excellent eye for detail, provided a vivid, accurate description: "Shiny black curls beneath her sequin-studded skull cap; a beauty spot on her right cheek; finely shaped nose, large dark eyes. Her dress: black, sleeveless....toeless, heel-less shoes; matching lipstick and nail polish." Was Mr. Sullivan blissfully unaware that a similar scheme had initiated the downward spiral in my existence? Did he simply have a mind that thought like Mother's?

Unfortunately, Mr. Sullivan was trying to bar the door well after the horse had strayed from the stable. I had already — under instructions — given three different versions of the torso murder to the police. These were the first short stories I ever concocted.

22

STORY ONE

Sunday-Monday, March 17 and 18

At first, I told the police exactly what happened. My husband had been kidnapped, I was summoned to fetch him after he had been warned about his big mouth, and only then discovered that he had been murdered. On the day after, one of the investigators, Mr. Wood, began with an extremely commonsensical question: “Mrs. Dick, why would this man call you to get you to drive him in your car with part of a body, when he already had it in his car?”

"The car couldn't stay. They had somewhere else to go."

"It is pretty hard to believe that this gang, having murdered your husband, having cut him up, and having got the body half way up the Mountain, would call you to drive the rest of the way. Why bring you into it at all?"

"They had a job to do in Toronto and alcohol to get in Windsor."

"But if they had the torso in the car up on the Mountain, they could have, in the time they waited for you to get there, driven along and dumped it over the embankment."

"Well, they claimed they had an another errand to do."

Annoyed but a bit triumphant in having demonstrated to me the illogicality of what I was telling him, Wood pressed me further: "When Romanelli told you it was part of John in the bag, were you glad that your husband had been done away with?"

"No, it was a pretty mean trick to break up a home."

"But he was your *husband*?" He said the last word as if he meant *enemy*.

So I answered him in kind. "Yes, but he had so many enemies."

Finding it impossible to keep the sneer out of his voice, he got to the heart of the matter: "Mrs. Dick, did you conspire with this man, this Romanelli, to murder your husband?"

"No." I answered him very deliberately.

"Were you to get any money for your part in it?"

"Well, I didn't like the idea, but he said something about settling up with me in a couple of weeks. I don't know why he said that."

"How much did he say?"

"Two hundred dollars ... 'For my trouble,' he said."

"When did he tell you that?"

"While I was driving."

"Up to that time you didn't expect any financial gain?"

"No."

"Did you get the two hundred?"

"Not even the smell of it."

Impatience now replaced sneering in Wood's voice. "Mrs. Dick, did you take any actual part in the murder of your husband?"

"No," I assured him.

STORY TWO

Wednesday, March 20

"I understand, Mrs. Dick," Wood began, "that you have been talking to my colleague Detective Preston and you want to give us some information in connection with the death of John Dick. Now, go ahead and tell us, so we can get it down on paper." This was Wood in his kindliest manner.

"Well, as you know, Bill Bohozuk detested my husband. They were bitter enemies." I paused: "Bill borrowed two hundred dollars from me."

"Did he say what he wanted the money for?"

"Yes, he was expecting a job to be done. The men doing the job needed two hundred as a down payment."

"What kind of job?"

"John had to be fixed."

"In what way?"

"Put out of business, and they had to have…."

He interrupted me: "What do you mean by that, put out of business?"

"Well, murdered, I guess."

"And who was to get the two hundred?"

"Well, I was to give it to Bill, and he was going to give it to the gang that had come through from Windsor. The two hundred was only a down payment. I gave Bill the money, but he returned it to me a few days later saying the men were too busy to do such a small job. He also told me the price had gone up to a thousand dollars."

"Did Romanelli tell you anything else about the murder when you were joyriding with him on the Mountain?" Wood now inquired, injecting a sarcastic tone into his voice.

"Yes, he told me that he and an associate had met John at the King George Hotel at 1:30 in the afternoon, had several beers, and offered to drive him to the top of the Mountain for another drink when the pub closed at two. The three of them drove and drank. John didn't notice the time until about 3:30; his shift began at 4:11. By now, they were on a deserted road, and he began accusing his companions of purposely keeping him late. John apparently cursed them: "I won't come out again with you sons of bitches, Dagos!" At that point, Romanelli let him have it."

"What do you mean by that?"

"He shot him, once in the back of the neck, once through the right eyeball."

"OK. Go on."

"From Glanford Street they came down to the city and went down to a home in the north end, where the Italians live. They stayed there for a little while disposing of parts of the limbs as there was no one home, and then about a quarter to five they had to start cleaning up."

"Why did they have to start cleaning up?"

"Because the person who lived in the house was arriving home."

"Now were you in the car with these men when this happened?"

"No, officer. Romanelli told me all this during the drive."

Changing his approach in order to confuse me, he asked me about John's missing limbs. Did I know where they were?

"They were burnt in a furnace. I don't know the address."

STORY THREE

Friday, March 22

I made this statement to the police, replacing the first two.

"On the day of the murder, I borrowed Bill Landeg's car and did some shopping. I met John on McNab between King and Market streets at 1:45 in the afternoon. He told me he had just returned from the Regal Hotel. He wanted to borrow twenty-five dollars. I told him I had no money. He went to the beverage room at the King George Hotel saying he had to meet a couple of fellows. I went to do some more shopping. I later saw my husband come out of the hotel with Romanelli and another man. I saw Bill Bohozuk's car on James Street near the Virginia Dare store. John and the two men were walking east. I wondered if John was about to be murdered.

"After I finished shopping I drove home, arriving there at four. Bohozuk called me: 'We've got him at last.' He wanted me to meet him at the Connaught as soon as possible. When I arrived at the Connaught, I was met by Romanelli and his companion. They gave me John's watch chain, some streetcar tickets, and a paper bag. 'These are some mementoes Bill thought you'd like to have.' Romanelli then asked to borrow the car. I agreed to this. He drove me home, let me out and drove away. Later, he called to tell me he was returning the car.

"He brought the car into the back lane. I remarked that there was a lot of blood on the car and he said that would come off all right. There was a blanket in the back of the car and it was covered with blood. Wrapped up in a piece of the cloth was a part of the face which was all smashed, and some other parts which he said they had tried to burn without success. Romanelli removed the parts from the car and put them in the garage. He told me I was too bloody slow and was very mad because he wanted to go back uptown. He was cleaning a gun and a knife and he also used some IT cleaning fluid to remove blood from his gabardine coat. After he had cleaned himself up he locked the door to the garage. The parts of the body he removed from the car were placed inside a bushel basket.

"We both got into the car. I intended to drive, but he got behind the wheel and backed the car southward out of the lane and drove to the Royal Connaught where he got out. I returned the car, parking it by the Grafton Garage. I walked up to the Royal Connaught alley and took a taxi home. I arrived home about 7:15 p.m. I went into the house and saw my mother. I told her John had been fixed, put out of business and she said, 'I knew Bohozuk was after him. So was your father.' I was expecting Bill or Romanelli to come and clean up the garage, but they didn't show up."

*****

I uttered these three conflicting, slightly overlapping narratives and, in the process, the police, not without just cause, became convinced I was a compulsive liar. Of more importance than the variants themselves are the events that transpired between the acts, the facts behind the fictions.

23

In books and movies, detectives never work alone. Sam Spade had partners, even though they tended, as in *The Maltese Falcon*, to get bumped off — thus adding the ingredient of revenge to the narrative. The masterful Sherlock Holmes was always accompanied by the blundering Watson. I should not have been altogether surprised, therefore, when the murder of John Dick was placed in the hands of the seasoned Charles Wood of the Criminal Investigation Branch of the Ontario Provincial Police in Toronto and the apparently kind, silent local, Clarence Preston, whose specialty before he encountered me was Morality.

After the night of my fateful drive with Mr. Romanelli, I waited in grim expectation of a visit from the police. Like everyone else in Hamilton, I had read a few days before in the *Spectator* about the mysterious partially clothed torso discovered by some frightened schoolboys. I suspected John's relations would be in touch with the police, and I realized it was only a matter of time before I would be interrogated. There was a comical irony at work: the coroner who performed the autopsy was named Dr. Deadman.

When John's relatives had phoned the house searching for him and before the story was in the newspaper, I fessed up to Mother, who now knew what I had been burning that evening. "I venture your father is at the bottom of this."That was her only response.

An hour before the arrival of Wood and Preston at my doorstep on Tuesday, March 19 — eleven days after John died and three days after the discovery of the torso — my father put in an unexpected visit at Carrick Street. During a family lunch, he announced that he was privy to some of the details of how John was murdered. For example, he informed me he knew all about my encounter with Mr. Romanelli.

"Well, if you know that, you know who ordered the execution."

"No, bairn. That I don't know. My contact — the man who phoned me at the HSR — told me that damned Silesian had been put out of his misery because he had been extremely indiscreet. Seems he was hiding in the bushes on James Street and saw some of the best-heeled gentlemen in the city frequenting your establishment. He named some of them. The man who paid to silence him was never mentioned. Dick died before he could implicate him."

Testily, Mother interrupted: "We're supposed to believe you had nothing to with the murder?"

"That's the truth, madam," he rejoined, nodding mockingly in her direction. "Not that I didn't have my reasons to be rid of him. He was telling some awful stories about me at the HSR."Then, looking around the room as if an unexpected person might have come in unawares, he proceed to tell me I was to tell the police exactly what I had done, although I was not to mention I had incinerated some of the remains.

"Why should I do what you tell me?"

A condescending smile that one gives a naughty child animated his face as he prepared to respond. Just then, the doorbell rang. I pulled myself up, checked to see if my slip was showing and walked into the hallway, where, for the first time, I saw, looking through the glass that filled half the door, Inspector Wood waiting for someone to answer his summons. Behind him were sergeants Preston and Farrow and Constable Mattick.

An elegant man. Too elegant to be a policeman. That was my first thought about Wood. He identified himself but before going any further, he complimented the furnishings in the room. "Shows remarkably good taste. Expensive. Very expensive in a subtle way. She must have hidden sources of wealth. Don't you think so, Preston?"

I am not sure the good sergeant had any taste, good or bad. A large messy bundle of a man, he mumbled something under his breath. Without further ado, Wood then looked at me: "You have probably read in the paper of the finding of a torso on the mountainside?"

I did not reply, although I could feel my face turning a bright red. He told me about the five children — Dave Reid, his sister Fiona, and Bob, Jim and Fred Weaver, accompanied by Dave's dog, Teddy — who had been hiking a long way from their homes in the west end of Hamilton. Earlier that day, they had come across dead — presumably diseased — pigs that had been dumped by farmers over the edge of the Mountain. Bob and Fred, who had wandered off on their own, came across the dead body, at first thinking it was merely another hog. Then, when the truth dawned on them, they became frightened and ran back to their companions at the edge of the Mountain, who returned with them to the spot. The band of children were not quite sure what to do; they wanted to report their discovery and they wanted to get home to their parents. They returned to the road to flag down a car. No one paid any attention to them. Finally, they formed a human chain across the lane. The man who was forced to stop promised to inform the police. Two hours later, the authorities arrived. "That torso has been identified as the body of your husband," Wood announced.

Wood's remarkably long nose and delicate, almost feminine facial features, together with his long, angular body, gave him the look of the whippets at the dog races. He frightened me, and I had not yet taken in my father's warning. My eyes flashed: "Don't look at me. I don't know anything about it."

The inspector looked offended, as if I had insulted him. "Sergeant Preston, the lady knows nothing. Does that surprise you, Sergeant? Shouldn't she know at least a little something?"

This time, the sergeant shook his head vigorously in the affirmative.

"Well," Wood announced, as he turned his head to examine me, "you had better put your coat on and come to police headquarters and we'll talk this over." Just then, my father walked into the room and identified himself to Wood. As it turned out, my father and Preston were old friends. The sergeant had been investigating my father for years but, in return for information on other suspected criminals, he had never pressed charges against him.

When my father — assuming the guise of the worried parent — asked if he could accompany me to the station, Wood told him to suit himself. Farrow and Mattick stayed behind to search the house. On the drive downtown, my father remained silent, but the imploring look in his countenance was hard to miss.

At the station, my father was left in the detectives' office, presided over by the sergeant of detectives, whereas Wood and Preston took me to an unoccupied Crown attorney's office. Various legal tomes were strewn on the table, but the thick dust that covered them showed they had not been consulted in a long while.

"Be a good chappie, Preston, and get a stenographer in here. Mrs. Dick and I will exchange pleasantries while we wait for you. You'd enjoy that, wouldn't you, Mrs. Dick? You enjoy talking to strange men?" There was nothing to which I could reasonably respond, but the conversation soon turned to my black Packard, which I told him I had sold two years before to Bill Landeg. I admitted that I borrowed the car back for a day or two at a time, the last occasion being March 4.

"You're being very coy with me, madam. It will be in your best interest to tell me the entire truth at once." This statement was issued brusquely as a military command. At that point, Preston, accompanied by the stenographer, returned to the room. Wood then cautioned me, and I began my first, long recitation of what I knew. As I have indicated, Wood cross-questioned me on the ridiculousness of the murderers asking me to convey another car to the Mountain. The real reason, I knew, was that I was to take the fall for John's death or, at the very least, to be fully implicated in it. I suspected Wood was fully aware of this line of reasoning, but he did not let on that he was thinking in this way.

"Do you know how your husband was murdered?"

"No, I am not sure."

"What do you mean you are not sure?"

"I wouldn't like to say in case I am wrong."

Then he startled me. "Who had the gun?"

"Well, I have no gun. I don't own a gun. *They* always carry them. They don't fool around. They might put a knife in my back or a bomb under my house."

"They, they, they. You're not being very helpful. I want you to take Sergeant Preston and myself on a tour of the drive you took on the evening of March 6. Are you willing to do that for us?"

I agreed, and the three of us set out fifteen minutes later with a driver. We went to the top of the James Street Incline. I showed them the spot where I had met up with the large sedan. Then, we continued south to Queensdale, turned east to Wellington, north on Wellington to Concession, and east on Concession right along to Mountain Brow Road. Just beyond where Flock Road intersects Mountain Brow, I pointed out the spot where Mr. Romanelli threw John's cap out of the car. We stopped, but the detectives could not find any sign of it. We got back in the car and continued on Mountain Brow Road in the direction of Albion Falls. When I saw the site where the body had been dumped, I told them to stop.

I can still feel the piercing coldness of that early March evening. Twilight slowly asserted itself as we drove up the Mountain, and we were enveloped in blackness during the descent. I sat next to Wood, who deliberately edged himself away from me, as if to avoid contamination. I suppose I cannot really blame him. A man who worked with evil all his life, he knew the thin line that separated himself from those he pursued. I hugged my Persian lamb coat.

As soon as we arrived back at the station, I was charged with vagrancy — at that time a police procedure for holding someone who was a suspect in a far more serious crime. The following morning, a Monday, I was arraigned before a magistrate. Wearing a broken check black and grey suit and a black tam, with my coat thrown over my shoulders, I stood in the prisoner's dock while my first lawyer, Mr. Walsh, pleaded for my release on bail. I was remanded in custody.

Later that day, my mother visited me. She began by telling me of the thorough searches that had been made to both the Carrick Street and Rosslyn Avenue houses. In the bedroom I shared with my mother, they had found a small snapshot of Bill, my bank book showing a balance of $720, and three of hers with just over ten thousand dollars. An arsenal of various guns and a revolver had been discovered at my father's place. Bill Landeg was interviewed about the Packard; he told the police about the note I had written him.

Mother gave me all this information in what was for her a normal, matter-of-fact way. Then, she softened her voice. "Your father came to see me this morning. I was out. He let himself into the house and was waiting for me when I got home. He has new instructions."

"New instructions! From whom?"

"Shush, dear. Don't let anybody hear you. From the person who phoned him before. Listen very carefully. You must tell the police that Bohozuk arranged the murder, perhaps even carried it out himself."

"That's a lie."

"That is of absolutely no account. If you refuse to implicate Bohozuk, he will be murdered. Same fate as John Dick. It's as simple as that. Your choice."

"I don't follow."

"Mr. Wood is a very clever fellow. A real Toronto busybody. It was some sort of accident that he was assigned to this case. The only way to outwit him is to confuse him and his cronies. He knows you may have had little or nothing to do with the murder, but he is going to try to use you to get to the bottom of it. Bohozuk is the red herring, as in Sherlock Holmes."

"Sherlock Holmes always knows a red herring."

"My dear, you'd better hope Mr. Wood doesn't." Then her smile became malicious: "You've always been such a diligent reader, pet. Now you've got to use your imagination to invent stories. I've given you the plot line; you do the embroidering."

This conversation with my mother paved the way for my second variant account in which Bohozuk was jealous of my husband and decided to do away with him. Since Wood had only straws to grasp at, he took the bait. In fact, he had hauled Bohozuk in for questioning earlier that day. A man easily inclined towards cynicism, Wood thought my new account plausible. As an explanation, it placed limits on the identity of the culprit rather than forcing the police to consider the possibility that John's big mouth had forced the hand of a powerful consort of mine. All in all, an ingenious manoeuvre. The police would be distracted — at least momentarily. The longer a mystery remains unsolved, the greater the chance of the criminal escaping detection.

On Thursday, March 21st, Wood and Preston returned to Carrick Street, where the good sergeant found a bushel basket filled with ashes. Just outside the garage doors, he also noticed a deep rut running at an angle of forty-five degrees, where a car had recently been driven up close to the garage. The gouge was filled with ashes. Later in the day, Dr. Deadman was summoned to assist in the removal of objects found in the garage.

My mother disliked Wood, but she found Preston congenial. She could talk at him without fear of interruption. On Wednesday, the day before, she told him, her estranged husband had let himself into the house while she was absent. When he learned that the police had searched the house, Donald had rushed upstairs to the attic. A little later, he shouted for her to bring him a screwdriver and hammer. She took them to him and waited, but, just as he was about to open a trunk, he noticed her, swore, and told her to get the hell out. While he was upstairs, detectives Farrow and Mattick came to fetch some of my clothing. Shortly afterwards, when Mother summoned father to supper, he had disappeared.

Intrigued by my mother's story, the good sergeant proceeded to the attic, where he came upon several unlocked empty suitcases and a lady's beige case. "Some of my daughter's books," was my mother's only comment. She had no idea where the key was. He forced the lock, revealing a burlap bag covering a small wicker meat basket, which contained a cardboard carton. The carton, filled with cement from which clothing protruded, emitted a ghastly smell, like decomposing flesh.

Sergeant Preston, placing a handkerchief over his face, informed my mother that he and Wood would examine the suitcase and its contents at the police station. There, in the presence of Deadman, the cement was chipped away. Among the contents was a blue leatherette zippered shopping bag. When the bag was unzipped, the police found the decomposed body of my son, clad in the tiny sweater coat I had knitted for him.

Having made this discovery, Wood and Preston decided to pay a further visit to Rosslyn Avenue, where they discovered a locker to which my father on their previous visit had claimed to have lost the key. When he was informed that the lock would be forced, he presented them with the missing key. Inside were two shotguns, a deer rifle, a .22 rifle and a hunting knife. In a brown hunting bag was $4,400 in cash. In the cellar, an axe and an eighteen-inch carpenter's strip saw were hanging on the wall; on a small nearby table was a black-handled butcher knife with grease on its fifteen-inch blade, "as if," Wood observed, "meat or something had recently been cut with it."

According to Wood, however, the most intriguing piece of evidence was the book — the August 5, 1944 issue of *Famous Detective Stories* — which he found on my father's bedside table. It contained this narrative, which the police red-pencilled:

Nearby were the tools of Dr. Zimmerly's barbaric surgery: a dull saw, a knife with blood dried on it, some smaller knives, none of which was clean, some bottles filled with narcotics, and a number of filthy rags. The old doctor lost no time in going to his gory chore. One by one he cut away the legs, the arms, the head. He worked like a butcher — first the knife, then the saw. The floor was wet with new blood before he finally finished. The dull sun of a new day had routed the night of horror before the bloody job was completed.

Wood did not have to be a genius to interpret this intriguing literary clue. Rather than a paucity of suspects, he now had two. The complication was that my father and Bohozuk were sworn enemies who never would have conspired to kill John Dick. Not a person to look gift horses in the mouth, Wood did not seem to consider that his case had quickly taken some extremely easy curves. Why had my mother volunteered information so fulsomely? Why was the cash at my father's house so accessible? Why was the book containing a description of a similar crime conveniently placed in his bedroom?

My mother informed me late on the same Thursday afternoon of the true circumstances surrounding the death of Peter David a year and a half earlier. My father had strangled the baby and later encased the baby in cement. I was in shock, unable to take anything in. She explained that the suitcase must have been at Rosslyn Avenue and then moved to Carrick Street by my father on the Wednesday before she discovered him in the house. She was also certain — based on what she had heard about the discoveries at father's house — that the murder of John Dick had taken place there. Perhaps my father had been one of the executioners? At the very least, she was convinced, he had been following orders.

Throughout her ramblings, my mother paid no attention to the obvious fact I was fixated on the true circumstances of the baby's death. I simply could not process the information and kept stumbling back to that irrevocable fact. "You knew all along ... you planned it ... you're a horrible old witch." In her matter-of-fact way, Mother understood everything I was saying, but this was not a topic for discussion.

"Keep your voice down. I have received instructions from the man who ordered everything. You must now inform the police that you did not meet Mr. Romanelli on the Mountain — that Bill told you what happened. You must confess merely to having assisted in the disposal of John Dick's face and limbs."

"Why should I do anything to help you?"

"Simple, my girl. Your precious Bill Bohozuk's life is still under threat, and you can revenge yourself on your father. If the police have too many suspects and too many circumstantial details, they'll never convict anyone of Dick's murder. Not even you. But you can blacken your father's name — and you can save Bohozuk."

In a whisper, she continued: "You must also tell the police that Bill killed the baby. To further confuse them."

On Friday, March 22, a dull, rainy late winter day, John's funeral was held at the United Mennonite Church in Vineland. According to the *Spectator*, "Dick's aged mother and his two sisters followed the flower-covered plain grey casket as the remains of the murder victim were carried to their last resting place in Vineland Cemetery." Although the authorities told me I could attend, I declined on the grounds I was unwell. Later that day, following Mother's instructions, I made my third statement to the police.

These were the circumstances that led to the contradictory accounts I gave to the police. All of a sudden, within six days, the police had two corpses and an abundance of clues that cancelled each other out. Utterly confused, the police charged both my father and Bohozuk with killing John Dick. Now three people had somehow conspired to kill the same man.

The murder of the baby was ascribed to my former lover. As instructed, I told the police I had taken a taxi from the hospital to the Royal Connaught Hotel, where I had arranged to meet Bohozuk. We got into his car, whereupon he said: "I will get rid of the little bastard," and he proceeded to strangle it by knotting a blanket around its neck. He then pushed the corpse into a small zipper bag and told me: "Here's the brat. I can't get rid of it until we start rowing in the spring." I took the bag home, where my father encased the body in cement.

Two gruesome murders. The only common dominator in the complicated mathematics the police were forced to employ was Evelyn Dick. *Cherchez la femme*. Yet, behind the death of John Dick and the story of Bohozuk's involvement with the death of the baby resided a brilliant legal intellect.

That mastermind had sent me, I now realize, a coded warning. Many years earlier, in October 1905, three lads from Hamilton's north end hiked up the Mountain to search the farmlands on the brow for chestnuts. At Limestone Ridge, they walked into a clump of hickory trees. Almost at once, they noticed a woman's boot sticking out from beneath a pile of leaves. A bit later, under a heap of thorn bush, they came upon the body of a woman, her head lying in a pool of blood. She had been shot in the head with a .32-calibre pistol just below the right ear. A handkerchief was stuffed in her mouth. Fashionably dressed in clothing available only in the States, she was a few months pregnant. The body of Miss X was taken to the morgue at Blanchard & Son, a funeral parlour, in downtown Hamilton. Before the woman was buried, more than ten thousand people streamed through that establishment to view her. She was never identified, her murderer never discovered. The *Spectator* was certain she was a prostitute. A man in Flint, Michigan eventually fessed up but recanted the following day, claiming to have been under the influence of drugs when he made his confession.

To this day, I am convinced that the murder of John Dick was contrived to bear similarities to Miss X's gruesome death. I had been spared — the parallel circumstances proclaimed — and might wish to take heed. The fact that John's huge penis was his only limb to survive was the perfect ritualistic warning to a prostitute who, like all members of her calling, earned her bread and butter servicing that part of the male anatomy. The mastermind must have been one of two clients, well versed in the history of Hamilton. To this day, I am uncertain which of those two clients it was. It had to be Judge X or the distinguished barrister, Mr. Y. They are both still alive. Even in the privacy of my study on this evening in 1999, I am frightened to write down their names in full.

24

For the next two weeks, I remained in jail — still held on the charge of vagrancy, a particularly strange charge since I was a property owner who also leased a flat. I cannot recall that time of my stay with any precision and, in this regard, I am not assisted in having my memory prompted by the late Marjorie Freeman Campbell's *Torso* (also published under the slightly less salacious title of *Unholy Matrimony*). Campbell, a native of Hamilton who wound up living in Toronto, became fascinated by all the complicated zigzags of the case and recorded verbatim many of the ensuing proceedings. In 1999, at the age of 79, I do not have instant recall. Part of me does not wish to dredge up the past, another is compelled to relive it daily. Memory, when filled with guilt and recrimination, is an onerous burden.

Wood and, therefore, Preston had become convinced that my father had murdered John Dick, abetted and assisted by Bohozuk. The evidence pointed in this particular direction, particularly the contents of the arsenal, the heavy traces of blood, and the intriguing episode in the book discovered at Rosslyn Avenue. However, my experience on the Mountain flew completely in the opposite direction, suggesting the murder had been perpetrated there.

If I was lying about my night ride, then another scenario could emerge: Bohozuk, provided with a weapon by my father, had done away with John Dick on the Mountain, returned to Carrick Street where the body was dismembered, drove the body back to the Mountain and disposed of it there. Mr. Romanelli and his companions were unacceptable to Wood's way of thinking; he wanted to be freed from them and, in order to do so, I had to recant their existence. In other words, he wanted me to lie in order to prove the truth he had reached in his deliberations.

On 11 April, having been left to my own devices for almost three weeks, I asked to see Preston. According to him, I greeted him with these words: "When are you going to bring the old man in? My father?"

"Why?" the man of few words rejoined.

"Why? Well, he is in it. He loaned Bohozuk his gun. I saw it." Then, pausing, I added: "You have got to help me."

"I am not able to help you. It is up to your lawyer. Is Bohozuk in this thing?"

"Absolutely. What can I do?"

"I cannot answer that. You are putting me on the spot, but if you want to talk, I will sit and listen. Why did you marry John Dick?"

"John was kind and lovable before marriage. He washed the dishes and brought me things hard to get, like soapflakes. After marriage he changed."

Abruptly, Preston moved the conversation in a new direction, one in which he was trying to eliminate the Italianate element.

"Were you in a barn?"

"No, on a side road."

"Do you mean to tell me this thing happened on a side road?"

"Sure, you will find some pop bottles and a ginger ale bottle which we left."

"That would be fine. We might get some fingerprints."

"Would it help if you found Bohozuk's prints on those bottles?"

"Well, it would certainly back up your story. What would you say if you were asked to go out and show us the spot?"

"With you alone?"

"No, not alone."

"Yes, I'll go. Do you want to go this morning?"

"I don't know. I'll see."

As this conversation ended, Preston handed me two chocolate bars, as a reward for being a co-operative witness. According to Wood and Preston, during the drive that afternoon, I changed the crime scenario completely; under instructions from Bohozuk, I lured John into my car, and the three of us drove up the Mountain. Bill shot John twice, covered the body, drove to Carrick Street, removed the body, and then drove me to the Connaught, where his car was parked.

At this point, the story of the torso murder begins to take on a Marx Brothers surrealist logic. Somehow my father removed the corpse from the garage on Carrick Street and dismembered it on Rosslyn Avenue. The burnings of the limbs took place on both Rosslyn Avenue and Carrick Street. At a later date, the torso was then dumped on the Mountain by Bohozuk and myself. This reconstruction ridiculously touches all possible bases.

This fourth variant was concocted by the detectives, not me. At the conclusion of that trip, I was asked if I would be willing to put this new account into writing. I supposedly agreed, was driven to the Ontario Provincial Police office but then changed my mind. In disgrace, I was returned to the Barton Street Jail.

What is true is that on the following morning I told my lawyer that I had been removed from the jail against my will and, while subjected to severe questioning, had been told a new scenario, to which Wood and Preston attempted to force my assent.

Almost two weeks later, my mother, father and Bill having been arrested for vagrancy, the four of us were presented for arraignment before Magistrate Burbridge. The *Spectator* thought Bill and I made a handsome couple. He wore a blue suit, blue shirt and a bright tie; I was "smartly dressed" in a fawn, fur-trimmed coat and black pancake beret. My mother's wardrobe — a black seal coat accompanied by a small brown tam — and my father's — a grey suit — obviously disappointed the observant, fashion-conscious journalist.

Although Wood and Preston had showed no interest in Peter David White, his murder was the first order of business that day. Dr. Deadman described in lurid detail the desiccated body of the baby: his dress, sweater, booties, shirt and the diaper held together by two rusted safety pins. At that point, the proceedings were closed to the public because, under prodding from Bill's lawyer, I was forced to provide a partial list of the citizenry of Hamilton I had kept company with.

"Is it not a fact that the father of that dead baby could have been one of four hundred men in this city?"

"No, not that many."

"Three hundred then?"

"Well, no."

"How many then? Tell the court how many men you had sexual intercourse with."

"A hundred and fifty maybe."

"One hundred and fifty men, any one of whom could have been the father of the child. Now Mrs. Dick, I want you to name those men for the court right here and now. Who are they?"

"Well," I said, looking in the direction of the magistrate, "his son for one."

"Are you indicating His Honour?"

"Indeed. The judge's son."

I then named two lawyers, a furrier, a druggist, a financier, a merchant, and two offspring of leading Hamilton families before the very startled and crimson-faced Burbridge interrupted me, ordering me to stop my tally at once.

Next, I was asked to testify against Bill. I refused to do so. An irate Magistrate Burbridge told me I would answer or be held in contempt. God help me, my pent-up anger at my former lover was so great that I uttered my greatest falsehood; I testified Bill was the father of the baby and had killed him. Up to that point, Bill had not looked in my direction. At that moment, he tried to do so, but he was unable to lift his head, so weighed down was he by the apparent absurdity and the spitefulness of what I claimed. When Burbridge committed him to trial, he simply stated: "I haven't a thing to do with this. I am innocent."

Immediately following the baby murder hearing, the preliminary hearing in the torso case was heard. A confusing array of findings was presented: the possible remains of John Dick — charred bones and teeth — found at Carrick Avenue; bloodstained black shoes at Rosslyn Avenue; the horde of cash and HSR tickets also found in my father's house. The *Spectator*, an ardent critic of the way in which the bus company habitually lost money, took special delight in highlighting this discovery.

On that day, I again implicated Bill in the murder of John Dick. After hearing a very confused array of so-called facts and vague assertions, Burbridge committed Bohozuk, my father and myself to trial for the murder of my husband. My mother was freed of the murder charge because of insufficient evidence but she was held as a material witness.

The same journalist who was intrigued by my wardrobe was also confused by the testimony he had heard, but he rejoiced in the proceedings: everywhere in Hamilton, he gleefully observed, "in beverage rooms, at lunch counters, in stores and offices, on streetcars and buses — the two murders are being argued and discussed, Rumours of all kinds abound, many wildly fantastic." In a way, I had brought the various elements in the community together. I was selling newspapers.

Four months later, in September, the Grand Jury returned a true bill on both indictments. The trial for the murder of John was set for the seventh of October, on which day the Crown moved to have me tried separately. When that request was granted, the other two accused and their counsel left the chambers. Up to this point, I had been represented by three different lawyers in turn. Only at this point did Mr. Sullivan begin to represent me. In addition to the instructions on hair, makeup and wardrobe he gave me at that time, he also jotted down for me his ground rules in selecting the jury.

Everything pertaining to the prospective juror needs to be questioned and weighed: his nationality, business, religion, politics, social standing, family ties, friends, habits of life and thoughts, and books and newspapers he reads.

Involved in it all is the juror's method of speech, the kind of clothes he wears, style of haircut, and above all, his business associates, residence, and origin.

An emotional, kindly and sympathetic man, if chosen as a juror, will place himself by his imagination in the dock; really, he is trying himself.

Retain Irish, English and Germans, agnostics, Jews. No prohibitionists, Calvinists, Lutherans, Baptists, or wealthy men.

You may defy all the rest of the rules if you can get a man who laughs. Few things in this world are of enough importance to warrant considering them seriously. A juror who laughs hates to find anyone guilty.

You want imaginative individuals. You are not interested in the morals of a juror. If a man is instinctively kind and sympathetic, take him.

Sullivan, I now realize, was the first genuine artist I ever encountered. He could have been a first-rate movie director or novelist. He had the uncanny ability to read people and to manipulate them.

25

Unfortunately for me and Mr. Sullivan, Judge Barlow was a prohibitionist, a Calvinist, and a wealthy man. I had often heard his name mentioned as a figure of both fun and contempt by several clients. Thin, short and spectral with a pointed perpetually red nose, he harboured disdain for everyone with whom he came into contact. Since he embodied the idea of fussiness, nothing could ever be quite right. He always spoke crisply, often harshly, to his clerks, the lawyers, even the jurors.

A stickler for rules, he proudly reminded the assembled congregation on the first day of the trial that Hamilton was the last city in the Commonwealth to insist that women wear hats in court.

He intended to enforce that regulation. Publicly, he had often stated his agreement with the principle that women were not really full citizens under the law and were rightly not allowed to sit on juries.

Barlow took special delight in the other singularities of the Hamilton assizes. The sheriff, attired in cock hat and with sword drawn, accompanied the judge to the carved walnut dais surmounted by a royal coat of arms. Barlow seated himself in one of the chairs — the other, slightly behind him and empty, was reserved for the King. Only a man and a city completely frightened that they had no special identities could cling so desperately to such antiquated customs.

In my direction, Barlow constantly squinted, as if his eyes could not quite take in the sight of such an abominable creature. Those belligerent looks betrayed his fear that he might, at any given moment, have to correct me for bad behaviour in his courtroom. From the outset, he was determined, I am sure, that I be punished for all my wicked actions preceding and leading up to the death of John Dick.

Most of the sensational aspects of the torso murder were well known to everyone in Hamilton and southern Ontario — the story had even reached the pages of *Time* and *Newsweek* in the States. Interest was now focused on the various participants in the drama, in how they told their stories.

Anna Kammerer, John's sister-in-law, whom I had never seen before, was smartly dressed in a sombre black suit. At John's instigation, she had phoned me once to have a friendly chat. Suffering from an abscessed tooth, I had been in bed and my voice had been garbled. Judge Barlow wrote this down, as if an important piece of evidence had been presented to the court. She then mentioned that she had phoned me twice after John's disappearance. During cross-examination, Mr. Sullivan forced her to admit that my estranged husband had spent all his spare time either stalking me on Carrick Avenue or at the Henson flat. Judge Barlow obviously did not consider this a significant piece of evidence and prissily told Mr. Sullivan to refrain from this type of questioning.

The prosecution staged a potentially heartbreaking moment when Joseph Visheau of the Windsor Hotel Coffee Shop told of my husband's last meal: "He wanted only a bowl of soup which we don't allow; we only serve full-course meals. But seeing I knew John, we catered to him. He didn't wait for his check but just flopped his money down and went off." Obviously hoping for some sort of reconciliation with his wife, the condemned man ate hastily. A less sentimental interpretation of John's behaviour is possible: he was always oppositional, never adhering to anybody's rules.

Robert Corbett, my boarder on Carrick Avenue, told of seeing me on the evening of the sixth of March attempting to put the Packard in the garage. In backing up and going forward, I collided with the doorpost, damaging the right hand running board. He went downstairs to help — a few minutes earlier, he had noticed an appalling odour — but my mother, who was already directing traffic, insisted he take Heather back into the house as it was snowing and the child had no coat on. My neighbours — looking at me through drawn blinds or lace curtains — corroborated Robert's testimony.

Under Mr. Sullivan's expert direction, my presence in the courtroom attracted a great deal of favourable attention, particularly my dark hair expertly coifed by a fellow prisoner. The public was grateful to me. Into their dull lives I brought excitement and drama which heretofore they could only see rendered on the silver screen. Any slight alteration in my appearance was newsworthy. In one piece, the journalist observed: "Her dress: black, sleeveless, perhaps revealing her gain in weight."

Another reporter said: "The accused is a woman possessing powerful, undeniable fascination." Even my slightest movements became subject for table-talk. One day, I wished a journalist "good morning". This became "as bright and crisp a good morning as the presiding justice himself might wish." Then he asked the usual question: "Everything going all right?" What else could I say but "fine." He wrote: "And she was off up the stairs to the second floor courtroom, moving easily between her friends and keepers, Mrs. Alice Hickmott, jail matron, and tall grey Officer Thomas Rouse."

And then there was the time the public hangman just happened to be visiting the Barton Street Jail. When he was introduced to me in my role of a potential customer, he gleefully instructed me to keep my chin up. Then, he proceeded to tell me I need not worry about being hanged at the jail and buried there. That distinction belonged to Benjamin Parrott, the thirty-year-old man who had split open the head of his sixty-year-old mother, Bridget. That murder had taken place many years before in broad daylight on the sidewalk in front of the family home.

Despite my weight gain, my legs were favourably compared in the press to those of Betty Grable. At Mr. Sullivan's instigation, I brought to court with me a large pad and pencil. During the laborious collection of evidence, I took notes diligently, occasionally passing a sheet of paper to my attorney. As I had seen in the movies, I would tap my teeth thoughtfully with a pencil before jotting down an observation.

Perhaps the most eagerly awaited witness was eleven-year-old Ralph Oakes, who had found John's bus driver's cap. In painstaking detail, he revealed he had come across it caught between two bushes beneath a railway bridge when he climbed down to watch a train pass. Since the cap was too big for him, the honest young man presented it to his mother who, in turn, insisted on giving it to the police. So, Ralph carefully put it in a bag, took it to school the next day for show-and-tell, and, later that day, took the bus to the nearest police station.

The surprise witness did not come as much of a shock to me. Mother had warned me she might have to allow herself to be called by the Crown. "Otherwise, my dear, they might detain me again, even put me on trial for John's death." She said this with a snicker — as if she had told a joke, but in her voice I could hear her steely determination to avoid further incarceration. On the afternoon she was summoned to the stand by the prosecutor, Mr. Rigney, Mother chose the dreariest possible outfit: brown cloth coat, brown felt hat, and dark polka-dotted dress; she also wore a choker. By costuming herself as a country mouse, she wanted to give the impression of the vast distance that lay between herself and her city-slicker daughter. With her black handbag firmly positioned beneath her arm, she spoke slowly and deliberately. She wanted to appear a commonplace woman of absolutely no intellectual capacity — or the ability to scheme and manipulate.

The camouflage worked perfectly. When Mother entered the witness stand, I glanced up at her for a second. Then I lowered my eyes, picked up my pad and made notes. Once or twice I polished the pair of reading glasses I carried with me but hardly ever used.

My mother's testimony began with her recounting of her disapproval of my marriage, of how John eventually moved to

Carrick Avenue, where the normal married life of the couple began. Almost at once, she had been perturbed — mainly for her granddaughter's sake — by the constant quarrelling that erupted between Evelyn and John. Then, she mentioned the mysterious phone calls her son-in-law received.

"John was having lunch with Evelyn and me when the phone rang. Evelyn answered. She called John to the phone. He talked for about ten minutes. When he returned to the table, he was shaking like a leaf. He couldn't hold his knife or fork. I excused myself and went upstairs. Later, I asked Evelyn about the call. She told me Bohozuk had been on the line. He had disguised his voice, but John knew it was him. He told John he would get him."

She then described the numerous threatening calls her son-in-law received. He began to absent himself from Carrick Avenue for two or three days at a time. On the third of February, he left for good. She spoke with him on the phone after that but never saw him again. Her final conversation with him had been on the fifth of March, the day before he vanished. Once again, he wanted to borrow money; she turned him down.

When she was asked about the events of the evening of the sixth of March, Mother told the assemblage about her annoyance at my attempt to get the Packard into the garage, "I said to her, 'You will never get that large car into this garage when it is so full of lumber, so get out of here.' She was furious with me, jumped into the car and backed it up. When she returned later that night, Evelyn was still very annoyed. I could tell by the twist of her mouth. She was starving but refused my offer of a late supper. We retired to the bed which we shared again after John's departure."

"Two days later, Heather and I went to Sherman Avenue to watch John's bus pass by. My granddaughter was very fond of her new father, very much enjoyed waving at him. But there was no John. When I arrived home, I said to my daughter, 'John is not working. He was not on his usual car.' Evelyn looked me straight in the face, 'Well, it's not likely he would be. You won't see him again.'

"My daughter's face turned bright red. 'Nothing has happened to him?' I asked. 'He has not been killed?'"

"There was a sneer on Evelyn's face when she answered me. 'Yes, John Dick is dead and you keep your mouth shut.'"

Mother's eyes gleamed behind the spectacles. In her quiet, masterful way, she had led her audience where she had determined they should be. Extremely audible gasps greeted her last pronouncement and immediately every eye in that large room was fastened on me. Judge Barlow was distracted. He found it difficult not to stare, but he had to keep control of the situation. "Order, order!" his attendants shouted.

The remainder of my mother's testimony did not reach that dramatic height. She told of my father's mysterious appearance on Carrick Avenue when he broke open the trunk in the attic, of her own husband's huge assortment of weapons, of John Dick's frequent, annoying requests for money.

When Mr. Sullivan cross-examined her, Mother admitted she herself had been arrested for her son-in-law's murder, then released on bond after thirteen days.

"So there is the possibility the police feel you are involved in John Dick's death?" my lawyer politely inquired.

"There *was* such a possibility," she countered him.

Mr. Sullivan smiled broadly in her direction. "Were you in the witness room this morning?"

"For about an hour and a half."

"Where did you go after that?"

"To the Crown attorney's office. I was there about fifteen minutes."

"Just enough time for a cosy little chat. And then you were brought here to offer evidence?"

"Correct."

Looking at the jury and then at my mother, Mr. Sullivan asked: "Was any inducement offered to you?"

"Oh, no."

Mr. Sullivan chuckled. "Any promises?"

"No, there were no promises." This time, Mr. Sullivan laughed in her face as he took his seat.

On the next day, *The Globe and Mail* carried an account of the end of that grim day:

And finally, a little past six, the still court was admonished into submission by Judge Barlow. The nightly witch hunt of Hamiltonians began again. It is impossible to adjudge the numbers which surrounded the court house, but last night it must have been in the thousands. It was the biggest mob yet. There was shouting as the mob swayed from door to door and red pinpoints of cigarette lights underlined the macabre scene.

Evelyn Dick was brought out the west door, and the mob surged in her direction. The glamorous-looking defendant always manages to look surprised by every evening's assembled throng as she gets into the car that drives her back to the Barton Street Jail. Children, anxious to get a good look at the evil seductress, push themselves forward to the head of the crowd. For a few moments, the police spotlight envelops her as she walks towards the car. Her hand shakes as she takes a cigarette from her mouth. But on her face, on this day of all days, there is a smile. Then darkness as the car slowly ambles away with its strange cargo.

Later that night, when Mother visited, I assured her: "You looked nice and, more importantly, you did not break down. You played your role to perfection."

26

Like the detectives before them, the Crown attorneys determined that the best way to convict me of John Dick's murder was to present a slew of evidence to the jury, even though the bits and pieces of the testimony were connected to me in only a peripheral way. My father had a large collection of guns and saws — therefore, I must have colluded with him to use some of those instruments to kill John. Or, my father had killed John, and I had assisted him. Such an approach, the province reasoned, would never hit the bull's eye, but, with any luck, it would lead to my conviction. And, just possibly, to the truth. Either way, justice would be seen to have been served.

Mr. Sullivan, obviously well aware of what was being perpetrated, tried to counter Mr. Rigney and his associates by suggesting that the evidence against me — most of it gained from my own lips — was inadmissible because it had been gained by coercion. In order to do this, Sullivan had to challenge the way in which Preston and Wood had obtained information from me. He insisted that prior to making potentially self-damaging statements, I had not been properly cautioned; he also maintained that a combination of threats and rewards had been used to wring incriminating statements from me.

When the trial had reached this junction, Judge Barlow was visibly shaken because he was well aware that Sullivan's best chance of saving me was approaching. In what was for him a halting way of speaking, he told the jury: "It now becomes necessary for me to make a ruling as to whether certain evidence is admissible or not admissible, in other words, as to whether it is evidence that you should hear. I must do this in your absence, of course."

Mr. Sullivan's first point of attack was my uneaten lunch on the day Woods and Preston had arrived to tell me of John's death. Preston admitted I had been given nothing to eat until five o'clock that evening, when I was finally charged with vagrancy. He heatedly denied having promised me a good meal if I confessed to my husband's murder. In turn, Wood told essentially the same story, although he explained he did not charge me with murder because he still did not know where he stood with the accused. He denied saying, "The sooner you explain things, the sooner you will get out."

During his cross-examination, Mr. Sullivan insisted I should have been charged with the murder of my husband rather than held under the bogus charge of vagrancy.

Barlow was swift in his reply: "She was not in custody on any charge; she was merely detained. Her statements to the police are completely admissible. A proper warning was given. Nothing was done that ought not to have been done." In subsequent testimony, Preston denied ever losing his temper, threatening to make me talk one way or the other, or opening a desk drawer in which I could clearly see a rubber hose.

In a turn of events that startled Barlow, Mr. Sullivan announced that his client would offer testimony in rebuttal. As I rose to take the witness box, the judge shook his head, either in exasperation at the legal manoeuvring of my counsel or in anticipation of my offering any kind of evidence which he would find creditable. On the twentieth of March, I explained, I was refused breakfast when I was summoned at daybreak from my cell. Preston had told me: "You'll get it when I am ready to give it to you."

"Were threats ever made against you by Preston or Wood?" my counsel inquired of me.

"Well, Detective Preston assured me the sooner I talked the sooner I would get home. He didn't really threaten me on that day. He said he had known of me since I was a child and hoped he could get me out of the mess I had made."

"He said he would help you if you talked?"

A furious Barlow interrupted him. "That is not what she said!"

"I'm sorry, my Lord," Sullivan assured him.

Mr. Rigney tried to make light of the situation by insinuating the greatest grievance I had with the police was the lack of meals provided at times pre-determined by myself. On the day in question — the twentieth of March — I admitted I had been given a lovely lunch.

"That's good," a now sarcastic Rigney reassured me. "What time did you have that lovely lunch, pray?"

"Well, I don't know."

"Well, I hope it was as soon as possible after you made your request?"

"Well, it wasn't long after."

"About noon, I suppose?"

"I guess so." Rigney sought the judge's eyes, which seemed to beam approval.

In his counter-rebuttal, Sergeant Preston sighed and then observed: "There are so many times that woman was hungry, I couldn't keep count of them."

Mr. Sullivan then turned his attention to the drive I had taken with the police up the Mountain. In gruesome detail, Wood recounted how I had described to him the way in which Bohozuk had fired his first shot at John's head, the bullet coming out the right eye. My lawyer, listening in silence to what he knew was a litany of lies I had composed, finally told the judge that the thirty-odd mile trip had to be considered an outing, that no warning was proffered to me, the resulting evidence therefore inadmissible. Quickly, Barlow ruled the information was given voluntarily and, was, therefore, fully admissible. The jury was summoned so that the trial proper could resume.

On Friday, the 13th of October, I celebrated my twenty-sixth birthday. On that morning, Mr. Sullivan arrived at the courthouse, carrying an assortment of heavily fragrant scarlet lilies and white carnations which had been left at his office with a card, "To Evelyn from an Admirer." I received over a hundred birthday cards plus an assortment of gifts: nylons, a strand of pearls with clustered pearl earrings, lipsticks, nail polish, facial preparations, bottles of perfume and eau de Cologne. I penned a note which was published in the *Spectator* the following week: "I would like to pay tribute to everyone, to the senders of letters, the senders of gifts, and to matrons and officers for kindness shown me during my custody." What I did not mention were the many death threats. One of the matrons told me of the sperm-impregnated black brassiere that had arrived: "Evelyn, it was still wet when I opened the parcel."

My missive caused a flood of "Letters to the Editor" — some of which railed against me, especially against my movie-star appearance. The newspaper contacted the inspector of prisons for Ontario who replied: "As a remanded prisoner there is no objection to another woman in the corridor helping Mrs. Dick to look presentable. Naturally a woman prisoner does not want to appear in Court looking like a tramp."

On the day when the floral tribute was bestowed upon me, I was anxious to get back to the Barton Street Jail in order to examine the card and study the signature. I was — and remain — convinced that the mastermind behind the John Dick murder had, as a sardonic twist, sent the flowers to me: Mr. Y, the lawyer, had twice presented me with the exact offering — identically coloured lilies and carnations. Twilight had just descended, and I clutched the bouquet closely to my person. I got out of the car quickly and walked smartly up the steps. Just as I reached the top, a turnkey at the door seized the flowers from me and tossed them in the direction of the crowd, who moved away to avoid contamination. They gasped, but they allowed the flowers to lie there in the gathering dusk, a red and white blur on the grey stone driveway.

I made one friend at Barton Street. Stella was a prostitute who had landed herself at the jail several times for soliciting. A woman of uncommon, delicate beauty, she did not look conventionally Italian because both her parents were born in villages north of Milan, where facial and bodily characteristics often display northern European features. Dissatisfied with the perfect railway timetabling instituted by Mussolini, the Viscontis immigrated to Canada in 1924, two years after Il Duce and his blackshirts marched on Rome. Stella's parents were simple, uneducated people, but they feared that demonic forces would be unleashed if the previously divided states of Italy were brought together by a man of the new leader's ruthless will.

At first, the Viscontis' new homeland promised salvation. Like many of the European immigrants who settled in Hamilton, they particularly loved spending Sundays at the Royal Botanical Gardens — then and now, the only cultural or natural institution in Hamilton that could defeat Toronto hands-down. The frame steel canopies — manufactured locally — which then sheltered the sidewalks of Hamilton reminded them of the covered colonnades in the small rustic towns of their youth. They sometimes travelled up the Mountain on the Saturdays in summer when bands performed at the sanatorium — the beds of the patients were wheeled out of the rooms, providing the patients with their own special balcony seats.

Mr. Visconti's job was hellish, but he endured it willingly. At the Dominion Foundries, he "teemed the heat," directing molten steel from a ladle into waiting ingot moulds. The cooled ingots were stripped from the moulds and then rolled into desired lengths and thicknesses. Like the other workers, Mr. Visconti was provided with neither faceguard nor safety suit while he stood completely exposed to flying sparks and explosions of red-hot steel.

Stella was born in 1924, the year the couple arrived in Hamilton. Four sisters followed her, the last born in 1930. The Viscontis were poor but extremely happy. At school, Stella was a precocious student, whose ability to write fluently and beautifully gave great pleasure to her parents and teachers. Although it was then uncommon for the children of immigrants to attend university, the Italian community in the city had, by the time Stella turned 12, determined that she was to enrol at St. Michael's College at the University of Toronto when she finished high school. From her earliest years, she told everybody who eagerly listened to her that she wanted to become a writer.

Until 1939 — just as the war started in Europe — everything remained on an even keel for the Viscontis. In October of that year Mr. Visconti fell to his death, consumed instantly in a bath of liquid steel. As her husband had not carried life insurance, Mrs. Visconti had to go out to work. Quite soon, she became a riveter at National Steel Car. The February 1942 issue of *The Car Builder* included this passage about her: "*Lucinda Visconti is a heater. Tongs in her right hand, her left on the handle of the heater, Lucinda places three cold black rivets in the copper jaws of her machine. In a moment they are white hot. Her foot presses down one of the pedals at the base of her machine, tongs grip the rivet firmly, she draws it out and flips her wrist. It has no sooner left her tongs than she has another in its place.*"

Since Mrs. Visconti was earning a decent salary, she was able to keep her five daughters in school. She was even able to afford to pay a housekeeper to look after the children in the afternoons until she arrived home from work at eight o'clock. Lucinda's work was mildly dangerous, but she thought she could survive it. But she did not survive the cervical cancer that carried her quickly and decisively away in February 1943.

Stella was 19 when her mother died. Her youngest sister was a mere 13. Until the time of her mother's death, Stella had been a devout Catholic, a reader of the lives of the saints. She had especially admired the Neapolitan Maria Goretti, the eleven-year-old admirer of the Blessed Virgin Mary who allowed herself to be murdered rather than be defiled by the eighteen-year-old handyman who coveted her. Like Maria Goretti, Stella was an idealist, one who was certain that everything would turn out well in God's divine plan if she could but see the way forward.

But there was no easy road ahead. She was expected to look after her sisters. Rather than going to university, Stella's parish priest crisply informed her that God's benign providence indicated that she was to find work in order to maintain a home for herself and the other four orphans. At first, Stella did what was expected of her, but, without really being aware of it, a rebellious streak began to assert itself. She became angry at the way life had treated her, no longer able to say to God: "Be it done to me according to Thy word."

At about this time, a shocked neighbour told her of the activities of the Widow Agostini, who — despite the premature death of her husband — was putting both her children through McMaster University. The Widow had even forbidden the children — both boys — to work during the school year. Mrs. Agostini obviously did not know her place in God's providential plan. The community felt that boys had no place in the halls of higher learning; the Widow was aiming far above her station. Such conduct would have been barely permissible had not the manner in which the Widow was supporting herself become known.

The Majestic Lunch on Barton Street East was the favourite spot of the male Jewish population of Hamilton. The professionals — doctors, lawyers, accountants, money lenders, and scrap metal dealers — frequented the place as did factory workers and pedlars. Many of the men spent their time playing euchre, pinochle and dominoes. Sometimes, when angry wives would appear at the front door, errant husbands would hop the fence at the rear and head reluctantly home.

The Widow Agostini's employment was at the Majestic. Every weekday afternoon — at one o'clock precisely — that slim, elegant woman would, clad completely in black, enter the restaurant, walk the length of the room and position herself in the booth adjacent to the washrooms. Sometimes, she knitted; sometimes, she darned socks. From time to time, a customer would walk down to her, glance at her and then walk into the woman's washroom. She would wait a minute or two and then enter that room. By that time, her client would have positioned himself in front of the sink and, keeping all his clothes on, would have unzipped his fly. The widow would kneel before him, remove his penis from its resting place and proceed to perform fellatio. From start to orgasm, most clients required fifteen minutes. The pleasure she gave to her clients was so intense that their moaning sounds would fill the Majestic. She left for home precisely at five o'clock. During her four-hour shift, she averaged seven customers. Her only overhead was the rental she paid to use the washroom which, without her presence, would have been unused.

Reports of the Widow's activities shocked her parish priest. Up to the time he upbraided her, she had attended Mass and taken Holy Communion daily. He told her she could no longer receive the sacrament. How could she receive the Body and Blood of Christ everyday when she was performing sex acts with her mouth? when she was obviously in a state of Mortal Sin? The Widow was not to be dissuaded from her new profession. She continued to attend Mass daily but was no longer a communicant.

When Stella heard of how the Widow had been threatened with excommunication, something within the young woman snapped. Her anger knew no bounds at what she now considered the ruthless interference of the Church into the activities of a local businesswoman. At about this time, Stella became a prostitute.

"I'm not a prostitute or — as you once described yourself — a call girl. I'm a whore. I do tricks and lots of them. Like the Widow, I suck some of the Johns, but most of the time I let the guys fuck me frontways or backwards. I don't use a room and I won't go anywhere with them — only cars and alleyways. That way it takes only fifteen minutes. That's why I've gotten arrested so many times. I've become a public nuisance."

"I would never have the courage to do what you've done. Those men could be dangerous."

"I've gotten lots of bruises and cuts. In my experience, men are interested in one thing only: getting rid of loads of spunk. Until they do that, they're restless and edgy. If you interfere with them then, they'll harm you. Once they've come, they're like contented pussycats."

"I know exactly what you mean. But I feel I'm never in the same room as my clients. It's like I'm not there. They're doing things to my body, but it's not me who's in that room."

"You're lucky. I've never had the ability to remove myself from the situation. I'm all too aware of what's happening." She paused, puffed on her cigarette and continued: "I now know one thing about myself: I hate men, each and every one of them." She lowered her voice: "To tell you the truth, I like women."

"I don't like men or women. I don't really like the sex thing one little bit."

"When you make a business out of sex, you lose all interest in it. I wish I never had to see another penis ever again."

"Amen to that. That is exactly what will happen in my particular case."

After three or four days, Stella was released from Barton Street. I lost track of her, but years afterwards I noticed — in the

Canadian publishing industry magazine *Quill & Quire* — that she had become a celebrated writer of Harlequin romances. More recently, I learned that she had moved from Hamilton to Alberta in 1950 where she had established a long-term relationship with another woman, a cattle rancher.

In Hamilton, the police had a long and distinguished career in allowing female murderers to evade them. Everyone on the force was well schooled in the Kinrade case. Thomas Kinrade, the principal of the Cannon Street School, lived in a comfortable red brick home with double veranda on Herkimer Street, not far from downtown; he owned a considerable amount of property inherited from his father in the poorer, east side of the city. The socially conscious Kinrade, his wife and his daughters — Ethel and Florence — frequently fed transients or gave them food tickets. On the evening of February 24, 1909, someone tried to break into their house. The next day, after her husband had left for work, Mrs. Kinrade, leaving her daughters in charge, walked to the police station to report the incident.

On her walk back home, Mrs. Kinrade's attention was attracted by the large crowd hovering about the bulletin in the window of a newspaper shop. To her horror, she discovered one of her daughters had been murdered.

At eleven that morning, Florence, the younger daughter, had answered the doorbell and confronted a young man of medium height, sandy brown hair, and a wispy moustache. Dressed in black and wearing a felt hat drawn down over his forehead, he peremptorily demanded food and money. Frightened by his insistent, nervous manner, she agreed to give him money. She allowed him into the vestibule, walked up the stairs to her bedroom, called to her sister to lock herself in her room, and retrieved a ten-dollar bill from her dresser drawer. At that point, although she heard what sounded like shots from a gun, she walked down the stairs, handed the bill to the stranger who left the house; then, she walked into the parlour and climbed out the window. At that point, the intruder — who had snuck back into the house — pounced upon her and pulled her back in; she escaped from him, ran out of the house, returned, and then ran across the street to tell a neighbour: "Ethel is shot, six times!"

Her count was inaccurate: seven bullets penetrated Ethel, four in the area of the head, three near the heart. Florence was an exceedingly poor witness to the events in which she had been a participant. She swooned when asked any question that attempted to make logical sense of what had occurred. She did not know how or where the intruder had come upon her sister; she had no idea why he would have shot Ethel; she did not know how she had arrived at the number six.

George Blackstock, the criminal lawyer turned Crown investigator, uncovered some fascinating information about Florence, who was very much the unfavoured of the two daughters. Unlike shy, retiring Ethel whose only occupation was that of rent-collector for her father, Florence was a concert singer of some distinction. In the autumn of 1908, she had taken lessons in the use of revolvers in preparation for a journey to Richmond, Virginia, where she had accepted an engagement to sing. While in the South, Florence — who was engaged to Montrose Wright, a divinity student from Toronto — had an affair with James Baum, an actor. Following her American interlude, her mother and sister had intercepted a brooch from the actor. Another strange piece in the puzzle: Mr. Blackstock was surprised by Mr. Kinrade's impromptu remark upon arriving home on the day of the murder: "I have expected something like this for a long time."

Hamilton gossip knew what the police were afraid to act upon. Florence, the black sheep of the family, had obviously murdered her sister. In so doing, she forced her prominent, well-heeled parents to protect her from the long arm of the law. In one mighty swoop, she became her parents' favourite. Sibling rivalry hardly ever carries itself to such bizarre extremes. Although the inquest found that Ethel had been shot by a person or persons unknown, the reliability of some of the evidence produced, they claimed, suggested that the case should not be closed.

Mr. and Mrs. Kinrade abandoned Hamilton. Florence married Wright and moved with him to Calgary; after his death in 1918, Florence returned to the concert hall — she even played Hamilton in the twenties. Later, she settled in California. I have always wondered: was there a steely sound to Florence's voice, a certain metallic edge that showed what a hard-hearted artist she was?

As the ending or climax of my own trial approached, even more people presented themselves each morning as spectators. One morning, they even managed to break a courtroom door off its hinges. Further mayhem ensued when the ladies' rooms were used as lunch rooms by groups of twenty or more until the court officials expelled them. Each morning, the mostly female assemblage in the crowded benches stood and leaned forward when my entourage of matrons and I entered the room. "Sit down!" the sheriff would bellow.

In a desperate attempt to stem the tide, Mr. Sullivan tried to insinuate that the police officers had engaged in unseemly conversations with me. In yet another cross-examination of Preston, he asked about my refusal to attend John's funeral.

"Were you on intimate enough terms with her to discuss the reason?"

"She discussed sex freely." For Preston the words "sex" and "intimate" were obviously synonymous.

Seizing his opening, Sullivan continued: "And she habitually discussed sex with you?"

"No, sir."

"You didn't tell her that it might be better for her if she did not attend the funeral and stayed behind to chat with you?"

"Not at all, sir."

"You did press her for a reason for not attending?"

"Yes, sir. The *Spectator* wanted that information. Then they couldn't use it."

"Well, what did she say?"

Preston blushed. "She was very unladylike." He looked at Barlow for encouragement, which was not withheld. She said, "I am very sick. I have used three pads already today."

Then Mr. Sullivan returned to the infamous trip up the Mountain. "You gave Mrs. Dick two chocolate bars before the trip, did you not?"

"Yes."

"An inducement to talk?"

"Certainly not. A courtesy. A little something to tide her over."

"You purchased some magazines for her at the outset of the trip?"

"At her request. She gave me the money for them."

"You provided her with a special chicken dinner at the police station before returning her to Barton Street?"

"That is accurate."

"Another inducement to talk? You've been trying to confuse her, hoping to get at the truth if you forced her to spin enough accounts."

Barlow, visibly displeased at the suggestion the police had tried to force me to produce conflicting variants of what had really happened, intercepted him. "You are harassing the witness. Cease from such unseemly behaviour in my courtroom." At that point, the sound of children playing on the lawn of Prince's Square filled the room. Now thoroughly outraged, the judge ordered all the windows firmly shut. I sat quietly sketching him and the other court officials. His small squirrel eyes narrowed, outraged that I appeared so unshattered.

Shortly thereafter, the Crown concluded its evidence. To utter silence, Mr. Sullivan rose, "My Lord, the defence is not offering any evidence." Somewhat relieved, Barlow replied: "That closes the case, gentlemen. We shall adjourn until ten o'clock tomorrow morning, at which time we will proceed with the addresses."

On the following morning, Mr. Weatherston, Mr. Sullivan's young associate, rose and, in the absence of the jury, said: "I should like to submit, my Lord, that there is not sufficient evidence in this case on which the jury can reasonably find...."

Calmly, Barlow interrupted him: "You should have made that motion yesterday when you announced you had no evidence to submit. Having failed to do so, the case was then closed. I shall not hear any arguments in this matter. We shall proceed with the addresses to the jury."

The jury was recalled. Even within the confines of the courtroom, the bright blue sky outside made its presence known. Behind the polished black walnut of the prisoner's bar, I sat slouched and disgruntled. Mother was supposed to have purchased a new outfit for me for these final moments, and she had not bothered to do so. "I have to look after Heather, pet. I have a lot of responsibilities." (As I write these words in 1999, I recall what a petty, small-minded young woman I was despite the tragedies that had rained down on me.)

The outset of that awful day had been brightened once again by a piece of the delicious sultana cake, baked by Constable Rouse's thoughtful wife — an admirer of mine — and presented to me every day by her husband. "Just a tidbit," Rouse assured the reporter from the *Spectator*. As usual, I greeted Mr. Rigney with a soft "good morning."

Mr. Sullivan had warned me well in advance that I was to pay no heed to his closing remarks. "I shall say things which I hope will gain the jury's sympathy and thus understanding. It is our only hope." Even then, I was not prepared for my lawyer's description of me as a creature of a "fertile, overactive intellect" who lived in a self-created fantasy world. Sometimes, he observed, creators of such inner retreats "never grow up, their dream world never disappears." His client, Mr. Sullivan assured the jury, was young, pretty, photogenic. "Mrs. Dick is basically an escapist who has tried hard to raise her station in life, reaching for a world other than her own." Thus far in his address, my lawyer could have been defending a writer like Oscar Wilde from the crime of excessive imagination.

Then, he changed his course abruptly, pointing to the lack of any real evidence against me. He tried to suggest Mother was a sort of demented female King Lear who had turned her back on her Cordelia-like only child. I was, he assured the jury, the victim of an unhappy home life, "perhaps not a very good condition for an impressionable girl to grow up in." Then he pointed at me, drew himself up, and proceeded:

"There has been nothing presented by the Crown to show that this little wisp of a woman could have committed the crime by herself, although she may have known of the crime after it was perpetrated. She could neither carry the body nor cut it up. The array of evidence you have heard does not make the accused a murderess. Although there are some threads connecting her to the case, that is all they are — threads. Meaningless strands. You cannot attribute any motive to her. Money, passion, love? All of these are absent. Why would she have wanted to kill her husband? The Crown has never answered this crucial question.

"Guilty or not guilty? There is a third view — the verdict must be not proven. Unless the Crown has brought home to you, without a shadow of a doubt, that Evelyn Dick is guilty of the murder of her husband — *I say murder* ! — I am convinced you will find her not guilty — which only means she has not been proved to be guilty." An eloquent response to the absurdities presented as evidence.

Mr. Rigney, well aware of the weaknesses in his own case, characterized me as a inherently deceitful person — the artist as liar. "Even her marriage certificate was a deception: she had no right either to the name of White or to the status of widow. A woman addicted to untruthfulness, she had practised deception even on the day she had exchanged wedding vows with John Dick."

Mr. Rigney's review of the evidence against me was mild-mannered in comparison to Barlow's charge to the jury. Those twelve men could come to any conclusion they deemed fit, but, he warned them, "any law that there is in this case is for me to judge, and it is my duty to interpret it to you and it is your duty to follow my interpretation of it." Pausing, and casting a spiteful glance in the direction of Sullivan, he continued: "If in the unlikely event I have made any mistaken rulings in this case or if I misinterpret the law to you in any way, it can be taken care of elsewhere, but not here."

As far as he was concerned, the Crown had proven its case: "even if you conclude beyond a reasonable doubt that she did not actually shoot John Dick, that someone else shot him and that she aided and abetted in that murder, then she is a principal and she is just as guilty as the person who fired the shot. She is equally guilty." He added: "You may not think so, but I think she possessed plenty of motive." With two quick thrusts, Barlow used his authority to puncture Mr. Sullivan's arguments.

The blue sky gave way to a late afternoon apricot glow as the jurors made their way out of the courtroom. I was escorted by the matrons to a dingy back room, where we could smoke and talk. A few hours later, I was told the court would recess until eight in the evening so Barlow could have his supper. I was given nothing to eat. At about nine, the constable came to fetch me: "The jury is ready to report."

As the constable, matron and myself entered the trial room, I was struck as never before with the contrast between the brightness of the lights in that chamber and the total void of blackness outside. After I seated myself, Mr. Sullivan came to the dock, offered me a chocolate bar, told me he was confident we had won and then took his seat. I consumed the bar quickly, just as Barlow entered the room and was escorted by his array of officialdom to his dais.

The crier announced that the court would now resume. The jurors entered slowly, more deliberately than usual, and, as was not their custom, avoided looking in my direction. I feared the worst. His Lordship warned the audience against any demonstration of emotion.

"Gentlemen of the Jury," asked the Registrar, "have you agreed upon a verdict?"

"We have, sir," the foreman Mr. Paupst assured him. "We have found the accused guilty, with a recommendation for mercy." He looked at me, tears welling up. The jury had not reached their sentence lightly.

Barlow interrupted my reflections: "Evelyn Dick, stand up!"

As I got to my feet, so did Mr. Sullivan. The judge would not tolerate this custom in my instance: "Sit down, Mr. Sullivan, please."

Then turning to me, Barlow asked: "Have you anything to say why sentence should not be passed upon you according to law."

Although I had not been instructed by my counsel in this matter, I knew justice had not been served. Moreover, I recalled Barlow's comment on the unlikely possibility he might have made any kind of error. Defiantly, I simply stated: "I want my case appealed."

If he was surprised, Barlow concealed that emotion. He informed the jury: "I don't see how you could have brought in any other verdict based on the evidence presented to you." Then, looking directly at me, he proceeded in an even voice: "Evelyn Dick, the sentence of this court upon you is that you be taken from here to the place whence you came, and there be kept in close confinement until the 7th of January in the year 1947, and upon that date you be taken to the place of execution and that you there be hanged by the neck until you are dead." Then the hint of a sneer could be heard in his final sentence: "And may the Lord have mercy upon your soul."

27

At my high school, the assembly prayed on my behalf. This offering was prefaced by a remark from the Mother Superior that I had once been a pupil at the school and deserved their "consideration *although a Presbyterian, a person of heinous morals, and someone who never inculcated Loretto values*." John Dick's family was magnanimous: "We hate the sin that has been committed but we do not hate the sinner." For them, capital punishment was simply the fulfillment of the moral law I had callously broken and that had to be rigorously enforced.

With the police clearing a path for me through the throng and the exploding flash bulbs, I slowly made my way to the waiting car the night of the verdict. Even after I had settled myself in and was waiting for the driver to take me and matron away, faces pressed themselves against the windows to catch a glimpse of the demon woman who had only now received her just desserts. Against the glass and in semi-darkness, the distorted countenances seemed to promise me their ever-present company in the deepest reaches of hell fire.

Time's caption was meant to be facetious: "Evelyn Dick: She went too far." The more sober *Newsweek* was matter-of-fact: "'Torso Girl' Sentenced to Hang." At the Barton Street Jail, I was transferred to a cell at the end of the corridor on the third — the top — floor, which had been isolated for the death watch by a made-to-order steel door. Tiny and windowless, my new room contained only one piece of furniture — a cot. In the corridor outside, on a chair facing the cell, three women kept around-the-clock surveillance in eight-hour shifts. Beyond that seated guard was a barred window, the only way in which I could monitor the weather. My reading was selected for me: *Photoplay* and *True Confessions* magazines. I pleaded for *The New Yorker* and that request was granted, although my wardens were amazed that a denizen of a prison in a medium-sized Canadian city should be interested in reading about the sophisticated goings-on in Manhattan. Books were frowned upon because the matrons did not wish to bother themselves to fetch and return them to the public library.

Before, my high-windowed cell at the Barton Street Jail had been one of several in a long corridor. I could see and easily talk with the occupant of the opposite cell. Now, I had to tell my guards when I wished to be accompanied to the toilet; my bath was at a specified time each day; I took a ten-minute walk outside with the matron on the day shift; my clothes were now prescribed; I took my meals alone on a small card table which was set up and then dismantled; the chair I sat upon to eat was available only at mealtimes. For most of the day, an animal on exhibit in a dreary zoo, I could pace the room or recline on the bed. My only consolation: because my room was brightly lit twenty-four hours a day, I slept in fits and starts and did not dream of the nightmare ride up the Mountain.

I asked Mother and Mr. Sullivan for food to supplement my meagre repasts and received fruit — and the occasional chocolate bar. I eventually added twenty-six pounds to my previous 109: that accomplishment filled columns in the *Spectator* on a regular basis. The weight gain was seen as divine retribution: I had lost the figure which had been the foundation of my life of crime. By implication, I was a gluttonous person, who now spent her entire existence gratifying herself through her stomach. These were the obvious wages of sin.

For over six months — since the day my lunch on Carrick Avenue had been interrupted by Wood and Preston — I had not seen my daughter. About two weeks after the conclusion of the trial, my mother announced that Heather would accompany her on her next visit. I cannot say I was overjoyed at the prospect of my only child seeing me in such dreary surroundings, but I did wish to see her, touch her. Allison, the matron on duty the day of that visit, was a cheerful soul, a tiny sparrow of uncomplicated, eager friendliness.

At first, I thought Mother had arrived at the appointed time by herself. Then I realized Heather was crouching behind her, hiding herself from my view. Beautifully dressed in a heavy blue wool coat, my daughter had grown slightly taller and looked lovely — my mother had obviously had the little girl's hair professionally styled in Shirley Temple curls.

"My little blue angel," I called to her. "Doesn't Wee Willie Winkie want to say hello to Mummy?"

Heather peered out from behind my mother and then retreated again. She glanced intently as Allison carried chairs into my cell. When the three of us were alone, Heather agreed to sit in the chair closest to mine.

"Mummy is so pleased to see her little lady."

Heather said nothing, occasionally turning around to search my mother's face.

Mother seemed embarrassed, a rare state of being for her. "Heather now calls me Mummy. She refers to you as Mother."

"How has that come about?"

"Well, Evelyn, every little girl has to have a Mummy who stays with her every day. She started to call me that, and I did not forbid her from doing so."

"What a wonderful reversal. You've been working on that change for a long time, well before John Dick arrived on the scene."

By now, Mother was angry. She could never bear even the slightest allocation of guilt. "You've never shown much interest in her. You're an unnatural mother, interested only in yourself, your own pleasures."

"Ah, but you devised those so-called pleasures. Some would say you were the unnatural mother. Like mother, like daughter."

This conversation, conducted in the most seemly, lady-like manner, quickly reached its climax. I indicated to Allison that my mother and daughter had unexpected obligations to which they must attend immediately. The interview concluded, I picked up the little girl in my arms, kissed her and bid her adieu. "Good-bye, Mother," she whispered as she hurriedly wiggled out of my arms. As soon as the cell door was closed, Heather took Mother's hand in hers.

"Heather's a gorgeous child, such a little lady," Allison assured me a minute later as she resumed her seat in front of me. I never beheld the flesh of my flesh again.

I launched the appeal in order to save my skin. I have to be frank about that, but I did have other sentiments. I felt defiant. I had not committed the crimes of which I was accused, and I was certain I had been found guilty because I was a fallen woman, who must bear the weight of the crimes she has unleashed in her community.

I was angry at the mysterious person — my former patron — who had set in track the series of events that had led to John Dick's death and in whose service my father — who had obviously dismembered the corpse — had been engaged. I was curious. Since I remained certain my father had not pulled the trigger of the gun, I vaguely hoped that the identity of the shooter — and thus his boss — would be revealed at a new trial. I also wanted to revenge myself on Barlow, who, Sullivan assured me, had made some atrocious judgements for which he could be rendered culpable on appeal. I cannot say I had any abstract sense that the cause of justice had been trampled upon, but that concern may have been operating at an unconscious level.

As soon as I was found guilty, the joint trial of my father and Bill Bohozuk resumed before Mr. Justice George Urquhart. On 17 October, the second day of those proceedings, I was summoned to testify. A drenching rain did nothing to forestall the huge crowd who sought admission to the courthouse that day. At three o'clock in the afternoon, I entered the chamber, glanced in Bill's direction, noticed my father's misty eyes, and took the witness stand. When the court registrar held up his Bible, I told him to put it down.

The judge asked me, "Do I understand that you refuse to give evidence and refuse to be sworn."

"That is correct. I have not had a chance to talk with my counsel."

Mr. Urquhart asked if I would "think the matter over until tomorrow morning," I nodded my head in reluctant agreement. When I discussed the matter with Mr. Sullivan — who, I am sure, was certain I had lied about Bohozuk's involvement in the case — he told me I must do what I considered to be in my best interest. "I might add, however, that whether or not you remain silent, I am certain Bohozuk will be exonerated. The evidence against him is not that strong and is completely contradictory." I also realized I would harm any chance of my appeal being granted if I revealed that Bohozuk — contrary to the evidence I had given the police — had had nothing to do with John's death. So on the next day, I again refused to offer testimony. Bill's lawyer wanted some punishment to be imposed upon me, but the judge — knowing he had no real power over a woman condemned to be executed — shrugged his shoulders, "A woman can always change her mind." He also decided to discharge the jury in the absence of my testimony and wait until a decision had been reached in my appeal. He reminded the lawyers that I could not be expected to offer evidence which might prejudice my own cause. A man of incredible finesse and tactfulness, Urquhart had been a client of mine.

Twenty-five grounds of appeal were mounted in Mr. Sullivan's brief to the Court of Appeal for Ontario, which set January 7 as the day for the hearing — the day on which I was to be executed. When Mr. Sullivan called their attention to the unsuitability of this date, Chief Justice Robertson postponed my hanging to February7.

At the appeal, a new lawyer assisted — according to *The Globe and Mail* — Mr. Sullivan. My mother claimed that the services of J.J. Robinette, later one of Canada's most eminent criminal lawyers, were obtained by her on my behalf: "A Christmas present for Evelyn." That was a boastful lie. I had seen brief mentions of the then-largely unknown attorney in the press and asked to meet with him just before Christmas 1946. I retained Robinette for two reasons. I was then involved in a nasty skirmish with Mr. Sullivan over legal fees. I had paid him $6,900, but he claimed I had agreed to pay him a total of

$7,500. More importantly, I was not certain the theatrical mode of defence had worked effectively and wondered if Robinette's mastery of the intricacies of the law might work more effectively.

During our ten-minute conversation after his hour's drive from Toronto to Hamilton, Robinette agreed to represent me. His biographer, Jack Batten, quotes him: "The reason I said I'd take her case was because I'd been following it in the newspapers and I wondered about those statements she gave to the police. It didn't strike me that they should've been admitted as evidence, and I thought I had a reasonable ground for appeal right there." He might have added that he was an extremely ambitious man and that a successful defence of me could do wonders for his prospects. A no-nonsense man with a dry wit, Robinette scoured my face intently. He seemed more interested in looking at — rather than listening to — me. Later, he told me he was sizing me up for the long battles ahead. On that day, he reminded me his approach would be different from Sullivan's.

"I do not believe in the couturier-approach to defending any client, male or female."

"You mean you're more hard-nosed than Mr. Sullivan?"

"I wouldn't put it quite that way. My talents — if I may label them such — are vastly different from his. He pointed Mr. Barlow and the jury in the right directions, but it led nowhere. He did not rebut the case against you in a logical-enough fashion. He made Barlow angry; he confused the jury; he forced the press to see you as a wronged Hedy Lamarr figure; he excited awe and envy. I work in a much more straightforward manner. I can promise you a thorough but sober representation."

At the appeal, Robinette attacked the outcome of the trial in three major ways: the unprofessional and biased conduct of Judge Barlow, the obvious fact that Donald MacLean was directly involved with the murder, and the absences of proper warnings in my various interviews with Wood and Preston. In their unanimous finding in my favour, the five justices ignored the evidence presented against Barlow and my father, but they agreed with Robinette about the conduct of the police, particularly their misuse of the charge of vagrancy as a cover with which to obtain incriminating statements.

My conviction having been set aside, I could once more be treated like an ordinary prisoner and released from isolation. After Mr. Sullivan visited me for the last time to tell me in detail the outcome of the appeal, he told the press: "She was feeling very happy at being allowed to mingle with the other girls. She looked pretty pale, with no makeup. She was wearing the ordinary jail dress with a red sweater over it. You members of the Fourth Estate better watch out. She's a serious young lady. She reads all the time and has been keeping a journal. She tells me she wants to become a writer when she leaves prison!" He guffawed and then went on to offer some other remarks, supposedly off the record: "She's hog-fat now" and "She eats like a horse." I am sure all those revelations were generated by my quarrel with him over money and by my firing of him. When his observations were made public, he said: "The reporter misunderstood me, but she is *not* slim."

Three weeks later, I appeared in court to testify in the now-resumed trial of my father and Bill. *The Globe and Mail* treated the event as fodder for a fashion column: "*Mrs. Dick, attractive widow of the torso murder victim, has apparently gained considerable weight since she was sentenced to hang and confined to solitary at Barton Street Jail. According to her mother, however, she will probably be able to get into the black silk dress she wore during her first trial. Over that she'll be wearing her grey kidskin coat.*" On the following day, my dress was described as *skin tight*; it was suggested that I could accurately be described as *short and fat*, but that my hair, under its sequined tam, looked *very smart*. On the other hand, the two males were *well fed, trimly clad, and in the best of condition*.

I was not asked, praise goodness, to offer testimony because it was determined on that day that my father, Bill and myself would go on trial together on February 24 during the spring assizes of 1947. On the first day of that trial, however, the Crown attorney argued successfully that the case of *The King v. Evelyn Dick* be once again sequestered from that of the other two defendants.

Mr. Robinette was pleased by that decision and immediately set about to take full advantage of the decision of the appeal court regarding the inadmissibility of the incriminating evidence supposedly extracted from me by Wood and Preston. In these attempts, he met a considerable match in James McRuer, the Chief Justice of the trial division of the Supreme Court of Ontario — and a bitter enemy of Chief Justice Robertson, who had written the decision granting my appeal. He forced Robinette to rehash *in camera* the case he made to the Supreme Court, made it obvious that he disagreed violently with their conclusion, but in the end, yielded, somewhat ungraciously: "I would not be obedient to the very express findings of the Court of Appeal if I were to admit any of the statements."

Strangely enough, my second, duller trial generated even more public interest than the first. Far larger crowds gathered to stare and hiss. In Hamilton, my detractors feared Robinette might be able, as it were, to get me off the hook. In an attempt to place me at the scene of the crime — now an extremely difficult feat — Mr. Rigney introduced a new witness, one Frank Boehler.

A tall, skinny, blond who did not look like he had attained the twenty years he claimed for himself, Boehler told of working on the farm of one James Hamilton situated on the Glanford Station Road on which I had alleged the murder had taken place. At about three o'clock on the afternoon of the murder — on March 6, 1946 — he had noticed a Black Packard parked on the right hand side of the road about a half a mile away. He had gone to the barn to tend to a sick cow, and, while returning to the house, saw the car again. A second later he heard two shots and then a third.

"There were two shots simultaneously, sir, both together, and then I walked towards the house and I was scraping my boots off in front of the door and I heard a third shot. They were quite loud and they were from a heavier calibre, either a rifle or a revolver."

Rigney asked him, "Why do you say that?"

"I have done a lot of hunting and have handled a lot of guns in my time and I can pretty well tell when a gun is fired whether it is a shotgun, rifle, or revolver, by the report of the shot."

Not thinking much of what he had heard, he returned to the house, picked up a cowboy magazine, went upstairs to his bedroom, where he lay on the bed for three quarters of an hour reading. At twenty to four, he went downstairs, put on his boots and looked out the window to see if it had stopped raining. The car was in the same place, but it was running — as he could see the exhaust. He went outside, picked up his milking cans, returned to the barn and began his chores.

"While I was in the barn I looked out the window and I saw a man coming into the driveway. He got nearly opposite the house and he kind of hesitated for a minute, and then walked towards the house. I stepped out of the barn door and asked him what he wanted. He came towards me, and I walked to meet him. He said the car was stuck in the road."

Since his work for Mr. Hamilton involved pulling out cars stuck in the mud, he offered his assistance. When Boehler could not get his tractor to start, he hooked up a team of horses and grabbed a rope. When he reached the Packard, he saw another man standing beside it and a woman in the car behind the driver's wheel. Boehler wrapped the chain around the bumper and the axle of the car and then went over to speak to the lady, who rolled her window down. He instructed her: "Don't start the car but place it in neutral." He towed the car about fifty-five yards. The man who had been standing by the car told him he had no money to give him but offered a cigarette. "No," the young man told him, "I got cigarettes of my own."

Asked by the prosecutor to describe the woman in the car, the witness remembered she was young with dark hair. While speaking with her, he had noticed two things: a package of cigarettes on her lap and an open handbag, out of which the handle of a revolver stuck out.

The snow was skipping against the high window panes of the courtroom, but that sound was completely drowned out as everyone listened intently to the witness.

Next, Rigney asked the young man: "Is there anything else you saw in the car when you were talking to the driver?"

"On the floor of the back seat there was part of a man's leg."

"Why do you say part?"

"I could see only part of it — the part below the knee, the calf of the leg and the foot. It was up against the right rear door and over against the seat, the cushion of the back seat."

"Were there any socks or anything on it?"

"There was a black oxford shoe and a black sock, and dark blue trousers or black — I couldn't vouch for the colour, sir. The shoe was directly under the window, leaning against the door. Toe up, heel down, leg placed as if part of a body lying flat on its back.

"Look around the room and see if you can identify the woman in the car you saw."

He nodded in my direction. Rigney inquired, "You mean the dark-haired woman in the black dress?"

"Yes."

The report in the following day's *Globe and Mail* is correct: "*There was a sigh of inhaled breath from the spectators. Mrs. Dick gazed directly at the witness and her black eyes flashed. Her colour heightened as she sat upright. Her full red lips parted and she framed a word which seemed to be, 'Liar!'*"

Mr. Robinette's questions to the witness were uttered so rapidly in machine-gun style that McRuer instructed him to allow the witness sufficient time to answer. My attorney shot back: "I intend to cross-examine this witness rigorously, my Lord." The audience snickered at this exchange, infuriating McRuer to the extent that he threatened to clear the court if the spectators insisted in treating the trial as something for their entertainment. Mr. Robinette did not change tactics.

"Did you testify in the previous trial?"

"No."

"Did you read about it in the papers or see pictures of the accused."

"Uh-huh."

"You never came forward? Did you feel this information would be of any assistance to the police?"

"Well, I didn't want to get involved."

"Did you mention this incident to anyone? Perhaps your employer at the farm?"

"No."

"Did you mention it to friends or members of your family?"

"No, I didn't."

"You claim to have seen what you describe. Yet, you read about the case and at no time breathed a word to anyone about this fantastical encounter. Why are you here today?"

"Well, I told a bit of it to a guy at the garage and I guess it came back to Inspector Wood and he found me."

"When was that?"

"A few weeks ago."

Having established firmly in the jury's mind that this bit of information had been collected by the policeman whose various interrogations of me were not allowed into evidence, Robinette changed the drift of his questioning.

"I understand you're a veteran, Mr. Boehler?"

"Yes, I am."

"Under what circumstances did you leave the army?"

"Honourable discharge."

"For what reason?"

"My health was bad."

"Was your health diagnosed as a mental condition?"

"Maybe."

"Where have you worked in the past two years?"

"Here and there, y'know. A few places."

"Isn't it true you've had over half a dozen jobs in that time?"

"I don't know. Maybe."

"Do you have a criminal record?"

"Yes."

"For what?"

"Possession of a revolver."

"Were you arrested last spring on the charge of forging your mother-in-law's name on cheques?"

"Yes."

Boehler was a madman — but one, I now realize, of a very unusual kind. Basically illiterate, he nevertheless conceived of himself as a story-teller, a true adherent of the oral tradition. He needed an audience and so he composed a narrative that allowed him access to the public. I had helped to unleash the well of creativity previously buried within him, but, an artist of a particularly ruthless kind, he did not mind if I lost my life in the process. I was the excuse for him to display his not inconsiderable talents.

His narrative line was ingenious. He had carefully read the court reports in the *Spectator* and injected himself into those events in a way difficult to dispute. If believed, he could all on his own have supplied the necessary information to put the hangman's noose around my neck. I suspect Wood performed substantive editing upon the story Boehler confessed to him — fine-tuning it for publication, as it were.

Mother followed Boehler to the stand. The hissing of the steam pipes warming the room made a thundering sound, but no one paid them any mind. The reporter for *The Globe and Mail* was so overcome with emotion that her prose took on an even more purple tincture than usual: "*It seemed an almost tangible struggle of wills. The mother and daughter continued to look at each other, one of them just out of her death cell, the other freed on the same murder charge. The resemblance between the two women was suddenly obvious. They have the same sharp black line of eyebrows, the sudden snapping black eyes. They are about the same height. However, where Mrs. MacLean has thin, taut lips, Evelyn's lower lip is full and protuberant, sticking out further and further when she becomes annoyed at the testimony.*" Even fifty years later, those sentences make me cringe, capturing as they do the many similarities — well beyond the physical — between Mother and myself.

Robinette made short-work of Mother when he asked: "Isn't it true that you yourself were originally charged in the murder of John Dick?" As soon as she replied in the affirmative, he rejoined: "And isn't it true that you are presently held on bond as a material witness for the Crown?" Then he shifted tactics: "Isn't it true you're a teller of tall tales? In other words, an accomplished liar? According to your neighbours, you don't know the difference between fiction and reality!"

"It's Evelyn who's the fiction writer in the family!"

"If that's so, isn't she her mother's daughter?"

"Stop badgering the witness!" the judge bellowed.

My lawyer's tactics in cross-examination and evidence suppression filled me with confidence, but, as one reporter put it, the whites of my eyes did gleam in horror after the jury retired after having been charged by McRuer. In his final comment to the jury, Robinette came perilously close to insulting me when he observed, "One would not hang a dog on the evidence you have heard." Despite my animadversion to being compared to a canine, I prayed he was correct.

I tried to hold myself up as I walked from the courtroom, but I alternately wept and vomited in the prisoner's room. A few hours later, we were summoned back for the jury's decision. None of those twelve men would look in my direction. I heard several people whisper: "They're going to hang her!"

Then, all of a sudden, I caught the eye of the youngest juror. He nervously returned my smile. The foreman announced I had been found not guilty. I raised my hands in triumph, then covered my face to hide the tears of joy that overpowered me. The Toronto *Daily Telegraph* truthfully claimed the men of Hamilton were relieved I had been acquitted whereas the women were greatly disappointed. The steel workers always supported the underdog, whereas their wives craved gentility. As I left court that evening, a skeletally ravished old woman waiting in the crowd hurled a bag full of icy mud at me.

My triumph was short-lived. Four days after I was acquitted, I was again in court to answer to the charge of murder in the death of Peter David White MacLean.

28

Public sentiment had to be appeased. My lawyer was a realist, supremely aware of the ways of the world. In his no-nonsense way, Mr. Robinette reminded me. "You have to pay a price for all the trouble you've caused. It all boils down to that simple fact. My job is to exact the smallest possible penalty from the blind goddess. But punishment there will be."

Although public sentiment in Hamilton had been evenly divided for and against me in the mysterious murder of John Dick, the same did not hold true in the case of the baby boy's death. When I was found not-guilty in John's case, many passing cars bestowed supportive honks as my car returned to Barton Street.

Local opinion wanted a sense of closure to the entire Evelyn Dick muddle. For many residents of Hamilton, I had been seen as a quasi-Robin Hood figure: I had slept with the rich, obtained their money, lived in a high style and, in general, taken advantage of my betters. Factory workers could identify with my plight. In this scenario, John Dick had been a nosy intruder who deserved what he got. Public will — fickle as it may be at the best of times — could not (I think rightly) view the murder of a baby in the same light — even if it could not be proven I had killed the child. After all I was his mother. I had an obligation to protect him. I had failed in a sacred duty.

How much evil can lurk in a human heart, especially one which seems on the surface so much like my own? That was the intriguing question I asked many citizens of Hamilton. A woman who prostitutes herself is simply flirting with Mammon. A dangerous game. A woman who conspires to murder her husband is simply doing what many other wives have dreamed of doing. But a woman who callously strangles a newborn? She is a monster.

She is also a mystery. Simply put, evil is a dark, dank, empty hole in the soul. No feelings reside there. Add the ingredient of the malevolent but attractive woman. Does her beauty camouflage her sinfulness? Or does she pay for her physical attributes by entering into a Faust-like deal with the devil? How can beauty be evil? These are unnerving questions; and I had the misfortune to pose them.

In order to lighten the forthcoming penalty, Mr. Robinette insisted I be interviewed by a psychiatrist, a so-called expert on the criminal mind. Today, such people attach the word "forensic" to themselves. When I was examined by Dr. Robert Alexander Finlayson, who had practised in Hamilton for twenty-three years, I was startled by his strange appearance. He was incredibly short — five feet at most — and almost as round in girth. Even those dimensions were rendered ordinary by his pure white hair, which trailed down his back to his waist; by his goatee, which gave him a Mephistopheles-like look; by the remains of several meals and the mounds of dandruff that had attached themselves to the shoulders and back of his three-piece black suit; and by the excessively condescending manner in which he spoke.

If he wanted to remind a casual acquaintance of the Falstaff who had been rejected by Henry V, he succeeded.

"Madam, your attorney has commissioned me to provide him with a candid profile of your psyche. I hope you will assist me in this noble endeavour."

"I shall be happy to do so. But I am curious to know why you say 'noble'?"

"You don't think too highly of yourself if you object to that word."

"No, I think you are using the adjective incorrectly."

"Are you always inclined to began a dispute with others as soon as you meet them?"

"No, not as a general rule."

"Good. Shall we begin?"

At that point, Finlayson showed me a series of ink blots. I must admit I was rendered a bit taciturn by this bizarre person, but I did respond to all the pictures he showed me. Soon, however, he was quite displeased when I remarked — in response to an ink blot that reminded me of the top of the Chrysler Building in Manhattan — that it looked like the top of a skyscraper. He obviously thought I was being evasive.

"Does it bring anything else to mind?"

"No, nothing I can think of."

"You are being less than honest with me. Think again."

"I'm sorry, but it looks like the top of a skyscraper."

He was now thoroughly exasperated. "It obviously reminds you of an erect penis, and you are unwilling to state the obvious."

"That would never have occurred to me."

"You have much knowledge of penises, do you not — in all kinds of sizes, circumcised and uncircumcised?"

He was obviously prurient. "I see no reason to discuss such matters with you."

"Again, you are being evasive."

"No. I don't see any point in talking about such things."

"Ah, you use the word 'point.' You are free-associating. 'Point' equals penis. Perhaps an erect one about to ejaculate." He paused. "Were you ever interfered with by your father?"

"I'm not sure. I think he may have fondled me, but I have little memory of any such incident." Obviously convinced I was circumventing him yet again, Finlayson quickly concluded the session. "I shall next see you in the halls of justice, Madam."

My next, more welcome, visitor was Rosie, whom I had not seen in over a year. Mother had told me that she and Stephen had married the previous summer. Although my old chum assured me of her complete happiness, something was amiss. Unlike me, she had lost a great deal of weight, and her habitual jolliness was forced. She was also wearing a great deal of pancake makeup — something she had never done before — and after a few minutes I could ascertain the powder was concealing a black and blue mark along her left cheek bone.

"I miss you so much, Evelyn. Nothing is the same without you."

"I feel the same way. Some of the girls in this corridor are very sweet, but I have not found a kindred spirit."

"What are your chances of getting out of here?"

"Not very good. I expect I'll be convicted of the baby's death."

"But there's no real evidence against you."

"That's true, but Mr. Robinette tells me I'll have to pay a price for all the trouble I've unleashed."

"Well, Stephen and I are completely behind you."

"And how is your husband?"

"Business is booming. There's a real demand for raw steel from the States, and his sales are excellent."

"How about other things?"

"You mean personal things?"

"Yes."

"You've never been Stephen's biggest fan, Evie, but I know that even you would be impressed at how much he's settled down. Become such an ordinary person." Her lie was made abundantly obvious when she unconsciously raised her hand to the concealed bruise.

"Don't be like me, Rosie. Take proper care of yourself. Don't let anybody tell you what to do."

My friend blushed. Knowing perfectly well how to encode this directive, she was grateful for the concern but resentful of the interference. A few minutes later, she stood up to take her leave. She came over to me, took my hands in hers, and kissed me. Her hot tears brushed my face.

Although Bohozuk and myself were jointly charged in the baby's death, my trial was held separately before Mr. Justice LeBel. Adding preliminary hearing, this was my fourth time within a year to occupy the prisoner's bench on a capital charge. Mother appeared as the first witness for the prosecution. She painstakingly listed the attire I had both made and purchased in anticipation of the baby's birth: a white embroidered dress, a slip, a vest, a pair of booties, a blue and white woolen jacket, and a blue and white bonnet. Her testimony then took a curious turn: "Before she went to the hospital, Evelyn told me she had made an arrangement with the Children's Aid to take the baby away from the hospital the day she was coming home." The Crown attorney asked if, to her knowledge, this had been done. "Dear me, I have no way of knowing, but I never saw my grandchild. Evelyn arrived home in the taxi by herself."

Robinette found it impossible to shake her during cross-examination, but he did elicit some potentially useful information.

"Your daughter was making every preparation for the normal care and delivery of an infant, wasn't she?"

"Yes, so I thought."

"And it was your husband, Donald MacLean, who said that that child was not to come in the house?"

"Yes."

"Did your husband ever say why he did not want that child in the house?"

"Well, we already had Heather there. He thought one baby was enough."

"Did you ever hear him say that to Evelyn?"

"Yes."

"Your husband broke into the attic on Carrick Avenue — the home occupied by you, your granddaughter and Evelyn at the time of the arrest — and ordered you away when you confronted him. Is this true?"

"Yes."

"What exactly did he say?"

"Told me to get the hell out of there."

Dr. Deadman testified about the state of the cadaver of the baby; various doctors offered evidence for and against me, but the most damaging evidence was provided by Samuel Henson, the owner of the apartments on James Street South. He told a startled court that he had voiced his objection to having two children on his premises when he had interviewed me as a potential tenant. "She told me I need not be concerned. The baby, she assured me, was dead within her womb." He was telling the truth, and Mr. Robinette wisely insinuated I had merely been "pulling Mr. Henson's leg because she wanted to obtain the tenancy of a wanted, hard-to-get apartment."

In his address to the jury, Mr. Robinette planted a seed in their minds — perhaps they should consider manslaughter as a reasonable verdict as opposed to first-degree murder? The Crown attorney tried emotional blackmail: "We hear a lot about the rights of the criminal and of the accused person these days, but we hear comparatively little about the rights of the rest of us." In his summation, LeBel was not opposed to the verdict of manslaughter, but he cautioned the jury: "We are not here to investigate or pass judgement upon the moral conduct of the accused. If you think her conduct has been immoral, you must not take that into consideration for a moment in your deliberations. This is a case of murder, not of morals." But he did point out that I had left hospital with a healthy, normal baby, who had vanished into thin air until a decomposed body of a newborn baby boy was found a few years later encased in cement in my bedroom on Carrick Avenue.

The Globe and Mail provided an interesting perspective on the final moments of the trial: "During the addresses Evelyn's face remained inscrutable. Not so the faces of the audience. They were quiet, but every point made by the lawyers was mirrored in their expressions. From the standpoint of audience reaction this trial had all the aspects of a mystery movie. But they do it better in the movies. The movie detective would have produced the driver who took Evelyn home from the hospital. Then we would find out whether she went straight home with the child, what she did, whom she saw — and the case would have been open and shut. In a Hollywood movie, the accused woman would have been telling the truth all along, and the real murderer would be brought swiftly to justice." My life did not imitate the movies on that day: I was found guilty of manslaughter.

Before sentence could be imposed, Mr. Robinette asked leave to provide evidence of a medical character, a request granted by LeBel. Immediately, Dr. Finlayson was called to the stand. The expert witness began by stating he could not possibly reveal the full findings of his examination of the convicted felon, nor would the complete array of those same findings be made public. They would remain in his custody, marked "Confidential," and would be available in future years to the authorities should the question of parole ever arise.

After that long-winded introduction, he claimed that the widow had "the mental age of about thirteen years, with a mental capacity of dull normal near the borderline between dull normal and moron. She possessed an excellent memory, but her general intelligence was substandard, her reasoning and judgement poor, and her vocabulary extremely limited." He continued: "Besides this retardation, she has a constitutional psychopathic personality. Such people have no feelings for their fellow human beings. They do not experience guilt or remorse. These people are notoriously difficult to train. I think the important thing here is the way this girl grew up, the constant sense of insecurity, of family trouble. She was allowed to do pretty well as she pleased. Behaviour problems are ninety-five per cent environment."

Following this testimony, Robinette pleaded with LeBel to disregard "the emotional disturbance suffered by the public and the resulting primitive desire for revenge" and, instead, to consider "the salvation of the accused." He also called the judge's attention to the case of the pitiful Maria McCabe, a twenty-year-old Irish domestic, who in 1883 in Hamilton was consigned to the gallows because she had drowned her illegitimate baby in a cistern. The judge who delivered the sentence broke into tears when he delivered the law's required verdict. Public outcry against the harsh penalty was so widespread that it was commuted to fourteen years in the Kingston penitentiary for women. When the young woman, who, like me, was interned at the Barton Street Jail, was given the good news of her change of fate, she was rendered mute, so extreme was her sense of relief and gratitude.

Mr. Robinette's stratagems backfired, as was painfully evident in LeBel's address to me after he directed me to stand: "You have been convicted of a horrible crime. If you are mentally ill or emotionally unstable — and there is no doubt from what Dr. Finlayson says that you are — you will be cared for in the place to which you will be confined in a better way than you have ever been up to this time. I rejoice that in cases such as yours there may be some hope of redemption. In pronouncing sentence today, however, I see nothing whatever that justifies me beyond the merciful view which the jury has taken of the evidence in this case. The sentence of this court is that you shall spend the rest of your natural life in penitentiary."

Even criminal lawyers of Mr. Robinette's stature cannot work miracles. He did the very best for me, although I hardly needed to be labelled moronic. Subsequently, after I refused once again to offer any testimony against the other two defendants, Bohozuk was unconditionally discharged and my father sent to prison for five years as a participant in the Dick murder. I was quickly removed to the prison for women in Kingston, Ontario.

I spent my last day and night in Hamilton by myself. No visitors were allowed. I found it difficult to sleep. When that mercy finally bestowed itself upon me, I was driving up Hamilton Mountain once again, taking all the same turns in the road, soon reaching the spot where I had encountered Mr. Romanelli.

The spot is deserted. I park the car, wait, and no one arrives. I smoke two cigarettes. I worry about John in my dream, and I am filled with anxiety for him yet again. I can't stop myself from experiencing that feeling even though I realize — in the midst of the dream — that I thought him an utter nuisance both alive and dead.

I stub out the last cigarette and get out of the car. Although there is no moonlight to guide me, I decide to wander into the woods. The pines have grown so close to each other that any attempt to penetrate them is difficult. My face becomes badly scratched, and blood drenches my hands. The strong smell of the pine tar is my only consolation, and even it threatens to overwhelm me. Slowly, and with tremendous difficulty, I move through the phalanx of trees, completely unaware of what direction I am heading.

Suddenly, the trees disappear. I approach a small white cottage with a green door. I hurry ahead and knock on the door. No one answers. Suddenly, I am certain some malignant spirit is behind me, but, when I turn around, I see only the trees that now encircle the building. I open the door cautiously and walk in.

The interior is not what I anticipate. The floor, walls and ceiling are white, and it is impossible to distinguish the borders between them. As I walk further, I now become aware that the building seems to be the size of an enormous cathedral, something on the scale of Chartres. I walk for ages, making no progress towards any object or piece of furniture. I am enveloped in whiteness.

Suddenly, I am aware of an object a few feet on the ground ahead of me. I proceed cautiously and see a baby, wrapped in white and blue woollen garments. I bend down and notice the smiling, radiant face of a small infant. I pick him up and take him to my bosom. His tiny body is stone cold.

29

"You'll have to be very careful when you first get to Kingston, dear. They don't like baby murderers. It's the unpardonable crime."

"If they've read about the case in the newspaper, they'll know I'm innocent."

Millicent, the friendliest of the guards at Barton Street, nodded her head sagely, half in agreement with me, half in astonishment at my naivety. "They all say they're innocent, honey."

The black Packard in which I was caged (in the back-seat, handcuffed to a matron) for the four hour drive from Hamilton to Kingston was an updated version of my former automobile. That grim irony did not escape me. From what I could see as we approached its outskirts, Kingston was a sleepy place, filled with monuments of war such as Fort Henry. Like myself, the small city had a colourful past.

The Prison for Women — known as P4W to inmates and guards — was constructed of limestone blocks so that it would blend into and resemble the other ancient buildings of the small city, including Queen's University. When I arrived at P4W, it was only a dozen years old and was successfully masquerading itself as part and parcel of the city whose most prized possession was old-fashioned gentility. The immense, tumbling structure with barred windows that suddenly loomed up before me that afternoon reminded me of an old medieval castle, one in which I, Rapunzel-like, was about to be confined.

The fairy-tale setting was rather comically contradicted by the sixteen foot high wall surrounding my new home; the wall was topped by ten feet of wire mesh fence, which was crowned by six strands of barbed wire. In case the wall proved insufficient in deterring wily inmates from climbing over it, the entire exterior was illuminated at night by huge electric lights placed at one-hundred-foot intervals. The excuse for all this: the female prisoners were not subjected to the indignity of guard towers built into the walls.

As soon as we arrived at the gate, my shackles were removed and my custodian, with whom I had not exchanged a single word, pushed me in the direction of a tall, nervous middle-aged woman, who introduced herself as Mrs. White, the sub-warden. With old-fashioned good manners, she asked me to accompany her to the office of Mrs. Nelson, the warden. We marched together into the grim mansion and along a long corridor, at the end of which was a door leading to a large, opulent office, completely lined with books. Mrs. Nelson, seated behind her desk, indicated with a brisk nod that I was to stand before her for inspection. Mrs. White immediately took her place behind her superior.

Although both women were natives of the British Isles, they were remarkable in their contrasts, perhaps my first clue on how well they functioned as a team. Mrs. Nelson spoke in a posh fashion, in the kind of marbled grandeur of the aristocracy. Yet, every so often, a harsh nasal or sibilant betrayed her Yorkshire birth. Her subordinate's plain North London accent was less intimidating. The warden was beautifully, simply, and expensively dressed in black and white; Mrs.

White's clothing may have been expensive but nothing matched — a magenta cardigan, a green blouse, a brown tweed skirt. Her makeup was messy and smudged, as if she had applied her lipstick, powder and creams hurriedly, paying absolutely no attention to the order in which they should be used. Although considerably older than myself (I guessed her to be in her mid-fifties), Mrs. Nelson was also obviously an avid fan of the silver screen: her hair was dyed a perfect dense black, her face powder applied uniformly, her lipstick — a perfect crimson — carefully painted on the lips.

Behind her desk was a placard with the following legend: "Fear not! I do not exact vengeance for evil, but compel you to be good. My hand is stern, but my heart is kind." (I later learned this motto is a translation from the Dutch of the words engraved over the entrance of the first prison built for women, the Spinhuis, which opened in 1645 in Amsterdam.) There was also an engraving of the kindly Elizabeth Fry reading from the Bible to female inmates during her 1813 tour of London's Newgate prison.

After I had been on display for a minute or two, Mrs. Nelson broke the silence. "Evelyn, I always interview a new prisoner as the first order of business when one arrives. It is my duty to receive you into our community." She stopped and peered into my eyes. "It is also my responsibility to caution you."

"Yes," Mrs. White proclaimed, "to welcome and to warn. Those are the goals of the first interview. Research has shown the prisoner must be greeted properly and, at the same time, reminded of the potential hazards that lie in her path."

"Exactly," Mrs. Nelson nodded in agreement. "As you can appreciate, Evelyn, I am fully responsible for you, and I take my obligations seriously. Some of the ladies — the inmates — refer to me as 'Mother Superior,' as if I were in charge of a convent of nuns. Perhaps they are having a bit of fun at my expense? As nicknames go, it is not a bad one."

"No, Mrs. Nelson, not meant unkindly by the ladies," her assistant reassured her.

"Well, let me continue along that line of thought. You, Evelyn, must see yourself as a postulant or novice who has joined a religious order. You may consider me demented for making such an outlandish comparison, but it is not one without merit. We are a closed community of women. I am in charge. You are here to follow my orders; if you do so, you will be rewarded."

"Amply rewarded," echoed the acolyte.

"Yes, you will find your life of forced enclosure a pleasant one. Although you will have little or no money, books or amusements can be readily acquired on your behalf. So if you follow the rules of obedience and poverty, your stay will be comfortable. For instance, I hope you will not follow the lead of those tiresome ladies who wrote love notes to male prisoners in the adjacent facility, placed them in water-proof cigarette packs, and flushed them down the toilet, where they were subsequently retrieved from the sewage outlets at the lake by the plumbing crew and distributed. It was a strange but effective postal system. I have quashed that particular infraction.

"In general, though, there is the question of chastity. Many of the women here lead sullied existences, whether writing missives to their male counterparts or engaging in illicit sexual activity. To be blunt, some of the women here have carnal knowledge of each other."

Mrs. White could not contain herself. "A great deal of research demonstrates clearly that many ladies of the night such as yourself are lesbians — that their profession destroys their interest in men as sexual partners."

"I am not a Sapphist," I assured them.

Mrs. White was nonplussed by my use of an expression she had thought out of the vocabulary range of any inmate. "My late husband, the eminent psychiatrist Dr. John White, conducted a great deal of research on this vexed issue. You can be honest with Mrs. Nelson and myself. We are prepared to turn a blind eye to such goings on. We know all about *commerce contre nature*, as the French so diplomatically phrase it."

"I am being blunt with you. I have little or no interest in sexual activity of any kind."

"So," Mrs. Nelson inquired, "I need not worry about making arrangements to have your cell door open on certain nights so that other prisoners might join you for a few hours?"

"Correct. You need not have any concern on that score." As I uttered those words, I could imagine Mrs. Nelson's white blouse a sort of wimple, her black skirt part of her habit; for a few seconds, I was transported back to Loretto Academy.

"So, we have reached an agreement regarding your fulfillment of the vows of poverty, chastity and obedience?"

"You have made yourself abundantly clear."

"And you are prepared to comply?"

"I have always been a dutiful daughter."

If Mrs. Nelson was taken aback by my claim, she did not show it. "I shall accept your word on trust, but in the event you choose to wander from the path I have ordained for you, I must sound a warning. The province has given me a mortgage on your life. For the next ten years or so, you are merely chattel at my disposal. If necessary, you can be bartered or sold willy-nilly. Govern yourself well, and you need not fear I shall abuse my power."

She waved her hand in the air, a signal for Mrs. White to take me on my way. On our way to collect my prison uniform, my companion congratulated me on my perfect manners — really, my readiness to comply with the regulations forced upon me. Although not placed in isolation, I was, she informed me, to be carefully segregated from the rest of the prisoners for at least two weeks, so they could slowly become accustomed to me, perhaps chat with me from a distance, allow me to assure them that I was not a baby murderer. She also took me on a tour of the facility.

We descended to the basement where the delouser room was located; I had been exempted from a visit to this chamber because "all the girls from Barton Street are always immaculately presented to us," Mrs. White assured me. There were also storerooms and a large sewing-room. In addition to the warden's office, the first floor consisted of a large receiving room, the kitchen, the matrons' mess hall and the doctor's office. On the second floor were the range and the wings.

The range consisted of two tiers of cells with bars across one end. I was sequestered in this older section, my cell consisting of a bed, dresser, toilet, sink and a row of bars serving as a door. After the range, amenable prisoners graduated to one of the two wings, where there were no cells, just simple rooms which contained, in addition to the basic ingredients of the range, a small desk, a wardrobe and a chair. Each door on the wings had a small window curtained on its exterior, allowing the guards easy viewing at any time. Toilets, sinks and baths were placed at the end of each wing, so that residents were allowed to have access to them at any time. No prison cell contained outside windows. Of course, all inmates yearned for the luxuries of the wings and so, it was hoped, adjusted their behaviour in order to merit this superior accommodation.

The pillows on my new bed were small and rock-like; the sheets were made of unbleached muslin; the mattress constructed of straw; the blankets of regulation army weight. Mrs. White waited while I removed the clothes I was wearing; she handed me a striped dress and a pair of shoes. I would be given underwear only when I was allowed to leave the range. (I later learned that undergarments and stockings were forbidden lest a new girl hang herself with them.) My new frock was a faded grey, the stripes having faded from much washing; its consistency had been reduced to that of a scrubbing cloth. The shoes were so large that I fell out of them as I walked.

Nighttime in jail or prison is incredibly frightening. My experience at Barton Street had terrifying moments, but my first impression of my new home was even worse. First, there was the stench of sweating bodies forced to breathe too closely to each other. Sharp, acrid stinks arose in waves now and then above the usual pervasive reek. These odours were of urine and faeces. In the middle of the night could be heard a cacophony of snoring sounds. I was, I told myself, in a black pit cut off from the world.

In Hamilton, I had been given decent, uninteresting food, although not very much of it. Now, there was even less, none of it enticing. On my third or fourth day, my breakfast corn flakes were one half cereal, the other half maggots eager to consume the cereal ahead of me. I later learned that some of the guards, nurses, and cooks routinely filched and plundered the commissary, laying claim to all the best provisions and, in the process, not being overly concerned about the safety of what they left behind.

My first excursion into the world of the prison was two hours per day in the sewing room, where the bed-coverings and clothing for P4W and the nearby men's prison were manufactured and repaired. My task was to wash and mend the sheets from the men's prison. This was a deeply repulsive task left to new arrivals, mainly because of the high amount of dry semen, urine stains and perspiration embedded in the bed linen.

"The perfect job for a whore," shouted Big Bertha, the obese woman seated next to me. "She's used to spunk. Put her mouth on a lot of pee holes in her time. Made the bastards sweat when they fucked her." Her comments were mild compared to those mouthed by the minuscule Goldie, who sat diametrically opposite me. "Nothing too bad can happen to a dame who kills babies. Baby pops out of her cunt and, hey presto, she smothers it! Then covers the body with cement and puts it in a suitcase. Sort of trophy or love cup. Right, dearie?"

During my first week in the sewing room, I made no reply to the taunts. None was really expected. A grim silence in my presence ensued. Within a few days, I was required to work full shifts. Mrs. Nelson, I later learned, had private contracts with manufacturers and used our labour to fulfill them.

Only at the beginning of the second week did I attempt to communicate with Goldie, to whom I whispered one afternoon when she came over to hand me some sheets to mend: "I love children. I am sick to death that I am separated from my daughter, Heather. I might never see her again. I would never kill a child of mine or anyone else." Her face did not register any acknowledgement of what I had said.

A few days later, during the ten-minute break we were allowed on our shift, she walked over to me. "A word to the wise. You must be careful of the Empress and her Shadow." She immediately retreated. On the following day, I approached her. "I do not know whom you are talking about." She turned her small, delicate face in my direction. "No one has told you?"

I assured her I had absolutely no clue as to the identity of these two creatures. She whispered: "I am giving you the lowdown on the head guard, June Morgan, and her stooge, Juliet Guilfoyle." I stared at her. "Still not know what I'm telling you? It's not that difficult a puzzle." Finally, she took pity on me, looked around and nodded her head in the direction of the stool next to hers. I sat down.

"Haven't you noticed the dope-addicts and the lady-lovers scuttling back to their cells before morning inspection?"

I hadn't been entirely sure of the noises I had heard towards dawn but now recognized them for what they were. "I guess so."

"Guess so? Those two spend the better part of the night with their favourite inmates. They even arrange to have special girls sent here from out of province. They've made this place sex-crazy. Nelson and White know what's going on, but they won't admit it, even though White has ordered saltpetre in the grub to keep the prisoners' drives down. Be careful the Empress and the Shadow don't drag you into their ring."

This turned out to be a well-placed warning because the Shadow, a tall well-built black woman let herself into my cell during the middle of the following night. "I've followed all your trials in the paper, dear. I guess I'm the big spider waiting for a tiny fly to get caught in her web. I'd really like to get to know you, although you've put on a hell of a lot of weight." When I told her I was not interested, she simply shrugged her shoulders. "There's a lot of fish to fry here, honey."

During next day's shift, I told Goldie what had happened. "Yeah, there's so many loaves of bread around here, they don't miss one or two holdouts. Another thing, though. Unless you're really desperate, stay away from the delivery area where the male prisoners drop off and collect the sheets and bedding. Only the toughest bulls are allowed in on that assignment — in fact, they'll kill to get that job. Those are the guys who don't do the homo stuff. They're here to get laid, and they're quick and brutal. The guards turn a blind eye to what they're doing — they think it calms those ruffians down. Gives them a release. Some of the girls line up to be serviced, but I imagine it's not very pleasant. Another word to the wise." I thanked her for the information and forever afterwards made certain that I made myself scarce when our next-door neighbours visited.

When my first two weeks were up, I was allowed to leave the range for the wings. My friendship with Goldie paved the way for my acceptance within my new community. There were a wide assortment of types, including Laura the Candy Kid, just seventeen years old, an experienced shoplifter, prostitute, and drug addict. As Goldie put it, Laura was as pretty as a picture. Then there was Old Lady Cumo, almost 82, who swore in German and smelled like a fish factory despite frequent, heavily abrasive scrubbings by the matrons. She had practised as an abortionist even before the First World War. Her best friend was Dora Coningsby, drug-addict and prostitute, her body completely needle-pocked. In their circle was Bugs, a burly old Irish woman of indeterminate age who smoked a pipe and swore like the proverbial trooper. She was a good friend of Big Bertha, who had addressed the first salvo in my direction. This ghastly looking, obese creature kept her mottled hair in curlers and wore her skirts and dresses above bare knees.

After about a month, my existence was simple enough. I rose early every morning, breakfasted in the commissary, worked a full eleven-hour shift from 7:30 until 6:30 (half an hour off for lunch), ate supper, took exercise for a half hour in the cold weather — two hours in the warmer — and then made my way to my cell for the night. Two months after my arrival in Kingston, I was transferred to another part of the wings, where I had more space and tranquillity. Some evenings I read for an hour or so, although the prison library consisted of less than a hundred books. Although it was difficult to obtain paper in the post-war years, I began to keep a diary.

At first, I kept pretty well to myself. I would smile at my fellow inmates — in the late forties there were only about forty-five of us. Only Rosie wrote to me on a regular basis. I had to be careful what I told her because our letters were read twice before being put into the post. Mother never wrote me; I knew nothing of Heather. When my father was finally convicted in the death of John Dick, I saw it in the papers.

I avoided controversy; I courted loneliness. Since I had always been a conformist, my existence was not entirely a living death. Since I had so little self-love, I had little self-pity. I informed myself constantly: you have reaped what you have sewn.

30

The Empress came by her nickname honestly. Obviously of German ancestry, she reminded me of the Marlene Dietrich character in *The Devil is a Woman*, the Josef von Sternberg film. The film poster for which showed a scheming yellow-haired Dietrich embraced by Cesar Romero, whose dark, regular features contrasted with his co-star's. Emblazoned on the poster is the seductress's motto: "Kiss Me ... and I'll break your heart!" Obviously, the illustration is perfectly emblematic: the virile handsome Latino will, in the course of the movie, be reduced to putty by the wily German. Although she lacked a foreign accent, June Morgan was immediately compelling, a Circe luring everyone with whom she comes into contact to their doom. She was not more than two inches over five feet and cadaverously thin. When she fixed her icy blue eyes — like Dietrich's, they were large and glaucomatous-looking — in your direction, you were reluctant to deny her anything.

The statuesque, almost six-foot Juliet Guilfoyle, perhaps ten years younger than the fortyish-looking Morgan, usually accompanied her boss on rounds. In every way, the Empress looked a bigger person than the black woman (in those days, we said "nigger woman" or — if we were being polite, "coloured woman" or "Negro woman").

The rumour was that the two had been lovers but now wandered further afield in pursuit of game. Thus, their frequent overnight stays at P4W. The two, always clad in white, wandered the range and the wings together every day, June doing all the talking, Juliet busily scribbling in her notepad. At first glance, it appeared as if the two were being attentive to those in their charge, but, in reality, the prisoners were placing orders, sometimes for necessary items, such as sanitary napkins and underwear, that the two women claimed could be supplied only when appropriate or for a negotiable fee.

At P4W, a Darwinian law of supply and demand — nature red in tooth and claw — was controlled by the Empress and her Shadow. Luxury items — such as soft pillows and blankets — were in their purview. They also took orders for special food, which would be delivered late at night. Of course, cigarettes and drugs were their most popular commodities. Sometimes, an inmate could exchange sexual favours in exchange for, say, a new brassiere. More often than not, the prisoner would have to give her scanty wages over to these two — or she would have to beg money from visiting relatives and friends.

As I got to know my fellow inmates, I realized I was always hearing the same story over and over again. As Millicent had observed, all the prisoners were guiltless. Many of them came from extremely poor families, where, like myself, they had experienced some sort of sexual intrusion. If not a father, then a teenage brother or an uncle or a family friend. Virtually all of them had left home at the age of 12 or 13. Some became streetwalkers, most worked in factories. All of them tended to have disastrous relationships with men, but many times they were behind bars because they had been hapless accessories to the crimes of their men friends.

Yvonne had been asleep in a hotel room after she had helped her boyfriend rob a bank. In the middle of the night, the door was battered down, a policeman made his way into the room and was shot dead by the boyfriend, who, in turn, was killed by another policeman. Yvonne was subsequently tried and convicted of second-degree murder, although she had been asleep when the policeman was shot. The judge at her trial informed her that she was, in society's eyes, just as guilty of the death of the policeman as her deceased boyfriend. According to the Parties Act, he told her, she should have been aware or known that a violent death might ensue from her activities earlier in the day. When he sentenced her, the judge gave her life imprisonment, although she technically owed the Board only fifteen years, and parole would be considered — and probably granted — after that period of time. In P4W, every prisoner talked of her obligation to the Board as if paying off a heavy mortgage.

My limited sense of camaraderie with my fellow inmates stemmed from a common point-of-view: we had done nothing wrong and, even if we had done something heinous, we really weren't responsible for our actions. A lot of double-thinking is what I would now label it. Somewhat philosophically, I began to consider the whole notion of blame. Although I endured a strong sense of guilt, I wondered if I could really blame everything on my parents, horrible as they had been. I may have started on this line of thought because I was trying, in a snobbish way, to segregate myself from the other wretches with whom I was confined. Perhaps my sense that I should own up to my responsibilities was a way of seeing myself as better — certainly more virtuous — than my compatriots.

The greed of the Empress and the Shadow niggled me, although a secret bank account in Buffalo, New York, allowed me to meet all their financial demands. All of my life I had been a silent witness to evil, but in this instance I rebelled. I was offended by the way those two miscreants preyed on the very young for sexual favours and refused to do anything to assist the older prisoners who had no money.

I requested an audience with Mrs. Nelson and Mrs. White. After waiting almost two weeks, I was given a brief appointment: when requesting — and paying for — the interview through the Empress, I indicated that I needed to speak to the warden in connection with an appeal being launched by Mr. Robinette.

As was the custom, I was required in the warden's presence to stand, as if a soldier at attention in the presence of a general. No inquiries were made as to my state of body or mind. The warden and her assistant were startled when I told them the real reason for my request to see them: unless they did something about the two head guards, I would inform Robinette of the true state of affairs at P4W. Mrs. Nelson did not respond well to blackmail.

"Evelyn, you have little knowledge of the ways of the world. I am perfectly aware of what June and Juliet are doing, but we live in a world of free enterprise. It's called capitalism. I cannot provide the prisoners with many of the necessities of life. Sometimes, even the basics are beyond my reach. They are useful coadjutors to me."

"Most assuredly," Mrs. White interrupted her, "we are doing our very best to help the prisoners. We can't do more."

I pointed out to them that much of the labour of myself and my fellow prisoners was undertaken for the public sector. Surely, someone was lining her pockets with this money?

Mrs. Nelson now became heated, her expensive accent giving way completely to coarse, North Country sounds. "I'm not going to be lectured on morality by a child killer!"

"The crime I am accused of has absolutely nothing to do with what we are talking about, which is abuse of power. *Your* abuse of power."

"As far as I am concerned, you have nothing to complain about."

"Perhaps you'd like to address that issue in a public forum? Mr. Robinette is on the verge of becoming one of Canada's foremost criminal lawyers. He likes to champion underdogs. He could start with all forty-six of us under your charge."

The warden had heard enough. "Mrs. White, remove this churlish woman from my sight."

As she accompanied me back to my cell, the under-warden assured me I had completely misunderstood the nature of the operations at P4W. June and Juliet interceded between the prisoners and the higher echelons of the administration. The best contemporary research suggested that modern wardens use underlings in this fashion. To put it bluntly: wheels had to be greased. I simply did not understand the latest trends in penology.

Then Mrs. White changed the direction of her monologue. She remembered I was an avid reader. We could stop on the way back to my cell at the prison library. "Just a small assortment of books. Perhaps you could find something there to your liking?" I accepted the bribe, and we stopped at the small alcove outside her office. I glanced quickly at the six or seven shelves, my eye attracted to what were obviously the oldest: an eight-volume set from 1768 of Richardson's *Clarissa*, originally published in 1748-9, over a million words in length.

"A masterpiece," Mrs. White assured me. "One of the greatest novels in English. It's about a wronged woman." At that point, having heard so much recently about the injustices inflicted upon women, I almost decided against the eight volumes. But something drew me to the name. Clarissa. Clarity. I removed the books from their resting place.

Sometimes, famous people are asked to name a work of literature that transformed their lives: what book left an indelible mark on your soul? In my case, the answer is Richardson's leisurely examination of the psyche of his tortured heroine.

The novelist was an ambitious man. He was a successful printer who wrote a book of letters upon which others could model their own correspondences. If one had a rich, shrewish old aunt living on the Sussex coast who repeatedly invited herself to your London home, Richardson had the perfect response for her, guaranteed to put her off and yet not offend her. A destitute niece in Yorkshire wrote asking for a handout: Richardson knew how to say no decisively and politely. From its commonplace beginnings, Richardson's imagination caught fire: he enjoyed imagining himself in difficult situations and then finding the perfect responses to rid himself of them. So he began writing fiction in the form of letters — an epistolary novel — in which he imagined himself as a poor servant girl whom the lecherous Mr. B wanted to seduce. In *Pamela*, he created a shrewd woman, one who refuses her employer's advances and manipulates him to the altar before they ever get into bed.

Clarissa is an altogether different kind of story. At the outset, the dashingly handsome Lovelace is courting Arabella Harlowe, the elder sister of Clarissa. When he meets and subsequently shifts his attention to Clarissa, the Harlowe family turns against him and — to a large degree — Clarissa, who, her parents and siblings determine, must marry Solmes, a fussy, much older and extremely wealthy merchant. Clarissa defies her parents and is locked up by them until she changes her mind. The wily Lovelace — completely smitten by Clarissa — offers to help her escape from the domestic tyranny imposed on her. He whisks her away to a brothel, which she assumes is a respectable lodging. Unwittingly, Clarissa has placed herself in the hands of another, even more rapacious enemy. She refuses her would-be lover/captor's advances and is eventually drugged and raped by him. Thrown completely asunder by the horrible chain of events that overtake her, Clarissa escapes, only to find herself trapped in a debtor's prison. She no longer wishes to live and, with considerable flourish, prepares herself for death.

At one level, Clarissa's story seems to be about a woman victimized by her family and by the man who supposedly loves her. The novel is particularly vivid in its description of Clarissa's loneliness, her self-imposed isolation, and her confinement in her home, a brothel and, finally, a prison.

After a while, reading the novel became compulsive for me, its claustrophobia — not unlike some of the settings I had lived in — removed me imaginatively for hours at a time from my own confinement. At first, I was puzzled by the heroine's single-minded wish to preserve her chastity — and her eagerness to surrender to death once it was violated. Read symbolically, her chastity represents a part of herself over which she rightly wishes to maintain control. Once penetrated sexually in a violent way, she wants to abandon her creaturehood. She has no reason to live. The book is not so much about Christian belief as it is about personal integrity.

As I feverishly consumed that book, I identified with Clarissa, badly treated by her parents and her lover. And, yet, that novel prodded me in a new direction. Clarissa dies because she is a rebel: She says no to her parents, her jealous brother and sister, and a possessive man. Clarissa is victimized, but — because she refuses to succumb to tyranny — she moves to a whole new level of existence. In dying, she preserves her essential self. There is nothing passive about Clarissa, although on the surface all she accomplishes is to write hundreds of letters examining her state of mind in its fluctuating conditions. At some level, the book spoke to me about my previous life, although its only direct effect on me was to fix my resolve to resume the diary I had begun in Hamilton, where I had haphazardly recorded some of the evidence presented against me and made observations on my existence on Barton Street.

One of my first entries in my prison diary was made twelve days after my encounter with Nelson and White.

Trouble falling asleep — suddenly, a glaring light in my face — then a hand near my head — my right shoulder yanked violently — "Get up! You're coming with me! Now! Get up now!" — I stumble up and see the Shadow hovering over me — "How many times do I have to tell you? Right now! Quick! You don't need to change." — My cell door is wide open and the Shadow pushes me out the door — an eerie yellowish light bathes the second floor corridors — we hurry down the stairs, and I am shoved in the direction of the warden's office, the door of which is open — the Shadow and I cross the threshold and make our way to the inner sanctum — the lamp on Nelson's desk sheds the only light in the room — the warden sits, White stands in her usual position behind her — the Shadow moves away from me to the edge of the room, where she takes her place in the darkness at the side of the Empress — the Empress tells Mrs. Nelson to "begin the meeting of the coven" — Mrs. Nelson clears her throat: "I don't know how you got that message to Mr. Robinette, Evelyn — I tell the truth — "I gave Gertie a message to give to her sister. Nothing strange about that." — She gives me a look of complete disdain: "He's going to visit you next week. That's why we're here." — She's embarrassed, put on the spot. Not sure where to go — the Empress intervenes: "You'd better tell her what *you've* decided to do." — "Alright, June. I know what I'm doing." Then she turns her face in my direction. "The wayward sisters will be leaving us in a month's time — they're taking jobs in British Columbia. So, if you keep your mouth closed, you need not worry about those two ladies in the future. Do we have a deal?" — I nod my head in full agreement and am accompanied back to my cell by a silent Mrs. White.

Two weeks later:

The Empress and her Shadow have become warden and sub-warden of the new maximum security prison for women on the outskirts of Vancouver — the two vixens have let all the prisoners know I played stool-pigeon — made it impossible for them to stay at P4W — with their customers, I'm even more unpopular than when I was simply a baby murderer.

Two weeks later:

Things have settled down — am only mildly hated — everything will be back to normal in a few more weeks — Clarissa's horrible nightmare existence haunts me — she felt guilty about being a nonconformist — knew she had a tendency to be self-destructive — how can anyone live like that? — what kind of strange man creates Clarissa? — must have imagined himself a woman — did he take on a female identity in order to know her from the skin outwards? — did he, like Lovelace, want to sleep with her? — did he want to penetrate her but she wound up penetrating him? — why does anyone bother to make up people in order to put them on to paper?

Since early girlhood I had been an avid reader; later, I used story-telling to entertain my clients. Always aware of the power of the written word, I had succumbed as a youngster to its powers and, very much like a musician quelling the savage beast, I had recycled the stories of others to feed the men with whom I endured sex. Reading *Clarissa* was a completely different experience, as if the spirit of a woman who never lived infiltrated the core of my being.

The impulse to record the events of my dreary existence in P4W was, I realized, not only an attempt to form a bond with Clarissa but also a way to appease her. We were both wounded, women who removed themselves from the sexual arena because such experiences were so deeply threatening. Clarissa was in essence a proto-feminist: her sensitivity to any kind of sexual activity was symptomatic of her conviction that she must discover her identity as a woman in isolation. I could not claim such lofty motives: my sexuality was cauterized — like living flesh burnt to a crisp — by my father's abuse. That strange word "schizoid" — the condition of wishing to remain alone from human contact — does not really apply to Richardson's heroine or myself. Sometimes, unfortunately, life gives us no alternative but retreat.

My regimented life at P4W was irrevocably changed when I had been there for almost six months. Mrs. White — with her passionate commitment to the three Rs of research, rehabilitation and reading — pushed books in my direction which were either about confinement — Dickens' *Little Dorrit,* Shakespeare's *Measure for Measure*, Diderot's *La Religieuse* — or written during confinement — Cervantes' *Don Quixote*, Bunyan's *Pilgrim's Progress*, Boethius's *Consolation of Philosophy*, Wilde's *De Profundis*.

She was a great admirer of the murderer Robert Stroud, the "bird-man of Alcatraz"; from his late teenage years until his death in 1963, he spent fifty-four years in prison. In 1933, he published *Diseases of Canaries* and, ten years later, *Digest of the Diseases of Birds*. He was a diligent reader and researcher who rehabilitated himself through his work on birds. Years before Burt Lancaster made him a folk-hero in the film biography of 1962, Stroud had written eloquently about the tiny creatures to whom he devoted his life. Mrs. White called my particular attention to this passage: "Years of work, of study, of careful observation; the lives of literally thousands of birds, the disappointments and heartbreaks of hundreds of blasted hopes have gone into these pages, almost every line, every word, is spattered with sweat and blood. For every truth I have outlined to you, I have blundered my way through a hundred errors. I have killed birds when it was almost as hard as killing one's children. I have had birds die in my hand when their death brought me greater sadness than that I have ever felt over the passing of a member of my own species. And I have dedicated all this to the proposition that fewer birds shall suffer and die because their diseases are not understood." Her eyes filled with tears, Mrs. White informed me how much her late, law-abiding husband had found a kindred spirit in Stroud. "A man after his own heart."

In me, Mrs. White had put her hands on the ideal candidate for rehabilitation. My native intelligence which had previously been doubted and my newfound ability to question authority sat well with her, if not with Nelson. If she nourished me on good literature, perhaps my pent-up abilities would be released, much in the same manner as the bird-man's? Or so she reasoned. When that initiative seemed to be working, she came to visit me one afternoon. As usual, her hair was dishevelled and her clothing an ill-fitting assortment of violently clashing colours. More than usually nervous as a cat in heat, she wrung her red, large-boned hands as she spoke.

"Evelyn, I have just spoken with Mrs. Nelson about something which you may find of interest." Full-stop. She scoured my eyes for at least twenty seconds. "I have informed the warden of the remarkable progress you have made in such a short space of time. In fact, I told her how much I admired the way you had challenged us, forced us to readjust our perspective in the matter of the wayward sisters, as Mrs. Nelson calls them. She refused to say anything on that thorny subject. 'Tell me what you have in mind, Janet,' she instructed me. So I mentioned how useful an instrument reading could be in the reform of our charges. Much more emotionally powerful than music. Much more didactic than pep talks or sermons. Having laid the groundwork, I suggested we do something about the so-called prison library, a hit-and-miss affair.

"At first, Gloria said little. Then, when I mentioned what an eager reader you had become, she started to take notice. 'You want her to become the prison librarian, don't you?' Yes, I admitted. 'Not a bad idea,' she replied, 'Such an activity might keep our friend out of harm's way. I don't have a lot of money to spend. But Evelyn could spend a few hundred dollars a year — and we could allow her eight hours a week away from the sewing room. Anything to keep her happy.'"

Mrs. White halted herself. "Well, what do you think, Evelyn? Interested?"

With an alacrity that surprised me, I told her I would welcome the challenge. "That would give me great pleasure. It is a task that really needs doing."(I almost said: "Be it done to me according to your word.")

"Precisely, Evelyn. Your rehabilitation would consist of helping to rehabilitate others. The Horatian principle. Literature delights us as it instructs us."

And so a whole new turn introduced itself into my prison years. I was assigned a small room in the basement, given an old beaten-up desk, provided with a barely serviceable typewriter and a supply of file cards and given time to teach myself the Dewey Decimal system. I received catalogues from Basil Blackwell in Oxford, from whom I purchased about forty books a year. On their breaks, my fellow prisoners were allowed to browse the collection during the two hours, four days a week, I kept the library open.

In order to buy the right books, I had to get to know my fellow prisoners more intimately than before. I had to understand what they wanted to read so that I could buy accordingly — mainly romance novels — but I felt an obligation to acquire some serious books that would edify — in so doing, I met my own needs. In my new capacity, I became the confidante of many women who, as they read stories, were anxious to tell me their own. As I discovered, stories beget stories.

31

Most of the stories I heard from the inmates were humdrum, accounts of missed opportunities, foul-ups, and indignities perpetrated by evil parents and even more vile husbands and men friends. In a very real sense, I was seeing shards of my own life in Hamilton, and witnessing accounts that bore many points of comparison to the genesis of my own life as a prostitute and, later, a convicted felon. My imagination having been sharpened by reading and diary-keeping, I developed a sympathetic ear for the tales of woe that were whispered to me in the library. More than the nearby chapel and the Catholic priest who once a week heard confessions and said Mass there, my little office became a confessional, where any prisoner was assured empathy and compassion. In large part, it was my own residue of guilt that made me a sympathetic witness to tragic lives.

I became more and more fascinated by the most ordinary falls into sin and crime. Like the collector who hungers for objects that look remarkably alike to an outsider, I was seeking further understanding of what had befallen me. Sometimes, you need to hear the same script over and over again before it finally makes its real emotional impact. I was thirsty for some sort of self-knowledge — I wanted to know what had made me into me.

Occasionally, I would cast autobiographical tales told to me into short narratives. The results occupied a strange no-man's land between fiction and non-fiction — the invented and the drearily real. Looking back at those first efforts, I now see that I simply could not turn them properly. Their dross remained dross in my hands. I lacked any kind of precision in transforming these accounts into good writing. Nevertheless, I had developed a craving to hear tales that I could write about.

My first break from this routine — although I did not realize it until years later, the turning point in my life as a writer — was my encounter with Eve, who arrived at Kingston in the summer of 1952. Like me, she was in her early thirties. I vividly recall how frail she looked, very much as I imagined Andersen's little match girl. A true white blonde, only her pale blue eyes and china complexion demarcated her from an albino. Miserably thin. Of normal height, she stooped when she walked and studiously avoided eye contact, even when revealing intimacies. Deeply passive, I thought to myself.

Eve — whose real name was Eva — had been born to elderly, wealthy parents in Vienna in 1922. The childless couple had been surprised by her arrival; they had given up hope of being blessed with a baby. Mr. Hoffman was a furrier, many of whose business associates were Jewish. The Hoffmans, both amateur violinists, frequently held musical evenings in their magnificent home on Huberstrasse, one street away from where Beethoven had spent his last years. Although the Hoffmans were Aryans and thus not threatened by the rise of the Nazis and the racial laws, both mother and father routinely received many of the newly proclaimed undesirables at their soirées.

In 1932, just as Eve turned 10, her mother and father precipitously decided to emigrate to Canada. Mrs. Hoffman's younger sister had settled in Toronto five years earlier, and business prospects in the rapidly expanding city were excellent. Afraid of the coming storm, Eve's parents wanted to settle somewhere where their only child could be raised in safety. Years later, they assured her, "we did it only for you, but, of course, we saved ourselves as well. 'Hog Town' is nevertheless a strange place for people from Wien to live. No coffee houses, no serious music, no interesting pictures to look at."

The kindly meant words carried a burden for the child as the impetus to immigrate had been fuelled because of her. In reality, her mother and father might have been murdered or lost everything they owned in the ravages of war, she later told herself. But she could not escape the burden of being the perfect daughter in order — to use her exact word — to propitiate the sacrifices made on her behalf.

At Bishop Strachan, Eve was a brilliant student, and no one was surprised when Karl and Maria determined that their daughter was to pursue higher education at Smith College in Northampton, Massachusetts, widely regarded as one of the finest colleges for women in all of North America. Karl told Eve that *his* choice of Smith over Bryn Mawr was determined by a careful examination of some crucial differences between the two. The women from Bryn Mawr were schooled better in Greek and Latin, but Smith seemed to turn out a more well-rounded *fraulein*.

At Smith, Eve was again an outstanding student. Although not as forward as some of her classmates, she nevertheless fit in to the long hours of study and the heavy party-going. On weekends, the girls were often bussed to nearby all-male colleges such as Amherst or Dartmouth for get-togethers — dances followed by heavy-petting. Sometimes, the men were bussed in to Northampton. At one of the Smith parties at the beginning of her sophomore year, Eve met Sam, a junior in economics at Amherst College.

Sam was not at first glance the most prepossessing of the men Eve had encountered. Of medium height and slightly overweight, his jet black hair and eyes nevertheless decisively drew attention to themselves. She could feel his charm and, she was certain, his goodness. They slept together the second time they saw each other. As it turned out, both had been virgins before that encounter. The more she knew him, Eve was convinced that no one but Sam would ever do for her. She made her mind up: she intended to marry him. They had been going steady for three months before Sam insisted they visit his parents in Yonker, just outside Manhattan. Eve was enthusiastic about this meeting, convinced she would uncover even more information about what made Sam so wonderful. The Stein home was large, opulent and decidedly grand — unlike the house in Toronto where she had been raised, the owners of this home put their wealth on display. For Eve, the furniture was too large, the colours of the rugs too bright. Yet, she adored Sam's parents immediately, although she was certain Hilda Stein was holding herself back when speaking with her. The visit went well enough, Eve was invited back, and when she and Sam parted for the school week, she felt even more confident about her future with him.

When Sam arrived at her dorm five days later, his face was crestfallen, all of the usual animation drained. His mother had been very upset by his attachment to Eve. The Steins did not mind their son seeing a non-Jewish girl, but they were repulsed by Eve's blondness, her Aryanness. Yes, they understood the Hoffmans had many Jewish friends, but the pure whiteness of Eve's skin was an abomination, especially in light of what was happening in Europe. Sam and Eve spent the weekend together, but Sam's courtliness had deserted him. A dutiful son, he was obviously not going to break with his parents. When they made love for the last time, Sam was so vigorous he hurt her, almost as if he were trying to wound her and thus make the break with her easier. Perhaps that's how he deals with guilt, she thought.

After Sam, there were no more boyfriends. Eve returned to Toronto when she finished at Smith. She took a job with Stabler's, a picture agency that supplied images for books, magazines and newspapers. Although she dealt with all manners of requests, Eve specialized in pictures showing disasters, natural and man-made. Publishers from all over the world began to use Stabler's because of Eve's knack of finding exactly the right painting or photograph to commemorate the tragic.

She had been at Stabler's for five years when Geoff Smith joined the firm. At first, she found his wildly handsome features annoying: he was simply too perfect to be human. After a while, succumbing to his charms, she spoke with him much more openly and readily. He asked her almost nothing about herself, but he told her a lot about himself, particularly about his marriage to the glamorous, exotic Pat, the only daughter of a Brazilian oilman and his Irish wife. "You must come to dinner," he often told her, but no invitation was forthcoming until the day Pat phoned the office to speak to her husband, who was away from the office. When Eve picked up the phone and offered to take a message, Pat thanked her and then became expansive, asking all kinds of questions. What did Eve do when she was not at work, who were her friends? Obviously displeased by the reticent responses she received, Pat peremptorily issued an invitation. "I fear you are hiding your talents under a bushel. We must have lunch together to discuss the situation. You can present yourself here next Tuesday." Although Eve was not aware of the existence of a situation, she was intrigued by Pat and agreed to meet her the following week.

On the phone, Pat spoke in a reticent, upper-class English accent, but Eve was not quite prepared for what her new acquaintance would look like. The thin, intensely white-faced woman who opened the door to her large Avenue Road apartment was at least six feet tall and had masses of flowing, Titian-red hair. After embracing Eve as if she were a long-lost friend, she exclaimed, "Geoff is completely wrong — the silly man doesn't understand women. You have loads of potential!" Having made this observation, she waved Eve into the flat, which was a monument to both International Modernism (chairs by Mies van der Rohe, a minimalist sofa of the Bauhaus variety) and art deco (two or three substantial Clarice Cliff Yo-Yo vases, white rugs by Syrie Maugham). The two styles were not comfortable with each other but somehow Pat had negotiated a truce between them.

Pat, who had answered the door in a red silk dressing gown, confessed that she always slept in, was not yet ready for the world, and ushered Eve into her bedroom. While Pat, seated at her dressing table, completed her toilet, Eve perched herself at the edge of the bed. Although she commanded Eve to "tell me all about yourself," Pat did most of the talking, the chief thread of which centred on her mourning for her father, who had passed away five years before. "They don't make men like that any more," she told Eve. "Geoff is very pretty — handsome, some would say — but he's just not as substantial as Daddy. I think about him all the time."

In the midst of a lot of chatter about herself, Pat skillfully asked pointed questions about Eve's life. "So you live with your parents —

aren't you a bit old for that?" And: "Why doesn't a woman of your beauty have a lover?" And, even more pointedly: "A woman of your age needs to be more experienced in the ways of the world. Why are you so stand-offish?" Eve sparred with Pat as best she could, avoiding any revelation about the past to escape her lips. Despite her new acquaintance's bossiness, Eve was enchanted by her, especially by her animal-like energy. Even at the outset of their strange friendship, Eve wondered why she was so attracted to this particular exotic creature. But she ignored all such doubts, so captivated was she. Soon, Eve became a satellite in Pat and Geoff's small circle, taking meals two or three times a week with them in small, chic restaurants.

Happy to have escaped her drab, unrewarding existence with her parents, Eve wanted to let herself go. So, she was particularly susceptible to Sean, Pat's Irish cousin from Dublin. A tall, well-built thirty-two year old doctor who had emigrated to Canada a year before, he was deeply fond of his cousin, who, he observed, was the sister his parents had never given him. Two days after they met, Sean phoned Eve to ask her to go out with him alone. She agreed and, within a week, the two became lovers, meeting always at his Rosedale flat. From the outset, Eve feared Sean might be feckless — she was also certain he was a bit of a rogue as far as women were concerned. Yet, the more she saw of him, the more she was able to see other sides, sides which rekindled memories of Sam.

Time reserved for Sean meant less time for Pat. After she had been seeing Sean for about a month, Eve was summoned to another lunch at Avenue Road. This time, Pat was much more agitated than usual. She was deeply depressed, could not get her princely father out of her mind. "He would have been the perfect lover for any woman," Pat observed. "So few would be worthy of him." After making this observation, Pat asked about Sean. In her habitual way, Eve was not very forthcoming. She enjoyed his company tremendously; they had many interests in common, especially the music of Chopin. Obviously displeased by the paucity of information coming her way, Pat became very direct. "He has very large coarse hands. He must have a huge penis." Eve blushed but did not respond to the implied question or the direction in which it was taking the conversation.

Shortly after this encounter, Sean stopped telephoning Eve. He was never in his flat when she phoned him; his secretary at his practice took messages, but no responses were forthcoming. For ten days, Eve did not see him. She was relieved when Pat called inviting her to supper in two days' time: "Sean will be here." Not having had even the slightest hint of discord in her relationship with him, Eve was not certain what she would encounter on the fateful evening she went to Avenue Road. Geoff answered the door and ushered her in; Pat was still getting herself ready and would be with them in a minute or two. While Eve and Geoff were sipping their cocktails, the doorbell rang. Although she was apprehensive, Eve was not quite prepared to encounter the woman accompanying Sean that evening. Elaine, a close friend of Pat's, was tall, elegantly dressed, and had masses of beautiful red hair. She was not quite as tall as Pat, and her tresses had achieved their colouring through chemistry. Nevertheless, Pat and Elaine bore a striking resemblance to each other, as if cut from the same cloth by the same tailor.

When Pat made her entrance, she bore down upon Elaine whom she kissed with a mighty flourish. She embraced Eve distractedly. For ever after, Eve was never certain how she survived the ensuing meal. To her, Sean was courteous but aloof. Elaine constantly made references to the excursions she had recently undertaken with him; the looks she gave him clearly indicated they had become lovers. Pat obviously approved of this new arrangement; as usual, Geoff had very little to say in the presence of his wife. Soon after coffee was served, Elaine said she must be going; she did not wish to be up too late. This remark was made in a sneering way as she looked at Sean. They left soon afterwards and, about twenty minutes later, Eve excused herself. She also had an early morning. As she said her goodbyes to her host and hostess, Eve was certain she could see the hint of a triumphant smirk on Pat's face.

Afterwards, Eve was never quite certain how much she consciously knew at the time — using a small hand pistol she removed from her father's study — she went to Avenue Road the following morning and shot Pat dead. Did she fire the pistol because her lover had been removed from her by a cruel, manipulative woman? Had Pat been toying with her all along? Did she kill Pat because she had been tricked into a kinky relationship in which she was to sleep with Sean and provide Pat with a full report so that some sort of taboo sexual affair between the two cousins could be consummated at a safe remove? Or did Eve kill her friend out of sheer frustration of having her lover removed from her? Did she shoot Pat because she wished she had murdered Sam's mother? Did she commit murder because she was simply fed up with being pushed around?

Karl and Maria provided the best legal counsel money could buy: they hired Mr. Robinette. Even a magician of his incredible dexterity could not pull rabbits out of this particular hat. Eve was found guilty of first-degree murder and sent to P4W for the remainder of her natural life. For a year, her parents would hire a car and driver to take them from Toronto to Kingston to visit their wayward daughter. Then, Karl died suddenly of a heart attack, and Maria was too depressed to make the trip by herself. Although she lived on for three years after the death of her husband, she never saw her daughter again.

Eve had no regrets about removing Pat from life. "She was a destructive person whose own sense of deprivation made her act cruelly to others." This was Eve's thumbnail description of what had happened. Of more concern to her was how she had lived her life with the elusive hope that others would like — or even love — her if she conformed to their expectations. A person without a sense of irony, Eve had no sense that Pat lacked the capability of looking at her, even noticing her.

Eve and I never became close friends, although we shared many intellectual interests. In her I saw a shadow of myself I intensely disliked. Perhaps she saw the same in me and was, likewise, repulsed? Unlike my reception when I first arrived at P4W, Eve was a female St. George to the other prisoners, someone who had slain a marauding tiger preying upon innocent villagers.

The only encounter I had with Eva in which any real intimacies were exchanged was in the library on the afternoon I recommended *Clarissa* to her. She had read it years before, she informed me, and was not certain she thought it deserved the status of "masterpiece" assigned to it. For one thing, she thought Richardson a crude manipulator of his heroine, who was, she observed, reduced to the status of a marionette in his hands. She also found Clarissa's lack of interest in sex disturbing. In addition, she saw Clarissa's life as a surrender to the death instinct. I told her my thoughts about him and his book were diametrically opposite to hers. But who was I to tell her she was wrong?

"I guess it all depends on which side of the fence you put yourself," she crisply told me. "I killed someone. I have no regrets for what I did. I did the world a favour." Then, she looked up at me. "I remember reading all the newspaper accounts of your various trials in the *Globe*. I was certain you didn't kill anyone. I still am. That's an important difference between us. I was a soldier who intercepted and shot the enemy. You were simply a decoy."

This remark may not have been meant as a put-down, but she was telling me that although many are called to become murderers, few are chosen. She and I existed in different leagues. The clear implication was that hers was the superior one.

32

Over the years, I established a friendly but sometimes uneasy relationship with Mrs. Nelson and Mrs. White. Although I obviously could never be assigned the status of an equal by this pair, they came to use me as a sort of fulcrum through whom they could negotiate with the other prisoners, who trusted me to act in their best interests. So I became a sort of half-way house between the very separate worlds of guards and prisoners. Since I never set myself up in business as the Empress had done, I could mediate with both sides without being seen to sully my hands. Moral stature — I possessed that elusive commodity in abundance.

Even when things are proceeding at an even keel, prison life is best described as enervating. There is simply nothing to do, and that can be very draining as well as depressing. That is the reason, I suspect, so much great literature has emerged from the experience of confinement. Cervantes created Quixote because he had to find a profitable way to spend his time. Breakfast, sewing room duty for two hours (I became an accomplished seamstress), a walk in the prison yard, lunch, library chores, another walk, early supper (five o'clock), reading in my room, lights out at ten. When I was fed up with reading, I made entries in my diary.

I was at P4W for eight years when Laura arrived there in 1955. She was a small, lithe creature, panther-like in her sleek, curving movements. Her face was arresting in a strange way, overpowering in its simple, unsophisticated, childlike beauty. In her, personality and appearance were in complete agreement. Except for the sensuousness of her walk, she seemed completely unaware of her mesmerizing physicality.

A full ten years younger than myself, her trial for murder in Toronto had aroused surprisingly little interest. Such a strange reason to murder anyone, the papers claimed. For a few days, the *Toronto Daily Star* was filled with the eerie story of her slaying of John Partridge, a high-school classmate, a man with whom she had never exchanged a single word before she murdered him.

At Jarvis Collegiate, Laura had been one of the *crème de la crème*, a member of the most elite band of girls. She gained entry into that circle because of her ravishing appearance. If she had been denied membership, the group's dominance might have been threatened — or extinguished. Some girls were known for intelligence, others for sexual inventiveness. Laura was the group's icon, a ripe physical symbol of all the values of her clique. In contrast, short, stocky Partridge was a misfit, a loner.

At school and at home, Laura had little to say. Her parents adored her, her elder brother was in awe of her. She was an average student, although her teachers complained — some bitterly — that she never participated in class discussions. When forced to conjugate a French verb or recite a theorem in geometry, she did so with great assurance. But she had very few words of her own in any instance. The proverbial silent woman.

"Ordinary": this was Laura's word to describe her early life. She did what was expected of her, even to the extent of marrying her brother's closest friend, handsome Bernie Daniels. Everyone agreed: they were the most attractive couple one could ever hope to meet. The only sorrow in Laura's life was her inability to conceive a child. Her family and friends were convinced she and Bernie would have had stunningly beautiful children. Perhaps such offspring would have been so devastatingly attractive that they would have been beyond the limits assigned to mere mortals. Such was the observation of more than one acquaintance.

There was another — but hidden — blight. From the time she turned 18, Laura was convinced some force was observing or following her. She never thought a person was actually trailing or stalking her, but she felt a presence of some sort. Never having heard anyone else voice such thoughts, she, as usual, kept her feelings to herself.

Laura's quiet life was disrupted the day she received a telephone call from Cynthia, one of the members of her high school set. Her old friend, now an arts journalist, had been startled when she visited the Hastings Gallery on Bloor Street to see an exhibit of nude drawings by John Partridge, the outcast who had been at school with them. "I didn't know you even knew him, much less posed for him." Laura told Cynthia there was some mistake. She had not seen Partridge in the six years that had intervened since high school. She had never posed for anyone. Cynthia, sure she had at last discovered hidden depths in Laura, was certain she was lying, especially as the police were on the verge of shutting the show down because of the supposed obscenity of the pictures.

Alarmed by what Cynthia told her, Laura decided to visit the gallery. As she walked in, the young woman sitting at the desk beamed a warm smile in her direction. "How nice to meet the model! I think John has done a splendid job, although I must say you look exactly like the drawings. Almost as if he had photographed you. He is a splendid draughtsman." Laura nodded weakly in her direction and began to tour the pictures. Without doubt, she was the model. The large mole at the top of her right shoulder was perfectly rendered; the way her left breast was markedly smaller than its companion was accurately done.

Quite soon, Laura lost interest in the question of verisimilitude. The woman in the pictures was touching herself in ways that had never occurred to Laura or her husband. Most disturbing were the renditions of Laura on her back, her legs arching up, her right hand plunging into a very wet-looking pudenda, her tongue archly pointing at the spectator, and her eyes bristling with lust. Those pictures frightened Laura. The face and body may have been hers, but she had never experienced such thoughts or performed such lewd actions.

After her inspection of the drawings, Laura accosted the young woman at the desk, telling her she had never posed for Partridge. What is more, she informed her that the drawings were obscene and should be removed from the walls and destroyed. "It's a bit late for regrets," the startled curator responded. "You're very beautiful. You've nothing to be ashamed of. I guess you didn't realize what a commotion these pictures would make." The young woman — obviously certain she was dealing with a model with a bad case of stage fright — could not be convinced of any of Laura's assertions. Finally, Laura asked for Partridge's address and phone number. Impossible, she was told: the artist was in Europe and wouldn't be back for at least six months.

Things went quickly from bad to worse. Having heard from one of his friends about the exhibition, Laura's husband visited the Hastings and then drove directly home, where he accused his wife of being the mistress of the degenerate artist. When she burst into tears and vehemently denied the charge, he struck her in the face and accused her of being no better than a prostitute. Although her parents and brother did not attend the exhibition, they heard enough about it to persuade them of Laura's dishonest, underhanded behaviour. Without any support from husband, family, or friends, Laura was completely cast asunder. Within a month, her previously tranquil, uneventful existence was in ruins. She left Toronto, took the train to Winnipeg, rented a small furnished room in the North End and took a job as a waitress at Main and Portage.

For three exceedingly long years, Laura kept to herself. She was friendly with several of her co-workers, but she avoided contact with everyone else. Routinely, she refused the many invitations she received to step out. Hers was a life of quiet desperation. That existence was suddenly disrupted one day when two or three customers sniggered at her in an embarrassed, furtive way. Later that day, Mr. Tompkins, the owner of the restaurant, called her into his office. "You could have told me you were posing for this garbage. Would have prepared me and everyone else." He handed her a copy of the x-rated girlie magazine, *America on Display*. As she looked at yet another series of nude renditions of herself — this time, photographs — Laura became utterly confused, burst into tears and told the boss that she had done no such thing. His tiny eyes squinted at her in disbelief. "Not posed for them? How's that possible? You're making things bloody difficult for me. You act like the Blessed Virgin Mary here at work and then look a right whore in these pix! Look at you, you're pawing yourself in these pictures. I've never seen that look in your eyes before."

As she studied the photos, Laura had to admit to herself that the woman was indeed herself. But how? She told Mr. Tompkins the story of the Hastings Gallery. He obviously wanted to believe her, but the evidence of his eyes prevented him from doing so. "You say the artist in Toronto was called John Partridge. Look at the credit for this portfolio: 'J.P.'"

Completely befuddled, employee and employer talked about the strange situation. Mr. Tompkins had heard of trick photography whereby, for example, the head of a celebrity was pasted on to the body of a naked person engaged in an unseemly act. But you could always search for tell-tale clues in such set-ups. These photos looked all too genuine. Tompkins obviously wanted to believe a very distraught Laura, but the look of doubt that crossed his face revealed his conviction she was lying. That evening, she finished her shift, took the streetcar home, packed the two suitcases that contained all her worldly possessions and, early the next morning, took the train to Vancouver.

Almost immediately, Laura found lodgings in Gastown and, a day later, a job as a waitress in a nearby greasy spoon. In Winnipeg, she had escaped the feeling of being trailed or followed. Only intermittently had the conviction that some unseen force was watching her surfaced. In Vancouver — where she changed her name to Lynne Davidson — most of her waking moments were consumed with the idea that Partridge was somehow spying on her. No longer, she reminded herself, had she the slightest memory of what he looked like. Any man in his early thirties could be he. She was frightened but felt she had nowhere to turn for help.

About a year after she had tried to settle in Vancouver, she saw a review in the *Sun* of an exhibit at the Art Gallery devoted to a series of oil portraits "in the grand style, very much in the manner of John Singer Sargent, by the Toronto painter and photographer John Partridge. The fourteen portraits on display — all of the mysterious Leslie Dyment, the Toronto heiress no one has ever heard of — show Partridge has taken his career to an entirely new level of achievement and sophistication. This is portraiture that bears comparison to Ingres. From the raw materials of his model, Partridge has fashioned a style of painting previously unknown in the Dominion. Previously celebrated as a technical wizard in the art of drawing and having gained notoriety as a photographer of naked women, Partridge has at last discovered the enormous extent of his talent."

No reproduction accompanied the notice, but Laura was quite certain of — as she entered the Gallery that afternoon — exactly what she would see. She did not even have to enter the rooms set aside for the exhibition. As soon as she approached the portals of the Gallery, she saw several women, obviously on their way home from the exhibition, nudge each other and glance in her direction.

The huge paintings — more in the manner of Reynolds than Sargent or Ingres — dominated the two rooms set aside for them. In some, Leslie Dyment stood full-length before the viewer arrayed in sumptuous evening gowns; in others, her face and shoulders filled the large canvases. The various stylings assigned to the model's dark black hair, the wide assortment of diamonds, rubies, emeralds and sapphires that adorned her, the dexterous folds and nuances in the silks in which she was clothed — all these glowed with the force of life. But they would have been inconsequential were it not for the face and body of Leslie Dyment, for the abundant charm which she bestowed on all the objects in her universe, her authority giving the objects the right to exist. "Breathtaking" was the word that came to Laura in the gallery that afternoon. And yet she was disheartened to see herself rendered as the queen of an empire she knew nothing about.

That afternoon, Laura spent an hour looking at the portraits of herself. The following morning she called the Gallery to discover the artist's whereabouts. He had, she was informed, flown back to Toronto a few days before. When she insisted on being given his address there, she was given the name of the gallery — Starling's —

that represented him. "We never give out personal information, madam." Later that day, Laura bought a small handgun from the pawn shop across the street from her restaurant and took the evening flight to Toronto. She took a room at the Park Plaza Hotel and began a daily vigil outside the gallery. No one going or coming bore the slightest resemblance to anyone she thought could be Partridge. Finally, she called Starling's, identifying herself as Lydia Dent. She had modelled for the great painter in the past and would like to offer her services to him again. As it turned out, the receptionist told her, John would be paying them a quick visit that afternoon at about three. Perhaps she could chat with him then?

Wearing her plain black raincoat, a kerchief tucked up around the lower half of her face, Laura positioned herself across the street from the gallery at quarter to three that afternoon. She only had to wait ten minutes for the yellow taxi to pull up in front of the gallery. The man who got out was obese, huge tortoiseshell glasses covering the upper half of his face. He paid the cabby, who pulled away quickly. Just as he reached the top step of the gallery, Laura ran across the street. "Mr. Partridge!" she shouted. "Is that you?" His concentration obviously disrupted, the artist looked in her direction and was startled to recognize the woman accosting him. He died instantly from the bullet that ripped through his heart. Laura remained there on the sidewalk, waiting calmly for the ambulance and the police to arrive.

Inspector Knox could not believe what Laura told him, could not fathom the confession she willingly offered. Partridge had stolen her identity — she had killed him in order to live. She could not have breathed, she assured him, a moment longer while he was in existence. The policeman reminded her that she hardly knew the painter, he had never threatened her, the only words they had ever exchanged were voiced by her just before she shot him at point-blank range. "Oh, but he murdered me over and over again. Took everything from me. He did not deserve to live." If Knox was flabbergasted by Laura's motive, her lawyer, Ian Browning, was even more put out. "Surely, he threatened you? Must have assaulted — even raped — you? Maybe you have amnesia?" She calmly assured him this was not the case.

Mr. Browning's incredulity diminished markedly once the personal papers of the murder victim became available. The artist's diary revealed that he had been obsessed with Laura from the time they were in the same class (Grade 10 Art) at Jarvis Collegiate. He had seen her in the nude because he had, as a teenager, spent many pleasurable evenings peeping into her bedroom window at her parents' home in Forest Hill. His knowledge of her face and body was so extensive that he had been able to make his drawings and then, subsequently, fake the photographs. At various times, in Toronto, Winnipeg and Vancouver, he had followed her; on more than a dozen occasions she had waited upon him. Having discovered this, Mr. Browning asked Laura: "Why did you kill him when you did? The portraits in Vancouver were innocuous." She thought carefully before she told him: "Once again, he remade me in an image that was not mine. He was always stealing from me. I was left with nothing."

Public opinion rendered Partridge into a monster of insensitivity, but Laura was, nevertheless, convicted of first-degree murder. Vengeance was the Lord's duty, said the jury and the Crown. Laura had overstepped herself. In those woebegone days, there were no feminists to champion her cause.

I think the technical word now used to describe a person like Laura is "schizoid." She had absolutely no interest in being around other people, not that she seemed to take much pleasure in her own company. Mrs. White, who took a motherly interest in Laura, often tried to engage her in conversation. She got nowhere. At that point, she asked if I would help bring Laura round.

"Round from what?"

"You can be awfully dense, Evelyn. Laura's trapped within herself. She needs to come to the surface. Otherwise ..."

"Otherwise what?"

"She'll become suicidal. All the best research indicators demonstrate that truism." Over the years, Mrs. Nelson and Mrs. White had unofficially added the designations "social worker" and "amateur shrink" to my prescribed tasks. In Laura's case, it turned out to be an impossible assignment.

For me, the strange thing about Laura was her resemblance to Gene Tierney, the supposedly murdered subject of Otto Preminger's *Laura*, which I saw at the Tivoli when it was released — two years before my own troubles began — in 1944. At that time, I had responded with cynical mirth to the famous throw-away line by Clifton Webb in the role of the writer Waldo Lydecker: "In my case, self-absorption is completely justified. I have never discussed any other subject quite so worthy of my attention."

There is a strange scene in that film when Clifton Webb, Vincent Price, Judith Anderson and Dana Andrews are assembled in a resplendent sitting room, the crowning touch of which is the portrait of the enigmatic Laura over the fireplace. In my mind's eye, I replayed that scene, trying to imagine what it must have been like for my Laura to walk into a large gallery filled with representations of herself. Dana Andrews, who plays the detective searching for the murderer of Laura, falls in love with the dead woman; John Partridge played a similar role in his Laura's life — he was obsessed with a remote girl and then woman. In trying to rid himself of his sexual feelings for her, he did two things: he became a first-class artist, in the process transforming himself into a miscreant. In the film, Laura — who shows up alive — turns out to be a milquetoast.

I did my best to talk with Laura, but it was slow-going. For one thing, she was not an avid reader and hardly ever visited the library. For another, Laura was remote, as if untouched by everything that had ever happened to her. Taking matters into my own hands. I suggested to Mrs. White that she rent *Laura* and show it on a Saturday night, the one evening a week the prisoners were shown a film. Maybe, I told her, that film would rouse her. She agreed.

Two weeks later, I sat behind my Laura during the film. Obviously never having seen it, she was struck by her own resemblance to Tierney. Like most of the inmates, she laughed at Waldo Lydecker's witticisms. She followed Dana Andrews' growing obsession with the dead woman, his startled discovery that Laura is alive, his involvement with her spoiled, wealthy friends, and his suspicion that Laura herself might be the murderer of the dead woman at first mistakenly identified as herself. She seemed taken aback with the discovery that Lydecker — infatuated with Laura — mistakenly killed the woman he thought was Laura and then, at the very end, is apprehended when he attempts to murder her for the second time. When Lydecker is mortally wounded, he has just a few seconds to reaffirm his undying love for Laura — "his better half" he labels her. If he could not have her, the writer was going to make sure no one else could. All for love, all for art.

Two days later, on Monday afternoon, I accosted Laura when she visited the library. "Did you enjoy the film the other night?"

"I liked the film. I'm not sure I could say I enjoyed it. Many people have told me that I look like Gene Tierney, but I had never seen even a photograph of her before the other night."

"You look very much like her."

"Yes. It spooked me. For minutes at a time, I thought I was looking at myself. That Laura is a bit like myself in other ways. She's what men want her to be — what they imagine her to be. That's really no excuse to fall in love with someone."

"No excuse?"

"That woman was totally uninteresting. The other day I came upon the word 'cipher' in a book. In the film, Laura's a zero, an absence. That's how I have also lived my life. The man I killed — he was like Waldo. Inconsequential, rodent-like. He was murdering me — he left me no option. Yet, he couldn't have seen anything in me to love — just a surface."

"He was taken with your beauty."

"Yes. And he didn't mind destroying me in the process. He was a sort of a cannibal, although he was eating me alive."

"Maybe you followed the only course open to you?"

"Some days I think that. Most of the time, I'm not so sure. I allowed him to direct the course of my life, responding as I did to his actions. He was the cat; I remained the mouse."

Laura did not say any more. Holding her head down even more than usual, she selected a book and left the library. Four days later, she was found dead in her cell, hanging from the ceiling. She had tied her single pair of nylon socks together and made them into a noose and rope.

After that, I decided to relinquish my role as inmate social worker. Mrs. White was unrepentant. "She had to be brought out of herself. We were doing the right thing."

"We may have been doing the right thing, Mrs. White, but Laura's dead. She was a passive creature her entire life. She didn't want to think about who she was. You and I forced her to do that."

"Yes, dear. I suppose we did. But human beings are thinking creatures."

"And women are often manipulated by men to act in certain ways."

Mrs. White would have none of my reservations. She certainly would not share any of the guilt I felt. I had encouraged Laura to reconsider her deep-seated passivity, to see her killing of Partridge as necessary to her well-being, her very existence. I had — under the instigation of one of my warders — encouraged Laura to break the mould. In so doing, I had forced her to kill herself. Years later, I tried to redeem myself by bringing her back to life in one of my first novels.

33

My closest friend during all my time at Kingston was Lydia, a woman twenty-five years older than myself. A mother figure, I suppose. Years before my arrival, she had assumed a key role at P4W in charge of the sewing room. Renowned for how quickly and efficiently she could turn her tiny, meticulous little hands to any task requiring a sewing machine, she was also a born teacher, one who deftly imparted her skills to others. Nevertheless, none of her charges — myself included — ever reached the same level of accomplishment as their instructor.

Small, wiry, her dark hair clipped severely short, she bore a distinct resemblance to my idea of a cockney. In another life, she might have been born within the sound of the bells of St Mary-le-Bow; in that bestowed upon her, she was born within the shadow of the Don Jail, where her father worked as a custodian and, later, a guard. He also travelled to Kingston from time to time, where he served as the public hangman.

Lydia's first recollections were of her father, Edward Jones, and their small, drafty, smelly one-bedroom flat. Tainted as those memories were by poverty, she recalled Edward as a kindly man who always made sure his little girl — whose mother had died giving birth to her — was looked after by kindly neighbours while he was at work. Often of an age to be Lydia's grandmother, those women adored her.

A week or so after she turned 6, her father married Wanda, a strange, brooding, sometimes violent woman. Edward was always kindly disposed towards his daughter, but Wanda's conduct went from one extreme to another. One day, she would assure the child that she was the perfect stepchild; on another, she would find fault with the little girl on a constant basis: Lydia did not help her clean the tenement, Lydia's (exceedingly neat) room was a pigsty, Lydia was not of a pleasant and easy disposition. These complaints were issued to Edward, who would then tactfully list his wife's complaints to his erring daughter. One day, he informed her: "Wanda has had a difficult life. She had expectations and they were dashed. That's why she flies off the handle. We must be tolerant." Wishing to please her father, Lydia nodded her head in sage agreement well beyond her years.

In rapid succession, Wanda gave birth to two sons, Edward and Evan. After each birth, Lydia noticed, Wanda would become listless, completely withdrawn, often talking utter nonsense. Lydia looked after the two youngsters, almost as if she were their foster mother rather than their half-sister. Then, when Evan was six months old, Wanda's "darknesses" (as she called them) completely took her over; in part, these were really severe migraines which sometimes lasted two or three days at a time; in part, the poor woman was hopelessly depressed, enclosed in a void of self-loathing. When she was not enduring the headaches, Wanda would be subject to violent mood swings. She began to drink heavily.

At school, Lydia was a brilliant student. Wanda took some pleasure in Lydia's remarkable abilities but she began to become even more harsh in her criticisms of her. Paradoxically, Wanda was thrilled by what the young girl could accomplish at the very same time that very success enraged her.

Seven long years of praise and criticism went by. When Lydia reached the end of Grade 8, Wanda, in consultation with Edward, informed her that she had to take a job to support the family. "My burdens are very heavy," Wanda told the teenager. "The doctor says I cannot work. Your father does not earn enough to keep us in this flat."

Lydia quit school, took a job at a mill, and became the family's principal breadwinner. She was allowed very little free time when she returned home of an evening — she was expected to cook the evening meal and to keep the tenement sparkling clean. On Sunday — her one day off — she was expected to wash and mend clothes. Wanda interfered with the attempts of would-be boyfriends to court Lydia. "They are not good enough for you, dear. You don't want to step out with the kind of young man who works in a factory." When Lydia pointed out that she was a young woman who worked in a factory, Wanda simply informed her that she was not really of such a place.

Wanda was far from being the traditional evil stepmother. Throughout Lydia's school years, she had praised her results highly, seeming to take pleasure in the girl's accomplishments. In fact, she had far higher expectations of her than she did of her two sons, who, when they went to school, were ordinary students. In her reading of fairy tales, Lydia was quite aware of how foster mothers often bedeviled the lives of their adopted children, usually advancing the causes of their own offspring over those of stepchildren. That's what *Cinderella* was all about, Lydia recalled. Yet, Wanda never acted in that way. She always expected the best of her adopted daughter. And unlike the evil woman who married the father of Hansel and Gretel, she did not try to abandon Lydia. Wanda certainly wanted — and needed — the money Lydia earned. But Wanda's motives seemed more complicated than simple greed.

The fettered life of the Jones family continued on a seesawing course for two more years until the day Lydia overheard a strange conversation at the mill between two workers — both elderly women — with whom she usually had little contact. She learned that Wanda was her real mother, Edward was not her real father. Edward had been infatuated with Wanda, who preferred another man — the son of the owner of the mill. During a brief affair; Eliot Drake had impregnated her. When Wanda gave birth to Lydia, Eliot, who had been whisked out of harm's way by his family, was living in Montreal. Wanda pleaded with Edward to look after Lydia so that she could follow her lover to Montreal. Six years later — all her efforts to resume her relationship with her lover having failed — she returned to Toronto.

Wanda did not feel it "fair" that a six-year-old be burdened with the arrival of her real mother. It would be better if Lydia thought she and Wanda did not share the same blood. She offered to do her best for her abandoned child and, as was his wont, Edward went along with her proposal. Wanda's feelings about Lydia were determined by her great love and her great hatred of Eliot. Like her father, Lydia was bright and intuitive — she even looked like him. Wanda hated Eliot for the way he had abandoned her, yet in Lydia she could see reflected all those qualities that had attracted her to her lost lover in the first place.

In a flash, Lydia understood her mother's motivations. She knew she could never live up to Wanda's high expectations; she knew that her mother's angry resentment stemmed from unresolved feelings about her real father; she was aware that she had been the victim of forces that had torn her mother apart. Yet something snapped in Lydia that day. When she begged off work and returned home early that afternoon, Wanda, alarmed that her wages would be lost, began to berate her. Lydia walked calmly over to the kitchen drawer, took out the large carving knife, walked over to the woman screaming abuse, and plunged the knife into her. Wanda died almost instantly.

When the police and, later, her lawyer asked why she had committed the crime, a startled and confused Lydia could not adequately respond. First of all, she blurted out something about never being able to meet high expectations. Then, turning her face towards her interrogators, she tried to help them to understand. "I didn't have a mother. I didn't have a stepmother. I had no one. I was nobody." She paused: "It was nobody who killed Wanda Jones."

Officialdom was not much interested in Lydia's strange reason for killing a defenceless woman. The psychiatrists who examined her asserted nothing was wrong with her mental health. She was certainly not legally insane, although these consultants spoke of something missing in her character. Since she was adjudged responsible for her actions, she was found guilty of first-degree murder at her trial and committed to life imprisonment. When I first encountered her in

1947, she was a woman of 51, who had been at Kingston since she was seventeen years old. Thirty-four years. An inconceivable amount of time for me to imagine. What a horrible life she has endured, I thought. Those were first impressions. And yet the more I knew her, the more I realized she was very contented. I might go as far as to claim that she was one of the few genuinely happy people I have ever met in my life.

"Mum": this was the nickname assigned by all the inmates to Lydia. If you had a problem, you asked her for help. Without my realizing it at the time (I was such an infernal blunderbuss), she had been secretly working with Mrs. Nelson and Mrs. White to overthrow the Empress and her Shadow. Although my interference produced the right result, Lydia would have succeeded eventually in ridding us of those two wretches. I later learned that my speculations about Mrs. Nelson using money from the sewing room for personal gain were completely unjustified. She and Lydia had devised the extra work in order to fund improvements at P4W.

Strange as it may seem, Lydia had the strange ability to accept people for exactly who they were. Since she was unfailingly friendly and never tried to refashion anyone, she was much beloved. Lydia was certainly not the kind of person to inform you that you had overthrown her apple cart. A year or so after the removal of the two women, she simply said: "You weren't to know other plans were afoot. Your heart was in the right place."

Lydia and I became good friends at about the time I became librarian. She told me about the desperately sordid conditions at the women's prison at Kingston where she had been lodged until 1934, the year P4W opened. According to her, Nelson had to be seen in context: she might seem an unduly forbidding person, but she had taken over from a head matron who had locked the women up, allowed them to exercise outside for ten minutes a day, fed them spoiled food, did not allow them to work, and, basically, treated the inmates are if they were large bulky parcels languishing in a warehouse.

At first, Lydia would visit me in my room once a week after dinner. This was the only completely free time in our busy days. In the beginning our conversations centred on Nelson and White, on how, as

I sarcastically put it, they made a perfect pair — White the flunky of the authoritarian Nelson, who kept her subordinate in check.

"I think you're right — up to a point."

"What point?"

"They work together well, they suit each other."

"Yes, but that's because White doesn't stand up to Nelson."

"You're still missing the point. When she was married, White obviously deferred to her husband — to his research. By temperament, she looks up to others. That is her nature. Nelson is a born dictator. She is determined to rule. When she was battling the Empress, she was dealing with a like-minded person. I became useful to her at that time — helping one tyrant overthrow another. She was furious with you because you were high-handed, acting as she might have done in a like situation. High-handed people don't like other high-handed people."

"Thanks for the compliment."

"Sorry, Evelyn. I didn't mean it quite like it sounded. Nelson is all about control, White is all about reflected glory. If you discover what really makes a person tick, you know everything about them. You know all about power because you had to adjust to it from the time of childhood. Your mother made sure of that."

I nodded in agreement. "So I know about power but am not powerful myself?"

"I didn't say that. You made adjustments. Simple as that."

"I'm sure you're right. I must have taken on both the Empress and Nelson because they reminded me of Mother. Maybe I was getting back at her by challenging those two."

"I'm sure you're right. At least you had something to react against."

"I don't know what you mean."

"As a child, I had a father. Later, I learned he was not my father. I didn't have a mother but was provided with an evil step-mother. Then, she turned out to be my real mother. I didn't really know who those people were. They said one thing, did another.

"During all my years here, I've relived my killing of Wanda over and over again. I can't bear to call her my mother. I must have been trying to be the good step-child but then that role was taken away from me. I was the child whose mother had disowned her."

"Maybe she wasn't capable of anything else?"

"Nonsense. She was a strong enough person to have taken charge of the situation. No, she didn't want to. Her hatred of my real father so overwhelmed her that she took revenge on me, his daughter. I can never forgive her, although I obviously should not have killed her." She stopped, looked around the room as if searching for some truth written on the blank walls, and then began again, finding it difficult to find the words she wanted. "She took revenge on me. I revenged myself. An eye for an eye." At that point, the tears began. "A person has to know where she stands. Otherwise, what's the point? You're either somebody or you're nobody. There is no other choice."

I got up, fetched a Kleenex and hugged Lydia as I dabbed her eyes. She nodded her thanks. That evening was a breakthrough in our friendship. After that, I felt free to tell her about Mother, especially my subservience to her. Whenever I raised that issue, Lydia would say one of two things. "Evelyn dear, you had no choice. Alexandra was a very controlling person, you were a young child, your father a molester." At other times, she saw beyond the excuses. "You were raised to be passive. You suffered from that upbringing. Now, you are a totally different person. Maybe you're ready to seize the day?" At first, I didn't know what she meant. How was I to change my life, make something different of it?

Prison walls are a most effective barrier. They keep the criminal out of general circulation. They can also rob the inmate of the capacity to change. Of course, the penal system is based on the general principle that leopards never get rid of their spots, tigers their stripes. Prison did not make Lydia a better person. She had always been more than decent. It gave her an anonymity that suited the circumstances of her early life. In one completely destructive moment, she had obliterated her past. In the present, she could afford to make peace with herself. That luxury evaded me. Eventually, my mortgage to the authorities would be discharged. I would be freed. Or, if I wanted to think of it in a different way, I would be free.

Strange to think of prison as a school for writing, but that's what it eventually became for me. And in this regard, Lydia was my muse because it was she who made me aware that the lives of society's female outcasts — like myself — could be a subject for fiction that I myself could write. Of course there was the more-than-honourable precedent of Daniel Defoe.

In her pleasantly bossy way, Lydia informed me one day that I should make the transition from reading books to making them. "You're completely different from all the other women here. The way you spend your time reading, thinking about things. You've been keeping a diary. You tell me you've tried to put some of your observations into stories. There's your future for you."

"Hardly. My writing starts and stops. A very bumpy ride that doesn't go anywhere."

"Beginner's faults. Practice makes perfect." This was said more like an order than an observation.

"For you, Lydia. You're never daunted. But writing is different from sewing. With a pattern you know where to begin and end. With those stories of mine I'm flying blind."

"I think you need to do a lot more gliding, my girl. Test your wings. Maybe you'll learn to soar."

"Or fall flat to the ground."

"Maybe. But you won't know until you try. You have your own point of view, I'll say that for you. And you have plenty of time on your hands to exploit your talent."

Exploit. That awful word again. During my first few years at P4W, I blamed myself for exploiting others. Then I began to think of myself as having been exploited by my parents. The idea of exploiting myself — my inner self — was repugnant to me. Another metaphor used by Lydia was also repulsive: one day, she told me to mine the gold lying hidden within me. Buried treasure. But I was a person who saw herself as essentially worthless. Nothing could be dug up that would be of any value.

I attempted to share this observation with Lydia, but she would have none of it. "The past is a foreign country from which you were expelled. Here, you can begin all over again."

34

The P4W in which I spent twelve years was vastly different from the prison described in Patricia Pearson's shocking *When She Was Bad* of 1997, a book I am sure in its lurid details is completely accurate: "On April 22, 1994, six inmates attacked four guards in a pre-planned escape attempt, outside B range.... The guards, all of whom were female, were put in choke holds, punched in the face, kicked in the stomach, stabbed with a hypodermic needles, and assaulted with scissors and a telephone ripped from the wall." This incident led to the shutdown of my former home in the summer of 1996.

In my experience, women in prison were occasionally violent, but I never witnessed the kind of events recounted by Pearson. My life in P4W was an altogether gentler affair. I am also tempted to add the word "rustic." We were withdrawn from the world; we suffered privations in dress and food; we had to work hard and diligently; we went to bed early and rose at dawn; we were not free to come and go as we pleased. In a closed environment such as ours, small events were easily magnified; tempers flared; harsh words were spoken on a regular basis. Yet, the idea of a close-knit community prevailed; the guards were not necessarily our enemies. When I skimmed Pearson's book, I could not make any kind of link between my life in the late forties and fifties and the prison experience of the nineties. I am not distorting the past, looking at it through rose-coloured glasses, or — heaven forbid! — romanticizing it. The world in which I existed in Kingston was remote from the real world and, like everything else in life, had its own hazards.

During those twelve long years, I thought of myself as serving time — paying for past mistakes. Only in retrospect do I see those years as a tedious apprenticeship in the art of fiction. A malicious sort of person might say of me: she learned to exchange one kind of lying for another. But that would be an unjust indictment. In my prison house, I studied the other women and, without really being conscious of what I was doing, I made shorthand notes that I would later expand into my first three novels based on the lives of Eve, Laura and Lydia. Those books are not as fictional as most of my readers and critics think.

My first novel — *Celia* (1974) — is based on Eva Hoffman's story. When Anita Brookner's *Look at Me* appeared ten years later, many reviewers commented on the similarity of my heroine to Brookner's Frances (Fanny). To what extent had Brookner been influenced by me? The consensus was that although *Celia* is a much more emotionally engaging narrative than Brookner's, it lacks the English writer's precisely beautiful, sometimes ornate use of language.

My recounting of the life of Laura Daniels in *Dahlia* (1976) became enormously popular in the United States, where the trial was never reported. American reviewers tended to see the book as an allegory, as an account of the tribulations to which women are subjected by men. In Canada, I was confronted by interviewers with the facts of Daniels' life. I admitted that the book was loosely based on that case but denied the book had any political or feminist agenda.

Lydia's story is the basis of the plot action of *Camilla* (1978). Although they are not thematically dissimilar, the remainder of my novels — twelve — are not taken directly from prison life.

My own particular form of writing was obviously influenced by the many books I read while a resident of Kingston. Perhaps an even greater source for my work lies in some of the films I saw during those sequestered years. Every Saturday night, our rickety old projector was rolled out of the storage room adjacent to the first-floor auditorium, three or four large cans of film were handed over to Cass, the guard who served as projectionist, and we were allowed an all too brief escape from our ordinary lives. In Hamilton, films had been a refuge; in prison, they were no longer an indulgence — they were a necessary lifeline to the outside world. In those two hours, I could forget my entire past life and my present sorrows.

Without noticing it, I began to see films differently, although I think the cinema itself had changed in the years following the Second World War. Star and siren movies gave way to those much more interested in the ways in which people actually led their lives — their hopes, their wishes, their fantasies, their indiscretions. The age of escapist fantasy had been replaced by the age of grim realism. Mind you, since the films I saw were chosen by Mrs. Nelson and Mrs. White, they had to have a strong educational bias to them. (The wages of sin, etc.)

Some of the films were simply boring family life sagas or costume dramas such as *Cheaper by the Dozen*, *Quo Vadis?*, *The Robe*, *The Ten Commandments*. There was *Sunset Boulevard* in which Gloria Swanson gave the performance of her lifetime as the self-absorbed, faded old actress. Yet when my mind wanders back to the films I saw in prison, I think of the actors and actresses who grabbed my attention. In particular, there is the Jimmy Stewart of *Rear Window* and *Vertigo*. In *Rear Window*, confined to a wheelchair because of an accident, he observes the activities in his low-rise apartment's courtyard; he uses his binoculars to spy on the people who live across the way from him. He witnesses what might be a murder and then uses his girlfriend (Grace Kelly) and an assortment of acquaintances and friends to gather further information for him. As a result, he is almost murdered.

Vertigo is the most repulsive film I have ever seen — I don't care what the film historians say about it. In the first half of the film, Stewart falls in love with Kim Novak's mysterious Madeleine; after she apparently dies, he comes upon Judy — also Kim Novak — whom he attempts to transform into the dead woman. He is harsh and cruel to Judy when she falters in following his most minute instruction as to how to dress and conduct herself like Madeleine, the woman she impersonated. The film is a depiction of obsessive love but more than that it is about the revenge men exact on women who do not occupy the pedestals assigned to them.

In *Mr. Deeds Goes to Washington* and *It's a Wonderful Life*, I had adored Stewart. In the two Hitchcock films I loathed him. Why?, I asked myself. Gradually, it dawned on me that in *Vertigo*, Stewart is a deeply passive person who — once his libido is fired up — becomes capable of great cruelty. As the wheelchair detective in *Rear Window*, he is restless, bored, waiting for something to happen. And then — in pursuit of the truth — almost winds up dead. Stewart's deep-seated passivity spoke to me. In him I saw a form of my youthful self, of the young woman who let others decide her life for her. When I became angry at him, I was, I now realize, merely activating my own self-loathing in being a similar sort of person.

The last film I saw before leaving prison in 1959 haunted me: *Nun's Story*, made into a film by Fred Zinnemann from the best-selling novel based on the real-life story of a Belgian nun, Marie-Louise Habets, is about a woman who, against her father's wishes, left home, became a nun, served as a missionary in the Congo and then abandoned the convent when she no longer felt she had a vocation in the service of God. Audrey Hepburn never gave a better performance. She completely inhabits the character, a person who is perfectly attuned to her own needs and to fulfilling them. She is a rebel, albeit one of a very strange stripe. When she decides to enter the convent, she dexterously tunes out her widowed father's imprecations to stay with him and look after her younger sisters; when she decides her vocation is over, she leaves. She is decisive in an extremely quiet way. This film spoke to me of the ways in which I had not lived my life in the past and of the necessity of becoming a truly independent person once I left Kingston. My fledgling interest in writing had bestowed on me a sense of a new self, but I knew it was going to be extremely difficult to maintain that self in the outside world.

As far as the outside world of Hamilton was concerned, they had one final glimpse of me in an article in the *Spectator* telling in glowing terms of my remarkable success during my first year at P4W playing the Christmas Angel in the annual pantomime. The not-so-subtle implication was that I was on the mend, well on the road to reformation: from whore to heavenly creature.

35

The outside world. What a strange concept that had become for me. What had once seemed ordinary was now bathed in an exotic glow. One constant was the dream, which had many variations at P4W. In one, I walk in broad daylight across a huge stretch of lawn heading towards a huge white church in the distance. After a lot of effort, I seem to be reaching the long set of stairs leading up to the portals. But then the perspective suddenly changes and I come to the sad realization I am making no progress in reaching my destination. My legs are heavy, I breathe heavily, my heart races. Often, that was the entire dream. I wake up exhausted, hardly able to drag myself through the following day.

Then there were the variations in which I reach the church's doors, which I swing open with considerable effort. The interior is deserted, the altar bare, a few comically coloured statues of the Blessed Virgin Mary and Saint Joseph being the only decorations on the walls. Then, off to my left, I see a set of stairs. I walk over to them and with considerable effort negotiate their steep, straight upward movement. I reach the belfry. I then wander over to the periphery and look down at the earth below, which now seems miles away. At that point, I turn to my right, where the baby is lying still, his bright blue eyes looking into mine. He gives me a wide smile and reaches his little hands up to me, signalling I should pick him up. When I do so, I cuddle him and become aware of the sweet smell emanating from him. I am happy; I am relieved. Then, I am aware of someone behind me. I turn around and can see, just beyond the large set of bells and their ropes, a figure in the shadows. Suddenly, that force lunges out at me and grabs the baby. I lose my balance and feel myself plunging towards the ground.

When I told Lydia of this new set of dreams, she was very reassuring. "Guilt, pure and simple. You feel responsible for the baby's death." She touches me on the cheek. "Something which was completely out of your control."

She was right. Yet, no matter how much my attempts at writing had become a buffer zone between myself and my past, the dreams reminded me that I remained the desperately frightened woman who had, from childhood, followed orders. The keeping of a diary can ward off feelings of despair, but it cannot completely vanquish those emotions. My struggle, I now realized, was to believe in myself as some sort of worthy human being.

Years after I had left there, Marjorie Campbell, while researching *Torso*, visited P4W: "Evelyn's record in Kingston was good. She accommodated herself to her changed conditions, got on well with Warden, Matron, and prison personnel, and became a confidante of her fellow inmates, always ready to listen to and give advice concerning their problems. Even today a staff member of that day recalls that Evelyn Dick was a 'nicer woman than many of the others. She had nice manners, never used bad language, and never behaved in a coarse or rude manner.'" Although stripped of any details that might indicate an inner life, the passage is accurate.

If in part a person begins a life of crime because she is bored, she soon learns that prison life is the fulfillment of her worse fears. The schedule had to be obeyed, otherwise, Mrs. Nelson assured us, chaos would gain the upper hand. Then where would we be?

Routine. Regularity. Dullness. Monotony. These are the words that still leap to mind when I think of my twelve years at P4W. During that time, I had only two visitors. I had been in Kingston for almost nine years when Rosie showed up unannounced one day. She had written to me regularly when I was on Barton Street, only half a dozen times since the transfer.

A bit matronly. That was my first (ungenerous) thought as I kissed and embraced her. Her bright yellow hair was as beautiful as ever, although tied up in a chignon. Her grey dress was so severely cut that her body's ample curves escaped the boundaries to which they were unnaturally confined. Simple pearl earings and a matching necklace were her only jewellery. I noticed immediately that she was no longer wearing a wedding ring.

"It's much more comfy here than I expected," she observed, as she looked around the large sitting room in which inmates received guests. I assured her that we were well treated. "Not exactly the lap of luxury, but it's not a bad place."

She smiled, acknowledging my feeble effort to assure her I was not suffering too much. I asked about her parents. Matter-of-factly she told me they had both died within the past eighteen months. She paused and then told me she had seen my mother in downtown Hamilton once in the intervening years.

"I was walking down Barton Street and almost bumped into her. 'Hello, Mrs. MacLean. Nice to see you.' She pretended not to see me, just continued on her way. Then, she and Heather vanished. No one has any idea where. A month or so before she disappeared, she made a funny sort of statement to a reporter from the *Spectator*: 'My husband and I left the farm at Beamsville because the work was too hard for me. But I've often wondered. In fact, I've wondered so many times — if we had stayed on the farm, would things have been different?' I thought it was a strange thing to say."

"Yes, almost like she's blaming Hamilton for what happened.

Mother always had to have a scapegoat. Her simple life in the country was disrupted by moving to the big city. She has an explanation for everything."

"And what about your father? He's next door at the men's prison, isn't he?"

"Yes. I guess so. To be honest, I've no reason to make contact with him. And he obviously feels the same way about me."

"You know, our parents were strange people. Crazy."

"Yes, but your mother and father were 'normal' crazy. Since my mother felt the world owed her a living, she felt deprived when there wasn't enough money. My father felt the same way. I told you years ago: he interfered with me when I was nine or ten. Mother threw him out of their bedroom. I shared a bed with her from that time onwards. Seemed normal at the time."

"My parents hated Jews and coloured people. Both groups were too uppity, taking over the world. Talked about kikes and niggers constantly. But that's as far as their insanity went. Evil words. Now, I've got a really crazy person to deal with. Stephen."

I met Rosie's eyes and only then did I notice the hint of black and blue showing through the heavy makeup on her right jaw. Once detected, the heavy bruising — as on her visit to me at Barton Street — was unmistakable.

"We're separated. But he phones all the time. Threatens me. If I don't come back, he says he'll kill me. If I go back, I know he'll kill me. I don't seem to have any choice."

"You could leave Hamilton. Escape."

"He'd find me. Sometimes I think he's my destiny. He's always been cruel to me, even from the time we first started going out. You know all about that."

"Yes. I remember. He's very nice looking. You were attracted to him. You didn't really know what he was really like."

"Now I know. I'm repenting at my leisure." A brief smile crossed her face. "But I should have got out early. Now I'm cornered."

According to Rosie, she had no option but to make some sort of truce with Stephen. If he agreed not to hit her, she would put her wedding band on again and return home. "Facing the consequences. I'll have to sleep in the bed I made, no matter how uncomfortable it is. Nothing else to do."

When I suggested a more radical surgery might be necessary, she looked at me as if I were a demented child and changed the subject. "Kingston's a pleasant little town. A funny place to build prisons." During the remainder of the afternoon, we gossiped about the nuns at Loretto Academy, school acquaintances, and movie stars. In rapid turn, she talked about Judy Garland's suicide attempt by cutting her throat with a piece of glass. "How can Dorothy from *The Wizard of Oz* want to do herself in? Must be her husband's fault. I see she's just filed for divorce." She mentioned that the court in Monaco had acquitted Errol Flynn of the charge of having sex with a seventeen-year-old girl. "I would have thought boys would be more his thing," she added. "Like us, movie stars have feet of clay. Their lives are not as glamorous as we make them out to be."

"Or as we *want* them to be," I replied.

That day, I realized all over again what a wonderful friend Rosie had been. And continued to be. She had never judged me harshly. In fact, she always tried to see things from my point of view. But an invisible wall had been built between us. I was upset at the way in which she was quite content to let things happen to her, no matter how horrible they might be. My new life was completely different from hers. When all was said and done, she was the caged animal.

I had also become something of a snob. Without realizing it, I had come to see life in literary terms. Clarissa Harlowe would never have allowed Stephen to abuse her physically or mentally. She would have stood up to him. I judged Rosie severely because she did not meet my new standards. Like Richardson's heroine, I preferred a life of isolation to that of involvement. If you become involved, you can be badly hurt. In a strait-jacketed way, I saw two alternatives. Pure black and white. I had no concept of greys. Or, for that matter, colours.

When we parted that day, I asked Rosie to keep in touch. She promised to mend her ways, to write regularly. I reminded her that I could only reply to letters I received. I could not initiate a correspondence. "Oh, is that why you never wrote to me after I stopped writing? That makes me feel better." We walked hand in hand to the door that separated my world from hers.

During the next twenty-four months, I was surprised not to hear from Rosie. I was so worried that, at Lydia's insistence, I asked Mrs. Nelson if I could write to my friend and was told that was an impossibility. "I can't do for one what I can't do for everyone." Out of sight was not quite out of mind — occasionally I thought of Rosie. Almost two years to the day of her visit, Maureen, one of the guards, came to my room to fetch me. "There's an old lady in the visitor's lounge for you."

I didn't know what to think. Mother? Would she suddenly turn up without any warning? My heart beat so rapidly I couldn't move for a minute or two. Then I thought I might faint. "I'll be right down," I assured Maureen, who looked aghast at my performance.

When I finally reached the lounge, the only person seated by herself was a tiny sparrow of a woman. Certainly not Mother. Who was this strange person? I walked towards her, staring into her face in an attempt to place her. It was no use. Obviously a stranger. Then I noticed the hands pockmarked with eczema. At that point, I hazarded a guess. "Mother St. John?"

"You were always extremely observant, Evelyn. But I am now Marian Smith. I left the order two years ago. I happened to be passing through Kingston today on my way to Montreal and decided to pay a call on my favourite student. I hope I haven't startled you? You look like you've seen a ghost."

"I was afraid Mother might be my mysterious visitor. Now I'm just plain relieved. And really happy to see you after all these years."

"It's been a long time. Twenty years? I was a young woman when I taught you at Loretto."

"Yes, many years. So much has happened to me. Or perhaps I should rephrase my statement? I allowed so much to happen to me."

"You had a very difficult childhood. I was startled when I read of your arrest, and I followed all three trials in the newspaper. I knew you weren't capable of murdering anyone. That almost goes without saying. I must confess I did wonder what had become of the sensitive little girl I had taught."

"What about you? I thought the convent was your life."

Marian looked around the room carefully before returning her gaze in my direction. "You know, this room reminds me of the foyer of the convent at Loretto Academy. The same kind of institutional furniture. The uniforms of the guards look like habits. The way the whole place is cut off from everything.

"I guess I saw my entire adult life as a self-imposed jail sentence. So I decided to get out. Live my life, as it were. But I may have left it too late. I have cancer and should be dead within a year. So I'm travelling, leaving for England by boat from Montreal tomorrow night. I plan to visit Jane Austen's home in Hampshire, Shakespeare's birthplace at Stratford-upon-Avon, and the Wordsworth cottage in the Lake District. That will allow me to bring my life to an appropriate conclusion."

I told my old teacher about my renewed interested in reading and then I told her I had begun, in the most tentative of ways, to fictionalize some of the stories the other prisoners had told me.

"Needless to say, I have become unreliable on the subject of vocations, but I always thought the life of the writer might be your true calling. You are not deeply intellectual but you are unusually sensitive and observant. I hope you pursue that path. Perhaps that is your salvation?"

Then we talked books for at least another hour, at which point Marian changed the direction of our conversation. "Did Rosie ever visit you here?"

"Yes. Once. Two years ago. She was not her old self. Very worried and depressed."

"She had every reason. She died six months ago. Shot to death by her estranged husband, who hanged himself in the room in which he murdered her. The incident was whitewashed in the newspapers. The couple were buried together in Holy Mother Church's consecrated ground. Poor woman. The circumstances of her martyrdom were removed from her. "

"I'm not surprised. But I am horrified. Did the *Spectator* cover the story up because of Stephen's family?"

"Exactly. Money talks — especially in Hamilton."

"Rosie was a dear girl. We were wee tiny bairns together on Rosslyn Avenue. Good pals since then, especially at Loretto."

"The world is a very wicked place, Evelyn. Sometimes the only goodness I can discover is between the covers of a book. Strange that there can be so many wonderful visions of the world in fiction and then the world itself is completely bankrupt of goodness."

"I have reached the same frightening conclusion. Reading and writing are the only realties that mean anything to me."

"Maybe you have to follow that observation to its logical conclusion?"

"I've been wondering if it's the only path open to me."

When she stood up to leave, Marian took a pair of gloves out of her handbag, put them on, and kissed me. "I suspect you shall do very well in your new life. You must say a prayer for me in mine." A year later, a few days before I left P4W, I saw the obituary in *The Globe and Mail* for "Marian Smith, previously known as Mother St. John, a true lover of literature."

PART THREE

Elizabeth Delamere

36

I boarded the trans-Canada express at Union Station in Toronto on the evening of October 12, 1959, the day I was released from P4W. Janet White drove me to Toronto. Earlier that week, she had arranged to collect the remaining money in my bank account in Buffalo — $412. She also bought a new wardrobe for me and helped me to dye my hair red. To the remaining money she added the two hundred dollars given to all parolees. So that evening I had just over five hundred dollars in cash before I purchased the train ticket.

Why settle in Vancouver? I asked myself many times that evening. Janet also made the same query. My response was simple enough: "I wish to go as far away from Ontario as humanly possible.

Besides, I have always liked the idea of a place that blends water with mountains."

"But Vancouver is such a dreary place, dear. Not a real city, no real culture. The Canadian equivalent of Australia. A lot of remittance men and undesirables there. Rains all the time."

Before she could inform me of the current status of research on the undesirability of Vancouver as a place to live, I was safely on board waving good-bye to her. When I kissed her, Janet blushed, obviously unused to any demonstration of emotion.

Nestled among my clothes in my large suitcase was my small archive: seven small diaries and four scribblers filled with notes, observations, and stories. As I waited for the train to leave the station, I began re-reading *Pilgrim's Progress*.

The notion of living in Vancouver had occurred to me when I read of the magnificent Carnegie Library Building built just after the turn of the century at Hastings and Main, next door to City Hall. During my time at P4W, the idea of a huge library where one could become lost in a world of books was entrancing. Confined for so long, I also hungered for a large city through which I could wander anonymously. So when the train finally pulled into Vancouver station, accompanied by two large suitcases, I asked a cabbie to take me to the Carnegie Building.

The shabbiness of the building and its immediate surroundings startled me. Unrealistically, I had expected a new Athens but all I saw was Skid Row, a plaintive collection of civic buildings that had seen far better days. Panhandlers roamed the neighbourhood; houses were in a bad state of repair; drugs — especially heroin — were freely available at many street corners. I did not know that during the Depression the Relief Camp Workers Union had occupied the building in May 1935. I was unaware that the Japanese — incarcerated during the Second World War — had not returned to this area. I hadn't realized that Main and Hastings was now segregated from the rest of the city. Gastown, a few blocks away, was another hideous mess.

I saw no evidence of what the Americans called "the San Francisco of the North." The water and the mountains were not readily visible. Even today, Canada's third largest city is thought to be an exceedingly glamorous place. That is so — if the constant, relentless, destructive powers of rain are forgotten. Many are the days without sunshine leading to depression and, sometimes, suicide.

My first instinct was to flee, stay in a hotel for a day or two, take my bearings and find another spot in which to live. If necessary, I thought, I could flee into the interior of British Columbia like Maggie Vardoe in Ethel Wilson's *Swamp Angel*, a book I had read in prison. But I had no idea how long it would take me to find work and on paper I had no real qualifications. Besides, I was a jail bird. Would any respectable business hire me? I might have to work as a waitress, a job that might not require me to divulge my true identity.

Frightened by my limited resources and dismal prospects, I walked a few blocks east and took a room on Alexander Street. The house, long broken into a rabbit warren of small rooms, smelled of grease, stale food and sweat. However, my new landlady, a women in her forties, was spiffy in her dress. Her hair colouring was from a bottle, but her lipstick and makeup were of the genteel variety. Of medium height and an olive complexion, she did not look like she had come down in the world.

"Take no account of the debris," Mrs. Skeffington announced a trifle grandly. "I am about to rid myself of some of the undesirables. A refined woman like yourself has nothing to fear. Within a day or two, an entirely new species of tenant will occupy these premises. People like yourself."

I wasn't sure where she was going to find such people, but I was exhausted and needed to sleep before collecting myself and perhaps finding other accommodation. Two weeks later I learned that my landlady had appeared on Alexander Street only the day before me. Recently widowed, she was a full-figured woman with magenta hair, creamy white skin and clear blue eyes. In contrast to her Amazonian girth, she carried herself in a delicate, ballet-like way. Emma, I was soon to discover, was a woman of extremes.

The house was the only legacy her slum landlord husband had left when he died suddenly. I was to be a member of a new dispensation. By and large, Emma — who had once been "on the game" but had reformed herself — was a woman of her word, although it took her over a month to build her new Jerusalem.

For the moment, I had a bed, a chest of drawers, and a washstand. My new home wasn't even as nice as what I was used to at P4W, but at least I could come and go as I pleased. A very new feeling, positively revolutionary — and I took advantage of that freedom. Early the next day, I toured the neighbourhood. The New Station Café was Chinese and pristine clean. The Chili Bar, around the corner from Vi's Steak House, catered to blacks and was open twenty-fours a day. (Two weeks later, I heard Mahalia Jackson sing there.) The other nearby black establishment was Harlem Nocturne. West of the Broadway Hotel was the White Lunch, a cafeteria with huge, broad windows looking into the street. There were chairs with steam-bent backs and steel-based tables with tin tops that you couldn't move. People lived there. They would get a cup of coffee and sit and sit and sit.

The language of my new streets I soon discovered was deeply imaginative: "blocks" were the wristwatches stolen off hapless tourists who happened to stray on to Hastings; "banana toes" were shoes; "bennies," Benzedrine. There was even "street poetry," strange words rhymed together in a stew of words; this genre was created by inmates in the British Columbia penal system and became a secret language among them once they returned to civilian life. Then there were the various conmen who worked the streets: "wangies," beggars who sold shoelaces, "timbers," who sold pencils, and the "blinkies" who had lost one or both eyes. These were at the higher end of this class system. Less elevated were the "grease tails," "jungle buzzards," and the "yeggs," the vagrants who didn't even pretend to any kind of genuine claim on the sympathies of the passers-by from whom they asked assistance.

There were many others. Plain and simple rubby-dubs. Failed prospectors reduced to mining the last glint of fool's gold in a bottle of rum. Crippled choker men from the interior. These were streets of broken dreams and criminal idleness. During my first stroll that afternoon, I also saw men and women dealing drugs and scoring tricks. The junkies congregated around Viaduct Drugs, in many ways the parish church. There were pawn shops, cinemas (all of which advertised midnight movies), a gay bar called The New Fountain and its brother establishment, Hastings Steam Bath. In comparison to Vancouver, Hamilton had been a very staid place. I was certain my parole officer would caution me against living in such a spot.

Although I had not given much thought to it, I had somehow imagined that person as someone out of the movies, perhaps a tough-guy outside, sentimental-man inside kind of person. Drew Smith defied all expectations. Almost seven feet tall in an era when basketball was not a big-time sport, his body was tubular in construction but stretched itself to resemble the letter S. His head and shoulder formed the top, his chest then sank inwards, his stomach stretched outwards whereupon his hips began an inward descent culminating in his sandal-clad feet that formed a perfect parallel line with his head and upper torso. Smith's hair resembled a very disorderly robin's nest, his clothing best described as tatty. He was not an authority figure. And he did not attempt to be one.

"Evelyn, I have heard many good things about you from Mrs. White. One of her best girls ever, she claims." He gestured for me to take a seat. He smiled, making no attempt to conceal missing and black-covered teeth. "I understand I do not have to worry about you. Have been assured you have no intention of becoming a working girl."

"I don't intend to become a street-walker or any kind of prostitute."

"Exactly. Am very relieved. That's where your troubles began."

"I'm well aware of that. You don't have to worry about my reverting to type."

"Perfect. And you don't mind Skid Row?"

"No. Do you?"

"Not at all. I live three doors down from you." He grinned: "Bet you didn't know that?" On reflection, I could have guessed. "No. My major concern is that you settle in on the West Coast. We're kind of different here, you know, from people back east. Don't give ourselves all your airs and graces."

"That's a relief."

He smiled. "We take people as they come. Have you ever read Malcolm Lowry? He died a few years back."

"I've meant to."

"No real need to, I suppose. He was a pal of mine. Settled here for a while. Out in Dollarton. The things he got up to. Once he was out walking with his wife. Right around here. They got into a fight. He took off. Disappeared down a street. Later that night, in the pouring rain, she ran him to ground. He'd taken refuge in a whorehouse, across the street from where you are. He'd sold his clothes for liquor and had only his shorts left. She climbed into bed with him to keep him warm. The next morning, the wife threatened the owner of the house, who had sold all of Malcolm's things: 'Get him some clothes or I'm calling the police.' A few minutes later the couple was back out on the street. Malcolm was wearing a suit with more moth holes than wool; the shoes they gave him were four sizes too big. He didn't care. All he wanted was a glass of beer! Needed his next fix." Perhaps thinking his anecdote not very edifying, he changed subjects. "Have you thought about what kind of job you want?"

"I suspect waitressing is all I'll be able to get. If I tell people who I really am, I don't imagine any respectable employer will want me."

"Not necessarily so. What kind of a job would you like? In a library?"

"That would be perfect."

"Have to start small. The public library on Robson is advertising for stackers, people who put the books back on the shelves. You would probably enjoy that environment." I agreed with him. He gave me the name of the librarian in charge of hiring at that branch, told me to tell the truth about my identity, but he suggested I might wish to create a false name for all other purposes. He even volunteered to obtain a social security card for me under any identity I assumed.

After the streetcar deposited me in front of the Robson Street Library about an hour later, I became confused. There seemed to be two libraries side-by-side. Then, I noticed one was a bookstore. What a strange thing to do, I thought. Imagine opening a bookstore next to a library. Intrigued by the apparent folly, I decided to inspect Duthie Books, the name indicated by the sign in the window. The place was bustling, the books arranged in attractive juxtapositions on tables, and five or six readers had hunched themselves against the wall, browsing as if the place were an extension of the library. The person in charge was a busy-as-a-bee man who seemed quite unperturbed by his non-paying guests. I asked him if he had a copy of *East Lynn*.

"That tear-jerker! Why would a sensible woman like yourself waste her time with a book like that?"

I smiled a little embarrassingly. "I know, I know. But it has its moments, even though they are overly sentimental."

"Are you a deeply emotional woman, given to tears at frequent, inconvenient moments?" This was said in the most genial and friendly of ways.

"No, not exactly how I would describe myself. A feeling reader."

"The best kind. Unfortunately, I do not have a copy of the classic you seek. I'm sure you'll find it next door."

"Yes. I'm heading that way." Not terribly sure of myself but now very curious, I decided to ask why the bookstore was located next to a library.

"The best possible place for a bookstore. I've been here almost ten years now, and, despite appearances, I've been thriving. I was a publisher's representative for years, always wanted to own a bookstore, these premises became available, and I decided to set up shop. The real readers go to libraries, I told myself, but they'll come to me for the books they want to own. Real readers have to own books. That's my philosophy. I've had a few hiccups but basically everything's gone well. Now, there's a new revolution. Paperbacks." He pointed to the back of the store, where I could see two or three workmen excavating the basement. "I'm going to open a paperback-only bookstore there in a week's time." Then, he switched subjects. "Are you a librarian, a writer perhaps?"

"I know a lot about building a library, but I have no professional qualifications. I was hoping to get a job next-door as a stacker."

"As a stacker? You seem a bit too refined for that kind of back-breaking work. Why don't you come here? Take a job at Duthie's? I need someone to help in the new section. By the way, I'm Bill Duthie."

I asked if we might retire to his office. "I haven't got much of one," he observed, as he pointed to a little hole in a nearby wall. We retreated there, and I made a full confession of my identity. He had read all about Evelyn Dick, but he was fairly certain that few people in British Columbia knew about the crimes and the trials. Then, he informed me: "I'm an excellent judge of character. Have gotten where I am through that. I have no hesitation in hiring you, but I think you need a new name. Should we put our heads together on that one?" Actually, he invented my new name on the spot. "You have a regal bearing and red hair. What about Elizabeth for a first name. One of my favourite writers is Walter Delamere, the poet and children's writer. Delamere has a very classy sound to it. What about Elizabeth Delamere?" And so my new self finally had a name.

37

Emma Skeffington turned out to be a trusted ally. No one in Skid Row cared who I was she informed me, but, like Drew Smith, she advised me it would behoove me to live under an assumed name. "It's the reporters you have to be careful of," she added. "They'll do you in. No need to attract that kind of notice." And so I became known as Elizabeth to everyone. Never Betty or Liz or Libby.

If used properly, a name can be a precious gift, a signifier of one's aspirations. In allowing myself to be called Elizabeth, I was telling myself to assume a regal aspect, to act as if I were a person of worth. Sometimes the actress becomes the person she is portraying. I wanted my new name to clothe me in a whole new identity.

Even then I knew I was going to have a lonely existence. I decided to set myself apart, never to be vulnerable again to the kind of meddling that had ruined my life. To many — then and now — I seemed distant and remote. I didn't necessarily want it that way; it had to be so. On occasion, I would let my guard down, but I did not wish to be destroyed by the past. Sometimes isolation is the only defence worth pursuing.

"Vancouver is a pretty girl who uses the wrong makeup. She's ripe, overdeveloped. A lot of men want to explore her curves. If she's ruined, they could care less." That was Emma's analysis of the civic history of my new neighbourhood. Bringing her metaphors closer to home, she added: "Older women — such as ourselves — know the wages of sin first-hand. By nature, we are pessimists. We also know how to survive." Perfectly aware of the importance of style as well as substance, my landlady — an admirer of Oscar Wilde — was supremely wise in the squiffy ways of the world. Under her tutelage, I became cautiously optimistic. Perhaps this was a place into which I could fit, live the quiet life that I felt fortune and fate owed me. I didn't have to be overly compliant, but I had to be exceedingly resourceful.

At work, I had many details to master. I had to learn to deal with publishers' representatives, the distraught authors who visited the shop to discover their books were not on the shelves, and the customers who craved help in their selection of books. Bill claimed I was exceedingly gracious to everyone, but I suspect he found me a bit frosty. I was always polite, almost always cordial, and many times very friendly. But anyone who felt I kept a large portion of myself in reserve was correct. I was not a person to wear her emotions on her sleeves. To many, the windowless basement rooms on Robson Street would have been a source of depression. To me, the work space was miraculous. It may have been a little like a prison, but I knew that every day I descended into that chamber I would be able to ascend again a few hours later, at lunchtime or at the end of the workday.

One of my first customers was a large, cumbersomely moving mountain of a woman perfectly attired in an elegant, tailored suit that would have done Queen Mary proud. With that monarch, she shared the same peachy complexion obtained by a masterly understanding of how to combine powders and rouges. Virtually identical slightly curled white hair and small, recessed but penetrating blue eyes. This person wore glasses rather than a pince-nez, but I was tempted to curtsy when she headed in my direction. She's going to be very starchy, I thought to myself. And indeed she was.

"I am Mrs. Wilson."

I nodded in agreement at this apparent truism.

"I am not at all pleased by the selection of titles that greets me in Duthie's basement. In fact, I am outraged."

I explained that we were still in the process of developing our selection. For instance, we were going to stock the entire Everyman's Library. "They're hard bounds but at paperback prices," I explained.

"You have anticipated my complaint, miss. Exactly what I was going to remonstrate with you about. You require more translations from the French and German down here. I feel very reassured by the information with which you have supplied me. If you will permit a crude metaphor, Vancouver needs culture to be injected directly into its clogged arteries." I nodded in agreement as the woman with considerable difficulty mounted the steps to the upper world.

A few minutes later, Bill Duthie came hurling down the stairs. "Ethel Wilson was very impressed with you. Informed me I had hired the ideal *coadjutor*. I think you will be invited to tea in a day or two. You must take the afternoon off when she requests your presence." This was an order from the boss, a role Bill was not usually comfortable with.

"You mean *the* Ethel Wilson?"

"Yes. But she is always Mrs. Wilson. You never take liberties with that woman. She is excessively formal. She can also be dangerous. I once accompanied her to a cocktail party where we bumped into Jack Wasserman, the gossip columnist for the *Sun*.

"'May I introduce Mr. Wasserman?' I offered in an offhand manner.

"There was a long pause. Then, in her slyest manner, she whispered: 'How do you do, Mr. Wasserman?'

"He said nothing. Mrs. Wilson stared ahead. I was left in a void and so I tried to fill it. 'Of course you read Mr. Wasserman's column?'

She looked at me askance: 'I don't have to answer your question. I don't need to tell you what I read or don't read.'

"Not sure what to do, I continued — very unsure of how much trouble I was letting myself in for: 'No, really, *do* you or *don't* you read the column?'

"'I have reached an age when I don't have to answer a question unless I want to!'

"Wasserman bowed politely in Mrs. Wilson's direction but gave me a sharp look. He made some innocuous remark in next day's paper about meeting Vancouver's literary grand dame. So forewarned is forearmed. The lady can be a mite difficult."

Sure enough, the summons came three days later. I have chosen the word "summons" carefully; I cannot call it an invitation. Mrs. Wilson's maid phoned Bill to tell him I would be received at four o'clock the following Monday afternoon. That weekend, I re-read *Swamp Angel* and *Hetty Dorval*; I read *Love and Salt Water* — published a few years before — for the first time.

Mrs. Wilson's formidable presence had been preparation of sorts for the high-ceilinged, resolutely old-fashioned flat in the West End. From her sitting room, she could see down into the waters of False Creek. She also had an unobstructed view of islands and mountains. The room was lined with books, oriental rugs were scattered everywhere over the hardwood floor, and a photograph of Winston Churchill and a pencil sketch by Burne-Jones graced the walls. A uniformed maid — I later learned her name was Phyllis Marshall, although her mistress always addressed her as Marshall — answered the door, took my coat and gloves, and then announced me to a room that appeared at first to be empty. After some effort, I could see a small bed at the far end of the room on which Mrs. Wilson was lying prone. She waved her hand in greeting and then used it to beckon me in her direction. "Hello Ducks," she called out. "I am delighted you are able to join me."

Although I never questioned her on the subject, I later learned that the arthritis in Mrs. Wilson's right hip was so bad on some days that she could barely walk. I took my seat close to her, at which point Marshall returned with the silver tea service. On that day I did not meet Wallace Wilson, my hostess's kindly physician husband.

That afternoon, I decided that Ethel was much more like Nell Severance than she had ever been like Maggie Vardoe. In *Swamp Angel*, elderly Nell is the owner of the revolver that gives the book its name. She is difficult, controlling, and utterly loveable. She also displays a sinister edge when she threatens Maggie's estranged husband. Nell is also unduly inquisitive about others; she is never content to mind her own business. I had been summoned to tea to be interrogated by Nell's creator.

Mrs. Wilson began on safe ground by quizzing me about books. I passed that test with flying colours, but then the real purpose of our meeting surfaced.

"I have observed that you have a very precise way of talking. Very crisp, right to the point. Have you always been like that?"

"I'm not sure. That skill seems to have come to me with age."

"You are still a young woman. Exactly how old are you?"

"Thirty-nine. Almost 40."

"And you are from Toronto I have been told."

"Near Toronto. Hamilton."

"The steel city? I have never been there. Why have you suddenly appeared in our midst? Why would a woman of your age and cultivation suddenly arrive on our doorstep? Are you a woman with a past?"

"You are a bit forward. I'm not sure I mind telling you about myself, but I've become fearful of sharing my secret with too many people. You are a writer, always looking for grist for her mill. Will you spare me?"

"My dear, you'll never know unless you confide in me."

Nell's curiosity in *Swamp Angel* was benign — if she liked the person she was interrogating. I decided she meant me no harm. And so for the next hour I told her my life history. No sign of amazement crossed her face, although she paid close attention to everything I said, once or twice interrupting me to ask for clarification. When I concluded, she pulled herself up slightly. "Dear, will you sort out my pillow?" she asked. When I finished doing so, she took my hands in hers and looked into my soul with her crystal blue eyes. "Like you, I am an immigrant to British Columbia, although I arrived here many years ago by way of South Africa and England. Both of us are outsiders — kindred spirits despite many differences." She stopped speaking and drew her shoulders up: "You have found a genuine confidante, Elizabeth." She should have added: "And a warm friend."

"Send me some of the pieces you've penned. I am most anxious to read them. Perhaps one of them could be turned into a short story?"

38

Two years ago, a reader of mine sent me a transcript of the following material in the Ethel Wilson archive at the University of British Columbia. I was as relieved to see these documents did not bare anything too revealing about my early history as I was touched by her generous words.

[Diary entry for 12 June 1960]

Some would say Elizabeth is strange. Some would call her withdrawn. The same adjectives are often applied to me — behind my back.

Recently, in confidence, she told me of her childhood and young womanhood. Before she began, she told me I would be shocked. When all was said, I was much surprised and profoundly saddened — but not shocked. The entire human condition is one of oppression and repression. Why should I be shocked that life has bestowed on this poor woman a goodly share of both?

[excerpt from a carbon copy of a typewritten letter to Earle Birney, October 14, 1962]

Dear Earle,

I have read and re-read with sympathetic pleasure a piece named "Prison Walls," by Elizabeth Delamere. I am sending you the typescript. Why my heart warmed and expanded towards Miss Delamere is because I have never before seen in print an admission of frailty or an honesty that is sympathetic to my own. Perhaps I am inordinately self-centred and simply see a reflection of myself in this woman?

[Handwritten draft of a letter of 4 October 1974, just after the publication of my first novel]

Dear Elizabeth,

What a darling you are to send me the glorious book, right from the fine texture and binding — the gold, the monogram, the paper, the type — the outside and then blazoning into the inside. I simply can't say all I feel. To me — it is just gorgeous. To me — despite all the suffering you describe so relentlessly — it is a *great* book. I believe some people could not read it because it is the very life of life, and they do not know about life.

Sitting here alone in the living room today — terribly worried about my health that continues to plummet — I imagined your early life. The despair of it all, the deep pain you endured, the humiliations, the unkindnesses poured on you by your mother and father, the very people who should have offered you consolation. You are very much like my dear Maggie in *Swamp Angel*, although she took off before she would have been forced to murder her beast of a husband.

Love can be a beautifully ferocious thing. You have endured only the ferocious — have never been allowed to touch the beauty. Is that why you write like an angel? Has the compensating grace sometimes given to those who suffer greatly been bestowed upon you? Yes. Most certainly. Much was taken away; much has now been given. Only you can decide if becoming a great writer is sufficient payment for the unhappinesses of the past. Lovingly, Ethel.

39

The hours long, the reward negligible. That was the painful lesson I learned soon after I began, at Ethel's instigation, to write with any kind of eye to publication. Since my working life consisted of the often difficult task of inciting would-be readers to purchase other people's stories, I often felt drained by the whole notion of creating my own. I also had to read a lot of books in order to talk about them. That took a lot of time. In many ways, I was overburdened by the book world, by the entire process of making books desirable to consumers. Moreover, I could only write in the evenings, on the few evenings after work when I did not have a book to read urgently. Having little confidence in getting anything published, I did not in my early days in Vancouver actively pursue the craft of writing.

During my afternoon visits with Ethel, I told her I was not a born writer. "Nonsense, dear. No one is simply given — hocus-pocus fashion — the act of conjuring a book from a hat. It takes a great deal of hard work. You have the raw talent. In embryo. You must apply yourself. Read and read. Avoid pretentiousness. Cultivate your interest in people — study them carefully at the bookstore — the nice customers, the old so-and-so's like me. You will instinctually know what to leave out — all good writers know about reticence."

These instructions, although kindly meant, were not helpful. I knew the stories I wanted to tell, but they were not yet inside me enough. Unwilling to be summoned like performing dogs, eager for reward and praise, they balked. The more I insisted, the more obdurate they became.

Emma Skeffington had no time for books. "A complete waste of time as far as I'm concerned," she bluntly informed me. Yet, she often asked me to use my employee discount to purchase self-help manuals (how to increase your self-esteem, how to become a more dynamic person, how to transform yourself into the powerful person you really are). Strangely enough, her idea of real culture was centred on the foreign films that were just beginning to attract attention in North America. She looked at me askance if I suggested going to *Breakfast at Tiffany's*, *Imitation of Life*, even *Lawrence of Arabia*. Her interest was entirely engaged by the "New Wave": Truffaut's *Jules et Jim*, Fellini's *La Dolce Vita*, Antonioni's *L'Avventura*. Hollywood films were, according to her, "pure schlock, formula films that tell us the same unrealistic things over and over again. Nauseating." If I attempted to tell her of my admiration for some of the stars in the ascent at that time — someone like Audrey Hepburn — she simply directed a look of complete incredulity in my direction and then let loose a string of invectives. She would always conclude her tirades with the same sentence: "You can go to that film by yourself!" I often did exactly that, but many an evening I accompanied her to the latest subtitled film to reach Vancouver.

After a while, I became a convert to the new cinema. I never had much time for the whirling camera shots and the anxiety-filled voice-overs. But those films, almost always about impossible human life struggles, never had final answers. Perhaps they were too ambivalent and ambiguous in their depiction of the human condition, but the faces, the bodies, the insurmountable problems were genuine.

In particular, I remember Bergman's *The Virgin Spring* wherein the young, chaste, beautiful girl is brutally raped and murdered. I have never forgotten the sequence where her mother and father see her mangled remains. Those parents take some consolation in religious belief, but Bergman does not: her cruel and unnecessary death is part and parcel of life's many grim realities.

After six months on Skid Row, I had put enough aside to move. I found the perfect place on Thurlow Street, a few blocks away from Duthie's on Robson. My second-floor apartment was a small one — tiny excuses for a bedroom and a washroom — but it had the advantage of an enormous living-cum-dining room with a large window that gave me a magnificent view of the water. The flat — above a men's clothing store — also allowed me a perfect view of the busy street and its shops. Directly opposite me was a pharmacy, a delicatessen, and a hardware store. Quite soon — after I had put aside another tidy sum — I had book cases built into every available corner of the room.

My next acquisition was a strange one for me: a cat. Not just an ordinary cat, it turned out. Casper, a Russian Blue, was a giant kitten who became an enormous cat. A creature of big paws but delicate feelings, he gave forth an enormous bellow if a visitor was careless enough to compliment me on my magnificent grey cat. Casper calmed down only when I explained to my startled visitor that the animal had a noble lineage, in fact considered himself a descendant of felines who had been attendants of the czars of Russia, and that he was very definitely blue in colour. Casper was also a very literary companion who approved of books. When I settled in my armchair to read, he seated himself at my feet, purring loudly his approval. If I wrote in an evening seated at the large table at the window, he would join me there, placing himself a foot or so away from my scribbler. At such times, the crescendo of his purrs assumed startling modulations in its rising and falling sounds.

My former landlady was Casper's most cherished guest. Emma despised all cats. Perfectly aware of this frailty, Casper showered her with the most gentlemanly of attentions when he approached her, even condescending to roll on his back in mock-submission the moment he beheld her. Emma was convinced he was making fun of her, but the cat had the makeup of a courtier. I think he wanted to convince her she must love him and, if that happened, wouldn't that open the door to all others of his species?

At Duthie's, Bill gave me more and more responsibility for stocking the paperback section, which thrived. I relished talking about books with young people, especially the bookish misfits who asked my advice about what books to read, their eyes wide as saucers as I told them I envied the pleasure they would experience meeting Defoe, Tolstoy or Cervantes for the first time. There were the hard-to-please customers, who automatically rejected every suggestion offered them in response to their earnest requests to help them find something exciting or new.

My favourite customer in those early days was a conservatively dressed, ultra-slim housewife with high cheek bones, brightly burning eyes, and a mischievous smile. She had lived in Africa for a number of years — had recently returned from there with her engineer husband and two small children — and had begun to write seriously in Ghana. She told me she hated the "whole goddamn racket" of writing fiction. "I can't stop myself, but it feels like I'm being torn apart from the inside. I hate myself for doing it. I'm like a moth drawn to the flame that will kill it." Mainly we talked writers, not writing. She was amazed that I liked John Galsworthy's *Forsyte Saga*. Much too upper-class for her, she assured me. "I consider myself a socialist." Once I told her I had literary ambitions of my own: "Kid, you're crazy if you go down that path. Take it from someone who has just about gone bonkers." I laughed; she smiled. Yet I knew very well she was telling me a desperate truth.

I never knew Margaret Laurence outside Duthie's, but I have never forgotten her description of the writing life as a bad habit, like cigarette smoking, that one could never get out of one's system. She always needed, she confessed, to have her daily fix. In those days, I had yet to succumb.

Once or twice she confided to me her thoughts about Vancouver as a literary backwater. "There's that booze hound, Malcolm Lowry, who croaked a few years ago. He used to live in a shack in Dollarton on the edge of this *great* metropolis. And there's friendly old Earle Birney. He's a decent poet but a first-class skirt chaser. Be careful of him when he comes in here. The only *real* writer in Vancouver is Mrs. Wilson.

"I'll have to leave Canada if I want to turn myself into any kind of real writer. I can't go to the States — I would become one of *them*. Maybe England. There's a semblance of a literary community there."

Nowadays, Laurence's comment seems awfully cynical, but she was correct. I had learned that the "San Francisco of the North" may have been much more lushly beautiful than Hamilton, but in the 1960s it had an identical village soul.

Within a year of settling in Vancouver, my life had assumed a comfortable rhythm. I liked my work and my flat. Emma was a congenial companion. My teas with Mrs. Wilson made me feel in touch with a living literary culture, although I doubted I could ever become part of that tradition myself. On the surface, everything was going well. But the dream visited me every night. Sometimes I frightened Casper, my bed companion, when I awoke from a particularly heinous variant. For that reason, I decided to consult Dr. Newman.

40

My first memory of Dr. Newman is of his small office in the Medical-Dental building on Georgia. The corridor leading to the consulting room was exceptionally narrow. In particular, I remember how difficult it was to avoid touching the eight prints of *Death* by Käthe Kollwitz — four on each side — that lined that meagre space. Afraid those eerie works of art — monumental yet deeply sombre etchings bitten deeply into the plate of men and women suffering from terminal malnutrition — might determine the mood for what went on in the room, I asked him on the first day why those depressing representations of the end of life were there. Of course, he did not answer the question. "Why do you think I put them there? What are your fantasies about them?"

All of this was asked in flat, accentless English. If there was German underneath it, I could not catch it. No harsh sibilants, no wheezing guttural noises. My interrogator was about my age, I guessed. Completely bald and round, he had large brown eyes that concealed all emotion.

As I looked around the consulting room, I was amazed at the bright, geometrically coloured rugs that covered the floor and the walls. Navajo, I guessed. A small desk and accompanying chair, an even tinier chair for patients, a large leather-covered, reclining chair for Newman, and the couch. These four articles of furniture were uneasily crowded into the room which, although it was not windowless might just as well have been. The shade — a dingy brown — was always completely drawn.

From Newman emanated several distinct smells of body odour, cigars, and the cologne by means of which he attempted to drown the other two. If the doctor was repulsed by what I eventually told him — after almost two long months — of the murder of John Dick, my various appearances in court, and my sojourn in P4W, he concealed those feelings. On the day I finally confessed, he asked: "Why have you come here? What can I do for you?"

"I feel completely lost. I have managed to establish some sort of equilibrium in my daily life, but I do not know where I am going."

"You feel lost in a dark wood?"

I was pleased he had read Dante. "Exactly. I have many questions about the past."

"This room might be the entirely appropriate place in which to interrogate your childhood and young adulthood. Is that what you are trying to tell me?" The last question was voiced impatiently. I nodded agreement.

"If you wish to pursue this matter in the kind of detail it requires, I am at your service. You would need to come four times a week faithfully." He stopped and, for the first time, looked directly into my eyes: "Are you prepared for that? It is very difficult work, extremely painful. I cannot promise the result will be to your liking."

"Will I become a more aware person?"

"Yes. I can promise that. But knowledge — especially self-knowledge — is often a heavy burden."

"I must understand my early life more clearly. At least, more accurately."

"Fine. We can begin next Monday."

My sessions with Dr. Newman were extremely predictable. I spoke for virtually the entire fifty minute duration of each meeting. Since I occupied the couch, Dr. Newman directly behind me, I only saw him for about twenty seconds each day when he answered the door to his office and then showed me out. I had a difficult time remembering what he looked like. At the outset, he would occasionally ask me to clarify a point. Or explain something I tried to skip over. "Did your father place his penis in your mouth? Did your mother touch your vagina when you two shared a bed? Did you experience sexual pleasure when you went to bed with one of your clients? Did Bill Bohozuk excite you sexually? Were you sexually attracted towards any of the women you knew at Kingston?"

Strange to say, I found these questions comforting, sensing that Dr. Newman was trying to come to some sort of scientific understanding. Most of the time he was resolutely silent. Whenever I asked a question, he always turned it back on me. Why did I want to know such a thing? He would then ask if I had fantasies about his real life as opposed to his existence in the room sitting behind me, pen and pad in hand, occasionally smoking a cigar or cigarette? His silence seemed cold when I told him I had little or no interest in such matters. What thoughts — if any — did I have of the "private" life I had no interest in? Surely I had some reflections on this aspect of his existence?

"Although I cannot tell where your slight accent comes from, I imagine you are from somewhere in middle Europe, that you are about five years older than me, that you may have been in a concentration camp, that your wife and children may have been murdered in the Holocaust, and that, like me, you are tormented by events you had little or no control over."

Dr. Newman did not reply. Throughout the remainder of that day, I felt guilty about voicing my fantasies. The silence in which he existed during the sessions was for my benefit, not supposed to be contaminated by his life. And yet I felt I had been cruel because, I was certain, my potted biography had hit the mark.

I was never embarrassed about the sexual details that emerged in the sessions. Now I remembered my father forcing me to attempt fellatio — but I was too young, my mouth too small. I could now recall Mother rubbing the hairs on my pudenda when I was 12 or 13. I knew all over again that the pleasures of the body had always been forbidden me. What began to bother me in a new way was the absolute distance between my body and my soul. I was so completely empty of the physical.

My deep-down humanity — if I can call it that — was concentrated on my children, all three of them. I would see a sixteen- or seventeen-year-old girl on the street and become convinced she was Heather: same colouring, same nose, same shape to the mouth. Two or three times I followed these teenagers in order to get a better look. After each close inspection I realized my error. Although I made the rational assumption that Heather was alive somewhere, probably in Ontario, I knew the two babies were dead, absolutely unrecoverable. When I got up some mornings, I felt like I lived in the kingdom of death. The world I would confront on such days was only a simulacrum — the real world was one of shadows, of murder, of prostitution, of dead and lost children.

Dr. Newman was very sparing in offering me interpretations. One afternoon, after I had been seeing him almost eighteen months, I had been talking about what I called my horrible crimes — the ensnarement of John Dick, the neglect of my baby son murdered by my father. Dr. Newman could not contain himself: "You have a profound misunderstanding of your past. You allowed others to coerce you into doing what you consider evil. In essence, you were a witness to evil and could do very little about it. Or so you thought. Your frailty is one you share with many others in this century: you witnessed evil and did little or nothing to stop it."

"You are saying I was a victim?"

"If you choose to employ that word, I won't object."

"What word would you use?"

"You are always looking for labels that mean little or nothing." His voice became darker, much more resonant. "When Hitler first came to power in Germany, his agenda was clear-cut. Most Jews did little or nothing to stop him. Later — when the worst atrocities were being committed — most Christians in the know were deeply passive, believing — perhaps rightly — that the monster could not be destroyed. So they became fellow-travellers.

They weren't arm in arm with Satan, but they tolerated his existence because he was so powerful."

"So I'm a fellow-traveller?"

"Again, you want a simple label. I am suggesting you had little control over what happened to you. You carry a heavy weight of unjustified guilt and must learn to jettison that burden. My job is to help you do exactly that." Having delivered himself of this observation, Dr. Newman was largely silent for almost a year.

41

Emma was extremely cynical of my visits to Dr. Newman. "You go there four times a week in order to talk to the walls! And, what's more, you pay good money for the privilege! I call that a waste of time."

I insisted that I found the process mysterious but helpful. "I'm getting a better handle on things."

"And getting your head shrunken in the process. What about books and movies as a way of self-understanding? That's how I use films. In them, I'm always seeing various parts of myself. That way I can think through certain parts of my life."

"Psychoanalysis is about putting all the pieces of the puzzle together. Integrating them."

"But no one does that in real life — complete the crossword puzzle that is their existence. What is more, I don't think they should do so."

That evening, Emma was reclining on my sofa, Casper as was his wont nestled in her bosom. Having learnt that any expression of disdain would simply make the cat more insistent in his wooing, she was studiously trying to pretend he wasn't there. Although she and I had become good friends over the years, we had widely differing views on most subjects. For her, the masterpiece of sixties' cinema was Buñuel's excessively cynical *Belle de Jour* about a bored Parisian housewife who becomes a prostitute. According to Emma, Buñuel was aware of the tremendous pleasures of the flesh at the very same time he satirized hedonistic indulgence. I told her I found the film tasteless and offensive.

"That's because you've always closed yourself off from the body. No wonder you don't care for *Belle*."

"I don't think that bored housewives become call girls. That's Buñuel's twisted, puerile view of the French bourgeoisie."

"What you are forgetting is that sex — even sex for money — can be fun." Very much in the manner of one of Ingres's odalisques, she stretched herself languidly, in the process dislodging an irate Casper. That evening Emma told me about her early life in greater detail than she had ever done before.

"I was a farm girl from Kelowna. Perfectly happy upbringing. Devoted but old-fashioned parents. I lost my cherry at the age of 13 to an older man, a migrant worker from the prairies who was helping out at the farm. Dad didn't know just how handy that guy really was.

"After high school, I was bored. Although I had a steady boyfriend, I couldn't see myself settling down. So, like many others of my generation, I arrived in Vancouver at the age of 18 in 1939, just as the war was on the verge of starting. Hitler was still a comic figure to most people; everyone listened to 'Fibber McGee and Molly' and 'Amos 'n' Andy' on the radio.

"There were all kinds of rumours that the city was a major recruitment centre for turning prairie girls into white slaves. No one ever tried to grab me off the street. I had little trouble getting factory work. I was a riveter at the factory that made the Blackburn Sharks, the warplanes. When work ran out there, I switched to the Boeing factory which made parts for the B-29 Superfortresses.

"Just after I arrived, some city hall gent I had met at a bar took me to the big shindig for the opening of the new Hotel Vancouver. The city now had its own sixteenth-century chateau sprawling a half-block over Georgia and Burrard. On that night, May 25, I was close enough to King George and Queen Elizabeth that I could have kissed them!

"Once the war started in earnest, there were blackouts, rumours about the hazards of drinking local water, and the exodus of the Japanese fuelled in part by fear of the power of the Black Dragon Society. One Japanese submarine did shell Estevan on the east coast of Vancouver Island, but by and large I didn't feel in great danger. All in all, I had a good war.

"I partied with Yvonne de Carlo who, after a long strenuous publicity campaign, was chosen by Hollywood to star in *Salome, Where She Danced*. Yvonne was hailed as 'The Most Beautiful Girl in the World.' That was strange because I thought in those days I was the most beautiful girl in the world!

"After Japan was bombed, life seemed to come to a standstill. All the excitement vanished. People became more serious, were intent on making money and leading stable lives. I had no such ambitions. I had lots of boyfriends, one right after the other. In those days, what I was looking for in a man was well expressed by Winston Churchill: 'It will be long, hard and there will be no withdrawal.' Sometimes my men friends overlapped, which led to some pretty awful fights. One knifing, no murders. Nowadays, the word 'slut' is given to such women, but it wasn't like that, even in the early fifties. But, gradually, I was still partying when all my friends had stopped. I was alone, desperately alone.

"I became very depressed, started drinking, couldn't work and went on the game. I made my pleasure my business. I did so exactly at the wrong time because in the wake of Senator McCarthy's witch hunts in the States, there was a corresponding clamping-down by the vice squads here. Vancouver's small-town mentality surfaced in full force. All of a sudden, I was part of the 'criminal element,' as city hall gracefully put it. Police Chief Mulligan was disturbed, he said, by the number of amateurs and housewives entering the profession; he was particularly offended that a number of women were setting up business in apartments in the West End near the Stock Exchange. He closed down thc production of Erskine Caldwell's *Tobacco Road* at the Avon. Not that the citizens of Vancouver weren't interested in sex: the mating habits and rate of reproduction of the penguins at Stanley Park's penguin pool when it opened in 1953 were chronicled in graphic detail in the newspapers.

"A city in search of some sort of cultural life. That was what Vancouver had become. There was Professor Francis, a tall, elongated pretzel of a man, clothed in a tattered overcoat with a dead flower in his lapel, who appeared at every single serious musical event. Joachim Foikis, the official town fool, received grants to keep him in business. There was the tall, fierce-looking 'Russian General' whose costume included a Balaclava helmet, tunic, and breeches; he strode through downtown clipping his jack boots with a riding crop.

"Two years before you showed up at my doorstep, I married Mr. Skeffington, who was fifteen years older than me. For many years, John had been a patron of mine. That is, he sought my services on an almost weekly basis. He had some lowly job on the docks, had been a life-long bachelor, and had — through frugal living (he never spent any money except for sex) — amassed a small fortune. The only trouble was that John was well-known to the Mob, although he was not a part of it. When he started to drink, he opened his mouth promiscuously. I warned him about keeping his trap shut. He would faithfully promise to heed my warnings. We had been married for a year and a half when John vanished into thin air. I called the police, who showed no interest in locating him. His body was dragged out of English Bay three weeks before you came here. The body was intact except for his penis, which had been dexterously removed with what seemed to the pathologist expert skill.

"When we first encountered each other, you remember, I had just taken over the house on Alexander. Since then I have attempted to be a good girl. I do not wish to attract the watchful eye of the Mob, I have enough money to keep myself in modest comfort, and just about the only sex I enjoy is at the movies. Marcello Mastroianni is now my heartthrob. The pitiful state to which I have been reduced. My life is merely sad; I'm not capable of tragedy."

The regrets were all there, but there was a complete absence of self-pity. When I told Emma of my sorrow at the way things had turned out for both us, she winked: "It's the way of the world. We're just animals, putting in time before we shuffle off."

My own favourite films were very different from Emma's: Truffaut's *The Wild Child* and Malle's *Lacombe Lucien*. In the first, a kindly doctor — played by Truffaut — tries to establish genuine communication between a boy raised by wolves and himself. In essence, an impossible task but one undertaken with compassion and gentleness. Malle's film is altogether different: Lucien is an ordinary, somewhat brutish boy who simply goes along with the Gestapo. Passively, he betrays and kills. He unthinkingly becomes embroiled in the evil of others.

When I told Dr. Newman about my encounter with Emma and, in the process, praised her naturalness, he broke his usual vow of silence.

"You have the tendency to make black and white distinctions. Emma is a more instinctual person than you, and you immediately put yourself down because you are not like her."

"She is much more alive than I am, more responsive to herself and, therefore, to others."

"Again, that is your reading of the situation. Once again, you place yourself in the worst possible light."

"Why shouldn't I? I am a person of little human warmth and even less feeling."

"Absolute nonsense!" This was the first time he had ever raised his voice. "You fail to see that there is a part of every human being that is determined by nature, not by nurture. Temperamentally, Emma has different responses to stimuli than you do. This does not make her a better or worse person than you are.

"I have been giving this a great deal of thought in the past six months. Perhaps I could offer you an interpretation?" I felt like telling him it was about time but kept my mouth shut. "Some women who are abused as children by a father, an uncle, a family friend, become promiscuous when they reach young adulthood. It's almost as if they take on the responsibility for the bad behaviour of their elders, can only catch a glimmer of self-worth by treating sex with men as a replaying of the initial trauma.

"Then, there are those victims who once they reach young adulthood — when sexual interest in men is natural — have absolutely no interest in such activity, even dislike it. I think you are a member of this group. The trauma of sexual interference on the part of both your parents cauterized your normal sexual feelings. You have told me that you would usually imagine yourself and your body somewhere else when you were having sexual intercourse with clients.

"Your attraction to Bill Bohozuk was very emotional but not strongly sex-driven. You have no interest in partaking of sexual activity. You have commented many times in amazement at how different your feelings about sex are from what you term 'normal people.'

"I think you and I must see this disinclination as in large part a constitutional adjustment your psyche made to unwarranted intrusion."

He sucked his breath in, as if uncertain he wanted to say more. Finally: "You have allowed yourself to wallow too long in totally unjustified self-loathing." His last remark was issued as if a command, a direction in which I must now turn. For me, the path ahead still seemed completely blocked.

42

I had known Ethel for about six years when Wallace Wilson died in 1966. I had met him about a dozen times. Always congenial, he routinely inquired about my adventures in the book trade. "Duthie isn't working you too hard, is he?" Sometimes he would ask me to recommend a recent potboiler. "If I wanted a really good read, what would you suggest?" I once pointed out to him that Dickens had written excellent page-turners. "Oh, I'm not up to that speed. Something simpler, Elizabeth, for me! Put your mind to it and give me a call. Or give the title to Ethel. Or, if you like, send it right over, and I'll pop a cheque to Duthie in the post!"

In contrast to Ethel, Wallace seemed an unduly ordinary person. But I think that was an essential key to their strong marriage. In their case, opposites attracted in a wonderful way. After Wallace died, Ethel wanted to follow him. Often she told me to prepare myself for the inevitable. "The next time you come here, I may have vanished. I long so for the day when I shall see him again." Once she assured me: "It won't be too long. I am confident my booking has been made — I must now be patient for the actual day and time to be set. I am optimistic that the Great Timetabler has me close to the top of his waiting list." For Ethel, there could be no life after Wallace. Her heart was broken.

In *Swamp Angel*, elderly Nell Severance, a widow of many years, mourns her late husband, many years dead. The intimacy that existed between them is suspended as she patiently waits for death to arrive. The odd thing is that *Swamp Angel* was published twelve years before Wallace died, almost as if Ethel, when she wrote that book, had foreseen her unhappy fate.

Suspended. That was exactly the right word to describe my own existence. I went to work, attended faithfully four times a week at Dr. Newman's, went to the cinema twice a week, usually accompanied by Emma. On the outside a remarkably plain life, one entirely devoid of great sensations. And yet within me the past lived uncomfortably. I was consumed by guilt about the children. And I even managed to feel a great deal of shame and — sometimes compassion — for what had happened to John Dick. Most nights in my dreams, I drove up the Mountain. Outwardly, I guess, I seemed a thoroughly reformed person, but the past still threw a menacing shadow over me.

A whitened sepulchre. In that awful image I summed myself up. No matter how subtly Dr. Newman suggested I was a victim, I resisted that interpretation.

Ethel implored me to write. "Force yourself, my girl!" or "Put what you know down on paper, Ducks! That's the trick!" Even in the midst of her own great sorrow and her longing for death, her eyes remained crystalline bright as she upbraided me: "The spark's there. You have to uncover it."

Increasingly, my non-writing became a concern of Dr. Newman's: "Perhaps Mrs. Wilson is correct. Perhaps you should switch from reader to writer. Much of your analysis has been about the switch from passive to active voice. Perhaps writing would allow you to find your true voice." Those perhapses had more than a dash of exhortation to them. Usually, I tried to be a compliant patient. In this instance, I was rebellious.

Invisible hurdles blocked me. I couldn't imagine a coherent storyline even though I knew all the plot details of, say, Lydia's life. Or the right words evaded me when I actually took pen to paper. Or the right shape for the story seemed lost in an unfathomable mist. So I drowned in a sea of ineptitude and timidity.

By 1964, the dream had a new variant. Instead of Mr. Romanelli waiting for me on the brow of the Mountain, John is there. His face more haggard than usual, he gives me a wan smile and thanks me for saving him. Before we drive home in the Packard, he informs me he has promised to do a favour for Romanelli for letting him off the hook. He points in the direction of the woods, indicating I should follow him. The sharp, sticky smell of the pines both overwhelms and comforts me as I penetrate them. I follow John closely but after a while the distance between us is considerable. I yell at him to slow down, but he does not hear me. He plunges ahead. The distance between us increases. Then, he vanishes. All of a sudden, any semblance of moonlight has vanished. Enveloped in a darkness so real I can touch it, I turn to my left and stagger on. Then I change direction but to no avail. My legs ache, I am thirsty, and I am about to burst into tears.

Then I see a break in the woods, a small clearing bathed in a bright yellow light. I head in that direction and, after what seems a good fifteen minutes, I reach the periphery. At first the tract of land seems empty. Then, as I walk around the edge, I notice a few spots of blood on the ground. I bend down to inspect them. When I stand back up, I am aware of a menacing force. I turn around and then see the bodies in the middle of the clearing: a young girl about 6 or 7 and two newborn babies, a boy and a girl. All three are naked and all have recently died. The two infants look as if they have been strangled — there is no blood near them, but their faces are a bright blue; the little girl's throat has been cut.

These variants of the dream intrigued Dr. Newman: "What do you make of the fact that John Dick leads you into the forest and then disappears?"

"Perhaps I feel less guilty about what happened to him? I no longer seem to have the need of reliving that part of that horrible night."

"Yes. That is very possible. What about the children?"

"Their deaths seem totally unrelated to me. I don't have the sense in the dream that I am responsible for their deaths."

"Why are they there then?"

"I feel incredibly sad when I see them. I mourn for them, for their blighted lives."

"When you look at the tiny corpses, you are in mourning for yourself, for your own sense of your early life having been spoiled by your mother and father's cruelty. You are much more in touch with what you had to endure as a young girl."

If this was progress — as Dr. Newman seemed to imply — I was not certain. When I told Emma of this particular interpretation by the analyst, she nodded her head in agreement: "I've been telling you the same thing for years. Him you believe. Me you ignore."

Father returned to Hamilton after he was released from Kingston in 1951, lived in cheap lodgings, worked intermittently as a parking-lot attendant, hinted to the *Spectator* that he might talk if anyone offered him enough money. He was destitute when he died in 1955. Mother died in Hamilton on July 7, 1964. From the early fifties until her death at the MacKenzie Nursing Home on Blake Street, she had moved — almost on a yearly basis — to various boarding houses and apartment buildings, each more ramshackle than the previous. Bill Duthie, who saw the obituary in *The Toronto Star*, mentioned that Heather had married and had a daughter, Maria. Mother left her entire estate of $11,000 to her granddaughter. Three years later, the same paper took notice of Heather's divorce, citing adultery as grounds and awarding sole custody of Maria to her.

Most days, Hamilton and what had happened there seemed swallowed in the mists of time. On others, I would sometimes wonder, when coming upon a young mother accompanied by a young girl on the street, if they were possibly Heather and Maria. I must admit my heart was pierced when, in a small piece in *The Vancouver Sun* that told the story of John Dick's death once again, Maria's in memoriam to Mother was quoted: "Her love was true; her heart was kind./ A better grandmother none could find." How could she be so blind to the truth? or had the commonplace piece of verse been supplied by the *Spectator*?

I had been living on Thurlow Street for about two years when Darrin rented the flat — even smaller than mine — directly above me. At that time, he was 24, a tall black man who had lived in Toronto from the age of 8 after he and his parents immigrated from Jamaica. He was the sort of man who made heads turn on the street. Although he was handsome, it was his sculpted muscularity that drew attention. Even more compelling than these attributes was his smile, the biggest and most spontaneous I have ever seen on any face. A bit older than the other students, he had been a track and field star as a teenager and had tried his hand at playing football professionally. After suffering a series of torn ligaments and hamstring pulls, he decided to go to university, where he was a business major. He had been an undergraduate for one year at Victoria College at the University of Toronto and then transferred to the University of British Columbia in order to see the west.

At first, my relationship with Darrin was casual. Twice I had to travel by train to San Francisco to attend booksellers' conferences Bill Duthie did not wish to attend. On both occasions, Darrin looked after Casper. Every December Darrin went east to visit his parents, and I would volunteer to look after the house plants he kept in the front window of his apartment. *Quid pro quo*. That was our relationship for three years. Over that stretch of time, I would often come across Darrin with women who would be entering or leaving his flat. The ladies would replace each other at about six-month intervals: a beautiful blonde named Michelle was succeeded by an equally attractive Eurasian named Susie and so on. I never gave much thought to Darrin or his love life, although over time I became very fond of him.

Our cosy arrangement had been in place for about four years the night Darrin knocked on my door and asked to speak to me. Ostensibly, he wanted advice about books to read. The reading material in his business courses was destroying his soul, and he needed to find more humanity. I offered some suggestions — novels by Greene, Faulkner, Maugham. He wrote all these down and told me he would be in the next day to buy them. He was about to stand up, but then stopped abruptly.

"Can I talk to you about something that's bothering me?"

"Of course," I assured him. I was certain I was going to hear about his problems with his then-girlfriend, a redhead named Jacquie.

"My father would kill me if he found out what I was up to."

"He would be upset that your girlfriend is white?"

"No. He wouldn't give a care about that. He's a tiny bit white himself — so's my mother. That's not the difficulty. I work as a hustler. That would kill him."

"A hustler?"

"A male prostitute. I have sex with men."

"I had no idea."

"You wouldn't. I never bring anyone here. I meet guys at bars, and my phone number is in circulation in the right circles. I get a lot of business. That's how I support myself. My mother and father have no money to speak of, and I have to earn money to stay in school."

I was both surprised and shocked, but I didn't want him to know it. "There's no way your father could find out."

"Maybe not. But I worry that the truth will come out."

"Not even remotely likely."

Rather than taking comfort from my assurance, Darrin seemed to become even more anxious about the predicament in which he saw himself. "I'm not a homosexual. When I do things with those fairies, I imagine I'm having sex with a girlfriend."

I wasn't much interested in what those things were, but he proceeded to enlighten me. "I take my clothes off for these guys and pose. I have a huge penis, and I let them suck on it. Sometimes, I masturbate or let them masturbate me. The sessions always end with the Johns masturbating while I pose some more for them."

It all seemed so neat and tidy — and loveless. Then, Darrin switched directions. "You know, it's like I'm not even occupying the same space as my clients. It's as if my body is in one place and my mind is somewhere else looking down on what my body is doing. A really strange sensation."

From my own first-hand experience, I knew exactly what Darrin was talking about, that sense of not being there. I saw no point in talking about my own brilliant career as a woman of pleasure. I didn't think it would help him. In fact, I wanted the conversation to be over, although I wanted to empathize with him in some way.

He thought I was sympathetic but uncomprehending. On that evening, he wanted someone to understand what had happened to him. "The other thing that my father doesn't know anything about began a few years after we had immigrated to Canada. Dad's older brother, Ronnie, arrived in Toronto four years before we did. He had been married three or four times, would get work at a factory, quit, be on pogie for a month or two, and then get another job. He was a nice enough fellow and always volunteered to take me out on various excursions, usually fishing. I was about twelve years old when it began.

"We had gone to some really remote spot in Scarborough, an inlet where there were supposed to be a lot of fish. We had no luck that day. By late afternoon, it was useless. We weren't going to catch anything.

"Uncle Ronnie was restless, bored. 'You know, Darrin, there's something you could do for me, if you were willing.' I really liked the guy. He had always been so friendly and generous. I told him I would do anything for him. 'Anything?,' he asked. Yes, I told him. 'Well, Darrin, would you mind if I took a look at your penis? I think you're growing a real man's wiener. Sometimes men like to touch each other's dicks. What do you say?' I was startled, mainly because I had no interest in doing any such thing. But, God help me, I did what he wanted. I pulled down my pants, removed my underpants and let him touch my penis. At first, he touched it gently but, almost before I knew it, he started sucking on it while, at the same time, he reached down to stroke his own member. After about five minutes, I reached orgasm. He took his mouth away and now staring at my penis, he manipulated himself until his hand was covered with his own sperm.

"For about two years, I saw my uncle once or twice a month. My parents didn't understand why I no longer cared much for Uncle Ronnie. I obviously couldn't tell them what he and I were doing together. When I was 15, I started to have sex with girls and finally told Ronnie I wasn't much interested in playing our little game any longer. I never threatened him; he never threatened me. 'If that's the way you want it, so be it.'

"So that game ended, and I never had sex with another man until two years ago. It all started when I guy propositioned me, offered me twenty dollars if I would let him suck me. One thing led to another."

"You're sick of all this. You want to stop?"

"Yeah. I want to stop. I've saved up — I don't need the money anymore."

"Then you've solved the problem."

"That's what I thought. I stopped six weeks ago. I'm no longer on the game. But in a way I don't at all understand, I miss it. Not the money. Not the sex."

Somehow or other, Darrin's self-esteem had gotten mixed up — or deeply confused — by his work as a prostitute. I couldn't remember similar emotions on my part, but I sensed he had somehow gotten trapped by what he had been doing. I wasn't sure what I could tell him that would be in any way useful.

"Perhaps these men offer you some sort of unconditional love? Perhaps you miss the admiration they express?"

"I've wondered about that. I now think I'm missing something irreplaceable, something I crave."

"I think you have to give yourself the same sort of veneration that was coming from your clients."

"The problem is that I don't know how to do that." He shook his head in anguish. I thought of suggesting he seek some sort of psychotherapy, but that evening did not seem the right moment to do so. Finally, he stood up, dislodging a sleeping Casper from his lap. He turned to me, kissed me on the forehead and went back upstairs.

The events of the following day did not allow me to think much about Darrin. I had been at work for about an hour when Bill Duthie came running downstairs. "Something awful's happened to Emma. The police have just called. I'll leave Steve and Julia in charge. I'll drive you down to her place. They wouldn't tell me anything more." When we reached Gas Town fifteen minutes later, five patrol cars and an ambulance were pulled up in front of Emma's house. We arrived just in time to see my friend carried out in a body bag and placed in the ambulance. Bill became hysterical whereas I stayed calm. To this day, I don't know how I remained so.

The story that emerged had a horrible simplicity to it. Emma was fussy about her house and those she allowed to reside there. Over the years, her tenants did not change all that rapidly. Despite the neighbourhood, she usually had a collection of two or three reliable women dwelling there. In any event, the day before Emma died, a young man had showed up at the house asking for his mother, a woman called Daisy Brown. Mrs. Brown was away for four or five days but, before leaving, she had asked her landlady if her son, Edward, could stay in her room for two or three days in her absence. Reluctantly, Emma had agreed to this arrangement and promptly welcomed Daisy's son to her establishment. On the following day, Emma entered her own living room, discovered Edward there, and calmly began a conversation with the intruder, who matter-of-factly took a small revolver from his pocket and shot her in the face. She died immediately. What Emma had not been told was that Edward was a paranoid schizophrenic who harboured many grudges against his mother.

I was in a state of shock. Despite her colourful past and her deteriorating neighbourhood, Emma had lived a quiet, exemplary existence, not one calculated to bring down the wrath of the gods. She and Mrs. Wilson had been my only two close friends in Vancouver. I felt so bereft that I was completely surprised when, four days after my late night conversation with Darrin, his girlfriend, Jacquie, showed up at my door. She had not heard from him in four days. That was unusual in itself but even stranger was the fact that his phone had gone unanswered — even in the middle of the night — during the same time span. When she called my attention to that detail, I remembered being awakened by his phone ringing incessantly during the middle of the previous three nights.

"Perhaps he was called away unexpectedly? A family emergency?"

"He would have told me. No reason not to."

"Do you want me to get in touch with our landlord?"

"No. But you have a key, don't you? He told me he had one made for you when you look after his place."

"Yes. It's around somewhere. Should I lend it to you?"

"No. That's too much like snooping on my part. Would you mind taking a look upstairs?"

So that's how I discovered the body hanging from the middle of the living room ceiling. Darrin had no clothes on except his blue jeans. He had used the only necktie — a bright paisley — he owned. In death, his body had a majestic, heroic simplicity to it, much like Michelangelo's *David*. His eyes were open, staring straight ahead as if confronting some dismal truth. There wasn't a note. He had been dead at least forty-eight hours when I discovered him. A fetid smell filled the room. Casper, who had accompanied me, squealed sharply and then retreated noisily down the stairs.

"You have had to endure a great deal recently. Almost beyond our human capacity to either accept or understand."

Those were Dr. Newman's words of comfort. They were both neutral and kindly. I told him: "I cannot make any sense out of what has happened."

"I agree with you. Some events defy explanation. However, I am in the business of attempting to explain the impossible, so you will have to forgive me if I do try to make some sense out of what seems so senseless. I have an obligation to assist you in this regard."

According to Dr. Newman, there is often a tragic accidentalness to life, things for which you could never prepare yourself. Emma must have reminded Edward of his mother against whom he harboured a number of grudges. She was at the wrong place at the wrong time. No one could have predicted what happened.

As for Darrin, Dr. Newman felt he had been badly depressed for some time. In confessing his past life to me, he was not consciously seeking either forgiveness or absolution. In putting things into words for the first time, however, he had come more in touch with what was disturbing him. Rather than obtaining any sense of freedom, he felt trapped. The sad truth, Dr. Newman maintained, was that Darrin's uncle had betrayed him, but he had done so only after the young man had become deeply attached to him.

"Darrin was correct: he was not a homosexual. But his uncle preyed upon his self-esteem, which may have been constitutionally vulnerable — paedophiles are often expert at such manoeuvres. As a man, Darrin had a normal sex life but when he became a prostitute, he began to re-enact the treacherous landscape of his youth. He got back in touch with how much he had craved his uncle's so-called love and how he had been forced to maintain it. Like many young people who suffer sexual abuse, Darrin separated his mind from his body performing sexual activities, but he reanimated the vulnerability his uncle had earlier exploited. Psychically, his male clients could not give him any real sense of self-esteem, nor could his girlfriends. In the past year or so, he confronted an abyss of emptiness carefully constructed for him years earlier. That's why he took his own life."

"You seem so self-assured in all these interpretations you offer."

"Never self-assured. You have suffered some recent traumatic experiences. I never met Emma or Darrin. In speaking about them with you, I am objectifying your subjective experiences, trying to explain them in a meaningful way. That is my job."

"You speak in a voice of great authority, as if you are completely beyond the fray of real life."

"You may be correct to complain about Olympian detachment but how otherwise could I presume to offer you any sustenance?"

"I have been wondering recently if you are giving me anything of value. Emma died because bad things simply and irrevocably happen. Darrin died because of a tragic flaw. Is that what you are saying?"

"In a nutshell."

"So what value is it to me to come here to be told things I could figure out for myself?"

"We all have blind spots. I am supposed to help you remove yours. Provide you with another pair of eyes. I also think you are consistently harsh with yourself. My job — from an objective point of view — is to disabuse you of false impressions you harbour about yourself."

"In order to set me free?"

"Yes." And then with a slight note of helplessness in the wake of my recalcitrance: "I live in hope of doing *exactly* that."

43

The whole exercise of analysis seemed increasingly meaningless. I was angry at myself for not taking a more active role in obtaining counselling for Darrin, for neglecting him after Emma died. Dr. Newman refused to countenance my suggestion that I could have done something to help Darrin. I also told myself that I should have insisted that Emma leave Gas Town, which had become an increasingly dangerous place to live through the sixties. When Dr. Newman reminded me that Emma had not died because she lived in Gas Town, I ignored him.

My own life seemed to have reached an uncomfortable stasis. I visited Mrs. Wilson regularly but, except for her — and the occasional meal with the Duthies — I lived a solitary existence. In 1972, the same year Emma and Darrin died, Mrs. Wilson's deteriorating health led her to take up residence at Arbutus Nursing Home, where she took her favourite books and pictures with her. Now confined to a wheelchair, she was not inordinately fond of the other inmates and craved every moment we spent together.

One afternoon, when we had made short work of the single tumbler of whisky that began each visit and were about to turn to tea, Mrs. Wilson mentioned to me how upset she had been to read the article in *The New York Times* about the psychoanalyst in Vancouver. The story had reduced her to tears.

"What analyst?," I asked.

"A man called Newman. The story is heartbreaking, has put everything into perspective for me."

I asked if I could see the story. "Certainly, darling. It's in the magazine section of last Sunday's *Times*." She pointed in the direction of the pile of newspapers in the corner of the room near her bed. "The one with Greta Garbo on the cover." I asked if I might borrow that issue. "Of course. No need to return it."

I don't know how I made it through the next hour. Usually I took the streetcar back and forth to the Arbutus. On this day, I asked the matron to call a taxi. The driver came within five minutes and I was back home in about twenty.

The story was astonishing, even in the wake of the many other Holocaust narratives I had already read. At first, however, the account seemed unduly ordinary. Ernst Newman, who was born in Stuttgart in 1916, had attended the gymnasium there. His prosperous father, who owned a factory that made pots and pans, insisted from the time his son was born that he was to be a medical man. As a child, Ernst had no such inclination but being, as he termed it, "a dutiful son," he allowed his father to make this decision for him. Ernst's own interests — as he told the American journalist — veered in the direction of music and books: "From childhood, I was fascinated by the "human sciences, the ways in which the imagination frames and reframes reality."

By the time Ernst was twenty, Hitler was in full command of Germany, and the extermination of Jews was beginning to be put into operation. The full horror that was to unfold evaded him. At that time, he did not wish to even imagine what later would seem such an obvious scenario. Certain, however, he would not be able to complete his medical studies, he did not pay them much mind. He stayed up late each evening, drank a lot and, in general, became something of a gadfly. "A particularly obnoxious form of nihilism took possession of my soul. Realizing I had no real future, I did not try to anchor myself in the present. For far too long, I had been an overly attentive child. When it manifested itself, my rebellion was of the deeply obnoxious variety. Terrified by what they beheld, my poor parents were filled with shame and anger. I was now the prodigal son."

For six months, Ernst's debauchery continued unchecked. That style of life was almost instantly cast asunder the day he met Rowena, the daughter of one of the publicans whose establishments he frequented. Her physical beauty played a great deal in what he termed his conversion. He met her purely by chance. One afternoon, he came across Herr Lasky accompanied by his daughter. Although the possessor of a lascivious tongue when serving his young clientele, the publican as paterfamilias was the model of propriety. He nodded curtly in Ernst's direction and ushered his daughter and himself away from the young man.

Ernst had fallen instantly in love. That evening, he penned a letter to Fraulein Lasky, whose given name he did not yet know. Fortunately for him, Rowena was also smitten and answered immediately. They arranged a meeting two days later and when, soon after, they confronted her father with the news of their engagement, he gave them his permission to marry. The Newmans, heretofore worried about their son's recent excesses, responded rhapsodically to the news of the forthcoming marriage. The couple married six months later and, almost nine months after that, their son, Peter, was born. Ernst continued in his medical studies, his newfound purpose in life enhancing the efforts he brought to the mastery of his chosen profession.

Up to this point, the life history of Ernst Newman had all the twists and turns of one of the Grimm brothers' happiest fairy tales. Unfortunately, the greatest blight of twentieth century history soon intervened. Ernst was forced to leave school, where he was now declared an undesirable. He worked for his father-in-law, until his tavern was shut down. Then, the small family of three — along with many other Jews — was expelled from the city limits and left to wander in the countryside. This state of affairs did not last long, as they were detained and after three days spent in confinement, they were separated: Rowena and Peter were placed in one work station, Ernst in another. Ernst was never sent to a concentration camp: he was dispatched to a small factory where medical supplies were manufactured. Rowena and Peter were not so fortunate, although they did not wind up in one of the infamous camps. Instead, Rowena was given work in a large abattoir. Women did not slaughter the animals, but they worked long hours cleaning out the innards of the dead creatures. Peter and the other children were left to their own devices in the cramped, lice-infested living quarters allocated to the workers. From 1942 to 1945, Ernst and Rowena were out of death's way, but their agony was that neither knew the fate of the other. Only at the end of the war did Ernst learn that his wife and son were safe in a small village in Switzerland near the border with Germany.

This information came in a typed letter sent to Ernst just after he had made it back to Stuttgart, where he learned that his in-laws had been murdered. He was happy to be with his parents, who had just returned from Switzerland, where they had been in exile since 1942, the year of Ernst's marriage. Not only had they survived, they had been fortunate enough to send a great deal of money out of Germany before the war. They were even more fortunate that they had placed those funds in trustworthy hands. Once again, they were people of both wealth and standing; and they had determined to settle in the new state of Israel.

The letter that contained the comforting information also told Ernst that the writer of the letter — one Herr Tarnopolsky — had obtained the safety of Rowena and Peter at considerable personal as well as financial cost to himself, and in: In order for Ernst to regain his loved ones, he would have to recompense Tarnopolsky for his troubles. The amount in question was the equivalent of $50,000. If he would present himself in Brig at the principal hotel there on the twelfth of September — in ten days' time — everything could be resolved to mutual satisfaction.

Ernst's parents felt the police should be contacted. They told their son: "This is the action of someone who knows of our great wealth. This is another crime about to be perpetuated against us, as Jews." Ernst was not so sure that the letter was, as his parents thought, a hoax. For one thing, the letter had contained small, intimate details about him that only a wife would know. He thought Mr. Tarnopolsky was criminally minded, but he was convinced Rowena and Peter were in his power. Against their better judgement, Ernst's parents gave him the money and on the eleventh, they saw him off at the train station.

The trip to Brig was short and uncomplicated. Nestled in the heart of the Alps, the scenery there was breathtaking in its simple magnificence. On the morning of the twelfth, Ernst received a telephone call at his hotel. He was to hire a car and travel with it in the direction of the huge glacier on the Hoffenstrasse pass; he was to leave at precisely three o'clock in the afternoon and should reach the lookout to the Glacier at about six, just after the sun had set. A car — a red Mercedes-Benz — would be awaiting his arrival. Rowena, Peter and Mr. Tarnopolsky would be the only occupants of the car; Mr. Tarnopolsky would greet him and receive the payment, only at which point would his wife and child be allowed to leave with him.

An organized man, Ernst left precisely at three. He had some trepidations, but, overall, his heart was filled with optimism. When speaking to Tarnopolsky on the phone, he had overheard Peter speaking to Rowena. They both sounded cheerful, obviously buoyed up by the prospect of being reunited with him. The drive was a pleasant one, the scenery refreshing in its rugged, often sublime, simplicity. At long last, he felt he could breathe again. He took in the air, felt it coursing down his lungs. The sun set just before six and not quite ten minutes later he saw the red Mercedes waiting for him, its bright beam lights welcoming him to the rendezvous point.

Ernst parked about twelve feet before the Mercedes, got out and walked towards it. Herr Tarnopolsky, meanwhile, was walking in his direction. He bowed in Ernst's direction, then clicked his heels. "I take it, Herr Newman, that you have the money with you?" Ernst reassured him that this was so. "Excellent. I see you are a man of your word. I am also a man of my word, but there has been a small change to the plan. Just as we were about to set out, your wife pleaded with me to allow her and your son to remain behind in the chalet we have been renting, just beyond the trees there." He pointed into the forest, where a small house could just barely be seen. "'It's too cold for my little boy, Herr Tarnopolsky. Let my husband fetch me from here, I beg you. I do not want my little boy to suffer any further tribulations.'

What can I say, Herr Newman? I am also a family man. I agreed to her proposition." Ernst was a bit suspicious, but he felt he had little choice but to turn the money over to Tarnopolsky, who, having clicked his heels once again, got into the Mercedes and drove away.

The walk to the chalet was fifteen minutes. The trees, bathed in full moonlight, gave off a strong but delicate smell. As Ernst got closer to the chalet, he noticed how beautifully constructed it was. He felt like a child who, having endured a series of horrible adventures, finally finds himself at an enchanted castle where he will be fully restored. He observed lights in the windows and, as he drew nearer, he noticed that the door was slightly ajar. He called aloud to his beloved wife, but no sound returned his greeting. In one final burst, he ran towards the door and pushed it in. He never forgot the sight that met his eyes: the room was completely devoid of furniture, but in the middle of the floor lay the nude, blood-covered bodies of his wife and child. They had obviously died within the hour. What is more, the look of agony on Rowena's face revealed all too well that she had been sexually violated; the little boy's open eyes also indicated that he had been a witness to unspeakable evil.

Ernst lost track of time. Eventually, he walked back to his car — it was now snowing — and drove to the nearest police station. The police insisted on driving him back to the chalet, from which the two corpses were soon removed. The perpetrator of the crime — Mr. Tarnopolsky — worked under a number of different aliases. The authorities were convinced his real name was Schneider, a Jew who had worked as a capo, an informant on other Jews, at Auschwitz. He was hated by the other prisoners, who had shunned him at the time of the liberation. He was a hunted man — one of the few Jews accused of war crimes — and had somehow made his way to Switzerland. He had committed two other hoaxes of this kind, killing four other people before Rowena and Peter.

The writer in the *Times* had obviously chosen to tell Newman's story because of its newsworthy elements, particularly how Jews sometimes preyed upon other Jews. The tone of the entire piece also made it obvious that Newman had not sought to have his story made public: he had co-operated only when the writer had told him she would tell the story with or without his assistance. At the end of the article, she summarized his life after that fateful day. With his parents' assistance, he had immigrated to England, completed his medical degree at Cambridge, qualified as a psychiatrist and later an analyst at the Maudsley in London and subsequently immigrated to Vancouver, British Columbia, where he had arrived in 1958, three years before I met him. The journalist — obviously hoping to end her story in a garish way — posed some provocative questions. "What if Tarnopolsky is captured and brought to justice?"

"He should be tried," Newman responded quietly.

"Executed?"

"Hardly a solution to replace one brutality with another."

"The horrible things that happened to you — the senseless, evil murders of your wife and child, all of this following in the wake of the Holocaust — doesn't this convince you that humankind is basically evil?"

I think his answer surprised her: "No. Not at all. There are many unfortunate, basically empty people who commit acts of unspeakable evil. There are an equally large number of people who spend their lives trying to undo such acts. I am also certain there are many people who spend their lives convinced they have committed evil acts whereas they have been merely caught up in the web of history. There are relatively few spiders; there are many harmless insects who get caught in their webs."

I called in sick the next day, a Monday. Bill was surprised — I had never taken a day off before. My appointment with Dr. Newman was at four in the afternoon, and I had no idea what I was going to say to him. One part of me shied away from admitting to him I had seen the article; I was afraid he would be angry at me for invading his privacy. Yet, how could he find fault with me? The article was in the *Times* for anyone to see. Then, my thoughts veered in another direction. How trivial and silly my own sufferings seemed in comparison to his. What right did I have to ask him to fix my heart when his was so more badly broken than my own?

Usually, I conducted myself as an unduly compliant patient. I did not argue with my therapist, although I sometimes politely disagreed with him. I was certainly not an emotional analysand, one whose sessions were filled with tears and recriminations. When I reached his office that Monday afternoon, I was certain my self-control would desert me. I even thought of returning home and waiting until Tuesday to see him.

I did not go away. When he answered the door, I noticed nothing different about him or the prints that lined the corridor. When I had settled myself on the couch, I made the dreaded admission. "I saw the piece in the *New York Times*."

"I didn't know if you read it."

"Usually I don't. Ethel Wilson mentioned the article to me. She had been very touched by it."

"What did you think of it?"

"It made me very sad. I was heart-broken for you, your wife and your child."

"Two of my patients have been very angry with me about that piece. According to them, I am supposed to have no life outside this office."

"Those people are worse off than me."

"Perhaps. Why were you heart-broken?"

"Because no one should have to endure the suffering you have experienced. Because all your hopes were dashed. Because of the sadness of the entire human condition in which such things happen."

"I have always known you capable of the gift of empathy. Now you have demonstrated that I was completely correct in my hypothesis."

I changed the subject slightly. "I have also been shaken by something else, something more personal to me."

"Yes?"

"My dreams about the events on the Mountain, about the strange house, about the children in that house. You actually lived what I imagined in those nightmares. When I first came here, you must have been unnerved by the conjunction of my dreams and your experience?"

"True. I was startled. On reflection, I put it all down to synchronicity. You were obviously meant to be my patient. I became convinced I might learn from you, the patient, about my own life. I also wondered if my own life experiences might make me a suitable guide to your inner world." He paused. "There is another thing. Sometimes, you know, we psychiatrists don't like to admit to ourselves that our patients can transform our lives."

When I left that afternoon, Dr. Newman had altered remarkably in appearance. He looked younger, leaner, more vulnerable. I even thought I saw the glint of a tear in his right eye.

My relationship with Dr. Newman changed after that session. Although he had been previously disinclined to offer me advice directly, he leapt with great alacrity on any pieces of instruction offered to me by Mrs. Wilson. "She is a great writer, one of the finest Canada has produced. If she thinks you have the makings of a writer, why should you continue to contradict her?"

In the last decade of her life, Ethel's health deteriorated rapidly. Every time I visited her, she was a shadow of the self at the previous encounter. She had retreated into herself so successfully that her delicate spirit was trapped in a hard shale of rock. She found it difficult to talk, a slur now invading her speech. She began to call me "Maggie" as if confusing fiction with fact. I never bothered to correct her. Sometimes, I simply held her hand. Her eyes would attempt to bring me into focus, but that was an increasingly difficult task for her.

Encouraged by Dr. Newman and the presence of Mrs. Wilson, I began the book that became *Celia*. Years later, journalists researching the beginnings of my writing life, would endlessly repeat the story of the various sightings of the lady seated in the big bay window, a large grey cat at the opposite end of the table from her, writing into her scribblers long into the night. At the time, I did not realize I had become such a source of fascination, especially to young people visiting Vancouver.

Almost a year to the day after my fateful encounter with Dr. Newman, I received the phone call that further altered my life. I had just returned from Duthie's, so it was early evening, about six-thirty. The voice on the other end of the line — resolutely English — asserted itself through a mass of crackling sounds.

"Miss Delamere? Is that Miss Delamere?"

"Yes. Speaking."

"This is Judith Smith at Penguin in London. I hope I'm calling at a reasonable time for you? It's the middle of the night here — I have stayed up in order to reach you."

"Yes. Your timing is perfect. I've just had your aerogramme acknowledging receipt of my manuscript — it arrived yesterday."

"Good, good. I'm delighted. I've just finished the book. I admire it ever so much." The last sentence was uttered in a gushy, totally un-English way of speaking. Then, the speaker seemed to catch herself. "I would like to make a publishing offer on the book. I assume I should negotiate with you? You don't mention the existence of an agent."

"No. I don't have an agent. To be honest, I didn't have any great expectations of getting the book published without a long struggle. It's the first extended piece of fiction I've ever written. You're my first reader."

"Perhaps I'm you're ideal reader?" She laughed, a bit breathlessly. "I'm saying that because I hope to convince you to sell me the book."

"I don't think I'll need much persuasion."

And that turned out to be correct. Judith has been my editor and publisher since that day in 1973, over twenty-five years ago.

A year later, in 1974, just after *Celia* was published, I concluded my analysis. Dr. Newman made the usual joke about having assisted in curing me of everything except life itself. Earlier, at the beginning of our final meeting, I presented him with a bouquet of blue roses, the most perfect specimens I could find in all of Vancouver.

"Blue roses?" He seemed startled more by the colour than the gift itself.

"They are called 'Blue Moons,' so rare is the colour in the rose family, as in *once in a blue moon*. Sports of nature, you might say."

"I know the first idiom but not the second. What is a 'sport of nature'?

"A plant or an animal which exhibits an abnormal variant from its parents. A spontaneous mutation."

"Interesting. The roses are very beautiful, but they have thorns."

Realizing that his unconsciousness may have gotten the better of him, he added: "I did not mean to be so insensitive, to imply that you are giving me a beautiful gift that might harm me. Rather, I should have simply thanked you." At that point, he cleared his throat: "I think you are like these roses. You have a genuine, radiant and rare beauty residing in your psyche. There is also a deep pain within you — the thorns of shame and guilt. The trick is to join the two forces together creatively. Perhaps your writing will do that for you?"

I remained in Vancouver until Ethel died at the end of 1980. In the last four years of her life, her bad health had almost completely removed her from existence. I prayed she spent that dream life reunited with Wallace. A few days after she passed away, Casper died quietly in his sleep.

Five years before, in 1975, I had given up my job at Duthie's to write full-time. I did not move to another home in Vancouver, although by 1980 I had published four novels, two of which had been optioned to Hollywood. Since many of the reviewers of my books had pointed out that my female characters were rendered in a series of finely crafted closeups worthy of a Josef von Sternberg or a George Cukor, I supposed it might be a fairly natural process for those books to be turned into films. Once or twice I have asked myself: did I become a writer because the kind of movies I loved as a young woman have completely disappeared?

On the West Coast I was in danger of becoming a celebrity, and I decided that my anonymity might be best preserved in a large, impersonal city like Toronto. So in January 1981 I moved here. When I boarded the plane on the twelfth of January, I wondered how really different I was as my sixty-first year approached from the relatively young woman who had settled on the coast twenty years before. Had the leopard lost any of her spots?

44

When I returned to Ontario from the West, I was on the verge of becoming rich. I purchased this two-bedroom condominium, immediately outfitting one of the bedrooms as a study. I also acquired two Hockneys and four Hodgkins in one fell swoop at Waddington's in Yorkville. Within a month, I had settled into my new nest and established the pattern that had — until five years ago — prevailed for the past twenty years. I lived in Toronto from January through to the end of May. During that time, I wrote, usually six hours a day.

Every other spring, I flew over to England with the manuscript of a new novel, stayed with Judith Smith who promptly read and edited it, and then I travelled, sometimes with Judith, sometimes alone. In alternate years, I took long trips to exotic places. I have visited every nook and cranny in central Europe and have gone much further afield: Morocco, Tangier, India, Japan, China.

I am usually away from Toronto for four or five months at a time. In the autumn, I am back in Toronto for about a month and then head south to the Caribbean until the end of December. I have only a handful of friends in Toronto, most of them young writers I have befriended. Kenji Ozu attributes his remarkable success to my assistance; he would have done quite well with or without me.

I want to avoid Toronto in winter, but that was the only time of year — in the past — I could be productive as a writer. Strange, but I could only draw something from myself when the landscape around me was in mourning, awaiting the rebirth of spring. Or perhaps the books were like lovely little lambs born every April and May? My cycle of creativity obviously craved winter's desolation, so dependent was it on bleakness to have any hope of saying something about redemption. I was like the Snow Queen imprisoned in her ivory tower, hoping the words I spun would release me from confinement.

Unlike the poor Lady of Shalott who only saw the world reflected in mirrors, no Lancelot made his way into my heart and forced me out of my tower. For years, I knew too much reality would kill me — as it did her. Yet, despite my best efforts, I can no longer write. That comfort has been withdrawn. I wish I knew why Elizabeth Delamere has not published a novel in four years.

I can no longer concentrate on my new book, my so-called autobiography. I am reduced to cutting out newspaper clippings and making diary entries. In my early days as a novelist, I could reread those entries and somehow transform them. Now they are obdurate to any attempt on my part to wave my magic wand in their direction. Circe doesn't live here any more. I am left with pure dross. No silk purses. Only sows' ears.

45

Hamilton Spectator, March 19, 1987

SPECULATION DEAD WOMAN WAS EVELYN DICK

BINBROOK — An elderly couple found dead in their Glanbrook home last night are believed to have been asphyxiated from a coal burning stove.

People have identified the deceased couple as Ethela McLean, 73, and Lino Bartollotti, 75. Police believe they have been dead for two or three days.

Mr. Bartollotti, clad only in underwear, was found slumped

around the coal stove which police believe contributed to the apparent asphyxiation. Mrs. McLean was clothed in a light dress and sweater. She lay face-down in a small pool of blood which he thought appeared to come from an injury due to a fall. Doug Turner, a neighbour, called police at six p.m. yesterday when he noticed the couple's mail had not been picked up for two days.

Their deaths have fuelled persistent speculation and rumours in the Binbrook area that the dead woman was actually Evelyn Dick, whose murder trial 40 years ago attracted international attention. Hamilton police say they are sceptical about these claims but confirmed they have sent the woman's fingerprints to Ottawa to compare them with Mrs. Dick's prints. Mr. Turner said he was convinced that the woman, five foot six inches tall, weighing about 130 pounds, who he had seen only on a few occasions during the last twenty years, was in fact Evelyn Dick.

Staff Sergeant Jim Willis said Mrs. McLean's daughter in Deep River, Ontario, has emphatically denied the claims that her mother is the notorious murderer.

Hamilton Spectator, March 20, 1987

DEATH BOUGHT HER ESCAPE FROM OTHER WOMAN'S GHOST

BINBROOK — Ethela McLean spent the last part of her life in the ghost of Evelyn Dick, the only woman ever sentenced to hang in Wentworth County.

Mrs. McLean, 73, died this week of apparent asphyxiation with her live-in companion Lino (Leo) Bartollotti, 75, in a small, run-down house on Hall Road, finally escaping the long-held suspicion she was Mrs. Dick.

"She never had the opportunity to deny it [the rumour]. No one ever came up and said, 'You're Evelyn Dick,' said Evelyn McCormack, a neighbour who lived across the street when the couple moved into the shack in 1964. "It never bothered me because I never believed it," she said. In the three times she met Mrs. McLean, Mrs. McCormack said the woman was always nice but was self-conscious because of her live-in relationship with Mr. Bartollotti. If she seemed to others to be hiding some dark secret, it was probably her discomfort that she wasn't married to the man she lived with, said Mrs. McCormack.

"A lot of people wanted to believe it was her, but it wasn't. There was never any reason to really suspect she was," said Margaret Garden, another neighbour.

The silence, coupled with certain similarities between the two women, kept the rumours alive. Although Evelyn Dick was slightly shorter than Mrs. McLean who was 5' 6", the two women were relatively small, attractive and looked about the same age, although Mrs. McLean was six years older.

Mrs. McLean appeared in the remote area of Binbrook two years after Evelyn Dick was released on parole. Patricia Carver, Mrs. McLean's only child from a broken marriage, who has lived in Deep River near Ottawa with her husband since 1965, cannot understand why anyone would mistake her mother for Mrs. Dick.

Hamilton Spectator, March 28, 1987

...AND NOW, THE OTHER EVELYN DICK

Evelyn Dick has spent the last 35 years trying to convince people that she isn't Evelyn Dick. Not that Evelyn Dick, at least.

Ever since she arrived in Hamilton from Scotland in 1952, the mention of her name has evoked a mixture of shock, surprise and embarrassment.

Her first experience came when she walked into the unemployment office in Hamilton to look for a job.

Born in 1934, she was only 18 at the time, spoke with a noticeable brogue and hadn't even heard of the other Evelyn Dick who had caused such a fuss in the Steel City six years earlier.

But it didn't take long for the word to spread, and soon workers were sliding up towards the front desk to get a look at her.

It didn't seem to matter that the real Evelyn Dick was securely locked away at the Women's Prison in Kingston at the time.

Her latest encounter with the other Evelyn Dick came 10 days ago after the *Spectator* carried a story about an elderly woman who died in a house fire in Binbrook

A few days later, the Mrs. Dick who lives in Hamilton and has her name listed in the phone book, was centred out again — when she went for a drink at the local Legion hall. The master of ceremonies pointed to her table and happily announced that rumours of her death had been greatly exaggerated.

Mrs. Dick, who is single and has three grown children, has learned to take all this frivolity in good humour and wouldn't think of changing her name. "Most people don't mean any harm and if they only thought about it for a minute, they'd realize it couldn't be me. The real Evelyn Dick wouldn't be using her own name and she probably would steer clear of the city," she said.

According to former prison warden, Janet White, Mrs. Dick had no connection with her family or anybody from Hamilton during her 11 years in prison.

Even if she returned to Hamilton tomorrow, she probably wouldn't look anything like she did when she was so prominently in the spotlight 40 years ago. But all this won't prevent stories about the real Mrs. Dick from popping up again, from time to time, as they have done for the last 30 years.

According to unconfirmed reports she has worked as a clerk at Eastgate Mall, was a waitress at Gulliver's Restaurant a few years ago, sold perfume at Eaton's and even underwent a period of shock therapy at Hamilton General Hospital. Last year, a local cabby told a *Spectator* reporter he knew Mrs. Dick well and drove her to Bingo games every Wednesday night.

Even if she appeared in person, Evelyn Dick might have trouble living up to her stories, so deeply etched is she in the psyche of this city.

Hamilton Spectator, October 5, 1991

THE STRANGE SAGA OF EVELYN DICK

The latest addition to the Evelyn Dick story centres around one Howard Gower, now 66. This episode begins late in 1948 at a watering hole called Basil's on Yonge Street in Toronto.

Gower is a man of property now. But back then he was an apprentice electrician. On that night, he was enjoying the beer and the company of a couple of pals.

They were undercover cops and they knew some inside stuff on the Dick case. Evelyn was in jail, but there was supposed to be a stash of money on the outside.

Maybe $100,000 — a fortune then. Those guys in the bar figured they knew exactly where it was.

Beer in their bellies, they set off for Harriston, straight south of Owen Sound. On a private little lake there, Evelyn Dick had a cottage.

The boys arrived about 5 a.m. They had sobered up by then and found no treasure. But they did discover a For Sale sign — Evelyn wasn't making any mortgage payments from Kingston.

Gower loved the looks of the place, especially the lake. The Indians called it Spirit Lake. White settlers called it Ghost Lake. It's nearly a half-mile long.

Gower had money, because his father had died. He bought Evelyn's lake and cottage for $2,500.

Not long after, some thugs paid him a visit. They told him to get lost, because they wanted to look around for a while. Gower had a shotgun handy. He waved it at them and they left.

They did return one day when he was out — he doesn't think they found anything.

One fine day around 1965 or so, a blonde arrived at Gower's door. Red shorts, halter top, hair right down her back. She had arrived in a black Olds, but the driver stayed in the car.

She told Gower he had a beautiful spot and asked if she could take a little wander. Sure thing, he said.

Then he realized that under all that blond hair, Evelyn Dick had returned. "I shadowed her all over the place. I don't think she knew I was watching." In the intervening years since she had vacationed there, Gower had built a house on top of the hill. "I'd bulldozed all over the place. It probably drove her nuts."

August 14, 1991

The clipping about Gower is of no consequence. Perhaps some

strange peroxide blonde did show up at his cottage and, from that, he spun his far-fetched yarn. The Evelyn Dick from Scotland seems to have weathered the confusion of names exceedingly well — seems a rather plucky sort of person.

I wish I could detach myself as easily from what happened to poor Ethela McLean. I can well imagine the many cruelties to which she was subjected — the funny looks, the whispers just as she turned her back. She suffered because of me (because she supposedly looked like me and because her name was similar to my maiden one), and now she is dead. I can do nothing to compensate her for the slings and arrows hurled at her.

October 10, 1991

I've been back in Ontario for almost ten years and have yet to visit Hamilton. No real pull to do so. And yet I've become increasingly fascinated by the prospect of seeing myself on stage. *How Could You, Mrs. Dick?* was first staged in my home town in 1989. The reviews of that version and the revival in the *Globe* and *Star* indicate I am treated fairly by Douglas Rodger, that the play implies not only that there may be many extenuating circumstances but also that I may be completely innocent of both homicides. I take comfort in that, but I'm also wondering what it would be like to see an actress playing me? Would I learn anything new about myself? I've been trying to banish this temptation but realize I am on the verge of giving in.

Part of me must be attracted to the danger. But what if Elizabeth Delamere is recognized and someone then figures out the relationship between her and Evelyn Dick? Or what if someone from my past sees and knows me? The risk may be negligible, but it is real. For two days, I can think of little else, am unable to write. Finally, I decide on an experiment. I shall go to Creed's and purchase black slacks and a cream blouse to accompany them. Elizabeth Delamere avoids trousers and has certainly never been photographed in them. Then, I'll buy one of those rinses, one that is easily washed away, at the pharmacy downstairs in my building. If I put a medium blond through my hair and pull it up, I'll be able to alter my public persona. With that adjustment, unusual costuming and perhaps a new lipstick colour — a florid orange that

Elizabeth Delamere would shun — I'll look like a new woman. Not like the well-known novelist. Whatever I do, I must be careful to blend in.

As a young woman, I "imitated" various sirens — Hayworth, Lamour, Grable; in middle age, I assumed a Katharine Hepburn no-nonsense guise; as an older woman, I do not much care what I look like. I must strive to resemble the role fate has assigned me.

When I telephone the Tivoli, they tell me I need not reserve a ticket. Just come along. I'm driving in from Toronto I inform the polite young man, and I don't wish to be turned away. No problem. Attendance has been brisk, but there are always at least fifty empty seats for each performance.

So I steel myself for this venture. I'll take a taxi down to the Elizabeth Street station, catch the GO bus, and then walk the two blocks from the station to the theatre. When I arrive, the city will be cloaked in early evening dusk. There will be little more than a hour before the performance begins, and, at its conclusion, I'll retreat quickly under the cover of darkness back to the station. Should be back home just before midnight.

The bus is more crowded than I anticipated. I realize I am travelling at the tail end of the rush hour. A dozen or so harried executives. A handful of McMaster students. Some professor-looking types. A huge assortment of the working poor, most of the males wearing baseball caps.

The entire highway is bordered by industrial parks. The journey through this nondescript semi-industrial landscape is mildly ugly, monumentally boring. Just as we reach the outer confines of Hamilton, the bay, accompanied by majestic woods and trees, comes into view. According to some, the most beautiful entry into any city in Canada. But first impressions are deceptive. On the other side of the bay, the steel mills pour their pollution into the water, huge tongues of flame lick the night sky.

The journey takes less than an hour. I've been so near and yet have kept myself so far away. As I alight from the bus, I realize it's been almost forty-five years since I've been here. How different will things look? Will I know my way around?

The bus station has not changed that much, neither have the once familiar buildings. Never in wonderful condition, they simply have been allowed to grow old gracelessly.

In my mind's eye, Hamilton is rendered in a medley of blacks and greys. Tonight, in the darkness, fantasy and reality are identical. Of course, if I had chosen to return in daylight, things might be different. Yet darkness gives an almost romantic glow to the ugliness of the inner core.

Despite the comfort of darkness, I am reminded all over again of the vast gulf between Hamilton and Toronto, of how the city has never really matured because of the looming, nearby presence of the metropolis. When I lived in Hamilton, there were two readily visible contrasting classes: the rich and the immigrant poor. The wealthy mined the city, in the process caring little about it. Toronto and its shops, galleries and theatres were a short drive away. Instantly, I feel not much has changed in this regard.

The Tivoli survives shabbily. The marquee needs repairing, and the ancient three-storied building into which the theatre was inserted in the thirties is lopsided. The Tivoli now exists as an old lady who, having gone on a binge, has ended up topsy-turvy. Once a movie palace, the Tivoli has been converted into a venue for live performances, an attempt by Sam Sniderman, the new owner, to inject energy into the city's blocked cultural arteries. The next-door Sam the Record Man store is, like its Toronto cousin, tawdry but welcoming. The nearby buildings on the street — a vast pawnbroking shop, a hair salon, a travel agency — have seen much better days.

Thankfully, I don't have too much time to wander about. I think of taking the ten-minute walk up James to the Henson Apartments but decide against doing so. I wander into the shopping centre, Jackson Square, a collection of mid-priced franchises, and then into Eaton's, which is adjacent. The last time I was in Hamilton, the city hall stood in this very space. In contrast to Toronto, the shoppers are badly dressed, have no flair or individuality in how they present themselves to the world.

At quarter to eight, I arrive back at the Tivoli. Only then do I remember that the old Opera House once occupied the space next to the Tivoli; the space has been taken over by a shabby little strip mall. Strange I didn't recall that at first. I enter the theatre and make my way to my seat. The proscenium is completely exposed with only a door at the back to allow the actors to enter and exit. I behold again the inverted spider-like chandeliers, the statues of Caesar Augustus and Minerva flanking the stage, the wall medallions of Mozart, Liszt, Beethoven, and Tchaikovsky. I remember what has vanished: the private boxes, wooden pillars, brass railings, sumptuous lobby with stained glass, and the long, mirrored hallway that took one from the box office into the theatre itself. The auditorium begins to fill up rapidly and, as I look around, I see young people, perhaps high school students, who have come to learn about the life history of their city's most nefarious criminal.

I now use eyeglasses to view distances, and when I put them on, I am amazed at how stripped down the interior is. I recall art deco sumptuousness, not the exposed, cracked brick that now envelops me. Battered from both the outside and the inside, the building had once been a wonderful refuge. Moving pictures had been my solace. Now, live actors and a minimal stage set. An entirely different reality, not one with which I feel comfortable.

As the auditorium darkens, two reporters, a man and a woman, begin to speak. He is convinced of Evelyn's guilt; the woman is not so sure — she has an entirely different vantage point. I am startled by the entrance of the hero-villain: the young woman looks a bit like me in those days, but she carries herself in an assertive, forward way of which I was never capable. She is aggressive, flirtatious, sassy. She bats her eyes at the detectives who question and cross-question her; she shrugs her shoulders in disdain; she controls her interrogators with the rapid movements of her cigarette; she even blows smoke in their faces.

"Smoke Gets in Your Eyes." The Jerome Kern melody wafts through the auditorium, helping the audience respond to the nostalgia of the recreation they are witnessing. Everything on stage happened almost fifty years ago when people wore funny clothes, listened to the radio, and drove around in huge cars. Yet, the aloof coldness of Evelyn, her refusal to admit to any involvement in two horrible deaths, and her indifference to others chill the audience.

Gradually, the play gets to me. I see myself as I was then. True, I was shyer and more hesitant — frequently stammering when questioned by the detectives — but protected from any real feelings.

As the play ends, the audience, drained from the experience they have witnessed, quickly leaves the auditorium. I stay in my seat, hardly able to move, so overcome am I by my hatred for the young woman I once was. Feeling deeply sorry for the failings of that creature, I notice an elderly couple slowly making their way up the aisle. The man is the nearest to me and, in a flash, I recognize Bill Bohozuk. The same majestic handsomeness as before, although time has taken its due. He stoops a little and his face is etched in the Rembrandt manner. His companion, a very attractive brunette a few years younger than himself, accompanies him. He waves his hands slowly in the air, obviously objecting to some aspect of the play, of how it failed to capture the past accurately. His face is animated and very red, tears glistening at the edge of each eye. Did I, I wonder, pass up my only chance for ordinary happiness — the wonderful dailiness that makes so many lives worth living — by rejecting that man? I brush away my own tears.

I wait for a few minutes and am the last person to leave the Tivoli. I make my way quickly to the bus station and leave a few minutes later for the return journey to Toronto. As the bus approaches the bay, the radiance of the full moon bathes the water and the trees.

March 14, 1999

Body parts were discovered in a garbage in an East Mountain home in Hamilton. Later, more human remains were found refrigerated in the kitchen of the same house. The *Spectator* claims Samuel Pirrera's wife went missing several years ago but the remains may be of a prostitute-companion of Pirrera. In any event, my picture has once again been plastered all over the newspaper. The link is a comparison of one gruesome murder in the past to the latest example of villainy.

And then there are the ridiculous comparisons of me to Homolka. Even the crimes I am accused of having perpetrated have no point of similarity to the activities of that hideous woman. She incited murder and then conducted herself as a member of an audience beholding the performance of a script she had, in large part, authored. When she revisited the house in St. Catharines where those poor girls were murdered, all she could think about was her furniture and makeup!

April 12, 1999

I don't really have a classic case of writer's block: I have written a long account of my life. But I can't transform it into fiction and — even if I managed to screw myself to that task — I couldn't publish it during my lifetime.

I never wanted to write this memoir, but I feel compelled to write about Evelyn Dick. If Elizabeth Delamere published such a book, she would be revealed to the world as a convicted felon. I cannot subject myself to that humiliation, but it is really the only story I have left to tell. Nothing else comes to me. No other scraps from the rag and bone shop of this heart.

The Globe and Mail, June 17, 1999

AFFLUENT FACADE MASKED FUGITIVE WITH A RADICAL PAST

Sara Jane Olson lived a comfortable life in St. Paul, sharing an ivy-covered house with her doctor husband and three daughters, enjoying success as an actor in local theatre.

But for the past 25 years — until her arrest by FBI agents yesterday — she was also a fugitive member of the Symbionese Liberation Army, a leftist radical group that kidnapped newspaper heiress Patricia Hearst 25 years ago in one of the most sensational stories of the 1970s. Ms. Olson's real name is Kathleen Anne Soliah. She had been wanted in Los Angeles since 1976, when she was indicted on conspiracy and explosive charges for allegedly placing pipe bombs under two police cars. FBI agents found Ms. Soliah, 52, after receiving tips from viewers of the TV program, America's Most Wanted, which featured her in a broadcast last month.

She had taken the last name of Olson, which is extremely common in Minnesota because of the large number of people of Scandinavian descent who settled in that state. Neighbours described her as a well-spoken and friendly woman, and an avid jogger and gardener. She had received good reviews for starring performances in local drama productions.

June 18, 1999

In the photograph reproduced on the front page of *The Globe and Mail*,

Kathleen Soliah stares into space. Her lips are tightly drawn, her freckles highlighted, her whispy hair is carelessly arranged. A true mug shot. There does not seem to be anyone home behind those sad blue eyes. Is she haunted by her past, relieved that the game is now up? Or is she unhappy because she is going to be deprived of her comfortable middle-class life with husband and children? Does she have pangs of guilt about the crimes she apparently committed during her troubled youth?

The photograph is an icon of the female criminal as cipher. For me, the strange thing is that Soliah was a rage-filled, rebellious young woman who obviously despised American middle-class values; her acts of rebellion included kidnapping, bank robbery and murder; she then went underground for twenty-five years living the kind of *Father Knows Best* lifestyle she had earlier tried to renounce. Was she angry at herself all those years when she made certain her lawn was immaculately clean like her neighbours' and participated in casserole dinners with them? or did she see the errors of her past ways and try to make amends by fitting in, by appearing to be normal?

Questions, questions, questions but I have absolutely no answers as I look at that photo. How would I explain myself if I were similarly outed? Simply say my novels were my good deeds, my acts of reparation? Would anyone believe me?

46

February 11, 2000

I find it increasingly difficult to say no to the gregarious Dolly, my publicist at Penguin. She hardly ever asks me to do anything, so attuned is she to how reluctant I am to be exposed to the publicity mill.

Against my better judgement, she had persuaded me to speak at a celebrity author luncheon in Hamilton. "The proceeds go the homeless. A very good cause. A member of the organizing committee will pick you up, drive you to Hamilton and then someone else will drive you home. You won't be away from home for more than five hours, six at most." I tell her OK, although it really isn't something I want to do. I'm not so much frightened as reluctant, have no wish to see Hamilton ever again.

The woman who calls for me drives a bright red, attention-getting BMW. When I have seated myself next to her, I notice her incredibly high forehead, Little Orphan Annie corkscrew curls and her steely little grey eyes which give me short, sharp glances as if subjecting me to x-rays. Although I'm a bit fearful of radiation poisoning, I try to make polite conversation. That proves to be a difficult task. I cannot have a conversation with her, however — she wishes to interrogate me.

"What do you think of Nadine Gordimer?" Before I can say anything, she tells me: "Nadine is the greatest woman writer of the century."

"You know Nadine Gordimer?"

"I've been to several readings. She's autographed all my copies of her books. I suppose you've met her?"

The question is said in a way to suggest that if I have met the great writer, I am unworthy of the honour. "Yes, two or three times. A very nice person."

"She's more than a *nice* person. She's someone with a social conscience." As she makes these statements, I notice that the accent has traces of South Africa under the Canadian sounds.

"You're from South Africa? You lived there during apartheid?"

This invitation seems to soothe Lucy, who proceeds to tell me about her former life of privilege, the black servants, and the horrible conditions of oppression she witnessed. Finally, she got out. I ask her how she made her escape. Her physician husband got a study visa for him to study gastroenterology. They went to live in London and later obtained landed immigrant status in Canada. In this country, Lucy is involved in a wide variety of charities. My suspicion is that she feels very guilty about leaving her homeland when it was even more troubled than it is today. She is doing penance.

We are half-way to Hamilton, and Lucy's autobiography ends rather abruptly. Travelling at a very high speed in the fast lane, she turns her face — now beet red — in my direction and stares at me. I wish she would keep her eyes on the road. "I was opposed to your being invited today."

Now we are really into it. I obviously want to contain her as much as possible — keep her calm — but I'm not really sure what to say. "I think you're referring to the fact that I am not as socially relevant an author as you would like."

"Exactly. You write about those women who have wretched, miserable lives. You're concerned about individual struggles and triumphs, but you say little or nothing about the status of women, poverty, overpopulation and unemployment. You avoid basic social concerns."

"That's because I know very little about such things. Besides, there are many fine writers, like Gordimer, who are comfortable writing about such issues."

"All authors have to be socially relevant. Shouldn't be published otherwise."

It would not do me any good to point out to Lucy that her mindset seems to me rather rigid, even fascist. We have now reached the outskirts of Hamilton and on this clear winter day — it is late February — the bay looks beautiful. I change the subject by asking her about the various pieces of natural beauty we are seeing. Well aware that I am trying to distract her, she co-operates in the charade I propose, now fully aware that it is probably not in her best interests to be rude to a visiting speaker.

Just as we enter the city, her cell phone beeps. It is her husband. Could she possibly pick up an x-ray at his office and take it to the literary lunch his colleague is attending? She agrees and then tells me we will have a brief detour. She exits at Main East, then turn left at Locke Street and then right at Herkimer. "My husband's office is just opposite St. Joseph's Hospital. I won't be more than five minutes." We proceed all the way down to the end of Herkimer, where it intersects with James. She scoots into the parking lot just before the two streets intersect. We are at the back of 215 James Street South, where I once had the apartment.

Before she steps out of the car, Lucy notices I am awestruck. "Very beautiful building. One of the three Henson apartments. Excellent example of late Victorian gothic. This one is particularly famous. Notorious is probably the better word." She looks at me, my eyes meeting hers. "Evelyn Dick lived here. Do you know who she is?"

"Vaguely. She murdered her husband?"

"Exactly. The torso murderer. A real degenerate." With that, Lucy gets out of the car, slams the door and leaves me. I look up at the gingerbread red gabble of the house, which resembles a building one might find in a watercolour to accompany a story by Perrault or Grimm. I can see one of the windows of my old flat — I remember looking down from there at John Dick, one of the last times I ever saw him. I was hardly a princess in the tower, I remind myself.

My mind wanders back to the badly named Nora Clench, one of the great violinists of the late nineteenth century. Born in St. Marys, Ontario, she had, at the age of 14, moved to Hamilton in 1882 in order to study with the renowned J.W. Baumann. Later, she moved to Europe, where she played before many heads of state. She returned to Hamilton in 1891, gave a splendid performance and never visited the city again. I have returned but no one knows who I really am. Would the city celebrate if they discovered my true identity, learned that I was a local girl who had done exceedingly well on the world's stage?

I wait ten minutes for Lucy and then, overcome by a sombre sort of curiosity, I get out of the car, walk the few feet to the end of Herkimer and go up the short flight of steps into the foyer of the building. The past is often an untouched landscape; here it is perfectly preserved. As before, the entrance contains an elaborate golden oak staircase leading to a landing filled with an enormous stained-glass window occupied by figures that look like they have stepped out of the Kelmscott Chaucer. The sun penetrates the glass, shooting colours out in all directions. The gleaming oak is bathed in magical tints. Once again, as so many years ago, I feel I have stepped into some mysterious chapel. The fallen woman in consecrated ground. Only the fragrance of incense is lacking.

My reverie is interrupted by Lucy rushing down the stairs, an enormous manila envelope in her right hand. "Curiosity killed the cat," she cheerfully assures me. We return to the car. The event goes well. I read for about half an hour, and there are the usual questions: why am I so interested in women criminals? doesn't writing about female convicts, for example, only marginalize women even more in society? The questions are polite but probing. Many of my responses I know by rote, could recite sleepwalking. Finally, the event is over, but there is a huge lineup of audience members who have purchased copies of my book and wish me to sign them. That takes a long time, although everything is concluded by 4:30. Lucy introduces me to her friend, Amanda, who will drive me back to Toronto.

This woman is also a forty-something South African. She is altogether more polite, but she is anxious, her nerves made worse by the weather. A major storm is approaching fast from Buffalo. We must be on our way immediately. I agree. When we reach the parking lot, the sun has deserted the day; we have gone abruptly into nighttime. We have been at the Sheraton in the downtown core. "We'll be on the highway in less than five minutes," Amanda assures me.

We set out and are proceeding to the entry to the highway when Amanda's cell phone rings. It's her nanny. One of her children — her youngest, a boy — has had an accident and is desperate to see her. She explains she cannot make it home for at least a few hours because she has to drive Ms. Delamere back to Toronto.

"Nonsense, you must attend to your son," I tell her. "I have no real urgency to be back home at a certain time."

She thanks me for my understanding and then explains we will have to change direction and go up the brow of the Mountain. "The weather's always worse up there than here, but we'll be fine," she assures me.

The snow has now picked up and is blowing fiercely causing white-outs. A few times, Amanda has to swerve to avoid a car coming into our lane from the opposite direction. Soon, we are at the top of the Mountain.

I remember March 6, 1946, over fifty years ago. There was snow on the ground although I did not drive through a storm. The moon and stars were also absent on that night. Amanda and I have now reached the exact spot on the Brow where I was to meet the Oldsmobile. This evening there is a car pulled to the opposite side of the road, its headlights beaming. So are its emergency lights. There is a small drive-in at the side of the road, Amanda tells me. "I'll see if I can help those people. Get close enough to see the license plate number." She says all this while pulling the car over. I ask: "Isn't it dangerous for you to get out of the car in a driving storm like this? You could get killed." Her anxieties having vanished, she assures me that is not the case. "I'll be fine. Just wait for me."

So there I sit as the past hurls itself down on me. I cannot see a thing. I am completely abandoned. What if Amanda doesn't return? My imagination leaps over all its usual boundaries. What if Mr. Romanelli is in that car? What if the corpse of John Dick is on the back seat? My heart races uncontrollably. After what seems an eternity, the door opens and Amanda seats herself and resumes control of the car. "They didn't have a cell phone. I've made a call. Help is on the way." We resume our journey. Her house is a further twenty minutes away, the little boy who fell cut himself badly but does not require stitches, the weather calms down, and at ten o'clock we leave for Toronto. I reach home at half past eleven.

I cannot settle. Some nights gentle ghosts of time passed inhabit my bedroom even before I go to sleep. That wonderful wild woman Emma Skeffington. Sweet, affectionate delicately blond Rosie. Mother St. John, the most erudite and feeling of Bluestockings. Dear Janet White and her relentless dedication to research. On other evenings, the guests are unwelcome. My sullen Mother attempts to instill herself; sometimes, she is accompanied by Detective Wood or Judge Barlow. On occasion, Father sits in my bedside chair. A malicious grin crosses his face; I break into a cold sweat. John Dick only visits me in dreams. I worry about Heather; I long to touch the dead babies. Tonight, as I look around my bedroom, I am absolutely alone. Total darkness.

October 11, 2000

I can never escape the facts of my early life. Truth is my persistent enemy: I can no longer write as I have become so dominated by the past. No truth liberates me. Sometimes, I think my writing has been some sort of huge defence mechanism against the past, a self-constructed barrier insulating me from my own reality. Now I no longer have the luxury of that escape.

Even more so than before, I am a well-known figure at the Carlton and Cumberland Cinemas and at the various reps, although I don't think any of the attendants at any of those places know my name. I am familiar to them because they see me on a regular basis. I am what is known as an art-house junkie.

I hardly ever attend any of the big American films. Ever since prostitution was glamourized in *American Gigolo* and *Pretty Woman*, I have no interest in the confections of Hollywood. I admire those films with an edge of menace, even though I found David Lynch's *Blue Velvet* frightening, especially those scenes when the protagonist is hidden in the closet watching the sado-masochist activities of Dennis Hopper. The best film I have seen in recent years is the Australian *Proof*, about the blind photographer. What a perfect metaphor for the contemporary artist: Without benefit of sight, he presents the world with perfectly realized renditions of the human condition. I know all about that kind of art.

October 15, 2000

The other night on *Showcase* I finally steeled myself to watch the documentary on Friedrich Tarnopolsky. Even before he was captured in Buenos Aires in 1997, the filmmaker had begun interviewing the victims, as he called them, the people whose lives had been irrevocably damaged by Tarnopolsky's kidnapping-murders. When the film was released in 1998, the controversy as to whether he should be executed or not had become rampant. In the film, Tarnopolsky looks a frail, bewildered old man. For the past twenty-five years, he had worked as a janitor in a government building in Brasilia. A minor but nevertheless highly regarded government employee. Always on time. Always meticulous in performing any task assigned to him. One could say he had — without benefit of prison — thoroughly reformed himself. Appearance and reality only became completely out of joint when his small apartment was searched and the children's pornography and snuff videos were discovered. At that point in his life, he had — as his lawyers pointed out — become merely a consumer of such material, certainly not someone who manufactured it.

The filmmaker interviewed Dr. Newman before and after the capture of Tarnopolsky. His opinions remained unchanged. Unlike all the other survivors, he did not wish Tarnopolsky destroyed and did not label him a monster. "Mr. Tarnopolsky suffers from a serious mental illness and should be treated accordingly. The task of society is to destroy the spiritual and cultural environment that freely allows behaviour like Mr. Tarnopolsky's unimpeded development. The real criminal is society — not some poor unfortunate like the man who killed my wife and child."

In a few days, I shall see Ernst for the first time in almost twenty years. What does he really think of his old patient? A genuine success story? Or the best example in his long career of the patient as sham?

Despite all the years I spent in treatment with Ernst, I have never been able to shake loose the conviction that a horrible deformity —

the Tarnopolsky side — dwells within me. In effect, Ernst told me I was a fool to believe such things. Now, in my eightieth year, I see an increasingly frail old woman and wonder if I am more sinned against than sinning? Some days I cling to that illusion. On others, I see only the monster.

PART FOUR

Ernst Newman

47

A week after Elizabeth died, her editor Judith Smith phoned me from London. Until the news broke, Smith had no definite ideas about Elizabeth's past life, although she had long suspected — because of information supplied in the novels — that her friend had some first-hand knowledge of prisons.

"I wondered if a parent, a relative or a close friend had been incarcerated and if Elizabeth had visited that person in prison." Although the two became close, she knew that her favourite author expected her not to pry into her past: "I could talk with Elizabeth about many things, but I instinctively knew her past was forbidden territory. She simply told me what she told everyone else: she had cared for ancient parents in Ontario, moved, when they died, to British Columbia in her late thirties, and began writing fiction when working at Duthie's. She never referred to her parents in conversation and obviously did not wish to be drawn into any discussion of them. I respected those limits. She was a very good friend, knew my own personal situation well and always made inquiries about the various problems — personal and professional — I told her about. Knowing she did not wish me to reciprocate, I accepted the situation as it unfolded.

"In retrospect, there was one extremely awkward matter that now explains itself. In 1996, I persuaded Elizabeth, who was staying with me in London, to accompany me to the Frankfurt Book Fair, the idea being that my house might be able to further increase her foreign sales — already excellent — if Elizabeth would assist us by putting in an appearance and talking up her books to various European publishers. Reluctantly, she agreed, and we held a big, extremely successful party for her. "Everything went very well until Anne Perry dropped in. The circumstances of her early life — the murder in New Zealand and all that — were already old-hat by then. In any event, Anne walked in, kissed me and I then introduced her to Elizabeth, who looked like she had seen a ghost. Her face blanched and she inhaled deeply. Unusual for her, she seemed lost for words, but she offered her hand to Anne, who took it, said a few words and then excused herself. Elizabeth was not exactly rude, but Anne must have assumed that she disapproved of her. I never discussed this small event with Elizabeth but, in retrospect, I now see that she was confronting an alter-ego, someone whose dangerous secret had become public property."

The other phone call I received was from the very distraught Japanese-Canadian writer, Kenji Ozu, a protegé of Elizabeth's. He felt the "whole situation has been blown out of proportion. What's the big deal? She wrote under an assumed name — she had every reason in the world to conceal her true identity. It's not anyone else's business." I explained that she was a convicted felon. Perhaps understandably, everyone wanted to know the full story.

"She was like a mother to me."

"You had no clue as to her real identity?"

"None whatsoever. In retrospect, I found her very stiff when we first met. Even before that, her two letters to me were curt. Polite but very distanced. 'Don't intrude,' they whispered. I was a polite young Japanese man, a person of the old school. I decided to stay away from her. Then, I thought of the books and knew there was a very feeling heart behind them. So I persisted. I guess I was more than a little bolshy.

"Even after she agreed to see me, I found her behaviour strange. She didn't make small talk. Not the slightest attempt to talk about anything but books. Even there, she confined her remarks to technique. Told me clearly, plainly and precisely what was wrong. Did not mince her words. An hour into the conversation, I began to think, 'This woman is very shy. She's even a bit unsure of herself. Her starchiness comes from insecurity. She's laying down the law, but she doesn't like to judge my work. She's really uncomfortable in the position I've placed her in.'

"Now that I'm older, I realize how calculating I was that afternoon. I decided to take my best shot at getting her to open up. I started to talk about the internment camp, the setting of the novel she had just read. At first, she didn't respond. Then, she began to wring her hands, then I noticed that the edges of her eyes had become bright red. She started to ask me about being in what she called prison.

"'Must have been awful for a young boy to grow up that way? Confined in that way. All your natural curiosity about the world stifled.'

"I assured her that had been the case. But then I mentioned how wonderful my parents had been. How they had endured a great deal of privation but assured me things would get better.

"'Yes, that must have made it easier to bear. Not having to endure your lot alone.'

"At that point, she told me that she had another appointment later that day. When I got up to leave, I took her hand and gave her a small kiss on the cheek. She smiled and walked me to the door. Ten days later, she phoned to invite me to dinner. We became close friends.

"We cared very deeply for each other. I never knew Evelyn Dick; I only knew Elizabeth Delamere."

On the small table next to Elizabeth's body in her suite at the Hotel Vancouver was the piece of paper which I had retrieved. She must have woken from the dream, scribbled on the paper and then gone back to bed, whereupon she died in her sleep.

Tonight the drive up the Mountain is accomplished with greater ease than usual. The way even seems a tiny bit brighter. There is a full moon. When I stop the Packard, the car awaiting me whisks away. For some reason, this does not bother me. As soon as I enter the woods, the smell of the pine tar is unusually sharp and dense, almost medicinal. I walk through it, bathing in its caressing touches. My body feels radiant, aching joyously from this soothing cleansing. My walk is a pleasant one, although my heart is racing uncontrollably.

The small white house stands majestically against the green pines. I imagine myself a young girl who has come across a small enchanted castle. I laugh at myself. This is more a cottage than a castle. You are not a child lost in the wood who has found help, I remind myself. You are not Little Red Riding Hood come to visit Grandmother only to discover that the evil wolf has eaten her. But I do feel awfully young, even vulnerable. But, I am absolutely certain, I have nothing to fear. Everything will be fine. There is a small brook running around the house, and I bend down to splash some water in my face. Then, I gather a mouthful of the water in my hands and drink it. The sparkling water refreshes me. I had not noticed before how parched I was.

As I make my way to the door, I see it is open. I knock but no one answers. I push it in a bit, still awaiting some response. When no one comes, I walk in. The interior is one enormous room painted a pale but true green. Each of the sides has many windows, perhaps seven or eight. Straight ahead is one enormous window reaching from floor to ceiling. From that opening I see a range of Alpine mountains separated from each other by streams of coursing water.

I am alone in the room. Then I feel a presence. I look around but see no one else occupying the space which is completely devoid of any furniture or decoration. I walk towards the large window and then hear a laughing sound behind my back. I turn around.

In the very middle of the chamber is a small table at which three children — two girls and a boy — are seated. They smile at me, their faces grinning as if they are concealing some great secret. I walk over to them and, as I approach, they rearrange themselves to accommodate me. I had not noticed the fourth chair which, nodding in my direction, the children beckon me to take. I sit down. As I inspect the faces of the children, I notice their complexions have a perfect, milky softness, their eyes a bright and true shine. The little boy sits opposite me. He joins hands with the girls on either side of him; then the two young ladies reach out to take mine. We sit there, looking at each other. I close my eyes. I feel the tender flesh of each girl's palm. The clear, delicate scent of the pines is overwhelming.

ACKNOWLEDGEMENTS

Marjorie Freeman Campbell's *Torso* (subsequently republished as *Unholy Matrimony*) is the only book-length study of Evelyn Dick. Campbell also wrote an excellent history of Hamilton: *A Mountain and a City*. I have also learned a great deal from Brian Henley's various books devoted to the history of Hamilton and from Paul Wilson's lively columns in the *Hamilton Spectator*. The following were very useful: Jack Batten's *Robinette: The Dean of Canadian Lawyers*, Vincent Burns' *Female Convict*, Owen Carrigan's *Crime and Punishment in Canada: A History*, Keith Edgar and Richard Daniel's *Evelyn Dick: The Tragic Story of an Emotional Degenerate*, Patricia Pearson's *When She Was Bad*, Douglas Rodger's *How Could You, Mrs. Dick?*, and John Weaver's *Crimes, Constables, and Courts: Order and Transgression in a Canadian City, 1816–1970*. Brian Henley and his staff at the Hamilton Public Library provided me with a wide array of documents, including many fascinating, unpublished photographs in the Local History collection.

Marc Côté, an editor's editor, was — as is his wont — both totally demanding and completely supportive.